Praise for
A DAGGER OF LIGHTNING

"Meredith R. Lyons delivers a fresh, science-fiction romance with dagger-sharp writing and lightning-quick wit to prove that sometimes being the chosen one means choosing yourself." —**Matthew Hubbard, author of *The Last Boyfriends Rules for Revenge***

"In her hotly anticipated follow-up to her award-winning debut, Lyons spins a wonderful fantasy epic with an unforgettable heroine, ingenious worldbuilding, and a page-turning plot. *A Dagger of Lightning* is guaranteed to leave an indelible impression on readers of speculative fiction. Fans of Jemisin, Hobb, and Grossman take note." —**Julian R. Vaca, Daytime Emmy award-winning writer and author of *The Memory Index***

"Meredith R. Lyons's *A Dagger of Lightning* hits you like a glass of sparkling rosé: a fizzy, flirty, and fun space opera about a satisfyingly badass forty-year-old chosen one whisked off to a planet of sidhe against her will. The tale shakes up classic tropes in a delightful potion that will keep you turning the page." —**Yume Kitasei, author of *The Stardust Grail***

"Meredith R. Lyons deftly mixes space opera, fantasy adventure, and paranormal romance into an irresistible combination in *A Dagger of Lightning*. Oh, and did I mention there's an unforgettable forty-something heroine? Get this book." —**Gwenda Bond, *New York Times* bestselling author of *The Frame-Up***

"Wildly original and wholly unexpected, Meredith R. Lyons' sophomore effort does not disappoint. I was swept away into the story just as Imogen was and rooted for her every step of the way as she gains back her sense of self and comes into her powers. Smart, sexy, and absolutely memorable, I can't wait to see what happens next." —**J. T. Ellison,** *New York Times* **bestselling author of** *A Very Bad Thing*

"*A Dagger of Lightning* begins with the mystery of a sci-fi novel, punches hard with the humor of a paranormal romance, and grows into a truly epic fantasy. If you like to have fun, this is the fantasy romance you need in your hands right now." —**Alisha Klapheke,** *USA Today* **bestselling author of the Dragons Rising series**

Praise for
GHOST TAMER

A 2024 IBPA Benjamin Franklin Award Gold Medal Winner
A 2024 IPPY Award Winner Gold Medal Winner

"Ghosts and the hunt for a possibly malevolent spirit sweep through the pages of Meredith R. Lyons's *Ghost Tamer*. In this fast-paced debut, a young woman discovers why she was the lucky one to survive a train crash while also facing, and conquering, shadows from her past that won't let her go." —**Georgina Cross, bestselling author of** *The Stepdaughter, Nanny Needed, One Night,* **and** *The Niece*

"Meredith R. Lyons' sizzling debut has a lot of heart and the perfect amount of snark. *Ghost Tamer* is a paranormal joyride!" —**James L'Etoile, award-winning author of** *Black Label, Dead Drop,* **and the Detective Penley series**

"Meredith R. Lyons' *Ghost Tamer* is a superbly-written and wholly original debut. A witty, fast-paced, and frightening supernatural thrill ride!"
—**Bruce Robert Coffin, award-winning author of the Detective Byron mysteries**

"*Ghost Tamer* is a page-turning must-read novel for fans of mystery, fantasy, and the supernatural. I can't wait for Lyons' next novel." —**Jeffrey James Higgins, award-winning author of *Furious and Unseen***

"Meredith R. Lyons writes with an intensity of emotion and an abundance of sass. Her debut novel *Ghost Tamer* has just the right mix of spunky and spooky. The pages turn all by themselves. It's uncanny." —**John DeDakis, writing coach, novelist, and former senior copy editor for CNN's *The Situation Room with Wolf Blitzer***

"I love this! Original, hilarious, and completely inspirational. Lyons has an incredible gift with dialogue, and *Ghost Tamer* is absolutely captivating. Touching, relatable, and haunting—in the best sense of the word. Do not miss this." —**Hank Phillippi Ryan, *USA Today* bestselling author of *The House Guest***

"Funny, poignant, spooky, and uniquely clever, *Ghost Tamer* is a remarkably assured debut from a bright light in the fantasy realm. Meredith R. Lyons is a name to watch, and this book is just plain cool from start to finish."
—**J. T. Ellison, *New York Times* bestselling author of *It's One Of Us***

"VERDICT: A paranormal thriller that offers thrills and chills in addition to a touching exploration of grief, love, and moving on." —***Library Journal***

A Dagger of Lightning

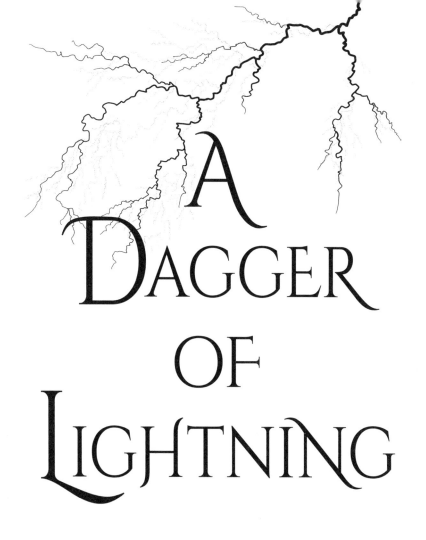

A Dagger of Lightning

Meredith R. Lyons

CamCat Books

CamCat Books
2810 Coliseum Centre Drive, Suite 300
Charlotte, NC 28217-4574

This is a work of fiction. Names, characters, places, and incidents are either products of the author's imagination or are used fictitiously.

© 2025 by Meredith R. Lyons

All rights reserved. Printed in the United States of America. No part of this book may be used or reproduced in any manner whatsoever without written permission except in the case of brief quotations embodied in critical articles and reviews. For information, address CamCat Books, 2810 Coliseum Centre Drive, Suite 300, Charlotte, NC 28217-4574.

Hardcover ISBN 9780744311570
Paperback ISBN 9780744311587
eBook ISBN 9780744311617
Audiobook ISBN 9780744311655

Library of Congress Control Number: 2024942819

Book and cover design by Maryann Appel

5   3   1   2   4

For Grandma.
I wouldn't be surprised to learn that she came from
some magical place.
And I hope she made it back there.

And for my dad.
He's pretty cool too.

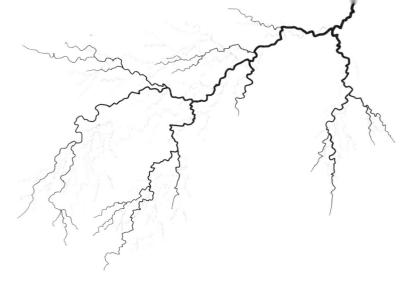

CHAPTER ONE

*If you don't know where you're going, fine,
just make sure you know what you're looking for.*
—Solange Aidair Delaney

"**I**m. Imogen! You're okay. You're all right, you're okay."

I awoke gasping, my ears throbbing as if my heart had established satellite locations. My eyes immediately locked onto a familiar shape, the feather swaying back and forth, dangling from the chain on our ceiling fan. *I'm safe. I'm in bed. With Keane. I'm okay.*

The orange glow of a street lamp filtered in through the open curtains. I reached up and lightly clasped Keane's forearm, his warm palm still gripping my shoulder, although he had stopped shaking me. I turned my head toward him, trying to take slower breaths. He'd angled himself just far enough away so that I wouldn't accidentally strike him. I must have been flailing.

"I'm awake. Sorry. Was I loud?" I never remembered these dreams when I woke. Only a sensation of falling and some vague knowledge that my grandfather had been there, either falling with me, or trying to keep me from falling, or ... something ...

"You didn't shout or anything this time, just thrashed around." Keane flopped back onto the pillows, sliding an arm beneath me and hauling me to his side. I let him, even though I was very warm and wanted air. The sheets beneath me were damp with sweat. I shoved the comforter down to my waist.

"Sorry I woke you. I've been trying to rest my ankle and didn't run yesterday." If my body was exhausted, my brain had less energy to run amok. I didn't process emotions the way most people did, and if I was unable to channel them physically, they liked to ambush me when I was unconscious.

"That's all right." Keane sighed, trailing his fingertips up and down my arm. Keane had been a good friend since college. Neither of us had ever married, in spite of cycling through many long-term relationships. At some point, after spending a mutual friend's wedding together as bridesmaid and groomsman for the umpteenth time, Keane had suggested that if we hadn't found anyone by forty, we should just wed each other. I'd drunkenly agreed. Now I was forty-five, Keane was nearly fifty, and six months ago he'd finally gotten my yes. I accepted a ring after insisting upon dating first, living together first, then living together for at least a year ... until I'd run out of excuses. There were none. Keane was great. We got along great. Sex wasn't bad. Cohabitating was cheaper and made maintaining a home easier. And it was nice being on his insurance plan.

Settling, Imogen. You're settling is what you're doing. She'd been gone sixteen years and I could still *hear* my grandmother's exhale, could practically see her tossing a gauzy scarf over a small-boned shoulder as she gave me a *look* from beneath her lashes.

But what was wrong with that at my age? I'd come to the conclusion that "true love" was a fantasy—although my grandparents had sure seemed to have it. Perhaps it wasn't in the cards for everyone. I'd looked around long enough. Fortunately, I'd never wanted kids, so I'd never felt that pressure.

"So, what are your plans for today?" Keane yawned, still lightly stroking my arm.

My stomach tightened. He had some kind of agenda. "Some more job applications, maybe—"

"You know, you don't have to get a job right away—"

"I *want* a job. I need to contribute—"

"I know, Im, and you will, but you don't need one in the next twenty-four hours. Your dad's coming in next week, and," he rolled toward me, "the guest room is still a mess."

My eyes dropped away from his. I turned my face skyward again and focused on the feather. "I know." The guest room would have been nice if it weren't for the large pile of cardboard boxes. All mine.

I *had* tried to whittle them down. But I didn't know what I'd need. I didn't know where I'd fit in this new place. Keane had received a dream job offer in New Orleans. He'd convinced me that this would be a great life for both of us. Wasn't I tired of the cold in Chicago? Wasn't I able to find friends wherever I went? Weren't we going to get married now? I had no good arguments, so I went with him. It made sense. We were engaged. Why not? I rolled my shoulders against the tightness threatening, trying to make a little more space between us. I didn't want to go through the boxes downstairs. Going through them meant getting rid of them, and I hated to let go of those little parts of myself.

I'd never found my calling. I liked to hop around. I was good at a lot of things, never great at any one thing. I never had a "tribe," but I was good at getting along. I'd find a job here too. Find things to like about it. I was good at adapting. I could wedge myself in.

Grandma would have told me to keep searching. *You're different, Imogen, and that's okay. But you have a place. We all do. You'll know it when you find it. Just keep looking.* Well, she wasn't here. Besides, maybe this would be it.

"Okay," I said, taking a deep breath. "I'll go through the boxes today. Try to put some away."

"You could make a donation pile too," Keane said, pulling the covers back up around us. "What about all that martial arts stuff? You haven't fought in over a decade."

Something twisted at my center. "I liked fighting though," I said, quietly. I had loved sparring. It was another effective outlet for emotions packed down too tightly. And I'd been good at it. Although I was technically too old to fight competitively anymore, I could still train. "Maybe we could find a place here, we could do it together—"

Keane chuckled. "I'm still sore from soccer two days ago." He yawned again and pulled me even closer, eliminating any space I'd created by wrapping his arms around me. He pressed a kiss to my forehead, one hand rubbing my back. "You know, I was thinking when your dad's here next week, we could set a date for the wedding. Like, an actual date. Maybe something in the fall."

I felt myself go rigid in his arms. "Not the fall," I said. Keane's hand stilled on my back, but he didn't let me go. This was the only thing I had ever pushed back on consistently.

"Imogen—"

"My grandma disappeared in the fall. I don't like the fall."

"Imogen." Impatience simmered under his voice. "Everyone on Earth has lost a grandparent—"

"Lost, yes, had one disappear, no."

His chest inflated against my arms where I was still smashed against him. He exhaled slowly. "She was one hundred and six, Im. You know she died. She probably left because your grandpa had just passed on and—"

"Her car was still there. All her stuff was still there. And she left me that message." The muscles between my shoulder blades tightened painfully.

Keane sighed. "She was quoting Stephen King."

I knew exactly where this conversation was going and how I would feel afterward, but I couldn't help it, I took the bait. "No, she said, 'There might be other worlds to see,' not 'There are other worlds than these,' there's a diff—"

"So she misquoted—" Keane cut himself off when I started pushing out of his embrace. "Okay, baby." His voice lifted on the second word like he was asking a question. He held me slightly away, pushed my short hair back from my face, then tilted my chin up so I was forced to look at him. "I know you don't like to talk about this, so I'm not going to push it but . . . it's always something. First, you wanted to wait until I was sure about the job, then you wanted to wait until after the move, and now I just feel like you're making excuses."

"Just not the fall," I said. "Any other season—"

"How about this summer then?"

It was already June. Summer was technically days away.

"You want to get married in summer in New Orleans?" Honestly, this far south it felt like summer had been sitting on us for months already.

He didn't answer, just stared into my eyes, his fingers still at my chin, his arm at my waist, still holding me to him. Keane knew how to wear me down. If it was this important to him . . . what difference did it really make when it happened?

"Fine. Summer," I said, although a surge of distress rippled beneath my skin. "We can talk about it when Dad's here."

"Really?" Keane grinned, the corners of his eyes crinkling. My heart softened. He really was a handsome guy. And he was good to me.

"Really," I said, smiling back.

He kissed me softly. "I love you, Imogen."

"I love you, too." The words came easy. We'd been saying them to each other as friends for decades. I forced another smile, the distress coalescing into eels tossing against my stomach. "I'm gonna head out for my run. The sun's gonna come up soon."

"Okay." He gave me a squeeze and released me. Keane knew what I was doing. And he was letting me. "Text me when you're close and I'll go out and get coffee for us." He snuggled back into the downy comforter.

"'Kay." I rolled out of bed and padded to the dresser in the soft brown light of near dawn. I snatched up some running shorts, a sports bra, and socks and slipped into the bathroom to get dressed. My sore Achilles still ached in spite of my rest day, but I ignored it. I couldn't get out of the house fast enough.

I stopped long enough to do a few heel drops on the front step to warm up my ankle before setting out, but that was it. The sky had lightened to pink by the time I hit the pavement. I loved the balmy June mornings. Although I was leery of hurricane season, I couldn't complain about the constant warm weather. No more treadmill-exclusive winters. I took off toward the levee. Running along the top at dawn was my new favorite way to greet the day.

I tried to shake off the tension from this morning's conversation as I ran. No one understood how hard I had taken my grandma's disappearance. We'd had a different bond. Even my father had said that he felt like an interloper sometimes when it was just the three of us together. I had a nagging feeling that Keane had used that attachment to push me into a speedy wedding. I shoved that thought away. If he had, it was done now.

My mother died when I was eight, which was about when I'd stopped emoting in the "normal way." I had to let it out physically. Running, fighting, acting. I wasn't usually a crier or a talker. Not unless things were *dire*, anyway. I think it was one of the things Keane liked about me. If something upset me, I waited until I felt safe to let it out, or I channeled it through my body.

Not for the first time, I wished my grandma was around so I could run this wedding thing by her. Ask her why I had these conflicting feelings about what was so obviously the right decision. I mean, I'd already followed the guy across the country.

Keep looking, Imogen. She would have leveled her green eyes at me. *Keep exploring. No need to pin yourself down to this one. You've got time. I don't care what anyone says.*

Nevermind that she'd met my grandfather at twenty-two and married him shortly after. Well, look where all that exploring had landed me. I had the most eclectic resume on the planet and was now a forty-five-year-old fiancée.

"Get outta my head, Grandma. Keane's great and I'm doing this." I turned up my music, ignored my aching ankle, and picked up the pace. Running was one thing I'd always done, always loved, and always been good at. And Keane was obviously the right choice. Wasn't he?

I'd only logged about three miles when I had to stop to stretch my protesting Achilles and glanced up at the rising sun. Good clouds today. I pulled my phone out of its pouch to take a picture and noticed a text message. Odd for this early. Maybe Keane needed something. I clicked on the app and my heart lifted a bit when I saw it was Al from our soccer team.

I liked Al, although I was surprised to receive a text from him at dawn. Keane and I had joined a rec league this spring to meet people and Al was another charming newcomer. We'd gotten close with the team and I'd enjoyed harmlessly flirting with Al, even though I was probably technically old enough to be his mother. He gave back as good as he got, which was fun for me, and he and Keane got along like a house on fire. Didn't hurt that he was easy on the eyes and fun to talk to. The first time the three of us had hung out alone, we'd stayed up until midnight. My 5 a.m. run the next morning had been rough, but I hadn't regretted it.

Al: Hey! I know it's early, but since you're an early bird, I took a chance you might be up. You feel like meeting for some coffee? My treat.

My finger hovered over the screen and I started walking toward the next trailhead, almost absently. Keane was supposed to get coffee for us later. But Al had never asked me to coffee before. Maybe he needed to talk. And if I was being honest with myself, I wanted someone to talk to who wasn't Keane. Seeing Al was always fun. It would give my morning a lift. And I was feeling a little reckless.

Me: I am up! On a levee run actually. Which coffee shop are you going to? I'm less than a mile from the next trailhead and I could run there.

Al: What trailhead are you near? I'll come meet you. We can go together!

Directions given, I tucked my phone away and continued my run, my pace a bit faster—in spite of my Achilles—in anticipation of seeing my friend. *Calm down*, I told the tendon. *We'll have a shorter run than planned and a nice rest at coffee.*

When I approached the trailhead, Al was already waiting. He waved.

I waved back, slowing to a walk as I reached him. He was strolling toward me. Wearing . . . a tunic and pants? Odd. His long blond hair was pulled neatly back and he was sporting the laid-back grin of a confident twenty-something without a care in the world. It was impossible not to smile back. I pulled my earbuds out of my ears and tucked them into the pouch with my phone, shutting off the music. "Hey! Fancy meeting you here. Do you live or . . . work around here?" I gestured to his attire. Come to think of it, Al had never mentioned where he worked or what he even did.

"Not exactly." He smiled and reached for my left hand as if to shake, which I automatically extended. He cupped it in both of his.

I laughed. "Sorry if my hand is sweaty."

"It's not." His amber eyes glittered. The wind blew his earthy, sandalwood scent in my direction. I was positive that I smelled of nothing but sweat, but if he noticed, he didn't seem to mind. "I'm glad you were out. Thanks for meeting up."

"Sure, how can I help?" I pushed sweaty strands of my choppy, chin-length hair out of my face with my free hand and planted my foot on a rock, taking advantage of the pause to stretch again. He clocked the movement.

"Ankle?"

"Always." I smiled, pulling slightly on my hand. He gave it a squeeze and let go. His eyes dropped to my engagement ring as his fingers brushed over it. "Ankle, shoulder, uterus . . . getting old is no fun."

He moved closer. "Maybe I can help with that."

"With . . . my ankle?" I stepped away from the rock, fiddling with the zipper on my pouch, a warning bell pinging. Was this weird? It felt weird. I glanced around for Al's car and realized there wasn't one. Had he walked here?

"Among other things." His gaze flicked to my fidgeting hands then bounced up to my face. Something flashed behind his eyes. "How'd you like to know more about your grandmother?"

I froze. My stomach turned in on itself. "What are you talking about?" I tried to remember if I'd ever talked to Al about her, riffled through my memories of post-game bar visits.

Al cleared his throat, eyes on my nervous fingers, speaking quickly as if he could sense that I was ready to bolt. "I knew her. And I know you want to know where she went and where she came from. I can tell you everything about her."

I stilled, my heart hammering. How was it possible that Keane and I had just been talking about her and Al would show up minutes later claiming to know what happened to her? Grandma would have called it a sign.

"I can tell you about where that part of your family originated and what they were like," Al spoke again when I remained silent. "And you'll get to learn everything you want about Solange."

He knows her name.

He glanced up at the sky, frowning, as if it were annoying him, then back at me. He tilted his head. The corners of his mouth turned up. "All you have to do is come with me."

"Come with you where?" Electricity bounced through my chest. *How could he know my grandma?* "Al, this is—"

His eyes flicked toward the sky again, brow furrowing. I followed his gaze. *Is it supposed to storm or something?* I saw nothing.

I shifted my weight from foot to foot. My heart desperately wanted answers. My atrophied practical side scratched at my subconscious, telling me something was off, urging me to ask more questions. "Can we go tomorrow? How far is it?"

"I have to go now, Im. I promise you'll learn all about Solange, but it has to be your choice to come. If you really want to know." He swallowed again, his jaw bunching with tension. "Some of it is probably going to be hard to hear. Up to you." He held out his hand to me. An invitation.

I hesitated. These were questions I had asked myself for so long. And was it possible . . . could she still be alive somewhere? *There might be other worlds to see . . .* No. That was ridiculous. But . . . if I could get closure . . .

"I do want to know." Why was I even trying to pretend? "Okay, I'll go." I could text Keane on the way. I reached for Al's hand. My fingers closed around his. "How far—"

He yanked me forward, pulling me hard against him. The earth fell away. The levee disappeared. We were plunged into blackness so thick it was almost tangible. I sucked in a sharp, panicked breath, my stomach lurching. There was no ground, no horizon, no sun, nothing but tumultuous current. Adrenaline punched through my veins as I instinctively scrabbled to cling to Al, the only solid, visible thing around me as we shot through a void of black wind. He hugged me tightly, chuckling. "You're okay, Im. I gotcha." I could do nothing but hang on as the entire world vanished.

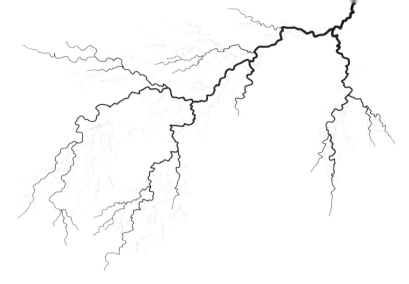

CHAPTER TWO

*It's how you handle the bad times,
not what those bad times are, that matters in the end.*
—Solange Aidair Delaney

Before I even had time to consider a "what the hell," we landed hard. My bad ankle received my full weight, and probably some of Al's. I couldn't hold back a yelp as pain clanged through my leg up to the hip. *Oh God, please don't let my Achilles have ruptured.* My leg buckled and Al hoisted me into his arms.

"Cutting it close, Aloysius. We need to head out *now*," barked an authoritative male voice. I tried to open eyes I had squeezed shut against the pain, but the room was so bright I only managed rapid blinking. I was able to discern at least five people in a cavernous space, with too-bright sunlight streaming in through enormous floor-to-ceiling windows, but no other details. My heart lodged in my throat.

Where am I?

"I'll remind you one final time: you have *no* rank on this ship and must follow the same rules as everyone else." The authoritative voice was pissed.

"I know, sorry." Al carried me briskly away, sounding anything but sorry. "She's hurt. If one of you can help, I want to turn her now, so she's comfortable."

"Al, what the fuck?" I bit out through the pain. I was still hanging on to him, my arms wrapped around his neck and shoulders. My entire body was trembling, and I couldn't get enough air into my lungs. I managed to open my eyes fully when we moved out of the bright room into a more reasonably lit hallway.

Al only squeezed me. "Bad part's almost over," he murmured and gave me a peck on the cheek. I smacked his shoulder, but there wasn't much behind it. My head was swimming.

The voice behind us said, "Llewellyn can help. I have enough people up here to get us going." Over Al's shoulder, I saw another gorgeous twenty-something striding from the bright room after us. As he got closer, I thought he looked like he could have been related to Al, only his long hair was dark red and he was taller, his muscles leaner. His face was edging to the irritated side of neutral.

"Thanks, Wells," Al tossed over his shoulder. "This is Imogen. Im, this is my brother. Imogen has a bad ankle. Among other things." He looked sideways at me, flashing his trademark rakish grin. "But she's still beautiful even when she's in pain."

"So not in the mood . . ." I puffed. I couldn't catch my breath. My ankle was throbbing. My heart raced. We passed by several identical doors, differentiated only by strange symbols above each one, along a seemingly endless corridor.

Al nudged one open, carried me into the small room, and gently set me down on some kind of narrow, padded table, the only furnishing. It reminded me of an exam table in a doctor's office.

I hissed as my foot made contact. "So, your name is Aloysius?" I gritted out, clenching my teeth, and trying to curb the now violent shaking taking over my body. Spots clustered in front of my eyes. I struggled to control my hyperventilating. "Well, *Aloysius*, I am about to lose my fucking shit. You said you'd explain . . ." I couldn't get my breath. *What kind of mess have you gotten yourself into now?*

"Leave it to Al to time everything poorly," Wells said as he entered the room and ambled around to the other side of the table, giving me a *what can you do?* smile, as if we were sharing a joke.

He was the most beautiful person I had ever seen. His eyes were the color of a sunset. Just a shade lighter than his hair. But there was something . . . *other* about him that I couldn't categorize. I stared at him as he moved to stand next to me and gently took my hand. His friendly smile dropped. "Al, she's shaking all over. She's clammy. I think she might be going into shock."

"Could be. Let's do it now." Al sounded completely unconcerned. He grabbed my other hand, took my chin between a thumb and forefinger, and pulled my face away from Wells. "Look right into my eyes, Im. You'll feel so much better in a second."

My eyes locked onto his. "Now," he said. The skin where my hands made contact with theirs heated up to an intolerable temperature. Every nerve in my body lit up and exploded as if my blood were made of lightning. I couldn't scream as the air was forced from my lungs. Then I was gone.

I woke slowly, becoming conscious before I was able to move. I was lying on something soft. A bed? I heard the sounds of someone reading nearby. How was I able to *hear* a perfectly still person reading? I tried to move, but my limbs weren't ready to respond. I took a deeper breath and could smell . . . *everything*. The pages of the book, the spicy, musky, male scent of the person holding it, the soap he had bathed with . . .

I tried to move again. *Am I paralyzed?* Panic clawed its way from my chest to my throat. *Are my other senses heightened because I—*

My foot twitched. Relief washed over me. I curled my fingers. Tried to move my head. It was so heavy. A tiny moan got stuck in my throat.

The person snapped his book shut. I heard him set it down and move closer to me. I desperately tried to open my eyes. Another whimper at the effort. My eyelids fluttered. I felt the bed sink next to my hip as he sat down beside me. *Where am I? WhereamIWhereAMI?* Gentle fingers brushed hair back from my face. I took another breath, tried again to open my eyes . . .

"That's it, Im. You can wake up. Everything's okay now." I recognized Al's voice. He continued gently stroking my face. I wanted him to stop. I wanted my goddamn body to respond to me so I could *throttle him.* He picked up my hand. "C'mon, Im. Almost there. Squeeze my hand, beautiful."

I tried to crush his hand. My fingers twitched. "That's it, good girl." *I am old enough to be your* mother, *pip-squeak,* I screamed internally. My eyelids fluttered. Fluttered. Blinked. Then opened. I would have yelped had my voice been awake.

Al was leaning over me, smiling as if Christmas had come early. He was still handsome, but . . . had somehow layered on that otherworldly beauty that I had been unable to put my finger on when I'd seen Wells. And not only that, I could see . . .

I could see individual threads in Al's tunic without trying. I could see grains of wood in the dresser on the other side of the room. There were flowing colors surrounding him. They were definitely attached to him, or emanating from him but . . . what were they? I blinked again, trying to clear my vision. *Did I hit my head?*

"There she is." Al cupped my cheek. "How's your ankle?"

My awareness instantly narrowed to my left ankle. I flexed and pointed my foot. No pain. No achiness. I rotated it 360 degrees. Nothing. Not even a click. "Seems okay . . ." I croaked. I cleared my throat. "Where—" Alarm squeezed my lungs, choking off my question. I struggled to push myself upright with stiff arms.

Al reached around my back, tucking his arm behind my shoulder, his palm supporting my neck, and helped me sit up. I wanted to shove him away but my arm buckled and I fell against him. I was wearing a short, gauzy, lilac dress. *Who the fuck changed my clothes?* Al's thumb idly stroked the side of my throat. I forced my elbows straight, locked my joints, and smacked him off. "Where am I? What did you do to me?"

The blue and green colors dancing around him brightened and sped up in response to the hardness in my voice, but soon resumed their slow swirling and cool palate. He smiled at me. It was the same charming smile Al had always wielded, but again . . . the *otherness* . . . His blond hair was down around his face, amber eyes bright.

"Told you I could help. You won't hurt anymore. Your body won't start sputtering out. Take a look . . ." He indicated a full-length mirror, surrounded by a beautiful silver frame, affixed to the wall behind him.

I shook my head, my heart hammering. "How long have I been out? I need—"

He swung my legs over the side of the bed and helped me stand up. My limbs felt oddly foreign. As if every bone in my body had lengthened, although I didn't feel taller compared to Al. My reflection in the mirror was a punch in the chest. Al kept his hand on my low back, nudging me forward.

My short, dark, wavy hair was still there, but that face . . . that *girl*. I hadn't seen that face in the mirror in at least twenty-five years. My lungs spasmed. I staggered closer, my hands pressed into the wall on either side of the mirror as I stared at this, this . . . wrinkle-free, smooth face. My eyebrows pulled up in shock, but my forehead didn't crease. I squeezed my eyes shut. When I opened them, my twenty-year-old self was still staring back.

No.

No, I had left this girl behind. I was not her anymore. My breath quickened. I hadn't realized how much I had loved my forty-five-year-old reflection. Yes, of course, I had religiously applied retinol moisturizers and cleansers and had enjoyed it when people exclaimed that I couldn't be a day over thirty-whatever, but *what the fuck.* Had Al Botoxed me or something?

I put my hand to my face. The reflection mimicked me. I pushed my cheek up. The corner of my eye didn't so much as crinkle. My heartbeat accelerated. My cheeks flushed a delicate pink. It was me from twenty-five years ago, and yet...

I had been a gorgeous kid, no doubt, but not like this. The *otherness* had claimed me too. I was speechless. My eyes darted around my reflection. Willfully ignoring the colors I could now see swirling around me, too. Obviously I had some kind of concussion. Then I caught sight of my own eyes and stilled.

Those were not my eyes.

I leaned closer. My eyes had always been dark brown, just like my dad's. They were now a deep violet. "What did you do to my eyes?" I rasped.

Al rubbed small circles between my shoulder blades. "Although yours were lovely, I did take some creative liberties there. That's the only spot." His calm smile in the reflection was maddening. It was as if he had designed me a dress to wear and had just altered it a bit in a sudden burst of creativity.

I touched a finger to the corner of my eye and noticed my hands. Slim, long—my fingers had never been long. I took a shaky breath, pushed my hands into my hair, and in doing so revealed my ears.

Ears which now tapered to a delicate point. *Spock ears?*

I tugged on one. It stayed firmly attached. My chest tightened.

I pushed back from the mirror, taking in my entire reflection. My limbs had felt foreign because they *were* foreign. I had always had long, toned arms, but my legs had been shorter, runner's legs. Not anymore. My entire body was lanky, graceful in the stupid purple dress. I clutched at my now narrow midsection. Before I'd been more of a newspaper shape, my torso long and rather waistless. There was a slight relief at finding the muscle tone still present but...

I whirled on Al. Heart hammering. "What have you done to me?" My voice broke. I felt my lower lip quiver and smashed my mouth into a hard line.

His eyes softened with sympathy, and the colors surrounding him changed subtly. *Is that his aura? Can I see auras now? Do Vulcans see auras?* He gently grasped my upper arms. "You've been made sidhe," he said, smiling again. He pushed his curtain of blond hair back behind one arching ear.

"What?" I yelped.

"Like your grandmother was."

"I'm sorry, *what*?" My brain was exploding.

"Before Solange was human, she was a sidhe for centuries. And now so are you. You'll never get old, at least, not like humans do. You'll heal quickly. And you have time to do all of those things you've always wanted to do."

A choked guffaw clattered up my throat. This was insanity! Keane was going to flip out when I told him. My blood chilled.

"Keane . . ." I whispered. *How long has Al had me here?* My imagination played a short movie of Keane waking up with the sun filtering too brightly through the window of our bedroom. Checking the clock, seeing that it was far too late. Throwing back the covers, calling my name . . .

Al's swaggering smile flickered. "He never had your energy, your drive. Your adventurous spirit. He's fine. He'll be sad for a bit, but he'll recover. You were wasted on Earth."

My stomach turned to stone. My spine stiffened. I slammed the heels of my palms into Al's shoulders and he staggered back. My proprioception was returning. This strange body was obeying me. "Take me back. Now."

"Calm down, you're just stunned, Im. You can't go back. Earth is a billion miles behind us and we won't be able to return for another century. Once you get used to everything, you'll be so much happier, I promise—"

My right cross arrowed to Al's nose, carrying all of my fear and anger with it. Apparently this body had absorbed the training of the previous one. My weight shift was perfect and my aim was dead on.

He caught my fist. Barely.

I didn't hesitate and followed up with a left elbow to his temple. He blocked, but I was gaining momentum, fueled by terror and a newly surfacing grief. Al defended effectively, but I was backing him up. Then he turned so quickly I didn't catch it between one blink and the next. He pinned me against a wall. I didn't have time to start jamming my fingers into pressure points before he said, "*Stop fighting me!*" His voice changed, ringing with a primal command that clanged through me. My body obeyed him. My limbs went pliant. I stopped fighting.

He blew out a breath, tension dropping out of his face. "There." He rubbed my arms. "I understand this is an adjustment but, Im, everything is going to be better for you now. I promise."

He slid an arm around me, guiding me back toward the bed. My mind screamed to pull back, to slap, to shove him away, but my body refused to fight him. *What the fuck is happening?* He guided me to a seat on the edge of the mattress, one arm hugging my waist. I couldn't make myself push him away. He brushed a stray lock of hair off my cheek and tucked it behind my ear.

"What did you just do to me?" My voice shook. Had he drugged me? I hadn't seen drugs. I didn't feel drugged. I forced myself to look into his eyes, my stomach flipping when I saw how close our faces were.

"Compulsion. Kroma. Humans don't have it." The corners of his mouth lifted. "You'll start to feel yours, too, don't worry, it just takes a while for your kroma to manifest and for you to gain control of it when it does."

As if possessing alien powers was one of my top priorities right now. *He's insane. I've allowed myself to be kidnapped by a crazy person,* I thought. But I had been physically changed somehow. And he had taken away my ability to fight with a word. *He could do anything he wants to me.* His eyes dipped to my lips. My throat closed. He looked back up at me, brushing his thumb across my cheek.

"Since I'm the one who found you and turned you, I'm responsible for you. And you're new. I can make sure you don't hurt yourself or anyone else as your kromas develop. We'll see what you end up with, but for right now, this is really safest. I can look out for you." His arm tightened around my waist. The hand at my cheek tilted my chin up. His thumb brushed across my lower lip and his gaze softened.

My body wouldn't pull back. I tried with all my might to shove him away but the most I was able to do was press my hands lightly to his chest.

He hugged me closer, tilting his head. I whimpered when I realized where this could go.

His hand stilled on my cheek. He dragged smoldering eyes away from my lips to meet mine. I saw his aura shift when he felt me trembling. "Too much?"

I nodded. My heart pounding in my ears.

He nodded back. "Okay." He kissed my cheek, skimmed his knuckles along my jaw. "You've had a big day. I can wait. You probably have questions, we can just talk—"

"I want to go home," I whispered, my voice shaking. I dropped my eyes from his. They landed on my hands, still pressed against his chest. My ring was gone. "Where is my ring?" My voice steadied. Hardened. An image flashed across my mind's eye: the sun setting behind Keane when he'd worked up the nerve to propose and slid that ring on my finger, our friends beaming around us . . .

"You know that marrying Keane would have been a mistake," Al said, rubbing my arm. His aura spun more quickly. As if he knew I was nearing an edge. "You let him talk you into it, but you knew it wasn't right. You're sidhe now. And you're free."

"You have a fucked-up idea of what freedom is," I said, my voice breaking.

The colors swirling around Al paused for a blink and a flash of ochre shot through them. *Guilt?* A part of my brain still tried to make sense of things. But his aura resumed its usual dance after only a moment. Whatever his motives, Al didn't truly believe or understand that he was hurting me.

"I'm going to give you a good life, Imogen. A *long* life." He gave me a squeeze, one hand resting on my bare shoulder, his thumb tracing circles over my skin. "I want to make you happy. I want you to be able to do everything you want. Solange was so gifted. I know you will be too."

"I *was* happy," I choked. *Oh God, what is happening?* "I *was* doing what I wanted. *I am engaged to Keane.* He's going to be freaking out right now, Al, c'mon . . ."

His eyes dropped from mine and his focus seemed to go internal. I wondered if I'd struck a chord somewhere. I latched on. "You were friends with Keane too," I said, my words coming out quick and breathless. "He's going to be devastated, Al, you don't want to do that to him. We were just about to set a date—"

"Im, I'm going to need you to keep a secret for a while." His throat bobbed.

"Okay, what secret?" My heart picked up its pace. *Does he want me to say that I won't tell anyone he took me? Sure, I'll tell him whatever the hell he wants, get home and go straight to the goddamn police...*

"You can't tell anyone when we met." Caution darkened his amber eyes when they found mine again.

I nodded, encouraging him. *Sure, I never fucking knew you. Get me home, asshole.*

He cleared his throat. "You can't tell them about Keane. You can't say that you didn't know you were coming with me to Molnair."

I blinked. "What the hell is Molnair?"

"That's where we're going," he said. "That's my country on Perimov. *Your* country. Where Solange was from. That's home."

I was thrown. "I don't understand."

Al plucked one of my hands from his chest, kissed it, then kept hold of it, running his thumb over my knuckles. My shoulders tensed.

"We're allowed eight months on Earth," he said. "We're supposed to find a potential partner with no less than six months to go or our search is terminated. It took me too long to find you, so I didn't have time to explain some things. But once I knew you, I couldn't leave you behind to fade away and die. So I . . . sped things up. I just need you to keep quiet about the fact that you were engaged, that you didn't know you were coming, and that we only met three months ago. Just for a while. Until we get home. And I promise I'll tell you all about Solange. You're so much like her, Imogen."

I sat stunned, my brain whirling. There was only one useful thing I picked up from what he said. If he wanted me to keep quiet, that meant there were other people here who wouldn't approve of what he was doing. And maybe not far away.

I couldn't fight, but I still had a voice.

I screamed.

Al clapped his hand over my mouth, but I didn't stop.

"Shhhh, Im, c'mon! Fuck." He pushed me down onto the bed, one hand still clamped over my mouth and stretched the other off to the side. A vial of silvery liquid flew into it. He pulled the cork out with his teeth, removed his hand from my mouth, and dumped the liquid in, covering my mouth and nose when he was done, forcing me to swallow. Once I had, he released me.

I coughed and gasped. Trying to catch my breath. Meanwhile, Al yanked back the covers and shoved me underneath them. "I'm sorry, Im. This is for the best. We'll get through this part."

My muscles went slack. My eyelids were impossibly heavy. "What . . ." I slurred.

Al knelt by the bed, tucking me in, brushing my hair back from my face. "Just a sleeping potion, Im. You'll feel better in the morning. We'll get breakfast. We can talk." He kissed my forehead. "I care about you so much, Imogen. We're going to be great together."

You barely know me, I thought, but no words came out. I fought the potion hard, but it had its hooks in me. I was still clinging to consciousness when I heard Al's door open.

"Did I hear screaming?" A male voice I'd heard before.

"Yeah, sorry, she had a nightmare," Al answered, still stroking my head. "I think she's a little disoriented. I gave her a sleeping potion, she should be fine now."

"If you're able to take your shift, I can sit and watch her for a bit," the voice said. "With your close call leaving orbit—"

"Yeah, that would probably be a good idea." Al tucked the covers tighter around me and dropped another kiss on my forehead. "Thanks, Wells."

The claws I had dug into consciousness slipped and I went under.

When I opened my eyes, Al was sitting next to me. As if he had been waiting for me to wake up.

"*Imogen, keep the secret,*" he said in that ringing voice.

My heart crumbled.

I knew I was lost.

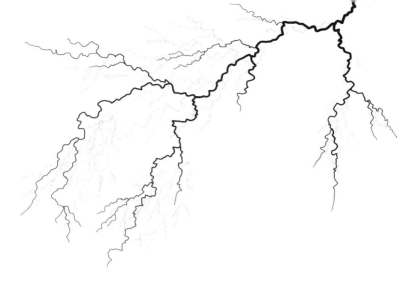

CHAPTER THREE

Do you think anything is what it's pretending to be?
Hell, I'm not even who I'm pretending to be half the time!
—Solange Aidair Delaney

Al brought me down one floor to the communal kitchen that morning for breakfast. The kitchen and common areas were one level below the crew quarters, he explained. Though I barely listened to him. He'd tried to get me to shower and change and I'd refused. I'd refused to do anything other than stare at the wall in his stupid, windowless room. My will had been taken from me. My life had been taken from me. What did it matter if I was clean? Some distant part of my brain still clocked the colors flowing around Al and tried to interpret them. Noticed that he was worried. At least that's what I thought those blue-blacks in his normal sea-green aura meant.

He hooked my arm around his and escorted me into the hallway. I didn't try to stop him. Perhaps I could get the lay of the land. Find a way to sneak out of here. By now there was probably a missing persons alert at least statewide. If the soccer team had noticed Al missing also, the police had probably put two and two together.

The curved hallways were narrow, windowless, bare. Our unshod feet padded over a textured floor that felt like fiberglass. It reminded me of being on a boat. "What is this place?" I asked.

They were the first words I'd spoken since he'd compelled me to keep the secret. Al's aura flared. He reached over with his other hand and squeezed my limp fingers. "This is our spaceship, Im. The *Promise*. It's what we use to travel to Earth and back every hundred years. Each deck is circular." He turned sharply and an unmarked door slid away to reveal a stairwell. Al guided me downward. "The main bridge, where we first came on board is above, and the kitchen is below—but you don't need to worry about it really. Only a couple more days and we'll be home." He rubbed my hand then dropped his arm to his side. The colors around him flashed more vibrantly. He grinned at me. I didn't smile back. I turned my gaze back to my surroundings. My stomach churning. Were we really in space? This made getting out much more difficult. *Maybe he's lying . . .*

At the next landing, another door whooshed open. Al pulled me into the kitchen, which was set up like an over-large galley. I had expected some kind of cafeteria, but this was more like an open concept cooking area. It reminded me of one of those sushi restaurants with the kitchen placed so diners can watch the chefs preparing the pretty little sushi rolls. The three sidhe manning the stoves appeared to be cooking with . . . magic? I blinked hard and stared.

One would float a kettle of something over to another, who would point at the hearth and ignite a fire with a snap of his fingers. Another sliced a loaf of bread by shooting transparent green blades at it that materialized with a flick of his wrist. The loaf separated into neat pieces wherever the colors touched. The few people eating this early were sitting at one of two long tables, either having a conversation with their neighbor, reading, or just concentrating on their food. As if what the three chefs were doing was completely mundane. I couldn't help watching the mystical cooking show. This was poking holes in a theory I'd been building that I was hypnotized somehow.

Then I felt Al tense and pulled my attention away. The redhead who'd helped Al turn me was strolling over to us. His brother.

"Hi, Wells," Al said. I wondered if his voice only sounded strained to me.

Wells smiled pleasantly as he approached. He was wearing a dark green button-down shirt with the sleeves rolled to his elbows, which, along with longer tunic-type shirts, seemed to be one of the main styles here. His sturdy dark pants had plenty of pockets. I would have taken a pair of those over the wispy dress I'd been stuck in. He had a cup of some kind of liquid that smelled . . . like coffee and yet, not . . . "Good morning," he said to both of us, then cocked his head toward me, putting a hand in his pocket. "Was the rest of your night better?"

I want to go home. I don't know him. I didn't ask to come here, I tried to say. But the words caught in my throat. All I could do was stare into his sunset-colored eyes. My mouth wouldn't even open.

Al cleared his throat, brushing a hand down his own sky-blue tunic. His was fancy, with gold accents at the cuffs and collar. "I think she's still a little groggy. We're just going to get something to go. I'll see you on the bridge later though." He tugged me along to the counter. "No meat except fish, right? Eggs are okay though?"

I swiveled to gaze behind us and found Wells still staring. His aura swirling with blue-blacks and orange-pinks. Concern and . . . curiosity?

Al put an arm around my shoulders and nudged my face forward with a thumb to my chin. "Look, Im." He pointed. "These are a little different from the muffins and croissants you're used to, but I think you'll like them. What looks good? I forget, do you like nuts?"

I stared blankly at the beautiful baked goods.

When I didn't speak, Al quickly ordered one of each item, two of the coffee-like drinks—which he called jatkis—and hustled me back to the room.

I wouldn't eat.

"Im, you have to get something in your stomach. You were out for days after we turned you." Al was sitting cross-legged on the floor in front of me, between me and the only exit. The room was windowless, like everywhere else, with a double bed built into the wall and floor, a nightstand on either side, similarly attached, a chest of drawers, a small bathroom, and one single chair. The chairs in these rooms were incongruous with the rest of the spartan décor, like antique, fabric-covered BarcaLoungers. I sat curled in the chair and stared at the floor, my warm jatki next to me on the nightstand, his on the floor by his knee. He had flattened the sack he'd carried the pastries in and lined them up on top of it. He picked up a cinnamon-colored, flakey oval and held it out to me. "Look, I know you're upset with me, but I promise, eventually, you'll thank me and you'll be glad you're in Molnair. You're going to love it there."

I refused to look at him. "I want to go home."

Al sighed and dropped his arm. He set down the pastry and buried his hands in his hair. "Im, we've been over this. There's no way to get you back. Not for another hundred years. Our collective kroma has to have an anchor and we depend on the movement of the stars and planets en route to get us there and home." He looked up and took my limp hand in both of his. "Please eat something, baby. It's been days."

I dragged my eyes up to his. "I don't care."

My whole life was gone. I might as well be dead already. Keane probably thought I was. Or he thought I'd run away. The ultimate wedding dodge. My stomach turned. I couldn't think of eating. I turned away and yanked my hand free.

Al's face broke, then hardened. His aura fractured around him as he grabbed a pastry and thrust it toward me. "Imogen. Either you eat it yourself, or I'll make you."

My stomach twisted. I held my breath. Which was worse? I imagined my body being compelled to eat . . . I snatched the food from his hand. "Fuck you," I seethed.

His aura cracked again. "You'll be better once we get home," he said. "You'll realize you belong there." I didn't know if he was trying to convince me or himself.

Al tried again to get me to shower and change. Only after he threatened to compel me did I capitulate. He spread all the clothes he'd brought for me out on the bed, many with the tags still on. I ground my teeth. He'd been planning my abduction long enough to go shopping. I had a choice between more feminine dresses or workout gear. I picked shorts and a tank top. Neither of them meant for casual wear. His jaw clenched but he must have decided not to argue in favor of getting me in the shower.

I breathed against the panic tightening my lungs as the hot water beat against my skin, vowing to find a way out. I had to at least try. There must be an escape pod or something. I took my time showering, drying off, and getting dressed.

I didn't want to go back into the bedroom. I stood in the tiny bathroom, fully dressed, my hair towel dried, and searched for an exit. Couldn't see an air vent. I checked the small cabinet. I checked the walls. I checked under the bathmat. No way to sneak out. I huddled in a corner on the floor and curled in on myself hugging my towel.

I flinched when Al opened the door several minutes later. His aura flared in surprise. The colors were brighter and easier to read since I'd eaten.

"C'mon, Im, get off the floor." He held out a hand.

Anger flooded through me. Frustration grated against my sternum. "Either take me home or leave me alone," I growled, but I did stand, disliking the disparity of him towering over me. "Better yet, just leave me alone and I'll find my own way home." Then, because I somehow knew it would get under his skin, I added, "I have a fiancé to get back to."

His eyes simmered as he dropped his hand. "You're behaving like a child," he said finally. "You didn't belong on Earth and you certainly didn't belong with Keane. You were more attracted to me than you ever were to him."

I threw the towel into his face as hard as I could. "I've been attracted to a lot of assholes, that doesn't mean they were good for me." I shimmied around him and stalked toward the door.

Between one blink and the next he was blocking my way. "Where do you think you're going?"

"Away from you." I tried to push past him.

He slammed his hand into the wall, blocking me with his arm. I glared up at him. He took a breath.

"Imogen, let's talk for a minute—"

There was a knock at the door.

Al glanced at it, then back to me. "Stay there. Just a second." He kept an eye on me as he crossed to the door and opened it only enough to speak to the person on the other side.

"Yeah," I heard him say. "Just let me get Imogen settled. Maybe ten ... fifteen minutes?"

What does he mean by "settled?" I scanned the room, furious at being unable to fight him. The bed had drawers built into the base, no way to scurry beneath it. I could shut myself back in the bathroom. There was no lock, but maybe I could hold the door long enough to scream. I could—

Al closed the door and leaned against it. "Imogen." His eyes lifted to mine. His aura had changed. A strange crimson color pushed through the sea greens and blues. "I have to take a shift, Im."

"I don't know what that means," I said, my voice hard. "You haven't explained anything to me."

He blinked. "We all take turns powering the ship with our kroma. I'm one of the more powerful people aboard. So is Wells, who you met. There are only a handful of people on board with our level of energy. They like at least one of us to be on duty when we're in difficult spots." He pushed off the door and took a step toward me. I backed up. "You've been pretty upset today and kind of volatile, so I'm going to suggest that you take a nap while

I'm gone." He reached out his hand and another vial of that silvery liquid appeared within his grasp.

"No!" I jumped onto the bed to avoid him and launched myself back toward the bathroom. I got one hand on the doorframe before he had me around the waist, pinning my other arm to my side. I kicked and my heel made contact with his shin.

I could fight.

Perhaps he can only compel one thing at a time. I redoubled my efforts, but he'd already brought me to the ground, using his weight to pin me down while he dosed me again.

"I'm sorry, Imogen," he panted as my body relaxed. "When you wake up, we'll talk about everything. I'll make time. I'll get Wells to take a double shift or something." He lifted himself off me and rolled me into his arms. "I promise you'll thank me someday."

"I'll always hate you," I breathed as my eyelids dropped shut.

When I awoke the room was dark. I was lying on my side and Al was curled around me, hugging me into the curve of his torso. I pushed out of his arms so hard I fell off the bed. He didn't stir. I noticed what looked like an empty bottle of wine on the nightstand. This was my lucky break.

My heart hammered against my ribcage. I didn't give myself a chance to second-guess. I grabbed the empty bottle and managed to locate the rubber stopper. I brought both into the bathroom, rinsed the bottle, and then filled it with water. Once stoppered, it was air tight. I wrapped it in a hand towel and nestled it in the sack of leftover pastries. Hopefully this would be enough to get me to Earth. Pending my ability to operate an escape pod.

Pending my successful location of an escape pod.

I slipped out of the room and shut the door behind me.

My sensitive new nose was pummeled with scents. I'd noticed this in the galley, but had been too overwhelmed to make sense of it. I stopped, focused, caught Al's scent. Other people's. A thrill shot up my spine. *I have a dog nose!* Many people had gone to my right, fewer had passed to my left. I went right. If there were going to be escape pods, they would probably be in some central location. I jogged down the hallway, my heart lighter than it had been since I was taken. I was doing something. I was getting out. I increased my speed.

I turned the corner and ran smack into Wells.

And fell right on my ass. Wells stumbled back a few steps but caught himself. "I'm sorry," I mumbled. Before I could get my feet underneath me, he bent down to offer me a hand up. "Thanks." I took his hand but kept my eyes down as I slowly stood. My face and neck burned with embarrassment.

"Imogen?"

I nodded. "Sorry for running into you," I said to the floor. I was sure that he had some kind of sidhe way of looking into my eyes and knowing that I was trying to run away.

Wells squeezed my hand and leaned down to catch my gaze. I was once again reminded of a sunset.

"Are you all right?" he asked.

"No," I said, and flinched. Was the compulsion gone? Could kroma wear off? I tried to follow up and say that I was kidnapped and wanted to go home. My jaw locked. I ground my teeth. *But there are* some *things I can say.* I tried to say Al had kidnapped me in every way I could think of. My mouth stayed firmly shut. I started shaking.

Wells scanned me from head to toe, my hand still lightly clasped in his. He finally sighed and said, "Let's get you back to Al."

"No!" I yanked my fingers out of his grasp and sprinted blindly down the hall. And crashed into Wells again. I stumbled but he caught me before I fell. *How did he move so quickly?* Had I starved myself so much that I was that slow? "I don't want to go back." I pulled against him and he released me immediately, but stood blocking my way.

"Did something happen?" His dark red brows pinched together, aura spinning blue-black.

"Yes," I said. A thrill shot up my spine. *Al took me from my life. I have a fiancé.* My mouth sealed shut again. I clenched my fists and blew out a breath.

"All right, Imogen—" Wells took a step toward me, I took a step back. He lifted his palms and retreated a half step. I looked him over. He was taller than Al, leaner, with a longer reach. Just as toned as his brother. And apparently very fast. I wasn't going to outrun him.

"Imogen, I need you to tell me what's wrong," he said gently.

Such a reasonable request.

"I can't," I spat, surprising myself. So I could tell him that I had restrictions. Interesting. I tried to remember all of the terms of "the secret." There had to be some way . . .

"You can't, or you won't?" Wells asked, his russet eyes fixed on me.

"Can't," I said clearly. "I keep trying—" My mouth sealed itself shut as soon as I thought of telling him what Al had done.

"So there's something wrong that you cannot tell me?"

"Yes," I said, blowing out a breath.

"And Al compelled you to keep this quiet?"

"Yes." My knees wobbled in relief.

"Imogen," Wells looked right at me, "did you want to leave Earth with Al?"

My lips clamped shut. I couldn't answer.

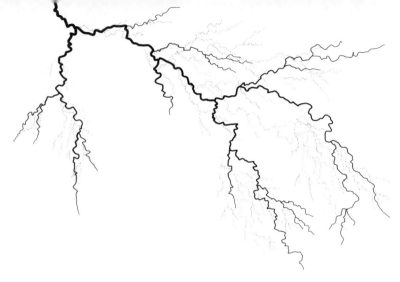

CHAPTER FOUR

There are always going to be horrible things going on. The trick is to find the people out there willing to do something about it. Stick with them. Be them.
—Solange Aidair Delaney

Wells coaxed me back up the hall to his room, promising me that he wouldn't bring me back to Al. I balked when I saw his room was right next door, but he patiently assured me that he could handle Al if it came to that. He left the door wide open so I wouldn't feel trapped.

His room was laid out like Al's in reverse. Wells's BarcaLounger was covered in books and clothes, which he shifted to the floor before offering me the seat. I dropped my sack of rations nearby and perched on the chair, hugging my knees to my chest.

"I'm just going to ask Captain Marc to come down," Wells said, sitting on the edge of the bed facing me. "If he's still awake, he might be able to remove the compulsion. Don't worry, he won't need to touch you." I watched in fascination as his aura separated above his head. He stared into the middle distance for several seconds, then sat back. His aura resumed its flow. "He's awake," he told me. "He'll be by shortly."

I blinked at him.

"I'm a telepath." One corner of his mouth lifted in a half smile.

"Oh," I said. "Neat."

He snorted. His eyes fell on the sack. He sniffed. "Do you have . . . baked goods in there?"

I flushed. "And water."

He locked eyes with me; I refused to look away, even as my face grew warmer. My escape idea seemed so idiotic now.

"Where were you going tonight?"

"Home." I blinked. I hadn't expected to be able to say anything. Then I realized that nothing I had done tonight was part of the secret.

Wells's aura tumbled through a rainbow array. "You mean . . . back to Earth?"

I nodded and dropped my eyes. *He's going to laugh at me and I'll deserve it.* How many half-baked escapades of mine had Keane had to rescue me from over the years? He was the planner, I was the doer. I could almost hear him chuckling, could picture him shaking his head at the thought of me running around an alien spaceship, hoping to find an escape pod with a bag of muffins. My heart cracked.

"How were you going to get back to Earth?" Wells was still watching me.

I shrugged. "I thought maybe I could find . . ." Escape pods sounded ludicrous. "A smaller ship on the bigger ship. Like a dinghy or something." I wanted to hide my face, but I refused to let myself.

"We don't have any," Wells said. "How were you going to operate it if we did? The ship is powered by kroma. I doubt you have control of yours yet—"

"Look, I didn't say it was a great plan." I dropped my legs and leaned back in the chair, letting my arms fall to the rolled armrests. "I just thought it might be my only chance to get away from him and I had to try."

"I'm not trying to disparage you, Imogen," Wells said, his aura swirling with pale blues. Sympathy? "I'm trying to understand. How did Al get you to agree to come?"

Once again, my jaw slammed shut over the words, trapping them inside. I shook my head. My stomach churned. My fingers dented the arms of the chair as I squirmed against the compulsion. A growl of frustration tore through my clenched teeth.

"All right, it's okay." Wells half-stood, as if he were going to cross to me and thought better of it. "Captain Marc will be here soon. I won't ask you any more questions until then. I'm sorry, I know it's frustrating."

"I hate this," I panted, keeping a firm leash on the swirl of emotions beating at my ribs. I didn't want to appear any more vulnerable than I already was.

"No one likes being compelled, Imogen," he said gently. "It's not something to be done lightly." He sighed, then added, "It doesn't tend to generate feelings of trust and goodwill when done for . . . selfish reasons."

A graceful, dark-complected sidhe rapped his knuckles on the open door. His head was fully shaved. His black eyebrows made handsome slashes over deep brown eyes. Wells waved him over the threshold, thanking him for coming.

"Tonight was far too dull anyway," he replied, glancing between the two of us. I recognized his voice from when Al first brought me on board. His dark eyes came to rest on Wells. "What's he done?"

"I'm not sure," he said, glancing at me. "He's compelled Imogen to keep it a secret." Wells stood and slid his hands into his pockets. "I ran into her trying to find a way back to Earth. She was terrified of being brought back to Al."

The captain rolled his eyes and stepped into the room. "I told Allistair I wouldn't tolerate his son's typical behavior on this expedition," he muttered, a crease forming between his eyebrows. He shook his head, his face softening as his eyes met mine. "Hello, Imogen. I'm Captain Marc. All right if I get closer?"

I nodded and forced myself to keep my chin up and my back straight, as much as I wanted to shrink away from Captain Marc's softly glowing hands. He didn't touch me, but came near enough that my skin warmed as he passed his hands near my head and chest. "Gods' bones, what's he done to you?" His brow furrowed. "Let's just see if we can pull it off, shall we?"

It was as if the skin on my throat was being tugged at. My jaw felt warm, then hot. My skin tingled, itched. I couldn't repress a head shake when my ears began buzzing.

"Can't do it," Marc said, dropping his hands and backing away, his mouth bracketed with tension. "He's done it well. How much of a stink would it cause if I threw him into the brig?"

He glanced at Wells, whose eyes widened. Captain Marc blew out a breath. "I know, not worth it. At any rate, we'll have to get him to remove it himself. I'll wake him, shall I?" He stormed into the hall. I heard Al's door crash open. I flinched. Pulled my legs up onto the chair. Saw Wells watching me and put them back down.

Wells looked like he was about to say something, but Marc hauled a disheveled Aloysius into the room.

Al saw me and sagged, the tightness dropping out of his face. "Imogen, where did you go?" He stepped toward me. "Thanks for finding her, I'll take—"

Captain Marc slammed a palm into Al's chest. "Aloysius, remove the compulsion."

Al froze. His face darkened. Amber eyes snapped up to mine. He took a breath. "Look," he said, quietly. "Just let me take her. I'll get her settled down. I'm sorry she—"

"Got out?" Marc spat. "I've been wondering why you haven't been bringing her into the common areas. The other twelve are happy to show off their partners, let them meet each other. I thought something was up. Remove the compulsion. Imogen is staying right where she is otherwise."

Al's aura spun faster and faster. "C'mon, Im." He held out a hand, his eyes bright with anxiety. "You don't want to stay here, do you?"

This time I didn't stop myself from pressing back into the chair and pulling my legs up in front of me.

Wells's face was stricken. "Al, what have you done to her?" he whispered.

Al's head snapped toward Wells. "Nothing!" I saw a black spike pierce his aura and wondered at it. "I—fine. Imogen, you can say whatever you want."

I felt it release me. Like stripping off a slightly undersized shirt. "I want to go home, I'm engaged, I have a family, I didn't want to leave . . ." Relief washed over me in overwhelming waves. I paused and took a shuddering breath.

Wells took a step toward Al and Marc. "Al." His voice was strained, his aura spinning with distress. "Tell me you didn't just . . . find a woman who looked remarkably like Solange and . . . take her."

Al folded his arms and dropped his shoulder against the door frame, glaring at the floor. "She's not some random person. She's Solange's granddaughter," he said.

"He promised to tell me why she disappeared. He said if I went with him . . ." I swallowed. "He never said I wouldn't be able to get back."

The other two were gaping at Al.

"Tell me you're not Solange Aidair Delaney's granddaughter," Captain Marc said, sagging against the wall as if he were dreading my answer.

"That would be lying," I said, narrowing my eyes in Al's direction. "And I'm not the liar here."

"Henry Delaney was your grandfather?" Captain Marc straightened again.

"Yeah." I sat up a little taller. Maybe I'd finally get some answers. "How do you know my grandparents?"

"Because," Wells's voice was edged, "Aloysius was very much in love with Solange Aidair when she was sidhe."

I sat all the way up. My feet dropped to the floor.

Wells's eyes flicked to Al, then back to me. "Solange gave up her immortality to be with Henry Delaney. It's incredibly rare for a sidhe to decide to go human rather than the other way around, but it has happened a few times. And generally, we respect the choice." Wells crossed his arms, turning to glare at Al—who glared right back, looking mutinous—and said, "We thought Al would never get over losing Solange. And apparently, he never did."

"What the fuck have you done, Aloysius?" The captain shook his head, rubbing his temples. "If *anyone* else had pulled a stunt like this—"

"Look, it wasn't entirely selfish," Al bit out. "Imogen is special. She's different. Solange's line was talented. Imogen is so much like her, I know she's going to be exceptional. And she belongs in Molnair. Once she sees it, she'll understand. She'll be happy."

These people all knew my grandmother? How? And how could Al have been in love with her? She had to have died when he was a kid...

Everything Al had said about being immortal eddied down into my mind like settling snow. She'd been sidhe before. If this was all true, it made a crazy kind of sense. How she'd seemed so certain about so many things. Seemed to have lived such a life before meeting my grandpa at twenty-two. Could she still be alive somewhere? Perhaps she hadn't died—just gone home. My head was spinning. The possibility that I truly might be unable to get back was hollowing out my insides, but if I could see her again... *Keane, this is the biggest mess I've ever been in...* Unnoticed by the three arguing sidhe, I curled into a tight shivering ball in the chair, trying to hold myself together. I needed to run, to move. But there was nowhere to go. I had no outlet.

"I knew Solange and I know Imogen," Al was saying. "I can make her happy. She'll be fine with me."

"You've certainly been doing a fantastic job," Wells snapped. "As evidenced by her running around the ship in the dead of night with a bag of pastries and water, trying to find a way back to Earth."

"I found her. I turned her. You can't take her from me—"

"I don't sense a mating bond," Captain Marc said coolly. "And I take great joy in reminding you *once again* that you have no rank on this ship, as per your father's agreement."

Everything spun around me. The world was tilting. I squeezed my eyes shut, hugging myself, and tried to focus on my body crushed into the fabric of the chair. My breath pulling in and out. But my world was crumbling into pieces. Nothing made sense. I had no true north. No Keane to ground me. No father. No grandma. No friends. No Earth. Nothing. I didn't even fully understand what I'd become. I was slipping away. My mind cocooned itself in numbing, protective folds of blackness and tucked me in.

When I came to, I was surrounded by warmth and a pleasant scent. I opened my eyes to find myself wrapped in a downy comforter, still curled in the chair, surrounded by silence. Except for someone else breathing deeply. I tensed. The rhythm of the breathing didn't change. Whoever it was, they were asleep. Not currently a threat. I dared to push myself to a seat.

I was still in Wells's room. It was dark, other than one nightstand lamp emitting a soft, warm light. The door was now closed. I panned the area from my nest. Wells was sprawled across the mattress, wearing the same black shirt, sleeves rolled to the elbows, and sturdy gray pants he had been wearing when I'd run into him. He appeared to have given up his comforter to me. My stomach growled loudly.

Wells inhaled deeply, then opened his eyes. I was again struck by their warm, ruddy color. When I'd first met Al, I'd thought his amber eyes were the most beautiful, unusual color I'd ever seen. Wells topped him, hands down. Although the fact that Wells had never kidnapped me may have subconsciously swayed my preference. He pushed himself upright, straightening his now quite rumpled shirt and running a hand through his long, red hair. "Good morning," he said. I thought I saw a faint flush along his cheekbones.

"Is it morning?" I asked. "I have no concept of time anymore. Why are there no windows here?"

"Safer," he replied, swinging his legs over the side of the bed. "There are a few places on the ship with windows if you want to—"

My stomach growled again. His eyes met mine, then he grabbed the sack of pastries—I noticed the wine bottle no longer weighed it down—and peered inside. "Do you want a day-old sweetbread or would you like to get something fresh from the kitchen?"

"I'm not hungry," I lied.

"Then you won't mind if I have one." Wells pulled a flakey pastry out of the bag and took a bite. My stomach protested loudly as the scent of the tart filling permeated the room. Wells swallowed his mouthful, long lashes flicking up as his eyes met mine. "I think you are hungry, Imogen. Why don't you want to eat?"

My throat worked against the saliva and bile fighting for dominance. "I'm hungry," I admitted, "but my stomach is upset. When I eat, I want to throw up."

His aura swirled with eddies of pale blues. He set down his half-finished pastry and tugged open the top nightstand drawer. "That's because you're . . . traumatized." He plucked something from within. "But you need to have something." He extended his open palm toward me. A small, rectangular brick, like a mini chocolate bar, sat in the center. "See if you can keep down a bite of this."

I gingerly picked it up and sniffed it. I was reminded of a Flintstones multivitamin. If someone had made a Flintstones-flavored power bar. "What is it?"

Wells retrieved his pastry. "A quick fix. We use them when we have to do a double shift to keep our kroma from tiring when we don't have time for an actual meal."

I nibbled on a corner. It wasn't bad. My stomach swirled, but didn't push back. My next bite was less cautious. We ate in silence for a few moments, unasked questions thickening the air between us. I waited until I'd swallowed the last bite of the quick fix before I asked, "How long have I been here?"

Wells paused in chewing his pastry. His throat worked as if he were having a difficult time swallowing before he answered. "A week. One of our weeks," he clarified. "Eight days."

My stomach flipped. I gripped the edges of the comforter, tugging it around me. "Everyone probably thinks I'm dead," I whispered, blinking against the stinging behind my eyes.

Wells froze, then set the remainder of his pastry to the side. His aura splashed with a dark orange. "Didn't Al put glamours on their memories or..." He trailed off when I furrowed my brow and frowned. "What exactly did Al tell you, Imogen?"

I couldn't repress a snort. "Well, he showed up on my running trail at the crack of dawn and said he could tell me what happened to my grandma. I just had to go with him." I pushed the duvet off my shoulders. "I didn't know it was a... forever type of thing. I didn't know he was going to change me. I thought he was just some guy from our soccer team."

I didn't need to read his aura. His face had paled. His knuckles were white where he gripped the edges of the bed. I could hear his heart galloping. I took a shot.

"I need to get home. Can't you just... turn me back and take me home?" I stared at him. The dark oranges and butter yellows tumbling through his aura were suddenly flooded with blues and indigos. "Please?" I refused to break eye contact.

His throat bobbed. He stood up. "Come with me." He offered his arm.

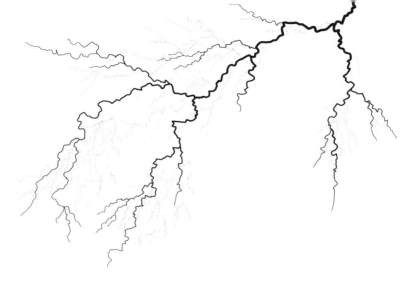

CHAPTER FIVE

Hope is a funny thing. Seems so harmless.
But it can crush.
—Solange Aidair Delaney

My heart leapt. I jumped up, bundled the comforter in my arms and set it back on the bed. I wrapped a shaking hand around Wells's arm and followed him into the hallway. *I can still fix this. I can get back in time. My dad will be so relieved.*

We turned right out of the room and marched past uniform door after uniform door, differentiated only by the sequential numbers above their frames. Everything was a nondescript off-white. We turned the corner where I'd run into Wells the night before and another endless hallway of doors stretched before us. "I can't turn you back, Imogen, at least not immediately," Wells explained quietly. We passed two other sidhe who looked at us curiously, but simply nodded to Wells as we squeezed around them. "It's a lot for the body to go through. If an attempt is made to reverse the turning too soon, death is a high possibility. Although a sidhe can be turned human, a person can only be turned in either direction once. It's why it sometimes takes several days to regain consciousness. Why no one wondered . . ." He cleared his throat. "We can revisit the idea of changing you back eventually if you like."

Ice coated my heart. But I lifted my chin. Fine. I wasn't human anymore. For now. The quick fix danced in my stomach. I corralled my emotions before they got a chance to run away with me. *Just get back to Earth first. Everything else can be worked out after.*

I'd find some way to explain my appearance. I'd be a little different. Okay. It's not like I wasn't used to being the new person or the odd one out. Keane would understand . . . No, he'd probably have a hard time understanding. But we'd get there. Everyone would just be relieved that I wasn't dead.

We made several turns, passing the stairwell that led to the kitchen. Still no windows. Wells paused at a larger stairwell and guided me upward. "Every one hundred years or so—Earth years, sometimes a bit longer on our end—we make a journey across several galaxies to find human partners to turn and bring back. The person being turned must want to come with us and we're required to explain certain things to them in advance."

"Why?" My fingers tightened on his arm. Dread squeezed my stomach. Why was he telling me this? "Why come take people at all?" We exited the stairwell into a long corridor.

"The short answer is that between time and kroma we stop reproducing after a few generations of pairing with pure sidhe only. It can take centuries for a sidhe pair to have a child even if there is a recently turned human in the family line. Usually, it's been made very clear to the person considering being turned that . . . this is a one-way trip. That's why usually younger, less . . . attached humans are chosen." He guided me around a corner. The light up ahead was subtly different. "Did you have children?" Wells asked softly.

"No, I never wanted any."

"And I assume Aloysius knew that when he took you?"

The hardness in his voice caught my attention. His eyes were blazing, staring straight ahead, jaw working.

"It's not something I kept secret," I said. He muttered something, but all I caught was "worse and worse" before my attention was captured by the vast space we entered. It looked like the control bridge of the Starship *Enterprise*, only without any computers. I scanned the room, stunned at its size. There were four people standing in a depressed section in the heart of the area, hands pressed into the tops of four pedestals in front of them, staring out the front window, each wearing a look of controlled concentration. I guessed that they were the ones powering the ship.

My jaw dropped as I stared around at the floor-to-ceiling windows that ringed the circular room and the endless vastness of starry space beyond them. Evenly spaced control chairs in front of these windows were half-occupied. The sidhe who filled them gazed out with a relaxed alertness, as if on watch during a quiet time. I examined them as Wells led me through the room toward a raised dais, front and center. Half of them had long, natural hair, like Al and Wells, the other half had definite statement haircuts. Some were even adorned with piercings.

Wells left me to wait at the foot of the short staircase leading up to the dais. He spoke to the sidhe with blue, spiked hair seated atop it for a moment, then waved me up. She eyed me curiously as I approached Wells, then swung her chair back to the front. Wells guided me over to a square pedestal off to one side and pressed a palm to its surface. I started when what looked like a holographic image of space appeared above his hand. I couldn't resist reaching out to touch it, expecting my hand to pass through. But when my finger brushed a planet, the view shifted, spinning that planet to the center. I snatched my hand back.

"Well, look at that," Wells said, waving a hand over the tiny cosmos and bringing it back to the previous view. "Your kroma is manifesting already. The map recognizes it at least." He kept one palm pressed to the top of the pedestal—I assumed his energy was powering the map—and with the other he drew my attention to a bright, slowly moving dot in the center of the tiny planets and stars. "This is the ship. Us." He flicked a finger and a red circle hugged the bright dot representing our ship. He passed his hand over the map, the stars blurred, and it shifted. When it stilled again, I recognized Earth.

My breath caught. I'd never felt so thrilled to see that blue-green globe gently spinning in star-studded blackness. The corners of my mouth turned up. I glanced at Wells and they dropped again at the brightness in his eyes, the sympathy swirling through his aura. "You obviously know what this is." He flicked his finger again and Earth was ringed in bright red. He dragged his hand away from the map and Earth receded ever so slowly.

And kept shrinking until I could only see a dot of red at the very edge of the Milky Way. The galaxy itself had moved all the way to the far end of the map. He drew my attention to the other side, where another tiny red dot floated. My throat closed.

"It's taken us eight days to get this far, using wormholes connected to stars that have already moved and shifted. I suspect that Al cut his retrieval of you so finely in order to avoid as many questions as possible. As it was, we really had only minutes to be underway before certain gateways closed, which would have left the entire populace on board in jeopardy of being stranded. We've been absent from our world for eight months. Supplies are nearly exhausted as we try to affect Earth as little as possible when we visit."

My stomach hollowed out as I watched him shift the map again. The red dot that was our ship took center stage. He flicked a finger and a lavender-blue planet, not far away, was circled with red. "That's Perimov," he said. The naked sympathy in his voice wrung my heart. "We'll be there tomorrow." He slid his hand from the pedestal and the image vanished. "I'm sorry, Imogen."

Wells ushered me back into the corridor and told me that, although Al had been confined to his room following the argument last night, he was due to start his shift on the bridge shortly. Wells assumed correctly that I wouldn't want to run into him.

I paid no attention to where we were going, clinging to Wells's arm and trying to breathe in and out. I was certain all the blood had drained from my face. I managed not to pass out, but my mind still spun.

"Are you all right?" Wells asked for the second time. "You're taking this better than I thought you would."

"I'm not . . ." My voice cracked. I cleared my throat and tried again. "I don't do emotions like normal people. I have a problem . . . crying or anything when I don't feel safe. Like unless I'm with family or something."

"That doesn't sound . . . easy."

I huffed a laugh that almost sounded real. I took a breath and noticed I had Wells's arm in a death grip. "Sorry." I willed my hand to relax, wincing at the crescent dents my fingernails had made on his skin. It can't have felt nice. "I usually go for a run, or spar, or—"

"Sparring? Actually sparring with another person?" The incredulous look on his face was mildly offensive.

"Is there a different kind of sparring?"

He half-smiled. "You just don't strike me as the punching and kicking type."

I stiffened. A spark flared in my chest. "I can fight," I bit out, glaring at Wells. "I was a three-time national champion of 'punching and kicking.'" I tossed air quotes around his turn of phrase with my free hand.

Something flashed behind his eyes and through his aura as he raised an eyebrow. "Is that so?" He stopped in the middle of the hallway and scanned me, nodding, then guided me in a new direction. What seemed to be athletic clothes appeared in midair in front of us and he caught them in his free hand. "I'll change when we get there. Fortunately, you're already dressed."

"Where are we going?" I asked. "Did you just . . . create gym clothes?"

He grinned. "I 'ported them from my room," he said. "I thought we'd let you attack something more interesting than my forearm. It might make you feel better. And we have time to kill before the meeting."

"What meeting?"

"Oh, right, of course you were . . ." Wells cleared his throat. "I apologize, Imogen. The meeting is to discuss how Al behaved toward you, give him a chance to enlighten us as to *why* he did what he did, and determine what is to be done about it. As soon as he left us last night, Captain Marc composed a message to the palace so the king can be informed as soon as we're in range. Al was allowed to come on the expedition because he's heir to the throne. He had to pass certain unconditional qualifications, but most who take this trip have been training for years. Once the heads of the expedition hear about his—"

"I'm sorry, I'm sorry." I tugged Wells to a stop. "Al is *what now*?"

"Oh, he didn't tell you that either?" Wells looked honestly amused for the first time. "How uncharacteristically modest of him."

"Please tell me that, whoever the current ruler is, they are in good health and expected to live forever," I said. Wells actually laughed out loud. "I'm *serious*." I continued to speak over him, although his genuine laughter almost made me smile. "I don't know how your kingdoms are generally run, but Al is . . . Al is the person that you do some light breaking and entering with when you've had too much whiskey and want to climb on a roof somewhere during a rainstorm. He is *not* the person you want in charge of policy and procedure that could affect an entire populace."

"For what it's worth," Wells guided us forward again, still smiling, "Al has been trained to rule his entire life. And he's not an idiot about *everything*." He gave me a sidelong glance. "Did you do that with Al? The . . . light breaking and entering?"

"Not with Al," I said with a touch of sass. He grinned. "I bet he would have done it if I'd suggested it, though."

The humor leached away. Wells blew out a breath, dropping his eyes. "I think he would do anything you asked him to do."

"Except leave me alone?"

He nodded. "Except that." After a beat he added, "You are a lot like your grandmother." He sighed, his next words so quiet I wasn't sure if they were meant for me. "You didn't stand a chance when he found you. Someone should have kept watch, anticipated this. *I* should have . . ." He trailed off, his aura swirling with guilt.

I swallowed, consciously keeping my fingers relaxed on his arm. "She wasn't a hundred and six when she died, then, was she?"

"No," Wells confirmed. "She was much older than that when she went to Earth to begin with."

"I always wondered why she seemed to know so much." I pulled in a deep breath, unable to shift the light twisting in my stomach as I asked, "Why did she disappear? We never found . . . a body. Al said he'd tell me. Is she still alive? Is—"

Wells was shaking his head. "When a very old sidhe—and Solange was very old . . ." He paused, his eyes flicking to mine then away again. "I'm assuming Henry died first?"

I nodded. "He was also one hundred and six. Not doing as well as she was, but . . ."

"Solange most likely chose to stop living once Henry was gone." He placed a hand over mine on his arm, gave it a squeeze, then dropped it back to his side. "When a very old sidhe dies, their magic leaves the body. Often all that's left is . . . dust. It doesn't always happen that way but I wouldn't be surprised in this situation."

My brows pulled together. "But she was human. At the time anyway."

He shrugged. "It's difficult to completely eradicate kroma from someone who was born with it. There may have been lingering traces . . . or perhaps she walked into the ocean. Either way, once turned, she wouldn't have made it much past a century in that body."

The twisting in my stomach wrung harder. There went that fleeting hope that I'd see her again. I tried to cling to the small comfort that I was going to the place she had originally lived. It made it slightly less threatening. At least I was finally getting the answers I'd basically traded my life for. I shoved that thought down. "Why did she go to Earth? Was she looking for someone to . . . turn and it just didn't go that way?"

"Actually, no. Solange was not interested in settling down. At all. She was a free spirit. It drove Al crazy, of course. She wouldn't attach herself to any one person, although she was happy to occasionally pair off with anyone she really liked, male or female, for months, or even years at a time."

"Was Al one of those people?" I asked, curious about my grandma's previous life. I'd always been close to her. It had rocked me when she disappeared in spite of her age. She'd seemed just fine and then . . . gone. I still had her last voice mail downloaded to my phone. My chest caved when I realized that was probably gone too.

"Off and on. Would have been more on if he'd had his way, but Solange never promised a lasting partnership. She didn't like to stay in one place. Liked to try different things and . . . different people. Al was convinced she'd eventually calm down and settle with him. He was certain a mating bond was going to pop up between them at any time."

I made a note to ask about this "mating bond" they kept mentioning. "Did you ever . . . ?"

"Gods' bones no." He laughed. "She was open to it, but it wouldn't have been worth the drama with Al. He saw us together one night when we were out as a group, and she started turning on the charm. I think she was just looking for a partner for the evening, but I heard about it from him for months any time I so much as breathed in the same room as her."

"Hm." *Possessive much?* Although I'd never seen my grandma so much as glance at anyone aside from my grandfather, certain stories she'd dropped and things she'd said had me certain she'd led a rather adventurous pre-grandpa life. "So she went to Earth to get a break from Al?"

Wells exploded into laughter again. He even stopped walking and leaned against the wall to catch his breath. After an initial flash of annoyance, I found myself enjoying the sound after buckets of nothing but strife. He had an infectious laugh.

"I'm sorry, Imogen. I can see why you would think that, but Al wasn't continually as bad with Solange as I'm sure it seems to you. This went on over several decades. Centuries even. He mostly let her do what she liked without comment—she wouldn't have tolerated him otherwise—he just wouldn't have been able to stand her being with me." I filed that information away. Wells continued, "He really was convinced she'd find her way back to him. To be fair, she usually did. But no, to answer your original question, she just wanted to see Earth. Wanted to see what it was like. Meet some humans, see what traveling on the ship was like. She didn't have an agenda. She wasn't planning on meeting Henry."

"But she did," I prompted when he paused.

"She did," he said, steering me down a stairwell. "And when she didn't come back..." He paused again. "We're here." He pushed open a door and I was momentarily distracted in taking in the layout of the training room. We were the only two people there.

"Be right back, I'm going to change."

I nodded as I stepped farther into the immense space. It was larger than I expected. It smelled like a gym. Mat dust. Lingering sweat. Something citrusy that I guessed must be a cleaning agent. Something metallic. Blood? There were a few rings for sparring just like gyms on Earth. Heavy bags in one corner. Weights in another. The racks of actual swords and shields were different, as well as the targets for what looked like archery and knife throwing, and a few tall posts and wooden circles that looked like they'd been incinerated... or something, but I was relieved that a few parts were familiar. I could confidently navigate at least bits and pieces of this room.

I couldn't help thinking that Keane would have loved this. He had once asked me if I'd rather go to space for a day or an all-expenses paid vacation anywhere on Earth for a week. I had picked the week without hesitation. Keane had picked space.

He would have been all over this ship, marveling over the way kroma powered it, asking a million questions about what kromatic energy entailed, chatting about wormholes, plastered to the windows, wanting to know how they were pressurized. He'd probably even ask to steer. Al should have kidnapped him instead.

Wells returned wearing a fairly standard t-shirt and what looked like gi pants. His long, red hair was pulled back, exposing his arching ears. I squashed the impulse to touch my own.

"Do you always wear pants when you work out?"

He blinked. "Yes." Then he turned to a nearby shelf which housed various weighted balls, rope, a colored tangle of cord like nothing I'd ever seen, and what looked like a mace. I glanced back at the heavy bags.

"So, there's boxing and stuff on your planet?"

"What were you expecting?" Wells pulled a box of hand wraps off a shelf and handed me a pair of red ones.

"I dunno, something... not like Earth." I unfurled one wrap and wound the fabric over my wrist and knuckles.

"You know, we initially all lived on Earth thousands of years ago." He picked a pair of black wraps for himself and replaced the box.

"I most certainly didn't know that, but I guess it's not the most surprising thing I've learned today." I smoothed a wrinkle in my wrap, flexing my fingers. "What happened when she didn't come back?"

"Hm?" Wells kept his eyes on his wraps.

"You thought I'd forget you were telling a story?" I started on the other hand. "What happened when she didn't come back?"

I'd finished both hands when he finally answered. "Without getting into detail that I'm not currently prepared for. Al was on suicide watch for... a long time. Which is also rare."

"Oh." The thought of charming, confident Al crushed by depression and heartbreak was difficult to wrap my head around. I found it hard to feel sympathy for him at the moment. But I could feel sympathy for the people close to him who had to deal with the fallout. "I'm sorry."

"It's all right, I should expect you to ask questions." He finished his hands. "So, what do you want to do? What will best assist your emotional processes? We can just hit bags for a while, we can spar if you want—"

"I haven't actually sparred with another person in like a decade," I told him. "My timing would be terrible."

"No it wouldn't," Wells said. "Anything you were good at when you were human you'll be good at again now. No matter how long ago it was that you were proficient."

I stared at him. "Anything I was ever good at in my *whole life*?"

He crossed his arms and leaned back against the shelf, his eyes dancing. "Oh, yes, I forgot. You're a ripe old forty-five. You might be good at a lot of things."

"Hell *yeah* I will. I did tons of shit," I said. "I've probably even forgotten stuff I used to be good at." His lips twitched as if holding back a smile. "How old are you?"

A corner of his mouth slid up. "Two hundred and fifty-one."

I blinked. "Well. That's. Yeah, I . . . I was totally gonna guess one seventy-five, two hundred. Somewhere. Around there." I could tell he was holding back laughter as I gaped at him. ". . . Holy shit, you're older than the United States of America."

His laugh finally broke free. He pushed off the shelf. "Let's warm up on bags. We can always hit each other afterward."

I followed him. "How old is Al?"

"Four hundred and twenty-eight."

"Jesus Christ," I whispered. "How old is Captain Marc?"

"That I don't know, actually. Very old though as he's done at least six trips to Earth."

I was doing the math in my head and choosing a bag when I realized something was missing. I glanced around. "Wait, don't we need like . . . boxing gloves or something?"

"Nope." Wells smiled at me. "The wraps will be enough to protect your wrists. You're much less breakable now than you were." Without another word, he turned and laid into his bag.

He was good.

Just watching his fluid combos, the sound of his fists connecting, my lips began to curve up in a wicked smile. I faced my own bag.

Oh, I remember this. This was fun.

I spent the next hour blissfully working up a sweat. The tightness in my chest, the eels in my stomach, the cracks in my heart; I exorcized them all. Although we were alone, I still wasn't comfortable enough with Wells for a full-blown meltdown, but a few tears did escape, hiding among the sweat. After an hour, I lost myself in fun imaginings: fighting off Al in the bedroom—compulsion be damned—then, even better, fighting him off on the levee and sprinting home triumphantly. I was deep into a fantasy about what I would like to do next time I saw him when a particularly vicious spinning hook kick split the bag.

"Oh, oops..."

I heard Wells stop and felt him watching as I wobbled on one leg and yanked my heel out of the bag. Cringing, I stopped it from swinging and poked at the rip I'd made, I glanced guiltily over my shoulder as Wells stepped away from his own bag.

"Sorry..." I said, although I experienced a flicker of pride upon noticing that the split was level with his eyes as he examined the damage.

"Interesting," was all he said, gliding a thumb along the tear. "You seem to be too much for the bags. Still have some energy?"

I considered only a moment. "Yes." I was keyed up now and didn't feel winded in the slightest. My blood was still up with residual Al-related anger but I was fully in control of my other emotions.

He angled his head toward the ring, eyebrows lifting. Challenge or question, I wasn't sure. His aura was swimming calmly, with little yellow bursts throughout. *Curiosity or excitement?* I wondered. I hadn't seen this kind of display before. I wondered if there was an aura reading manual somewhere.

"Sparring? With you?" I clarified. "You're much taller than I am."

Russet eyes flashed. "Scared?"

I crossed my arms. *Yes*, I admitted only to myself. Wondering if he could read the trepidation in my own aura. However, sparring was the ultimate emotional cleanse. You couldn't think about anything else when sparring. "What are the rules?" I asked.

He grinned, then turned and walked toward the ring. "Weapons or no weapons?"

"Let's do no weapons," I said, swinging my arms casually as I followed. As if sparring with live blades was something I—or any sane human—had regular experience with. I'd worked with rubber training knives and sticks, and although I was proficient, weapons had never been my strength.

"All right, then the rules are pretty simple. No attacking with power, although you most likely wouldn't be able to do that yet anyway, no kill shots—"

"Aw shucks," I said.

"—no serious attempts at maiming—"

"Again with the unreasonable restrictions."

He grinned but kept talking. "—stop at a verbal 'yield,' a physical tap out, or first blood. Any questions?" He stepped halfway through the ropes, holding them open for me.

I climbed into the ring, my stomach tightening with nervous excitement, but my hands were steady. "First blood," I muttered to myself. "This is completely insane." Then louder as I turned to face him, "Nope, how do we know when to—"

The words were barely out of my mouth when Wells fired a jab right at my face.

My vision changed.

The world slid into slow motion. Everything except for me. I shifted into fighting stance and easily slipped my head out of the way of his jab... cross... hook... uppercut. I parried his next jab, sliding off to the outside of his arm, shifting my weight to my back foot and kicking his lead leg across his centerline. He stumbled, but caught himself. The world resumed its normal pace.

"Not bad," he said. "A little on the defensive side but—"

I launched a front kick straight at his jaw. As soon as I lifted my foot, the world—apart from me—slowed down again. He brought up his forearms to block just in time, but I managed to pull my foot back and redirect the strike to tag him in the stomach before stepping off to his right and following up with a back leg roundhouse to his left side. If Wells had been holding back before, he stopped now. The cadence of our sparring sped up. He got his strikes in, but I was kicking ass. It was *fun*. There was no room in my brain for anything outside of the two of us in the ring. Several minutes in, I remembered I was supposed to be going for first blood. I'd been following my human sparring instincts. Avoiding hurting him. I pressed harder, but Wells wasn't a pushover.

After fifteen minutes, both of us were tiring, neither backing off. A five-minute round would have been excruciating when I was human. I was searching in earnest for a good opening when I noticed his aura. The steady pulse of bronze determination was dimming slightly as he tired, but... there were gold flashes occasionally. *What are* those? I watched for a few seconds before I realized: his aura was telegraphing his moves.

I acted on the hunch and the tables turned rapidly. I was blocking attempts before he finished making them. Anticipating strikes with counterstrikes before he had moved. No longer was he able to get anything through my guard. I took him down to the mat once ... twice ... three times before faking another takedown and coming around with a spinning backfist. It connected perfectly with his nose, knocking him completely off balance.

First blood achieved.

Wells landed on his tailbone. This time he didn't spring back up. One hand flew to his nose. He pulled it away and gazed at the blood on his fingers. His aura splooshed with surprise.

The world spun back to normal.

"I'm sorry!" I blurted even though I knew that was the goal.

"Are you kidding? That was brilliant." He extended his right hand to one side and a small, clean towel from a stack near the ring flew into it. He wiped off the blood, the bleeding already stopped. His nose looked completely normal. "You're better than I expected. Even for a ... what was it? Former national champion of punching and kicking?"

"I'm better than *I* expected. I was all right, but I was never that good before." I stretched my hand toward the towel stack, imitating Wells. As soon as I focused on pulling a towel toward me, a light fizzy sensation tickled my fingertips. A towel flopped off the top of the stack, landing on the floor like a limp fish. "Dammit." I tried again. It may have wiggled.

Wells summoned the poor towel himself and tossed it to me. I mumbled my thanks and mopped my sweaty face. Wells remained sitting on the canvas. Staring at me.

"What?"

"You said you weren't that good before?" He leaned back on a hand and rested his other elbow on a bent knee. His aura had changed, the colors shifting, concern, surprise . . . something else . . .

"I mean, I was above average," I said, feeling a need to defend my former self. "But I wasn't like . . . as awesome as I apparently am now." *Maybe I am good at weapons.* I thought, forgetting Wells's aura and glancing over at the racks across the room. I tossed my sweaty towel over an even sweatier shoulder and reached out toward a dagger. The fingertip tingles started up immediately and I *yanked*. It clattered to the ground. Wells let me continue to try this time until, after five exhausting jolts across the floor, I had the weapon in my hand. "Why do I suck at this," I muttered, flipping the dagger into the air and catching it by the hilt.

"You're just learning. Not everything is going to come as easily as combat apparently does, but—"

"There you two are. I've been looking all over . . ." Al was striding across the training room, smiling.

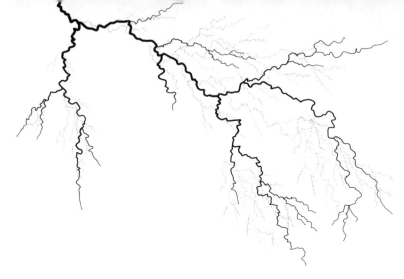

CHAPTER SIX

Always carry an equalizer.
—*Solange Aidair Delaney*

Reality came crashing into the room in Al's wake. Any residual endorphin buzz I'd been riding fled.

My throat tightened and I took two steps back from the ropes before I wrenched myself under control. I turned slightly away, giving Al a shoulder view, then continued coolly playing with the dagger. Wells flipped his towel over to a blood-free area and mopped the sweat off his face and neck before standing and walking closer to where Al stood next to the ring. He tossed his towel into a nearby hamper. "It turns out that Imogen is an incredibly skilled fighter."

"Really?" Al's eyes flashed as he grinned at me. "I didn't know that."

I refused to make eye contact. My skin felt itchy and hot as I spun to examine the targets on the far end of the room. "The things you don't know about me, Al, would probably fill several books," I said, willing ice into my voice.

Unfazed, he leaned on the top rope, resting his chin on his crossed arms and stared at me. I felt his eyes tracking me as if they burned the side of my face. "I can't wait to read them all."

My jaw clenched. I narrowed my focus on the farthest target, keeping my gaze locked on it while I tossed the dagger skyward. The world slowed for me. As the knife spun back into my line of vision I pulled my arm back, waiting for the hilt to level out, the blade to angle toward my goal, then thrust the heel of my hand into the pommel, striking precisely at the center point. My arm shot out in a perfectly straight line from shoulder to wrist, fingers flexed back out of the way. The dagger kept going and the world sped back up. The three of us watched as it thunked straight into the bullseye.

"Interesting," Wells said again, studying me as he unwrapped his hands, his aura pulsing strangely once more.

"Nice, Im," Al said, as if I had just shown him a cute drawing. "Wells, it's your turn on the bridge. I'll take over babysitting Im." He smiled at me and held out a hand. "C'mon let's get you showered off."

My spine locked. Throat closed up. I stopped breathing. I made no move to go near him. In my peripheral vision, I saw Wells's aura split again. My entire body was rigid. It was an effort not to back away from Al's outstretched hand.

"You're lucky she'd already thrown the dagger," Wells said mildly, his aura resuming its normal flow. "I'll take Imogen to clean off. You're doing a double shift. You had days off while you were waiting for her to wake up."

"I haven't seen her at all this morning—"

"You'll see her at the meeting."

Al glowered. "I haven't eaten."

"So wink up to the kitchen and grab a block on your way up if you don't have a spare one on you. I've just spoken to Captain Marc and he agrees that you working a double might go a little way toward smoothing over some irritations caused by your recent . . . choices." Wells finished unwrapping his hands and tossed the wad of damp wraps into the hamper; his expression was neutral, but his aura flashed with irritation.

Al took two steps closer to Wells, staring hard into his brother's face. "What are you doing?" he bit out under his breath.

Wells glared back, matching Al's tone. "What I always do, Aloysius. It'd be nice if I could have a break occasionally."

A muscle bunched in Al's jaw, then he backed away from the ring. He looked at me, frustration warring with the disappointment stamped across his face, his aura swirling with longing, then he... vanished.

I blinked.

Wells crossed over and tugged on one of my hand wraps. "Do you want to take these off?"

"Are you going to explain that to me?" I said, pointing to the spot where Al had been.

When I made no move to remove them, Wells began unwrapping the hand he'd tugged on. "What, Al? He—oh, you mean the winking out. Of course. Don't get excited, it takes years to learn. Handy though. Especially when you want to leave in a snit."

I gasped. "*That's* how you caught me in the hallway. Oh, that's a relief."

He grinned, "Well it was easier than running after you. What did you think was happening?" A final yank and the wrap was free. I unfroze and hastily unwound the other one.

"I just thought I'd gotten really slow from not eating or something," I said, following him over to the side of the ring where we tossed the wraps in the hamper with my towel before clambering out. This time I insisted on holding the ropes for him. Babysitting me indeed.

Wells was quiet until we reached the door. His aura spinning faster. He held it open for me, then offered me his arm. "Imogen, how long have you been awake? And by that I mean, since you were turned."

Even as I took his arm, I felt my shoulders curling forward, my head dropping. I forced myself to straighten. Lifted my chin. "I don't know. I don't know how long those sleeping potions put me out—"

"How many times did he dose you?"

"Twice. The first time was pretty soon after I woke up initially. He compelled me to stop fighting him so I started screaming."

Wells swore under his breath. "I knew something was off. We just never guessed—" He glanced at me. "I'm sorry, Imogen. Marc and I thought something was strange when you seemed to be sleeping so much. Al just said you were older than most humans we turn and it had taken more out of you. We should have pushed. Nothing like this has ever happened before. Al should have—"

"Seems like there's a lot Al should or shouldn't have done," I said crisply. "Does he usually just do whatever the hell he wants and damn the consequences?"

"No . . ." Wells's face was blank.

I saw a black spike through his aura. "Was that a lie?" *Is that what those mean?* "Did you just lie to me?"

"Aren't you perceptive." Wells sighed. "Al does get away with more than he should. In fact, I think Solange may be the only . . . situation that hasn't worked out the way he wanted."

We turned down a hallway I now recognized. My shoulders crept toward my ears. Wells must have felt my growing rigidity. "Al's not there right now, but you can shower in my room if you'd prefer."

"I would prefer."

He looked me over. "I can step in and grab some clothes for you if you don't want to go in at all."

"Thank you."

Minutes later I was pawing carefully through the clothes spread out on Wells's bed. I'd found some underwear but . . .

"Was this all that was there?" And after he nodded, "Why are there only dresses and workout clothes?"

"You don't wear dresses?" Wells asked from where he was crouched on the floor, attempting to sort through the pile of items he had dumped off the chair.

"Not most of the time." I lifted a dress. Waved it slightly back and forth. "These are all . . . kinda . . . floaty I dunno." Another short, strappy, feminine number in a pale blue. *Does* everything *have to be uncomfortable? Can't I at least have some goddamn pants?*

Wells cleared his throat then refocused on his pile, grabbing two jackets. "Solange liked dresses." He scooted past me to a small closet sunk into the wall.

"So unfortunate for everyone involved that she's dead," I said, realizing as I spoke that I sounded remarkably like my irreverent grandmother. My heart did a little bob and weave.

Wells shut the closet door, jackets now stowed, and edged around me to the dresser. "Normally, anyone being turned gets a chance to pack their own things. Al must have bought those for you on Earth." He dug through a drawer, handed me a plain t-shirt of his own, then scooped a pair of running shorts out of the pile on the bed. "Take these and get into the shower. I'll see what I can dig up for you later, otherwise you might have to wear dresses for a day or two."

"Okay, thanks." I tried to smile at him. "It's not like worse things haven't happened to me lately." I took a closer look at the shirt he'd handed me. "Do you seriously have Express for Men on your planet?"

"You think we spend eight months on Earth and don't go shopping?" He didn't turn from where he was arranging his books on top of a nightstand. "Everyone's allowed to bring a few things back. Research purposes." The tips of his ears were pink.

I snorted, a grin breaking free, then slipped into the bathroom and shut the door.

When I emerged, freshly scrubbed, Wells's room was considerably neater. He'd gone ahead and packed some things, he'd explained. We'd be arriving at our destination in the morning. My stomach swooped, but I steered my thoughts hard in another direction. Not ready for those emotions.

While Wells showered, I folded the remaining clothes, then left them on the bed, not sure what else to do with them, and scanned the room for a distraction. Every time I was faced with really looking at my situation, my mind veered sharply away, as if avoiding driving off a cliff. I examined the books, now in an orderly stack atop the nightstand. None of them looked like light reading. I reached my hand out and focused on the top volume.

The entire pile toppled onto the floor.

I hurried over, cursing under my breath, and shoved them back atop the nightstand in what I hoped was the correct order, then pulled the first title off the pile and settled sideways over the chair, flinging my knees over one armrest, propping the book open against them, and leaning back against the other. It read almost like a textbook on sidhe history. Had it been a similar volume on Earth, I probably would have found it dry and only cracked it to find specific information.

Current circumstances being as they were, I found it fascinating and sank wholly into it. Perhaps I'd learn something useful about where I was going. And apparently where a rather significant branch of my family had originated from. Better than continuing to try and navigate everything blind at any rate.

I barely registered Wells when he reappeared. I didn't even look up from the book until he spoke. "Does your hair just . . . do that?"

"What?" I looked up briefly. "Oh, yeah, if I let it air dry, it's just kind of all over the place. I'm tired of fighting it, so I let it have its way. No grays yet, so . . . bonus." I returned to the paragraph I was trying to finish.

"You probably won't get any gray hair for a very long time."

I acknowledged that with a grunt, ignoring my somersaulting stomach, and pushed myself back into the book. *Avoid avoid avoid.*

"I've never seen anyone so engrossed in a history book." Wells took the folded clothes and placed them on top of his dresser before perching on the edge of the bed. "Find anything interesting?"

"Well, so far nothing in here about time travel, so . . ." I flipped the page with a snap.

He snorted, then leaned forward, resting his elbows on his knees. "If the secrets of time travel were in that book and you hypothetically managed to jump back to eight days ago, don't you think that Al might follow you? Although, I supposed you'd be forewarned..."

"Oh, I wouldn't just jump back eight days," I said, meeting his sparkling eyes. "I'd go all the way back twenty years or so and ask my grandma what the fuck."

He barked a laugh. "You'd say 'fuck' in front of your grandmother?"

"I already did once." I gazed back at the book without seeing the words, smiling at the memory.

"And what was her reaction?"

My eyes flicked up to see Wells's aura dancing with the golden pinks I was starting to recognize as curiosity. He had known my grandmother. Probably pretty well if she ran around with Al that often. I closed the book.

"Well, I was about fourteen and she was on the landline—telephone. You know what that is? Good—anyway, so when she hung up I said . . ." I cleared my throat and pitched my voice higher in imitation of my younger self, "'Grandma! Did you just say fuck?' To which she replied . . ." I straightened my spine and smoothed my face, taking on my grandmother's old Hollywood grace and cadence, "'No, honey, I said, 'fuck you, you fucking fuck,' and then she tossed her scarf over a shoulder, said, 'Don't tell your father,' and swept from the room."

Wells's smirk had spread to a broad smile. "Who was she on the phone with?"

"To this day I have no idea."

"You looked *just* like her for a second. You even sounded like her." My eyes dropped away from his as my smile slipped. As if sensing my mood drift, he shifted gears. "And did you tell your father?"

"Oh, absolutely not. I was no tattletale. And he had enough going on." I toyed with the frayed corner of the book.

"What about your mother?"

"She died when I was eight, so I spent a lot of time at my grandparents' place."

"I'm sorry," he said.

I glanced at him. "It's okay, it was all a long time ago." I swung my legs off the chair's arm and sat up properly.

"I don't mean to cause you additional discomfort with personal questions." His eyes bounced up to mine. "I can't help but be curious about how Solange ended up. It's so strange to think of her as a grandmother..."

"Well, she was fantastic," I said, setting the book back on the stack. "She was funny, she let me do all kinds of crazy things, and never lied to me. Oh, wait. No, that's not true, I guess she did."

Awkward silence descended like a sudden fog.

My stomach growled audibly.

"It keeps doing that," I sighed.

One corner of Wells's mouth lifted. "You keep not feeding it." He grabbed the sack of pastries. "We have about fifteen minutes. Do you want to go to the kitchens or—"

"No, thank you, I don't want to see people. I'll just take one of those things."

He peered into the sack. "Make sure you have something substantial after the meeting," he said, lining up the remaining pastries on the nightstand.

I went for a dark brown one just to be bold. It was loaf shaped, but fit in my hand. "What's going to happen to me at this meeting? I don't have to go with Al, right?"

He lifted his eyes from the remaining two pastries. "You don't want to be a princess?"

I intentionally took an obnoxious bite of the little loaf and spoke around it. "Do I look like a princess to you?"

He snorted, grabbed a pastry for himself, and leaned back on the bed. "This is uncharted territory, Imogen. We've never had anyone turned against their will. Molnairians strive to treat humans with respect, which is what sets us apart from the Sephryans."

I swallowed my bite. "The what now?"

"There's another country of sidhe on our planet who don't believe it's natural to turn humans. They maintain a colony on Perimov and keep them in a contained village—no one without some kind of kromatic ability is able to leave—specifically to ensure the continuation of the species. Sidhe genes are dominant, so . . . they take the children that result from those relationships and integrate them into sidhe society." He busied himself removing a wrapper from his pastry.

A sharp inhale lodged a bit of loaf in my windpipe. I had to set my last bite down as I choked. "Seriously?" I rasped out as Wells retrieved a cup of water from the bathroom.

"Molnair and Sephrya both originated on Earth," he said, taking his seat and giving me time to compose myself. "The other countries on Perimov are comprised of different sorts of creatures. Molnair and Sephrya split millennia ago, largely because of this massive difference in opinion, but in general the Sephryans were traditionalists in regard to how they felt kroma should be used." He popped the last of his pastry in his mouth, then stood to wrap up the final one that neither of us had taken. "It sparked the Wind War which ended up involving beings from every country on Perimov. The other countries banded together afterward and promised to eject our race from the planet if a conflict of that scale ever erupted again. What Al has done is now widely known throughout the ship. A lot of people are upset by how you've been . . . wronged."

I forced myself to finish the last bite of my pastry. To chew in spite of how dry my mouth had become, and choke it down. I stared at the floor. Regardless of the outcome of this meeting, I wouldn't get to go home. A fact that my mind still hadn't come to grips with. And kroma? If I had been offered any kind of superpowers a week ago, I would have said *hell yes* without question. But I'd been gagged by "kroma," knocked out with potions, and captured by "winking" before I'd so much as learned a magic word. Although I was beginning to think that magic words weren't a thing. Whatever it was, kroma was scary. And I didn't understand it.

"What is it, Imogen?" Wells said gently. "What are you afraid of?"

I had unconsciously hunched forward, pressing my elbows against my knees. I lifted my gaze from the floor. "Literally everything," I said. I realized

I was shaking and hoped he couldn't see it. "I've had things done to me in the past few days that I didn't know were possible. I . . . really and truly have no idea what is going to happen to me. At all. I don't even really know what I am anymore or even what I'm capable of. So, yeah, I'm scared of absolutely everything." I dropped my eyes back to my clasped hands.

I flinched when Wells reached over and touched my forearm. "I'm sorry that this has been your introduction to this life, Imogen." His eyes were level with mine when I looked up. "Solange would have let us all have it for allowing you to be treated this way. I shudder to think of what she would have done." He held out his hand, palm up. "On her behalf, I promise you have nothing to be frightened of at this meeting." The left corner of his mouth twitched upward. "You have at least one friend, Imogen."

I did my best to smile back. "Thanks."

I placed my hand in his.

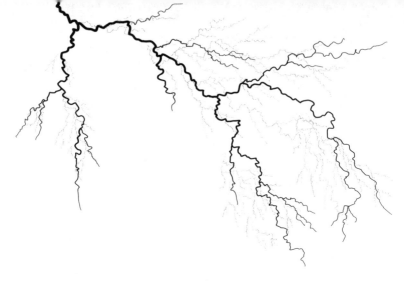

CHAPTER SEVEN

*What are you gonna do, stop people talking? People are gonna talk.
All you can control is how you listen. How you internalize it.*
—Solange Aidair Delaney

Wells asked me to please change into one of the dresses for the duration of the meeting and I acquiesced with minimal grumbling, assuming he didn't want his brother—or anyone else—seeing me in one of his shirts and jumping to conclusions. I picked a deep purple one, as it was one of the least "floaty"—being little more than a shift—then almost stripped when my reflection in the mirror made me physically flinch.

"What was that about?" Wells asked, waiting by the door.

I edged closer to the mirror again, as if I was peering into a lion's den. "This is only the second time I've really looked . . ." The dress punched up the violet color of my eyes. I shook myself, then stepped away from the mirror and crossed to Wells without meeting his gaze. "Al changed my eyes. Freaks me out a little."

He lifted a hand as if he would tilt my face up, then stopped and put it in his pocket. "What did he change?"

I shrugged, as if I could shed the tension draped around me. "They used to be brown. Like my dad's. Not sure whose they are now." I looked up at him. "We can go, I'm fine."

His face hardened, then smoothed out. "They're your grandmother's eyes."

"No." I felt my eyebrows drawing together. "She had green eyes."

He shook his head and held out his arm to me. I took it, letting him lead me into the hall. "When a person is turned, they sometimes ask for small . . . alterations. Less freckles. Remove a birthmark. Things like that. Solange asked for green eyes. To fit in more, I believe. Al doesn't know that."

"Then how do you know that?" I asked.

"Because I was there when she was turned."

I stopped walking so suddenly I pulled him off balance.

"Hold. Up!" I said. "When were you going to get around to dropping this little nugget of information?"

He rolled his eyes skyward and tugged me forward again. "If I were required to tell you everything that you don't know about everyone involved in this little drama in less than twenty-four hours, neither of us would sleep and I would lose my voice."

"Okay, but *that*—"

"Is not really that big a deal."

"Not a big *deal* he says!" I tried to stop him again but he didn't even slow, muttering something about being on time. "Who turned her?"

A muscle feathered in his jaw. He wouldn't look at me. "The training room is actually the largest area on the ship, so we'll be meeting there."

"Oh, I don't give two shits where we're meeting and you *know* that." He was moving quickly down the corridors now. Even after lengthening my own stride, I struggled to keep pace. "You turned her, didn't you? Does Al know? Who else was there? Was my grandpa there? Okay you really have to slow down." I released his arm and fell behind a few steps.

He glanced up and down the corridor, then jerked his chin at me as he stepped into an alcove off to the side. I followed, wedging myself in between Wells and a storage cabinet. He leaned forward, his palms meeting the wall on either side of my head. "Yes, I turned her," he whispered roughly. "With Captain Marc. She asked for us both specifically. No, Al has no idea and we're going to keep it that way. Yes, Henry was there, we did it at his house. It's where she wanted to wake up. We left afterward. That's the last I ever saw of her. If it's all right with you I'd like to pause this conversation until after the meeting. If possible, with the inclusion of alcohol."

I nodded mutely. For a moment we stared at each other, both of us breathing slightly harder than usual. My gaze locked on his russet eyes, one strand of silky, dark red hair had fallen forward. I had the strangest urge to tuck it back, push my fingers through it . . .

He blew out a breath, dropped his hands, ushered me back into the corridor, and offered his arm again. I took it and we walked at a reasonable pace.

Wells's aura was a tumult of emotion, moving too quickly for me to make sense of. His eyes distant, his focus drawn inward. I chewed my lower lip. I hadn't meant to upset him.

"Have I mentioned how much I appreciate that there's booze in this galaxy?" I said under my breath.

Wells puffed a tiny laugh. His aura slowed.

Just before we reached the door to the training room, I looked up at him. "Once we've got that alcohol," I said quietly, "remind me to ask you what it's like to have played a part in my eventual existence."

One corner of his mouth lifted. He winked at me, then opened the door.

It was all I could do to keep walking forward, my fingers tightening convulsively on Wells's arm. "Why are there so many people here?" I whispered.

I had been expecting to see just Al and Captain Marc. Maybe one or two other people of rank. But there were easily thirty people milling around. Most had already taken seats in a large cluster of chairs off by the targets.

(I noticed someone had removed my dagger.) Others were standing and chatting with those sitting or with Captain Marc who was leaning against one of the rings, a small table set out in front of him. All heads swiveled toward us when we walked in. There was a two-second hush in conversation and then it started up again slightly louder than before.

Wells cleared his throat and gave my hand a reassuring pat. "Al broke a lot of rules when he did what he did. A lot of these people are county leaders or others who passed the selection process. Some came back with a partner, some didn't, some are just on the crew, but they all worked hard to be here." Captain Marc was still deep in discussion with four serious-looking sidhe. Wells stopped a few feet away. "I think a random sampling was allowed to attend today. Of course, some had to work."

A quick scan of the room told me Al hadn't yet arrived. Captain Marc ended his conversation and waved us over. "Any idea where he is?" The captain practically sighed the entire question.

"No, sir, we came straight here." Wells glanced at me. "But I would have thought—"

Al winked in, appearing feet from us. He panned the area, stopping when he saw me, lines of tension disappearing as his face broke into a smile. He closed the distance between us in two steps. "Hey, Im, what have you—"

I backed hard away, yanking my arm from Wells's more forcefully than I intended. My legs hit the ring behind me. Captain Marc stopped Al with a hand to his shoulder.

"Aloysius, how nice of you to join us. If you and Llewellyn would take a seat over there," he gestured to two chairs on the opposite side of the table and several feet back, "we can get started. Imogen, if you wouldn't mind sitting here beside me."

Al didn't immediately follow his brother to the seats indicated. Instead he stepped closer to Captain Marc. They were nearly the same height, but the frost in the captain's gaze gave him a little extra something. Al's throat bobbed, but his voice was steel when he muttered, "I thought this was going to be a private meeting?"

Captain Marc's smile didn't reach his eyes. "You were incorrect. Sit."

Al's jaw clenched and I wondered if he was used to some kind of "your highness" or something that the captain wasn't giving him. His chest rose as he took a long breath and blew it out, but he did finally turn and drop, sprawling, into the chair beside Wells.

Captain Marc remained standing, waving any stragglers to their spots. I took the seat he indicated, happy to have a physical barrier between me and Al. Once I had settled myself, Captain Marc addressed the crowd.

I stared at my clasped hands resting on the metal tabletop, watching my knuckles turn white while Captain Marc explained why we were here and the known facts of what Al had done. Hearing him lay it out in crisp narrative had every muscle in my body tensing. I forced my shoulders away from my ears and lifted my eyes.

My gaze collided with Wells's and my breath caught. One corner of his mouth turned up, as if he were trying to reassure me, but his eyes were shining with worry. I pushed some excuse for a smile back and checked out the assembled.

Many of their auras were dancing with the autumnal colors I now associated with irritation. A few flashed with spritzes of curiosity. Some seemed outright hostile. I gathered it was directed at Al. Peeking over at him, I saw his aura flowing with its usual sea tones, although there were a few flashes of butter yellow interspersed, which I thought could be nervousness. He watched me with his steady amber gaze, a slight upturn of his mouth.

I pulled my attention back to what Captain Marc was saying, something about questioning Al and instructing him not to lie.

"You can't just take him at his word," someone called out from the group. "To really be sure he's not lying, you'd have to compel him."

Another voice chimed in. "We've taken too much of what he's said at face value. The very reason he's here proves that he's comfortable with deception and duplicity."

There were a few shouts and murmurs of agreement. Captain Marc seemed to be taking the room's temperature. Al stiffened when he heard someone say something about how his royal status shouldn't exempt him from compulsion.

"Can't you just . . . *see* when he's lying?" I asked, almost to myself. Captain Marc's attention snapped to me. The crowd quieted so suddenly that I flushed. My eyes flicked up to the captain's as I cleared my throat. "Like, with his aura?"

Any remaining murmuring ceased and I was uncomfortably aware that everyone was staring at me. The auras now spiking with curiosity and confusion. I'd said something wrong. My face burned. "Are . . . are they not called auras? Is it called something else?"

Captain Marc sat down next to me. Still speaking loudly enough so that everyone could hear him, but addressing only me, he said, "Explain what you're seeing, Imogen."

I knew my face must have been brick red, but I forced myself to keep my eyes up. "The colors around everyone. The ones that change with people's moods? And they . . . change when someone lies? Is that not . . . does everyone not see those?"

"How long have you been seeing auras?" Captain Marc asked. No hint of disbelief in his voice or in the colors floating around him.

"Since I woke up," I told him. "I figured it was just . . . part of the . . . package."

"It's a rare gift, but not unheard of." He smiled at me. "Let's test it out, shall we? I am eight hundred years old."

I saw the black spike. "Lie."

His smile broadened. "I am *over* eight hundred years old."

"Not a lie." I didn't have time to mentally wrap my head around his age before he continued with his experiment.

Captain Marc turned to Wells. "Llewellyn. Say something. True or false."

I looked at Wells for the first time since my aura proclamation. His was now swimming with an array of fascinating colors. "Oh, well . . . winter is my favorite season."

"Lie," I said. "Although, who likes winter really?"

A few titters from the crowd and then Captain Marc called on four more random people to spout off statements. Lie, truth, lie, lie. People seemed to be enjoying it a bit. Like I had a neat parlor trick.

Al spoke up. "Wells is my brother."

A *brown* spike. "Oh!" How to interpret that? "Not . . . completely a lie? But I thought you were brothers? How is somebody *kind of* your sibling?"

"They're half-brothers," Captain Marc said. "Which I suppose you hadn't learned yet."

I shook my head.

"Were you a psychic when you were a human?" the captain asked.

"Ha, no," I said. "I would have liked to have seen this coming." Another sprinkle of laughter. My stomach flipped. I guess it was amusing if it wasn't you. "But what I'm doing isn't reading the past or the future, it's just . . . seeing what's there right now."

"You're an empath," Wells said.

"*That* I have been called before. But I never saw auras before."

"It seems like some abilities have been heightened," Captain Marc said. His eyes flicked to Wells's for an instant before returning to me. Al's aura flared, catching my attention, his smile deepening. As if I was proving him right in some way.

"Interesting," Wells said.

My head snapped toward him. "You keep using that word." I was unable to resist sliding into an Inigo Montoya cadence, even as it crushed my heart to know that no one would get the reference. "I do not think it means what you think it means."

To my utter joy and relief, there was a chortle of delight from the group. I looked over and spotted a sunny, tanned blonde, her arm looped around the elbow of the rather regal female sidhe next to her, whose skin was so dark it shone. The sunny blonde grinned at me.

"I appreciate you," I said to her, not caring what anyone else thought. Her grin spread and crinkled her nose. I wondered where on Earth she had been pulled from.

After it had been satisfactorily established that I was a sidhe lie detector, one of the serious sidhe that Captain Marc had been talking to prior to the meeting stood up.

"Use Imogen," he said. He was one of those with anime hair, purple spikes and an undercut, sporting an eyebrow ring. He wore dark, well-tailored clothing and was obviously a person of some influence. "We can be sure she won't let him get away with a lie."

There were several exclamations of agreement. Captain Marc turned to me and put a hand on my shoulder. "Is that something you're emotionally up for, Imogen?" he asked quietly. "It would be convenient to avoid compelling him. When you compel someone not to lie in general, they sometimes stop speaking altogether. Almost the opposite of what you endured. But we don't want to impose—"

"I'll do it, it's fine," I said, even though my intestines were in knots. Although the thought of Al being compelled in front of all these people was vindictively delicious, I didn't want him getting away with anything. "I'd be seeing it happen anyway, so I may as well just say what I see."

The captain nodded, then a slow smile spread across his face, his eyes locking on mine. "And can we trust that you'll give us an *accurate* account of what you see?"

I blinked. It legit hadn't occurred to me to lie just to get Al in trouble, but I could see why he asked. "Yes," I said clearly. "I think everything Al did will be pretty obvious without any help from me."

"Would you swear it?" he asked, his dark eyes serious.

I stopped myself from agreeing immediately and ran a quick mental eye over every fantasy movie I'd ever seen where someone had sworn to something and been turned into a toad or tricked out of years of their life. I didn't know the rules here, but I figured as long as I actually told the truth regarding the specific thing I was swearing about, it shouldn't bounce back on me.

"I absolutely swear to tell the truth about the auras I see around Al during this meeting." There, that oughta cover it.

Captain Marc glanced toward the assembled. I caught a few short nods. "Good enough," he said, and set about questioning Al. The main issue seemed to be that he might have used his position as prince to wrangle his way onto the ship, with the full intention of finding a human to replace Solange, whether said human wanted to go or not.

"No, I didn't go to get Imogen specifically. How could I have even known she existed?" Al lifted his palms and shrugged.

Captain Marc glanced at me to see if I had any objections before continuing. "So, you went with the intention of finding a willing human partner. *Any* willing human partner?"

"Yes."

"Partly true," I said.

Al grimaced at me. Captain Marc leaned back in his chair crossing his arms. "Now we're getting somewhere. What was your additional intention, Aloysius?"

Al's aura shifted, the normal relaxed, confident sea greens mixing with pinks and browns. He looked down at his knees. "I was pretty sure that Solange wouldn't be . . . alive." His throat bobbed. "But I thought maybe I could go see where she was buried. *If* she was buried. Maybe find out . . . how she lived . . . I don't know."

Al glanced at Captain Marc, who waved his hand in a circular "go on" motion. Al sighed. Wells was leaning back in the chair next to him, watching.

"I found out that she'd had some kids. I thought it might be interesting to go meet them. See if they were anything like her. It took me a while to get to them all. Chester was the youngest."

Electricity flashed up my spine when he mentioned my father.

"I tracked him down and found a way to meet him in a bar one night."

The electricity cascaded into gooseflesh, dancing over my skin. Dad always had a beer on Friday night at his favorite watering hole. Now that he'd retired it was like clockwork. It wouldn't have been difficult for Al to casually run into him.

"He was all right. He didn't look like her much. Didn't act much like her. Kind of bland—"

"My father is the kindest person on the *planet*," I blurted, unable to stop myself. "And he probably thinks I've been *murdered* now thanks to you." My voice quivered on the last word. I snapped my mouth shut and leaned back, dropping my eyes to the table in front of me. I didn't want to see all of the auras swirling with pity and sympathy.

"What happened after you met Imogen's father?" Captain Marc asked. I noticed that he said "Imogen's father" and not "Solange's son."

"I talked to him for a while. He told me he had a daughter. Showed me some pictures. Said she'd just moved to New Orleans." I looked up to find Al staring at me. "She looked just like her. She was the only one out of all of them. I . . . just wanted to see her."

"Half true," I breathed. Wells squeezed his eyes shut.

"So, I went to New Orleans . . . it took me a while but I found Imogen—"

"When was this? When did you find her?" Captain Marc's voice went sharp.

Al flushed but didn't break eye contact with the captain. Wells stared at him.

"How long. Had you been. On Earth?" The captain leaned forward, resting his elbows on the table.

"I had three months left," Al muttered.

"Oh, Al . . ." Wells dropped his face into his hand. Angry murmurs punched from the crowd.

Captain Marc half stood, one fist pressed into the tabletop, the other hand extended, palm up. A stack of papers dropped into it. "These are the reports you've been turning into us since," he glanced at the topmost one, "six months before departure to the day."

Al didn't drop his eyes, but his aura shuddered.

Captain Marc laid the reports on the table and paged through them, fully standing. "Humans form bonds quickly, but under six months is not enough time. You were *well aware* of this."

"Yes," Al admitted. Wells looked like he was going to be sick.

"Meaning three months of these reports are falsified."

There was a general outcry, which the captain allowed for a few moments, glaring at Al, whose knee bobbed a few times, but otherwise met Marc's gaze stoically. Marc held a palm out to the assembled and turned to Wells as they quieted. "Llewellyn, were you aware of this?"

"I had no idea, sir." Wells's voice was hoarse.

"True," I said.

"Aloysius, do you have anything to offer in your defense?"

"The reports aren't entirely false," he said. "Yes, I made it sound like I was talking to Imogen alone, but I got to know several of her cousins first. I never mentioned a name. I knew they didn't have . . . that they weren't who I was looking for. I found out about Imogen from her father at four months. You can see, that's when I began including her name and picture—"

"That you undoubtedly took from her father."

Al blew a breath through his nose. "As soon as I met her, I knew."

"And yet you gave her no time, no choice, you've left everyone she was connected to devastated—"

"Don't you understand what she is?" Al sliced a hand in my direction. "A human descended from a sidhe. She could be the one the legends mention."

Another uproar broke out. Several people stood. It took Captain Marc a few seconds of glaring at the crowd to restore order.

"That is a Sephryan legend," the captain said coldly. "They are the ones that take children from humans."

"But any human and sidhe pairing produces a sidhe child," Al persisted, completely unabashed. "Sephrya has never had a human born of a sidhe."

"Imogen was born of a human," Marc said. He opened his mouth to go on, but Al cut him off.

"Solange's body was never found," he said. "Ask Imogen. Ask her how old both her *human* grandfather and Solange were when they died. They were both in their hundreds. Rare for humans. If you ask me, Solange hadn't lost all of her kroma when she was turned. She was still part sidhe. And Imogen is a human descended from sidhe. Her powers are going to be exceptional and she's going to be the turning point."

Captain Marc looked at me.

"He's not lying," I said. Although I wondered if that meant the actual statement was true, or merely if the person stating it believed they were speaking the truth.

"And Imogen's cousins? Aunts or uncles? Why Imogen—"

"Few of them were young enough to survive being turned," Al said, as if he'd been through my entire family tree and dismissed them all. "All the rest were married with kids. And Imogen was the only one who—"

"Looked exactly like your former love interest?" Captain Marc's voice was steel. Wells closed his eyes as if in pain.

"Everyone knows that Sephrya has been increasingly volatile toward us lately and no one wants another Wind War. A human descendant of a sidhe will be the key to bringing peace," Al went on. "Imogen didn't fit on Earth, but I knew as soon as her father told me about her, as soon as I learned how Solange disappeared, that she was the one. It took me too long to find her, I didn't have time to explain things to her, but I couldn't just leave her there to die."

"Abducting a human on the basis of an unproved legend is still—"

"She has a spark. Imogen is *different*." Al was on the edge of his chair, aura spiking, his amber eyes darkening. "Im, I couldn't leave you there to die. And you liked me right away. I know you did, I could smell it—"

"*Everyone* liked you, Al!" I smacked my hands on the table. "You were happy and fun and easy to talk to. *Keane* liked you. He was talking about inviting you on our next road trip, introducing you to his niece . . ." I closed my eyes and bit my lower lip, forcing tears back before saying, "You didn't care about us at all, did you?"

"Care about you? I risked all of this for you, Imogen, I *love* you." He leaned forward, hands clutching his knees, flashing amber eyes locked on mine. "And you know you wanted more than friendship—"

"All right, enough." Captain Marc mercifully cut Al off before he could say something to trigger the explosion simmering just beneath my skin. Wells was slowly shaking his head, staring off into the middle distance. The captain continued, "I sent a message to the palace as soon as we were in range." He took a deep breath. Exhaled slowly. "The expedition heads and I will be convening to put procedures in place against a repeat of this . . . disaster. Aloysius, I would think it goes without saying, but I'm learning that with you nothing goes without saying: you are banned from any future expeditions to Earth. Indefinitely."

There were some satisfied murmurs among those gathered. Al just pressed his lips into a thin line and nodded once without looking at anyone. Wells continued to stare at nothing, arms folded across his chest.

"I received communication from the palace just before this meeting with regard to who will be responsible for Imogen until she has control of her kroma and has adjusted to life in Molnair . . ." Captain Marc produced an official looking document, broke the red wax seal, and unfolded the thick paper as we watched.

My breath caught and my stomach turned inside out. I hadn't considered what would happen to me after we had landed. Hadn't realized that someone would need to be "responsible" for me. I instinctively bridled at the implication that I couldn't take care of myself, but it made sense. I had no idea what this body was capable of yet, or how to responsibly direct any powers that I might or might not possess. And I had no idea how to support myself or make my way in this completely alien society that I'd be trapped in for at least a century. I forced slow breaths in and out as I watched Captain Marc's dark eyes scan the document swiftly, a crease forming between his eyebrows.

"The king has stated that since Aloysius brought her into this situation, it is unfair to foist her upon anyone else. The palace will provide for Imogen's care, including housing . . ."

A buzzing filled my ears. It was difficult to breathe. Did this mean what I thought it meant? My gaze flicked to Al. No longer the least bit cowed;

he looked like he had just been given everything he wanted. His aura practically glowed, and when he looked at me . . . I felt like a rabbit in a snare. I yanked my focus back to Captain Marc, desperately hoping I had misunderstood something.

". . . since Aloysius was responsible for turning Imogen, he will be responsible for ensuring she is able to successfully join society . . ."

My insides turned to concrete. I couldn't draw breath. Couldn't think. Couldn't move. *They're just going to* give *me to Al?* I saw a horrific path laid out in front of me. One where I was trapped in a palace—a palace where Al was the prince and heir and got whatever he wanted—where he could compel me to do whatever he liked until I broke and stopped fighting. Where I would only learn what he wanted me to learn. Where he might even eventually Stockholm me into loving him back. Or at least acting like I did. For centuries upon centuries. I doubted he'd let me go back on the next expedition. I scented my own terror drenching the air around me.

Captain Marc continued to read about Al taking responsibility for what he had done. I looked wildly around the room; troubled looks decorated some of the faces, and a few of them were whispering among themselves, but no one came to my aid. I had never smelled my own fear before. Whether it was because I had lacked the capabilities or because I had never been this afraid, I didn't know.

My gaze landed on Al and Wells. Al radiated relief and elation, his aura practically luminous. He'd gotten away with murder. And he was getting what he wanted. Wells . . . Wells looked like he was about to walk the plank.

"I'll take responsibility for her," Wells interrupted, then winced, even before Al's head whipped toward him.

"What was that, Llewellyn?" Captain Marc said mildly, as if Wells was simply volunteering to be the designated driver for the evening.

"I am also responsible for turning Imogen," Wells said clearly, although he was looking more and more like he had eaten bad sushi. "She didn't choose to come here. She didn't choose to be turned. I think she should at least have a choice as to where she starts her new life. Even if her options are currently limited." His eyes swept to mine. "I don't live in a palace, just so you know."

"Excellent points." Captain Marc turned to me. "Imogen, your choice. Who would you prefer as a guide while you adjust to your new situation?"

Al's expression morphed from triumph to desperation. His gaze collided with mine, eyes pleading, then flashed me that charming smile. "C'mon, baby..."

"I'll go with Wells."

Al deflated.

"Done." Captain Marc pushed his chair back and stood. "If the expedition heads would speak with me briefly... everyone else, have a good meal and rest well. Battle stations at first shift." He crossed to speak with the same four serious sidhe he had been conversing with when we arrived. They appeared slightly less tense.

I hesitantly pushed back from the table and stood. Everyone was milling around. Some exited right away in groups or pairs, others lingered to chat; Al was in the midst of a quiet, but furious diatribe directed at Wells, who was resignedly listening, looking as if he were questioning two-hundred-and-fifty-one years of life choices that had led him to this moment.

Someone touched my arm.

"Hi, I'm Cilla." It was the pretty blonde who had enjoyed my *Princess Bride* reference. Her voice was a sultry alto in contrast to her beachy, tanned appearance.

"Imogen," I said, pushing my frozen face into a smile.

"I get the impression everything is going to be pretty hectic tomorrow, so in case I didn't get the chance, I wanted to introduce myself. I'm from LA. Originally." She smiled. "Anyway, once you get settled, if you ever wanted to get coffee or something—"

"Do they have—?"

"Oh, they have jatki. It's basically the same thing. Caffeinated and everything. I definitely checked."

My smile softened into something more genuine.

"Anyway, we could reminisce about Earth and human stuff. I promise to laugh at your pop culture jokes. I love those old eighties movies. All movies really." Flashing another impish grin, she sauntered off to join the tall, dark sidhe waiting for her. Her smile was a stunning gleam of white as she pulled Cilla into a hug. They walked out with their arms around each other. The contrast of their light and dark beauties together was breathtaking.

I was still staring after them when Wells came up to me. "Ready to go? I think a drink is definitely on the agenda."

I pointed at the female pair. "I thought like . . . creating the next generation was the main reason—"

"Oh, they'll have children," Wells said, following my gaze. "Zoe wants a big family. This is her fourth search."

I felt my brow furrow, still watching Cilla and Zoe, who were almost to the door.

"Right, I forgot," Wells said. "A female pair can have children together. It takes some doing, and they can only bear other females—we're working on that—but they can reproduce. And since they're both capable of it, they can take turns being pregnant if they want."

"Division of labor. Nice," I quipped before I could stop myself.

While I was busy gawking at the stunning couple, Wells offered his arm and I took it automatically. He started forward and I followed.

"Thanks, by the way," I said.

He was quiet for a beat. His aura changing colors so quickly I couldn't make sense of it. "You're welcome," he said at last, and pushed the door open for me.

I stopped myself from glancing back to see what had become of Al.

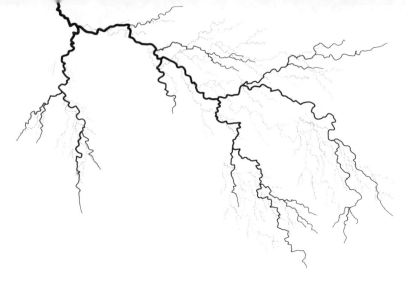

CHAPTER EIGHT

Dear Heavens, what would we do without wine?
—*Solange Aidair Delaney*

Although it was early for dinner, Wells asked if I'd like to get something from the kitchen and bring it up to the room to eat when we were hungry. I agreed. The kitchen was virtually empty as we passed through—which sadly meant less culinary kromatics in the cooking area—and I waited while Wells pointed to several things behind the counter. He was eventually handed a large sack and then offered me his arm again. We marched briskly down the hall to his room, meeting no one on the way, which I assumed was his goal. I certainly wasn't going to argue. I'd been stared at enough today.

When he opened the door to his room, it stopped partway, blocked by a cot that had been wedged into the only available space. "Well, that was fast," he said, gesturing for me to squeeze in first.

"I guess a spare room wasn't an option?" I said as I shimmied through the doorway.

"There aren't any," he replied, handing me the sack before pulling himself through and shutting the door behind him. "No wasted space on a ship. And anyone recently turned shouldn't be unmonitored for long periods anyway. The assumption is you'd be happy to share with your partner but..."

I grunted in response and suppressed a shudder at how close I'd come to being back with Al. *I'd've refused,* I told myself. *I would have slept in the kitchen or the training room. Fuck that.* I set the sack at the foot of the bed, then clambered over the cot to squeeze myself into the chair, now wedged against the wall in between the nightstand and dresser. I found my running shorts from earlier on top of the dresser and pulled them on under the dress. An indigo pulse of Wells's kroma floated the nightstand's lamp—cordless, how did they light these things?—to the dresser top, along with the stack of books. He hauled the sack to the head of the bed. Meanwhile I had put the t-shirt back on and removed the dress underneath it. I let it drop to the tiny space of floor between the dresser and chair.

Wells pulled a bottle of wine out of the sack and set it on the nightstand between us.

"Oh, thank Christ." I scooped it into my arms and hugged it. He half smiled. I inspected the bottle; it was identical to the one I'd seen in Al's room. No label with a rubber stopper.

"There are barrels of wine in the hold. All of the bottles are washed and reused." Wells pulled out two earthenware cups with no handles and something in wrapping that smelled like cheese. "I thought we could have a snack first. Unless you want the entire meal right away?"

"No thanks. I want to *feel* this first glass of wine." I handed him the bottle, unsure how to remove the stopper without making a mess.

"I'm in agreement with you there." His aura eddied with blue-black and ochre. I wondered if I should ask about what Al said to him—yelled at him—or leave it alone. He unstoppered the wine and poured two cups, then unwrapped the cheese and set a knife next to it. "I'll find the bread in a moment, it's in here somewhere. Anyway," he lifted his cup, "salute. To our temporary cohabitation."

I imitated him, lifting my glass then taking an exploratory sip. The wine was good. Yay. I took a longer one. "Is Al mad at you?"

He took another swig then dug around in the sack while he answered. "Not . . . really. He's upset that he doesn't get you to himself, of course, but he obviously realized this was a possibility, as evidenced by his efforts to keep you hidden until disembarkation. I think he feels that if you're with me he'll at least have some . . . access to you." He pulled out the bread—it was slightly squashed—and cut a few slices of cheese.

Eels raced around in my stomach as I asked, "And will he? Have 'access' to me?"

Wells tore off a piece of bread and paired it with a slice of cheese. "Only if you agree to see him. There's no point in lying to you though, he will try. And as you've noticed, Al does tend to get away with more because of who he is, but I will do my best to circumvent that. I was serious about wanting you to have a choice, Imogen."

The eels settled down. I fixed some bread and cheese for myself. For a minute we ate and drank in silence, each wading through our own thoughts. The bread and cheese were finished and we were on our second cups of wine when I asked, "So, when Captain Marc said 'battle stations,' that was a hyperbole, right?"

Wells was mid-drink and raised his eyebrows at me over his cup. He swallowed loudly. "Oh, fuck, Imogen, I forget how much you don't know."

"How nice for you." I took a gulp of my own wine. He had not agreed that it was a hyperbole. Maybe he didn't know what hyperbole meant.

He shook his head. "No, there are literal battle stations, but we only have a . . . I'd say sixty-forty percent chance of being attacked—"

"When you say sixty-forty," I said, helping myself to another swig, "which is the sixty in your world?"

"Sixty is that we'll be attacked but—"

"Wells." I set down my cup, twisting to face him fully. "I don't know if you got the chance to visit Vegas while you were prancing around on Earth—"

"Prancing?"

"—but those are *terrible* odds."

"I resent the implication that I was prancing."

"Put a pin in it, we can get to what you did when you were cavorting around—"

"Now I'm cavorting?"

"—on my pale blue dot after we discuss the fact that we might be attacked in a few hours and I'd like to know what the hell *that* looks like." I tossed back the rest of my wine and held out my cup for more. He took it.

He downed the rest of his own, placed his cup next to mine, and retrieved the bottle. "I don't know that I should give you any more, you've been so insulting."

I narrowed my eyes and mouthed "battle stations."

He smirked and refilled the cups. "You've heard us mention Sephrya a few times now?" He handed mine back.

I took it. "The kidnappers?"

He coughed, but didn't contradict me. "Once we'd established ourselves on Perimov, they felt continuing to push kromatic space exploration was unnecessary and unnatural. Hypocritically, centuries later, they'd like to know how we manage to get to Earth and back with such precision. As we don't agree with how they'd use that knowledge, we keep it secret. Sephrya is a much larger country and—other than our significant kromatic advances—they have more resources than Molnair. It irritates them that they can't buy or barter for our secrets and Molnair largely believes it serves them right as they chose to stop progressing. Quite frankly, there's been a grudge between the two countries since we split. So, often they'll try to down a returning ship, either because our technology is blasphemous or because we won't share it. The narrative flips occasionally. Technically, sixty miles above the ground is under no jurisdiction. They can do whatever they like until we cross into our specific airspace. If they follow us from there, it's a formal declaration of war, which both sides dance around continually." No doubt noting my horrified expression, he added, "Nothing for you to be concerned about, these attacks are usually for show more than anything. It's just people throwing kroma at each other, which is why all of the strongest are resting right now."

"So, they're all for show, but the strongest people are resting in preparation for battle stations first thing in the morning, sixty-forty chance."

He squeezed his eyes shut, huffing a breath through his nose. "What is it you actually want to know, Imogen?"

My brows dropped. "Shall I draw up a list? What kind of kroma? What's our likelihood of death percentage? What will I be doing? What will you be doing?" I took a sip of wine. "Also, as . . . horrifying as it is that they keep a herd of humans trapped, if they already have them, why would they want to be able to go to Earth?"

Wells grabbed the bottle and waved his hand for me to extend my glass. He topped me off and poured the last bit into his cup. "Thank the gods I thought to get two," he said, pulling another bottle out of the sack.

"Wait, don't you have to do battle stations in the morning? Isn't it like, twelve hours bottle-to-throttle?"

Wells blinked at me, then leaned forward, eyes flashing. "I'm not sure exactly what you meant, but I think you were concerned about my ability to fight in the morning after a few cups of wine, so let me assure you that I'll be fine. I got us a big dinner." He leaned back. I wasn't aware until that moment that I'd been enjoying his scent. "To answer your question about Sephrya . . . imagine, if you will, a race of sidhe that already considers humanity to be nothing better than cattle—in spite of the fact that their own race would become extinct without them—imagine what they might do if they were able to descend upon Earth as they wished. Simply kidnap a few hundred people every so often? Or perhaps take over the entire planet? Regardless, it would make what Al did to you look like a kindness."

I sipped silently for a beat, digesting that.

"What legend was Al talking about?" I asked, swirling my wine and extending my legs off the chair and onto the cot.

Wells stared at my bare legs for a second, blinked hard, then pulled the sack of food toward himself.

"You're right, we should just eat. No point in getting too drunk and probably better to get to sleep early. I can answer your questions while we have dinner."

Dinner turned out to be vegetarian sandwiches for me and sandwiches with meat for Wells. There was also some kind of seafood—which Wells promised me was an actual sea creature, because I'd never heard of a cephlaang before—fried and chopped into bite sized pieces with a spicy dipping sauce. A purply dipping sauce. But the cephlaang tasted kind of like a breaded scallop ring—not calamari as I'd been expecting—and the sauce was *awesome*.

"There's a legend," Wells's words were clipped, "which not too many people take seriously, that a human descended from a sidhe will arrive during a time of conflict to restore balance to our people." He devoured half a sandwich in about two bites. "Sound like something you're up for?"

"No, thank you," I said, munching on my third bite of cephlaang. "Why does Al take it seriously if no one else does?"

The corners of his mouth turned down as he prepared to attack the second half of his sandwich. "He went to a psychic after Solange left who told him that the human of legend would take up residence in the palace and have a great influence on his life."

"Oh dear lord," I said.

"Quite." He washed down his sandwich with a healthy swig of wine, eyes narrowed, aura simmering.

I decided to change the subject. "So tell me about this mating bond thing. Sounds like a juicy piece of business."

Wells started choking.

"That's what you get for inhaling an entire sandwich in four bites." I leaned forward, setting my glass down. "Do you need some water?"

He shook his head and managed to take another sip of wine. "You caught me by surprise with that question." He gave me a half smile, a flush blooming across his cheekbones. "A mating bond is . . . a bridge between two connected souls. Once joined, the pair are bonded for life, always in tune with each other. To forcibly separate a mated pair is considered cruel and criminal. And the bond only occurs once. The connection is permanent. They're forever linked." He appeared to contemplate his wine. "Al was probably hoping one would spring up between the two of you before he was found out."

"But I barely know him," I said, my stomach clenching. Being forever linked to Al was not appealing. "How does it—what does it—"

I must have been wearing my apprehension on my face because Wells cut me off. "Although it can happen quickly, there's always an emotional connection first. And even so, it doesn't happen with every pair; it's actually quite rare. There are plenty of happily partnered couples who live their entire lives together unbonded. It tends to happen when the match is . . . incredibly balanced, in terms of kromatic ability and . . ." he cleared his throat, "the potential for strong children."

"Would you know? If it happened? Is there like a . . . test or something?" I took a fortifying slug of wine.

"A bonded pair can be sensed. From what I understand, a male usually feels it immediately. Regardless of if the pairing is heterosexual or otherwise. For females it can be more gradual. Once both parties are aware of the bond, it can be sensed by just about anyone around them."

"How does it get . . . accepted?"

He raised his eyebrows.

"Oh. Right. Fucking. How silly of me."

He snorted.

I watched his aura while working through my own sandwich. A thick slice of some yellow vegetable comprised the "meat." Something between a cucumber and a tomato. Crunchy on the edges, but with a dense, watery center. "Were you looking for your own partner on this trip?"

"I was," Wells said, unwrapping a second sandwich.

"And you didn't find one?"

"Obviously."

That might have been a personal question, I thought belatedly. "I'm sorry."

He shrugged. "It's uncommon to find a partner on your first expedition."

"But you were on the last one. The one my grandma was on."

"Yes, but I was only crew then." He was already halfway through his second sandwich. He was a sandwich killing champion. "In most cases, the first time you go to Earth, you're on crew, not on active search."

"So, you just stay on the ship?"

"No, not at all. You're on the ship more than those who are on search, but you have shifts, like everyone else. That's the point. Get to know what life on the ship is like and get a feel for what humans are like without the pressure of trying to find a partner." He had slaughtered *two sandwiches* while somehow having a conversation. I was still working on my first. Having apparently eaten his fill, Wells leaned back against the pillows, balancing his cup on his belly.

I slid my legs underneath the cot's blankets and moved the pillow to my side to lean on. "You said in *most* cases you're just part of the crew the first time you go to Earth . . ."

I intentionally let my sentence hang, waiting to see if he would say it or make me ask the question, watching his aura the entire time. Only a few red shoots of anger, which surprised me. I was starting to wonder if Wells lived for cleaning up Al's messes.

"Well, you know one exception. And I doubt that will ever happen again. The other is if you were originally from Earth." Confusion must have registered on my face because he continued, "As much as it would make a fantastic love story to say that every pairing that came out of these expeditions lasted forever, it sometimes takes former mortals several decades to adjust to the fact that they no longer have a mere century or less to make do with. Occasionally pairings that worked well when the Earthling was in one mindset changed when they were able to wrap their head around the fact that they actually had a lot more time." Wells drained his wine and refilled it, passing the bottle to me without so much as a querying glance to see if I wanted more. I took it.

"No one will ever know Earth better than a former Earthling," Wells said. "That's the theory, anyway. So, any who are unattached three months before launch are allowed to participate in partner training."

"How many are on this one?"

"None. They don't often come." Wells sipped his wine.

"Why?"

"You'd have to ask one of them. Or better yet, maybe you'll tell me in one hundred years. If you chose to remain sidhe, that is."

"When can I get . . . re-humanized?" I forced myself to ask.

"It would be best to wait until you are back on Earth. In one hundred years. You'd need to remain sidhe to live that long and it's very dangerous to be a powerless human in a world of creatures with various energetic powers," he said softly. "Ask any human residing in Sephrya."

"And there's no way to go back early?" It was getting harder to breathe. I locked my reactions down as best I could. I was not going to break down in front of a veritable stranger.

"I'm sorry, Imogen," Wells said. "We can make some inquiries in a few decades, if you like. Kromatic advances happen every day . . ."

But it was unlikely. We were quiet for several moments while I tucked those emotions away. *Stuff your sorrys in a sack,* my grandma used to say. She was talking about useless apologies, but it still came to mind when I actively compartmentalized.

"You should eat at least one more sandwich," Wells said, going for his *third*.

I considered it for a moment. I'd had a lot of wine and not much food the past several days, I should probably take his advice. I peeked into the bag. "Jesus, how many did you get?"

"You can have some tomorrow during re-entry," he said between bites. "I'll be bringing some with me also. I have no idea how long it will take

A Dagger of Lightning

if we're attacked. And this is awkward, but are you okay sleeping in what you're wearing? It doesn't appear that Al got you any night clothes—" I growled. "—and I'm running low on clean shirts."

"This is good, I'm perfectly comfortable," I said, stifling a yawn. "Has this just been the longest day ever or are days longer where you're from?"

He chuckled. "It's been a pretty long day. It wouldn't hurt either of us to get to bed early if you're tired. I'm certainly not going to insist we stay up just to finish this bottle."

"I can finish it tomorrow while we're being attacked. I can just sit in here and read your crazy history books, drink wine, eat sandwiches, and wear all of your shirts."

"All of them?"

"Only the clean ones. But all at the same time." I looked at my wine cup. It was still fairly full. I'd better get busy if we were shutting down soon. I took a sizable swallow.

"How are my history books weird?" Wells straightened back into a sitting position facing me and applied himself to his own cup.

"Well, maybe it's not the history books so much as this history." I pushed myself upright. "And I'm not even halfway through. Would you like a for instance? That law on page 47."

"I'm afraid I don't have every page memorized."

"No? I do. But let's just say that I'll be careful not to mate with a deer in the Briarwood forest during the full moon."

Wells barked a laugh and reached a hand up toward the dresser. "Move your head," he said. I did and the book zoomed past me into his hand. He turned to the page. "Well, I wonder who fucked up how and made that a law . . ." His eyes bounced up to mine. "How far did you get in this?"

"Page 164."

He flipped a few pages. "Tell me something on page 128."

"Oh, that was a good one. The Great Honey Wars of the first century. Good to know Earth isn't the only planet that screwed up in regard to our honeybees." I glanced over; he was staring at the page, his aura shot with golden rays of surprise. "Before you ask, no, I didn't intend on memorizing the book. It just happened."

He snapped the book shut and kroma'ed it back to the dresser.

I shifted my head out of the way as it passed.

"Did you have this kind of memory bef—"

"No. I had a *good* memory. I remembered more than most people and memorization was always easy for me, but I didn't have an eidetic or photographic memory before." I stared at my wine.

"Interesting," he said.

"Oh my God, if you say that one more time without elaborating, I am going to tackle you out of pure frustration."

He laughed and tossed back the rest of his cup. "Fair enough." He set it on the nightstand. "Imogen, do you remember when I told you that anything you were good at—"

"Anything I was good at as a human I'd be good at again now. I do." I tossed back my wine and set my cup beside his. Neither of us made a move to get more.

"I also told you that your powers won't have started to manifest." I nodded. He went on, "When a human is turned, all of their talents and abilities—even the neglected ones—will be . . . honed to their sharpest. And some do manage to improve these abilities with regular practice as they live their lives. However, they don't awake from turning with talents in excess of their previous capabilities. And they don't usually start wielding even the smallest expressions of their kroma as quickly as you have."

"What about if a sidhe was turned into a human and then she had a baby and then her baby had a baby and then that baby was turned . . ."

He gave me his half smile. "I guess we'll find out, won't we? You're the first."

"I hate going first," I muttered.

Wells grinned. "Do you want to go to bed early, then?"

"Yes," I said. "I'm tired of consciousness. I'll take the cot."

"No, Imogen, take the bed, I insist."

"I'm not having this argument. You actually have to do . . . battle stations in the morning. I don't have to do anything aside from eat sandwiches apparently. I'm likely to fall asleep in ten seconds even if I was lying on the floor." I glanced up; he looked like he might be marshaling a comeback, so I kept talking. "Look, I don't want to die in some magical sidhe dogfight tomorrow because you didn't get a good night's sleep, so really this is pure selfishness on my part."

I was rewarded with a half-smile. "Kroma isn't magic. Magic implies . . . haphazardly bestowed gifts. Kroma is energy present in all sidhe, honed, trained—"

"You say potato, I say potahto. I'll take first dibs on washing up in exchange." I scooted off to brush my teeth.

When I returned, Wells had restoppered the wine and cleared up the detritus from our meal. I clambered right into the cot, just in case chivalry should rear its ugly head, but he didn't argue as he went to take his turn cleaning up. I was asleep before he had finished.

Keane was searching for me. Face pale. Hair disheveled. Frantic. Tearing through the house, shouting my name.

"I'm right here!" I cried. "Keane, I'm right here! I'm fine!"

He ran right past me, eyes wide and panicked. I tried to follow but my legs moved as if I were slogging through mud. I tried to call out to him again but my throat closed up over the words. I coughed, but it only constricted tighter.

Keane sprinted past me again, not seeing me. "Imogen? Imogen!"

Here! Here! I tried to say, but I was choking now and could barely pull an inhale past the tightness in my throat. Keane grabbed the car keys and bolted out the door. I floundered in his wake, my legs like anchors. I crawled after him, wheezing, but he didn't see me. He pulled the car away and I collapsed in the driveway, unable to speak or draw breath.

"Imogen! *Imogen!*"

My eyes snapped open. Wells had a vice grip on my upper arms, hauling me to a sitting position. I was choking in real life. *It's a laryngospasm. You'll be fine in sixty to ninety seconds. Just keep trying to pull in air,* I told myself. Even as I clutched Wells's arms hard enough to bruise, trying to suck breath through any tiny space that remained in my airway. Laryngospasms aren't deadly, but they are terrifying. Both for the person having one and for whoever has to watch them drowning on dry land for a minute and a half.

"Imogen!" Wells gave me a little shake. "I'm going to compel you to breathe, okay?"

I nodded vigorously.

"*Take a breath.*"

My vocal cords mercifully relaxed their stranglehold on my larynx. I pulled in a deep breath, then started coughing.

"*Take another.*"

My lungs obeyed. My heart gradually slowed out of its gallop. My fingertips unburied themselves from Wells's forearms. He compelled two more breaths before he was satisfied and let me pant and cough on my own. He released one of my arms to push back the mass of hair that had obscured my face.

"Are you all right?"

"Yes," I panted. "Thank you."

"What . . . were you having a nightmare?" Although his grip had slackened, Wells still clasped my right arm, as if he were afraid I might topple over. My own hand rested loosely on his forearm.

"No, well, yes, I was having a nightmare, but . . ." I shook my head. "The suffocating thing's called a laryngospasm and I used to get them before . . . Basically your vocal cords spasm and cut off your airway. Mine always seem to happen at night. I got them more frequently when I was a child, but I still get surprised by one every couple of years. Nice to know they've followed me into immortality."

Wells blew out a breath. The orange panic in his aura ebbing away. "It's not uncommon for previous handicaps to be enhanced just as talents are."

"Well, that fucking sucks."

Wells half-smiled. "All right," he patted my arm, "you're moving to the bed."

"What? No, that's not necess—"

"I'm not having this argument."

I raised my eyebrows.

He smirked. "Look, I have to be up in less than an hour. You don't. If you move to the bed, there's less chance I'll wake you when I leave. You need more sleep right after you're turned."

I didn't know if that last bit was a bill of goods he was trying to sell me or not, but I nodded my acquiescence and let him help me over to the bed. "Only because I'm impressed you threw my own words back at me in less than twenty-four hours."

"Ha!" He released my arm once I was settled down and tossed the covers over me. "Tuck yourself in, high maintenance female."

I chuckled deep in my throat as I arranged the blankets to my liking. Noticing as I did so that I was now surrounded by his scent. *I have to find out what soap he uses.* "I'm sorry I'm so high maintenance," I said sincerely. He hadn't asked to be stuck in this mess any more than I had.

"It's all right," he said, fully settled in himself. "You haven't exactly been doing it on purpose."

"Wells?"

"Hm?"

"If I'm ever suffocating in any way, shape, or form? You have my *blanket permission* to compel me to breathe."

"Noted." I heard the smile in his voice. "Now go to sleep Imogen. I have a mystical dogfight to rest up for. Or whatever it was you called it."

CHAPTER NINE

Don't hold back, my girl. You show them exactly who you are. I don't give two shits if it scares them or anyone around you. You do not pretend to be less. It's a waste of fucking time.
—Solange Aidair Delaney

The rest of my evening was mercifully nightmare free. When I woke, Wells was indeed gone and so was the cot. I sat up in bed, rubbed the sleep from my eyes, then stared at my fingers. The fourth digit on my left hand looked barren. *I need to get my ring back from Al,* I thought. *Even if I'll never see Keane again, it's mine.* I sat in stillness for a moment, thoughts and feelings tumbling through me. It was the first time I'd been alone since being pulled from Earth. I didn't try to sort through or make sense of the swirl of emotions crashing into me like ever increasing waves. I just let them go. Until they lodged in my stomach, my throat, my chest. Tears formed. *Don't get pulled under. You've got to survive this.*

I flung back the covers and stomped to the bathroom, twisting the sink faucet and cupping my hands beneath the water. One part of my brain registered the absence of pain in my left ankle. The tears pushed free, as if sensing I was finally alone. I repeatedly splashed cool water over my face. When they didn't stop, I wet a hand towel and pressed it to my eyes and neck, trying to calm my flushed skin.

When my mother died, I'd developed an aversion to crying. My father had still been hospitalized and some well-meaning relative sent me to school. I still don't remember exactly what set me off, but I'd been asked to put something on the board, had started crying, and couldn't stop. I was pulled out of class and eventually they sorted out what had happened and called someone to take me home, but some of the other kids had smelled blood in the water and never let me forget my meltdown. A few even tried to trigger me into repeating it. Since then, I'd kept everything locked down unless I was in a safe place or a very private place. I'd developed a sense of humor to deflect tension when things got too hot. Yes, I'd been told it was unhealthy, but I'd been doing it for decades and I had no plans to change.

I had pulled off my now soaked shirt, the tears subsiding into sniffles, when the first shudder rocked the ship. I stumbled. A sound like rolling thunder cascaded the length of the hull. *Just people throwing kroma at each other my ass.*

A tingle of adrenaline washed over my limbs as I dropped the wet shirt and yanked open dresser drawers until I found my clothes. Nothing would convince me to wear any of the ultra-feminine dresses while we were being attacked, regardless of if I were doing any actual fighting or not. I didn't feel like traipsing around in a strappy yoga top either. I shucked off my shorts, poured myself into a set of plain black running tights, and dug through Wells's clothes. He *was* running low on t-shirts, but I found a dark blue V-neck and threw it on.

I yanked open the door and practically fell into the hallway as another tremor ricocheted through the ship. I scanned the corridors to either side of me, searching for some sign of another person. I saw no one. All other doorways remained firmly closed. *Was I seriously supposed to sleep through this?* I wondered where Wells was. Where these "battle stations" were. I needed to see what was happening. There had to be a window somewhere.

I chose a direction and jogged down the hallway. Almost unconsciously, I cataloged different scents as they hit my now incredibly perceptive nose. I found a faint trace of Wells from when he passed through this morning and locked on to it. I wanted to get where I could see something before another blast hit. I tracked him turn by turn, darting up a stairwell, my heart pounding as I sped up, thrilled by the speed in my legs, my painless ankle, and the complete lack of soreness from sparring yesterday.

Terse, clipped voices reached my ears and I galloped toward them. Another turn and I could see sunlight at the end of a corridor. *Yes! A window!* I charged forward, skidding to a stop at the entrance to the bridge. I scanned the room, stunned at its brightness, my new eyes adjusting rapidly.

The energy was completely different from when Wells had brought me in before. The four people powering the ship were glaring out the front windshield, each wearing a look of grim determination. Everyone else was standing in front of the floor-to-ceiling windows. The control chairs near each person were vacant and completely ignored.

Bursts of movement flashed about the room. Individuals at the window threw dramatic flourishes at some *things* shooting by outside, trails of color echoing the movements of their hands and blasting out toward their targets. Mainly sleek, silver, bean-shaped pods, dozens of them, zipping every which way beyond the windows. Blasts of their own kroma spit out from dark, gleaming slashes across the nose of each pod, trying to pierce the holes in our defenses. Captain Marc manned the raised dais, sleeves of his rust-colored tunic shoved up to the elbows, his hands thrust out in a Hadoken-like gesture, corded muscles in his forearms straining, as if he were trying to push through something in front of us. He occasionally barked out an order, but his concentration remained ahead.

"Imogen!"

I whipped my head toward the right side of the room and saw Al, standing near Wells, looking for the first time like he was not happy to see me.

At the sound of my name, Wells turned away from the window, following his brother's gaze, and locked eyes with me. His entire body sagged and his expression shifted into that long-suffering, pained look I'd only seen before when Al had said something idiotic.

"*Focus!*" Captain Marc shouted as a blast of fuchsia speared toward the gap created by a distracted Al and Wells. Wells pivoted toward the window, crossed his wrists, and pushed out an indigo shield. It only partially deflected the blow and I fell to my knees when the room was rocked by the impact.

Al winked over and hauled me up by an arm, dragging me forward and shoving me into the seat between Wells and himself. "What the *hell* is she doing up here? Didn't you tell her to stay put?" He turned back to the window, flinging out pine-green balls of kroma toward a particularly aggressive pod speeding through space beside us. One of the blasts finally connected with its stern. It spun wildly end over end, colliding with one of its comrades before dropping out of sight.

Wells spun my chair toward him, grabbed its harness, and roughly buckled me in. "I assumed that it went without saying," he answered Al, then glared at me. "Congratulations. You're now purposefully high maintenance." He spun my chair back to face the window and launched a volley of indigo spheres at a group of six pods in tight formation, converging on our side of the ship. Each sphere found its mark and four of the six went down with gaping holes in their hulls; the other two managed to swerve and avoid full impact, the glancing blows still sending them spinning away.

I was riveted. Each person's power had a signature color, so I was always able to see when Wells or Al was firing without taking my eyes off the aerial display unfolding before me. We were being attacked by hundreds of little pods, zipping around us from all sides, seeking openings in our shields or weaknesses in our offensive line. Occasionally a larger vessel would charge by and fire at us, but they stayed so far out of range that deflecting their attacks didn't cause our fighters too much strain.

I didn't care that Al and Wells were irritated with me. Potential death by kromatic explosion aside, this was fascinating. I didn't regret finding my way to the bridge. Staying locked in Wells's room with no idea what was happening had been far more terrifying. I pulled my gaze from the battle outside to focus on the dramatic hand gestures everyone was making. *I wonder if I'll be able to do that shit.*

Suddenly, a larger vehicle rose up from below, directly in front of us. Three times the size of the silver pods, with sharp, chevron-shaped wings and a long narrow nose, it resembled an angry vulture, and it was no longer out of range.

A bright wall of kromatic energy rushed toward us before either Al or Wells could refocus enough to defend. I flinched, instinctively bringing my arms up, wrists crossed, to block my face . . . and an enormous, glittering, blue-black shield pulsed from my body, spreading wide to arch in front of the window, completely deflecting the blast.

Al and Wells gaped at me.

"Watch out!" I hollered, pointing at the gigantic attack ship, which was now kamikaze-ing toward us. Al and Wells snapped back toward the window, simultaneously slicing their arms through the air. I imitated them. Three blade-like projections, pine-green, blue-black, and indigo sheared through the charging vessel, cleaving it into three sections, which slowly separated from each other before gently floating away or being blasted apart by kromatic crossfire.

"YIPPEE KI YAY, MOTHERFUCKER!" I crowed, thrusting my fists into the air. "Who's high maintenance *now*?"

"Llewellyn!" barked Captain Marc, still pressing on an invisible barrier in front of us. Beads of sweat clustered on his shining pate, sliding down his sepia temples. His tunic clung to his shoulders, dark with perspiration. "How did she learn that?"

"Ask her." Wells tossed a deadly indigo frisbee through the dark windshield of a pod. "I certainly didn't teach her."

"What, like it's hard?" I snapped, unable to resist being a little snotty. "I just saw what you were doing and did it."

"Get her up here! She's fresh," the captain ordered.

Wells nodded at Al and spun my chair to face himself. Al shifted to cover both of their spots, throwing a rapid fire of pine-green projectiles while Wells thumbed the release on the harness and hauled me to my feet. His face betrayed nothing, but his aura pulsed with bronze determination, fractured occasionally with the autumn colors of irritation, and edged with the swirling cools of concern. He turned me around, planted a hand on my spine, and propelled me toward the dais. "Let's see what you can do, little show-off," he muttered, giving me a shove and then stalking back to his place. I flipped him off and stepped up next to Captain Marc.

"Watch what I'm doing, Imogen," he said, not taking his eyes from that space in front of him. I watched. His golden kroma oozed from his body in a relentless flow, pouring down the arrow-straight lines of his arms and spearing out from between the connected heels of his hands, his fingers curled back and out of the way, his palms thrust forward. I followed the line of his energy to the window and beyond and got my first glimpse of the planet.

We were close enough so that it filled the window, the curve of the horizon only just visible at the top. The green and purple landmass we approached loomed larger and larger, surrounded by sparkling blue ocean. My breath caught in my throat. It was beautiful. Pulling my focus back to the captain's aura was an effort, but once I saw what he was doing, the emotional surge I'd felt was wiped away. We were entering the atmosphere. And Marc's energy was the shield preventing us from burning up.

The pods and attack cruisers increased in activity around us. *They want to pull his focus*, I thought. *They want us to burn.* I snapped my wrists together, thrust my arms forward, and *pushed*. In my peripheral vision, I saw the colors of my kroma shrink into me and coalesce. A blue-black beam shot from my palms, arrowing alongside the captain's energy, then blooming out, my dark, glittering shield spreading out in front of his own.

"Brilliant," Captain Marc muttered. "Keep your focus only on this, Imogen."

I nodded, vaguely aware of my skin heating with the effort. One part of my brain registered the surprised murmurings around me, but I did as the captain had said and kept my focus on maintaining the shield. The planet filled the screen, its horizon no longer visible. A rhythmic shuddering rumbled throughout the ship as we entered the atmosphere. I forced myself to take deep inhales and slow exhales. I felt Captain Marc pull his energy back slightly. Testing.

"Imogen, can you hold?" he asked. "Three minutes at most."

I nodded again, and felt the load increase as the rest of his shield dropped away. He remained beside me for a few seconds more. What he saw must have satisfied him. He stepped off the dais.

I narrowed my concentration to a razor-edged awareness. I was the shield. Anything existing beyond the shield was not a concern. Some part of my mind clocked the aching in my arms, the tightness in my shoulders, the trembling in my legs . . . then dismissed them. My eardrums absorbed words as Captain Marc asked for, and received, a quick fix block. My eyes registered motion as he stepped up to the windows immediately in front of me, standing just beneath my beam of energy, but my world remained the shield and nothing else.

I did not allow myself to flinch when Captain Marc clapped his hands together, then thrust them outward and to the sides, flinging a golden wall of energy in every direction. Every pod, vessel, and cruiser that it touched disintegrated. I barely noted the burst of whooping and cheering peppered throughout the room. My arms vibrated just as steadily as the ship, my shield glowing with friction. Sweat poured down my face in rivers. Still, I forced slow exhales, deep inhales.

Captain Marc had collapsed against the window, breathing heavily, aura dim. After a moment, he staggered back up the dais beside me. "Almost there, Imogen. My kroma is wiped, you'll have to hold. Just a few more seconds . . ."

I didn't have spare energy to nod. I pushed every last bit of myself into my shield. I felt my core contracting with effort. My breaths shuddered; I could no longer control them. I dug deep inside myself and pulled up all my reserves, holding nothing back. The heat, the pressure, the shuddering intensified to an unbearable level. I was certain I was going to collapse. I gritted my teeth, a groan pushing its way up my throat . . . then we were through. I welcomed the release of resistance like a cool breeze on the most humid summer day.

"You're done, Imogen, we're through," Captain Marc said. I dropped my arms, my shield vanishing instantly, and looked at him. He was smiling broadly. "Well done!"

My knees buckled and collapsed, kneecaps meeting the floor with a thud. Captain Marc smacked a hand to my shoulder in time to keep me from face planting. Every inch of my body was slick with sweat. My hair plastered to my head, the ends curling under my jaw and sticking to the side of my face. The captain called Wells over.

"Take our little prodigy to sit down and catch her breath. Then get her something to eat and a shower. Landing should be a breeze from here." He squeezed my shoulder as I felt Wells's broad hands slide under my arms and lift me onto my feet. The captain smiled at me before collapsing into his own chair and rotating it to the front. "And Llewellyn . . ." he said without looking back at us. "Don't let her out of your sight."

Wells steered me to the nearest chair and plunked me down. Al watched from where he was taking a turn powering the ship and looking hacked off about it. Wells wiped his palms down the sides of his pants to rid them of my sweat. "Is that my shirt?"

"My shirt now," I responded weakly. "This color is excellent on me."

He rolled his eyes. I tried to read his aura, but had trouble focusing. Wells reached a hand toward the center of the room near the sunken power station and a clean towel flew into it. He picked up my arm and dried it off, then placed two fingers at my wrist, monitoring my pulse. "Did you eat?"

"Oh, no. I forgot," I said. Another eye roll, this time accompanied by an exasperated grimace. "Your face is going to get stuck that way," I panted. My breath wouldn't come back.

Wells was not amused. "Speaking of faces, dry yours off." He tossed me the towel. It hit me in the nose before falling into my lap.

"Mean," I puffed, swiping the towel across my face with my free hand. Wells was still checking my pulse. Probably waiting for my heart to stop racing. A petite, strawberry-blond sidhe with a pixie cut trotted up to him. She cut a sideways glance in my direction and muttered to Wells before placing something in his hand. She gave me a nervous smile and ran back to her place.

"Here." Wells turned over the wrist he was gripping and smacked the block she had given him into my palm. "Eat this."

I shoved the entire thing into my mouth. It was heavenly. I let my head fall back against the headrest as I chewed, moaning around the explosion of wondrous flavor erupting over my tongue. The rest of my body went completely limp in the chair.

"Would it be too much to ask for a little decorum?"

I swallowed. "I can't help it. That was amazing. What flavor was that one?"

"They're all the same flavor, Imogen, you're just incredibly depleted." His words were clipped. "How do you feel?"

"Pale. I feel pale. Can I just take a nap here?"

"No." Wells wrapped a hand around my dry arm and hauled me out of the chair, catching the towel before it tumbled from my lap and roughly swiping off my other arm and neck before tossing it to the ground and tugging me toward the exit by my wrist.

As we passed Al, he took one palm off the pedestal he was manning and reached for me. "Wait, Imogen—"

I lurched away from his hand, colliding with Wells.

"AL-OH-WISH-US!" bellowed Captain Marc, stretching Al's name into four long syllables. Al smacked his hand back onto his pedestal, glowering up at the captain like a cat who had been trying to steal from the table and been caught. Captain Marc was still sagging in his chair, but his eyes glinted dangerously. "Once again, I will ask you to resist the urge to interact with Imogen until you are off this ship and no longer my responsibility. It's only a few more hours and it will stave off days of intestinal distress for me." He slowly turned his chair back to the front of the room muttering, "Gods' *bones.*"

Wells pulled me along quickly until we were out of the room and had made our first turn down another corridor. Only then did he slow down to an easier pace. I was feeling better after the block, but that wasn't saying much. Wells frequently had to catch me when my knees buckled and lean me against a wall for a few seconds to rest. It was during one of these breaks that he finally deigned to speak to me. "You couldn't have just stayed in the room." It wasn't a question. It was an accusation.

I, however, was buzzing. Recently used kroma lit up my exhausted synapses and made me a little punchy. "It's okay," I said, pushing a grin up at him. "I hear the subtext beneath your crabby words. 'That was cool as hell, Imogen. You totally did some awesome space magic and were much more helpful there than sitting in the room wondering what the hell was going on.'"

"If you keep up that cocky attitude, I'm going to hand you back to Al," Wells bit out. The smile slid off my face. He opened his mouth to say something else, then snapped it shut, shaking his head. He grabbed my upper arm and yanked me off the wall.

I was getting tired of being hauled around by my arm like a naughty toddler. I twisted against him, but he only gripped tighter. I bit back a yelp as his fingers ground muscle against bone. "What's *up* with you?"

"You tell me. Read my aura or whatever the fuck you do." Wow, he was *pissed.*

"I can't right now. The colors are going too fast and my brain is too tired."

He glanced down at me, scanning my face. His eyes softened minutely. He slowed his pace almost imperceptibly and loosened his crushing grip on my arm but didn't speak.

I could tell we were close to the room when the scent of the sandwiches hit me, my mouth immediately watering. Wells opened the door and shoved me inside, keeping hold of me until he had shut the door behind him. Like I was going to make a break for it or something. As soon as I was free, I dropped to the floor in front of the food sack and tore it open. I fell onto the first sandwich like a feral dog on a ham hock, barely peeling the wrapping off in time. I hadn't even finished chewing before I pulled out the next one, my fingers trembling as I unwrapped it, my movements frenetic. As if the sandwich were going to disappear if I didn't get to it in time. Wells set a cup of water on the floor by my knee.

"Drink that," was all he said.

Some part of me wanted Wells to like me again, so I slammed the cup of water back before starting on the second sandwich. He silently refilled it and set it back in the same spot. I crammed the last bit of the sandwich into my mouth, barely leaving myself room to chew and picked up the cup. As soon as my maw was clear, I gulped the water down, then handed the cup back to Wells. He didn't look at me as he took it and crossed to the bathroom. I got out the last sandwich, flopping sideways to the floor as I unwrapped it.

The next thing I knew, Wells was gently shaking my shoulder. "Imogen. You have to get into the shower." He pulled the sandwich I had fallen asleep unwrapping out of my hand. "You can have this when you're out."

I had no idea how long he had let me lie there, but I felt bleary-eyed. Like I'd been out for hours. My wet hair belied this. I pushed my upper body off the floor, my lungs dragging in deeper breaths with the effort. "Shower means standing. Are there no baths in this world?"

"Not on the ship. You can have all the baths you want when we're planet side."

I stared at the floor, propped up on my hands. "All the baths I want. What a time to be alive."

"Okay." Wells marched into the bathroom and started the water, then came back and hauled me to my feet. "Let's go."

I caught a glimpse of myself in the mirror over the sink. I looked like *Pulp Fiction* Uma Thurman post drug overdose. Wells pushed me into the middle of the bathroom, facing away from him. He took one of my hands and hooked it around the towel rack, then yanked my pants down to my knees, leaving my underwear in place. He removed my balancing hand, spun me around, pushed me to sit on the toilet lid, then peeled the pants the rest of the way off.

"Arms up."

I obeyed. He stripped the shirt off me and let it drop to the floor with a wet smack, then pulled me back up and faced me toward the shower. "You do the rest. I'm coming back to check on you in three minutes if you don't answer when I knock." He left, unhooking my bra with a snap of his fingers on the way out, and shutting the door behind him.

I finished my shower with minimal drama. Wells let me borrow his last clean t-shirt, eliciting a promise that I would wear a dress for disembarkation. I was so tired—and a bit cowed by how fed up he was with me—that I agreed immediately. He was no longer snappish and his tone had quieted, but he still hadn't looked me in the eye. I was sitting up in bed, covers over my legs, munching on the remaining sandwich. This one I was able to eat at a normal speed like a civilized being. Wells was perched on the edge of the chair, elbows on his knees, fingers interlaced, staring into the middle distance. I chewed and swallowed my last bite, trying desperately to keep my eyes from falling shut. I wanted to figure out what was going on with Wells and I still couldn't focus enough to read his aura. I marveled at the fact that I already relied on this new talent so heavily.

Glancing at Wells, I fortified myself with a sip of water, then cleared my throat. "In my defense, you didn't tell me not to leave the room."

Wells lifted his hands and slowly sank his face into them.

"Well, you didn't!" I couldn't understand what I had done to elicit this level of shade. "And you made it sound like this wasn't a big deal. 'Just people throwing kroma at each other' or some shit."

"Oh, Imogen," he groaned, propping his chin on his fists and shutting his eyes.

"What? Oh, Imogen *what*?" I lobbed the sandwich wrapper at the waste basket. Surprised when I made it. "Two points." I refocused on Wells, who was at least looking at me now. "I'm putting tremendous effort into not passing out before I figure out what I did to piss you off so much, Wells, but I don't know how long I'm going to have a choice in the matter." I set my cup on the nightstand.

He sighed deeply. Then stood up, pushed the chair around next to the bed to face me, and sat back down. "For starters, you should not have come onto the bridge during an active battle."

"Okay, well that wasn't my original intention, I just wanted to find a window to see what was happening."

"*Why*, Imogen, why did you have to see what was happening? Why couldn't you have just stayed here? I told you everything was going to be fine."

"Because it was scary!" I said, startled when the threat of tears burned behind my eyes. "You didn't tell me that the entire ship was going to shake like an earthquake whenever we got blasted. You didn't tell me we were going to vibrate like a goddamn jackhammer when we entered the atmosphere."

Wells looked like he'd been smacked. He stared at me without speaking for a moment. I shoved a non-existent tear out of the corner of my eye with the heel of my hand, but otherwise stared right back. His eyes dropped to the duvet.

"I apologize, Imogen. I'd forgotten how that can feel when you've never experienced it before." His finger traced the decorative pattern embossed on the covers. "As usual, you fall victim to the fact that you weren't taken conventionally. Most newly turned sidhe have their partners with them during re-entry." His sunset eyes flicked up to mine briefly, then back down to the bed. "And that wasn't a normal attack."

I flung up my hands and let them splat back onto the downy covers. "So why are you so pissed at me?"

"I'm—" His brows contracted and he blinked as he scanned the room for a few seconds. His aura swirled but the colors were too muted for me to read them. They seemed to fade in tandem with my exhaustion. Wells grabbed my hand, sandwiched it between both of his, and met my eyes. "I'm not . . . really angry with *you*, Imogen. Yes, I am frustrated with . . . how you behaved today and the . . . I'm concerned about the fallout that's likely to occur because of what you've done but—"

"Let's just pause right there, shall we?" I said, pressing his bottom hand into the duvet. "How I *behaved*? Okay, I shouldn't have gone onto the bridge, but once I figured out what was going on . . . I'm sorry, I kicked fucking ass! And the fallout—?"

"Will be the result of you 'kicking fucking ass' as you like to put it." He sighed. "Imogen, how do you feel right now? An hour after holding that shield for five minutes?"

"As soon as we stop talking, I will fall asleep hard and never look back."

"Exactly. You seem to . . . I don't know, have a talent for imitation, at least when it comes to combat. You see something done once and then you can do it. You're *still* so new. You have no idea how to control your energy flow. You don't know how much to keep in reserve. You don't know how to block if someone tries to pull energy *from* you. What you did today was so dangerous and yet you have no idea—"

"But Captain Marc—"

"Captain Marc's first priority is the success of the mission and the safety of the general populace on board." He squeezed my hand. "I told you that it wasn't a normal attack. They hit us much harder than they've ever done before. Marc saw what you were doing and took a gamble to get us into the atmosphere and friendly airspace quickly and safely. He risked both of you in doing so. Only *you* weren't aware of it.

"I'm . . . *upset* because from the moment I assumed responsibility for you, *my* first priority has been keeping you safe. Getting you to where you can stand on your own in our world in a fulfilling and healthy way." He shook his head, his top hand briefly rubbing mine. "And you just blew past me, Imogen. I'm concerned I've bitten off more than I can chew with you. I want you to have autonomy, but I don't know how to keep you safe until you're able to achieve it. And there's so much that you don't understand.

I'm constantly forgetting to explain important bits to you. I just—" He shook his head.

"You mentioned potential fallout from my bad-assery?" I wanted to take more time, as he was obviously struggling with this, but I was fading so fast.

"Everyone in that room saw what you did today," he said, his eyes on our hands. "Not one other person on this ship could have held that shield for Marc. Even Al and I together couldn't have done it. Learning how to control kroma at that level—much less generate that *amount* of kroma—takes centuries of training. You somehow perceived what he was doing and you . . . did it." His voice dropped to a whisper. "And it could have killed you, Imogen."

We were getting somewhere. I allowed myself to fall back against the pillows. "What does that mean that everyone saw?"

He sighed. "You're unattached. It's not a secret what Al has done. By the time we land, everyone will know your name. *If* word begins to spread about your lack of a partner, everyone is going to want you. Combined with the knowledge of your abilities, it could get ugly. Every small state in Molnair—probably even a few individuals among the nobility—they're going to want you for themselves. To tie you into their courts or to weaponize. Control of someone with your level of power would tempt several very influential houses."

Oh.

"I don't suppose we could take out an advertising campaign to let everyone know that I have little interest in those things?" My blinks were taking longer. My eyes felt so scratchy.

Wells smiled at me, although it didn't reach his eyes. "You will be relatively safe in Molnair, Imogen. But—and I know it grates against your independent nature—I need you to run things by me. Listen to me. If I tell you to do something, I promise it has to do with your safety. And always ask as many questions as you like. That part at least, I know you're happy to do."

There was a sudden loud, insistent hammering at the door. Wells got up to answer it. Between long blinks I saw that someone had handed him a slip of paper. His face smoothed to blankness as he said, "I understand. I'll make sure we're ready."

CHAPTER TEN

If you find someone you can truly trust, don't let go.
—Henry Delaney

I'm not sure how long he let me sleep. When I woke it felt like I had only just shut my eyes. In that time, Wells had packed up the entire room with the exception of one dress for me. And some ridiculous shoes.

"I thought we didn't wear shoes here. I liked that! I was here for it!"

"We don't wear shoes on the ship. They can scuff," Wells said patiently, placing the blue silk flats in front of my feet. "We do wear them when we go into the city. There are any manner of things you could step on."

"Like what kind of things? Glass? Rocks? Bugs? Do you have millipedes? I hate millipedes. Actually, anything with more than six legs really bothers me. Are there spiders here? I don't like spiders. Are they poisonous? Do you have snakes? Dogs? Are there dogs here? Are there trees?"

Wells put a hand on my shoulder, looking a bit shell-shocked.

"Okay, slow down." His eyebrows dropped, creasing the space between them. "Did Al tell you anything?"

I broke eye contact and wiggled my feet into the useless coverings. "I'm going to assume that any question that starts with 'did Al tell you' is rhetorical." Once I had them encased, I looked up at him again. "Sorry for vomiting questions at you. I've never been to a different planet before."

He squeezed my shoulder before dropping his hand and putting it in his pocket. "Our ancestors did originally come from Earth, so it won't be a complete shock. There are trees. The air is cleaner since we don't rely on fossil fuels. It's springtime, so it shouldn't be too hot. We'll be walking through a city, so yes, there might be glass or rocks. I don't think we have millipedes."

"Spiders?"

"We do have spiders."

"I will not suffer a spider to live."

He snorted. "Any other questions?"

"Why did you change? You're all fancy now." I gave him a once over. His t-shirt and utilitarian pants had been replaced by a dark green tunic with black details and dark pants. "Do people dress like this all the time here? Am I going to have to wear dresses all. The. Time?"

He grinned and I caught at least one dimple. "It's a mix. You'll see some fabrics and styles that are similar to what you're used to. And no, you don't have to wear dresses all the time." He turned to pull the door open. "I changed because we'll be going to the palace straight from the parade—"

"Hold. Up." I smacked my hand against the door, slamming it shut. "There's a fucking *parade*?"

"This does only happen every one hundred years, Imogen, and we are gone for eight months and generally get attacked every time we return. It's a bit of an event when we safely land. Why did you think we had to leave in order?"

"Because that's how you leave planes! And trains and ships." I dropped my head and sighed. "I hate everything."

"It's only a bit of walking, Imogen, I promise it won't hurt." He pulled his other hand out of his pocket, ostensibly to remove mine from the door, and dislodged several small, colored packets which fluttered to the floor. He ducked down quickly to retrieve them, but not quite fast enough to hide how red his ears went.

My hand slid from the door, horrifying parade momentarily forgotten. "What are those things?" I was pretty sure I recognized at least one of them.

"Just something Varklev dropped off when he was giving us our positions," he muttered, avoiding my gaze as he straightened and attempted to shove the packets into his pocket.

I snagged one. "Is this . . . Splenda? Are you hoarding sugar packets?"

He gave me a flat look and extended his hand. "I'll have that back please." His face just grew more and more crimson.

I shook the packet between two fingers and tilted my head to the side. This was de*light*ful. "Wells. Why do you have sugar packets in your pockets?"

He sighed and dropped his hand. "If you must know, you little pest, I collect them."

"You collect sugar packets?" I barely kept myself from squealing. "Did you start this last time?"

"Of course not, they didn't have these last time. Their sugar was in jars just like ours," he said. "I started with tea sachets."

A squeal of delight escaped me, which he ignored.

"The packets were a new thing this trip and I thought the two went well together."

Somehow my jaw dropped open while still smiling, my fingers wrapped around the little yellow rectangle.

Wells was completely crimson. "You look demented."

"I'm sorry, this is just the most precious thing ever. You collect sugar and tea packets because of course you do." I pinched the one I held and tilted my head to study it. "Can I use this in my coff—"

"Imogen, NO! I only have two of that one!" The horror on Wells's face snapped the final thread tethering my decency. I bust out laughing. He rolled his eyes and crossed his arms, glaring at me, although I could tell he was having a hard time holding back a smile.

"I'm sorry, here." When he didn't move to take it, I tucked the Splenda into his pocket, doing a poor job of stifling my giggles. "I'm sorry for teasing you, it's just so freaking adorable." I lifted my gaze to his. "Will you show me all your century old tea sachets?"

His expression relaxed a fraction, his lips twitched, and those sunset eyes glinted. "Absolutely not."

"I said I was sorry, please let me see Sachets Through the Ages." Without thinking I reached out and curled my fingers around his forearms. Our eyes met and this time my own face flushed.

He tilted his head. "If you will promise not to drink them."

"I have no interest in drinking one-hundred-year-old tea leaves." I gave his arms a squeeze, then dropped my hands. "I have *great* interest in exploring your quirky collection."

"As long as you're respectful." He finally uncrossed, reaching for the door and offering his arm. Some of the flush had receded and a soft smile still turned his lips up at the corners. "People bring me tea and sugar packets from other countries that I don't get to go to. There might even be some you haven't seen."

"That sounds cool," I said, my smile fading as I took his arm. I debated asking if we could just wait until everyone else had left and sneak out when the parade was done, but I knew the answer. I followed him out of the room for the last time.

The corridors were busy. Initially, most people simply scooted around us, intent on their errands, but as we edged closer to the disembarkation point the crowds grew thicker. And more and more of them were turning around to gawk at me. I hung on to Wells's arm like a toddler with a security blanket and tried to ignore the stares. Which were now occasionally punctuated with whispers and not-so-subtly pointed fingers. Wells did a better job of pretending he didn't notice. While we walked, he explained to me that the parade was basically everyone on the ship walking up the main thoroughfare of the city—in some specified order—while the gathered crowds celebrated and got a good look at us.

Just pretend it's a marathon, I thought. *Only we're all walking.* I'd run the Chicago Marathon years ago and had marveled that cheering crowds lined literally every inch of the 26.2-mile course without a gap between them. I wondered if all the Earthlings were going in the same group. Maybe I'd get a chance to see Cilla.

"Once we're done with the actual parade route," Wells said as he guided me through the training room, which had been cleared of all equipment and was now set up as a kind of corral with different colored flags indicating where certain groups should wait, "we're to meet with King Allestair and Captain Marc. Al will be there too, just so you're aware, but he'll likely be getting chewed out, so you should enjoy that."

Even the entertaining thought of Al getting royally chewed out—literally!—didn't make the prospect of an audience with the king any less nerve-racking. I'd asked and there was no way out of it. No way to postpone it. No way for me to wait outside the door and let them hash it out sans me. I was going and going immediately.

Wells guided us to stand with the group clumped around a silver flag. I glanced around to see if I could spot Cilla, but had to stop searching when I continually met the eyes of strangers staring at me, pointing at me, or nudging their companions to look at me.

It didn't help that the group we were standing with kept angling themselves in odd ways so that they could watch me without being obvious about it. I dropped my eyes to the ground, let my hair fall around my face, and scooted closer to Wells.

"Oh, keep your head up, the sooner they get a good look at you the sooner they'll go back to minding their own business," Wells said in a slightly louder than necessary voice, which at least had an effect on those immediately surrounding us. Some of them flushed, but they all either straightened themselves and kept their eyes forward or struck up a conversation with their immediate neighbors to pretend they hadn't been gawking.

A Dagger of Lightning

A metallic groaning at the far end of the training room snagged my attention and I saw a sliver of daylight through a slowly widening horizontal crack in the far wall. "Oh, good." Wells patted my hands, which were both wrapped around his arm like it was my life raft. "Not too long now, we'll file out in order."

The trembling started in my knees as I watched the group closest to the blinding rectangle of daylight shuffle forward. I did not want to walk through an entire city of people staring at me and being very loud. I did not want to go to a palace and meet some king, whether he was going to ream Al out or not. By the time the first group was nothing but vanishing silhouettes against the yawning hold door, my entire body was vibrating.

Wells glanced down at me. "Are you cold?"

I shook my head, my eyes fixed on the door and the second group moving toward it.

"Hmmm." Wells followed the line of my gaze. "Why don't you ask me some questions? Anything you want to know about. Make things less . . . intimidating?"

This was a solid plan. He was right. The unknown was always scarier. But I didn't want to think about what I was walking into. I didn't want to deal with it. I didn't want to anticipate it any more than I already was. I just wanted it to be over. All of it.

"What did you do when you were on Earth?" I asked, my voice quivering slightly. "Besides collect tea and sugar." Another group shifted forward and the rest of us moved along the wall, filing relentlessly toward the exit.

"That . . . well that's not what I thought you'd ask about." He guided me forward with the rest of our group.

"I know, but it's what I want to talk about. Once you realized you weren't going to find anybody, what did you do with the rest of your time?" *Inhale deep. Exhale slow. Inhale deep. Exhale slow.*

Wells shrugged. "Saw the Grand Canyon . . . went to look at the Eiffel Tower . . . went to the movies . . ."

"Do you speak French?" I tore my eyes from the looming opening and focused on him.

Wells gave me that half smile. "I speak all languages, Imogen. And so do you."

I stilled. "Tell me more right now!"

His smile grew. "Did you think you were speaking English this entire time?"

"I . . . I . . . I . . . what the hell else would I speak? What am I speaking? Are we not? I need more. More info." We were ambling closer to the door, but I was no longer paying attention. My shaking was subsiding.

He outright laughed. A few people from our group looked our way and then quickly turned back around. "Think of something in English. A song, a rhyme, something ingrained. Don't say it out loud, just think it. Then say it."

I thought of "Twinkle Twinkle Little Star." As I thought the lyrics in my head, I could clearly tell that they were not part of the language I had been conversing in for the past day and a half. "Twinkle, twinkle, little star . . ." I sang under my breath in the new language. "Holy shit," I whispered. Then I focused and sang again, "Brille, brille, petite etoile . . . holy crap I speak French!" Wells was chuckling; my eyes shot to his. "But I could understand you when Al brought me on board . . ."

"Then we *were* speaking English. It's the etiquette whenever we bring a new human on board that anyone in their hearing will speak their primary language until they're turned. It's less overwhelming that way."

I processed this, mentally turning over "Twinkle Twinkle Little Star" in every language I could think of until the sounds of a large crowd brought me back into the present. We were closer to the door and I could hear the gathered multitudes outside. My spine stiffened. I felt my breath shortening. Thoughts of various languages tumbled from my brain.

"What movie did you see?" I asked, trying to lengthen my exhales.

"Hm? Oh . . . wow that was an experience. They've changed considerably from last time. It was some weird thing about a human who grew claws out of his hands . . . and another . . . strange person who annoyed him . . ."

"*Deadpool & Wolverine*? Did you seriously see *Deadpool & Wolverine*? Oh, that was a *fantastic* movie! So much better than I thought it was going to be," I said, running through the plot in my mind.

Wells didn't look convinced. "I had no idea what was happening. It was very . . . loud. And very violent. The two main humans fought about . . . everything. There were a lot of very bizarre characters . . . and off-color jokes."

"I suppose if you'd never seen any of the other ones, it wouldn't be as fun. If that was your first movie since the '20s . . ." I chuckled and patted his arm. "You poor thing." I opened my mouth to tell him that I would be happy to do a Marvel movie marathon with him then snapped it shut. That was Wells's first movie in this century. Which meant there were no movies here. I swallowed against the tears burning the back of my throat. *No more movies is the least of your losses,* I told myself.

Wells noticed my mood shift. "What is it?"

"I'm going to miss Netflix," I said, *and my fiancé and my family and everything comforting and familiar.* I tried to keep the crushing sadness from my voice. Breaking down in public was not an option. "Do you have any kind of . . . television? . . . streaming . . . Anything like a movie? Computers? Phones—" I glanced around the crowd and realized how different it was to be standing in a huge line of people, disembarking a vessel, and no one was calling anyone, checking messages, checking social media . . .

"Gods' bones, those things." Wells rolled his eyes. "What a nightmare. There was nothing remotely like that the last time. The prep team had to go down, obtain one for every person attempting to search for a partner, set it up, and show us how to use it. Al was one of the only ones who became remotely proficient at it. I was happy to hand mine back. No, we don't have anything like that." He shuddered. "The humans who did come had to leave all of that behind. So cumbersome anyway. Why would you need . . . Imogen?"

"I'm fine," I lied. My heart hammered as I scanned for a bathroom, a shadowy corner, anywhere I could take a minute. My throat was burning, my breath was hitching and I could not, *would not,* break down here. "It's just different. I'll get used to it . . ."

They're staring at me, they're all staring at me. I panned the area, pulling my arm from Wells's as I spun in a tight circle. "Is there a bathroom?" My voice emerged high and squeaky. My breath came in shorter and shorter bursts. My emotions needed release and there was nowhere to run. Nothing to hit. Nowhere to hide and panic quietly and safely. My eyes began to burn and my panic hit level ten. *No, Imogen, no! They're looking at you, if you break down—*

Wells gently caught my arm and pulled me into a hug. Surprised, I hugged him back, my fingers clinging to the folds of his tunic like claws. I hid my burning face against his chest. He wrapped one arm around my shoulders and placed one hand on the back of my head.

"Breathe with me," he whispered.

I closed my eyes, felt his chest expand beneath my cheek, and did my best to match my breath to his. Tears pricked the corners of my eyes. I squeezed them shut as hard as I could, turned my face further into Wells's shirt, but I couldn't continue to breathe and hold them back. The floodgates opened and there was nothing I could do. My stomach turned over; I wanted to flee but knew there was nowhere to go, and my entire body was shaking. But Wells just murmured softly in English, encouraging me to breathe as he gently stroked my hair.

I sensed people shuffling around us and knew our group was continuing toward the entrance. Wells didn't move. Didn't rush me or remind me of where we were. He waited until the hitching in my breathing stopped and my grip on his shirt relaxed, then gave my shoulders a squeeze and gently held me back to look at me.

"You're not too bad," he said, angling my face up and swiping the remnants of tears off each cheek with his thumbs. "No one will notice." He smiled and tension I didn't even realize I was holding dropped from my shoulders. "You think you can stand to head out now? We can wait a few minutes if you need to."

I blew out a breath, shaken, but nodded. I had never been one to prolong inevitable agony. "Let's get it over with." I took his arm again and we strode forward to catch up to our group just as they were poised to walk down the massive gangway. My legs continued trembling. I idly wondered how many calories traumatic shivering burned.

The crowd outside was deafening. Captain Marc stood just to the side of the exit, barking directions; we were two steps from the gangplank and then...

Al stepped up to my other side. "Hey, Im. Hey, Wells," he said, smiling as if he'd just run into us in the park or something. He seemed oblivious to the glances he drew from one or two of the people surrounding us.

Captain Marc leveled a death glare at Al that would have sent me running if it had been directed at me, but Al just smiled pleasantly back.

"I'm practically off the ship." He gestured to the gangway. "The sooner I go, the sooner you'll be rid of me."

I had never seen a full body eye roll before, but Captain Marc did an excellent job. "Very. Well. Get out of my sight. The three of you. I'll see you at the foot of the mountain."

The one good thing that could be said about Al's sudden appearance was that I was no longer focused on the crowd lining the street as we stepped out into the bright sunlight. I was once again clinging to Wells's arm with both of my own, afraid that if I left a limb unattended Al would be tempted to snatch it. I checked Wells's face occasionally, but he had it set into a pleasantly neutral mask that told me nothing. I tried to read his aura, but there were too many jacked-up, excited auras flashing around me. I would have had to focus intently to read one, and most were transparent as I still wasn't one hundred percent after my superpower morning.

The noise was deafening. And my new ears were so sensitive. My new nose was assaulted with too many scents. Everything was brighter, crisper, *more*... it was like the saturation level had been bumped.

Wells tilted his mouth toward my ear. "Breathe." I felt his ribs expand next to my arm. I matched him.

After a few breaths, I steadied, adjusted enough to take in my surroundings rather than feeling bombarded by them.

It reminded me of Mardi Gras, only cleaner and without the floats, throws, and copious inebriation.

Crowds crushed up along the curb, stopped at a shimmering barrier lining the length of the route. I assumed it was a shield to prevent people from running into the multi-colored street.

The road was paved in cobblestones of all colors and wide enough for a vehicle, though Wells said there were no fossil fuels. When I asked him about it, he said that horses—I was ecstatic to learn their ancestors had brought horses to Perimov—and another animal called a trenunch, were used to haul things too large to 'port, summon, or wink. And to ride. "Because it's fun." There were buildings, but more reminiscent of a European city than the skyscrapers of the United States. Nothing seemed taller than six stories. Apartments and townhomes along the route had people clumped on balconies to watch us go by. The air felt like silk on my skin. What I took at first to be clumps of weird, fluttering decorations splashed between the buildings turned out to be trees with brightly colored leaves. Blues, pinks, lavenders. Almost like enormous hydrangeas.

Al was in his element—I could now completely believe him to be the crown prince—waving at people, that one-thousand-watt smile fully unleashed, occasionally jogging over to the side to shake someone's hand or sign something. Always trotting back over to us afterward, grinning at me like I was in on the fun.

After a few blocks I started to relax. This wasn't intolerable. The sun was shining, the weather was warm but not hot. I could simply focus on the finish line, just like a race. I didn't have to interact with anyone, Al was in his own world, this was fine. *Just get through this. One thing at a time.*

Then Al started pushing the envelope. He'd wave to someone in the crowd and at the same time touch my shoulder. Come back to us after a sojourn and brush the back of his hand down my arm. I didn't realize Wells was clocking these little touches until he folded his other hand over mine and gave Al a quick, hard glance. Nothing that anyone in the crowd would notice, but a warning to his brother to stay in line.

Al wasn't good at staying in line.

We passed a large stage near the end of the route, a small raked seating area atop it, like bleachers at a sports event, with fifteen or so sidhe perched within. All dressed to the nines and exuding wealth and influence. The rest of the crowd had faded away, but I couldn't shove these people into the background. I felt as if they were all shifting their gazes toward me as we approached. I pressed closer to Wells, turned away from their faces, and focused on the lavender sky—*isn't that totally wild and pretty? Look at that*—but I was unable to stop my fingertips from digging into his forearm.

The instant we crossed directly in front of this stage Al appeared, grabbed my face, and planted a kiss on my mouth. I reflexively tightened my grip on Wells, but Al released me and trotted off to greet someone before either of us could react. Wells's eyes blazed crimson, his jaw clenched, and his brows dropped. But he wiped the expression quickly. I felt his ribs expand in a slow breath as he once again placed his hand atop mine, this time leaving it.

Then I *heard* him telepathically speak to Al.

You will not use her as your statement piece. Do you have any idea how terrified she is right now?

Al glanced back at us, smirked, then turned back to whoever he was talking to. *She looks fine to me. She's tougher than you think.*

If you touch her one more time, I don't care what it looks like, we will *have a problem and I am not above having it out in the middle of your crowd of admirers.*

Al was facing away from us, but his shoulders tensed. He stopped mid route to whatever group of people he was heading to dazzle, as if he were contemplating storming back to us. Then he shrugged and loped off ahead. *Fine. See you at home. Just remember she's not yours.*

Wells stiffened. *She's certainly not yours either,* he retorted. His aura shifted as he cut off contact.

I was still reeling from the violation in conjunction with the new ability to hear telepathic communication—*Does this mean that* I'm *telepathic?*—

when Wells spoke to me, leaning down so that I could hear him above the crowd.

"He'll leave you alone for the rest of the parade. If he doesn't, I'll kick his ass, which he won't want to risk being viewed publicly. He's showing off and trying to send a message."

"What kind of message?" I asked, tilting my face toward his ear and raising my voice. I considered telling him that I'd understood his chat with Al in case it would be easier to talk that way, but he was already answering me.

"Only thirteen humans were turned on this trip; everyone will already know your names and descriptions, and they'll know who brought each of you on board. That information is logged as soon as you've been retrieved and it's with the first message that goes out once we're in range. What I'm not sure of—and we're certain to find out in a few minutes—is how many of the details regarding . . . this charming situation have leaked out. For you to be walking with me and not Al would definitely sway beliefs in one direction, but if he stays close, touches you occasionally, it sends a different message. You're still his, I'm merely being helpful. Watching after you while he runs around being princely." He sighed deeply and muttered something that I didn't catch. I tugged on his arm and asked him to repeat himself. "I'm just dreading the sensational level of gossip when people find out that you're Solange Aidair Delaney's granddaughter."

I was so done with this parade. It was all I could do not to lay my head against Wells's arm and snooze while we walked. He pointed out an archway in the distance. Once we passed underneath, everyone would meet their families and go their separate ways. Parade over. Yay. It still looked like it was half a mile away.

"If you did get in a fight with Al in the middle of the street, *could* you kick his ass?"

"Oh, absolutely. I've been kicking his ass since I turned seventy-five." Not a hint of swagger, just stating a fact.

"How old was Al when you were seventy-five?" I asked, trying to distract myself from the exhaustion leaching into my bones.

Wells tilted his head, his gaze shifting into the middle distance. "Huh. Two hundred and fifty-two. About the same age I am now."

"So is Al just not that good or are you especially awesome?"

He laughed—and wow did it light up his face—and shifted his sunset gaze toward me, eyes glittering. "Al is no slouch when it comes to fighting." His grin expanded. "But it's not for nothing that I'm the youngest General of the King's Armies to have ever held the position."

I blinked. "Hang on . . ."

He was still smiling. "Yes?"

"Are you saying . . . that a forty-five-year-old, brand-new whippersnapper got first blood in her very first fight with the two-hundred-and-fifty-one-year-old, very experienced, person in charge of all the fighting in the country?"

A surprised guffaw burst from Wells. "Yes. Congratulations, you are once again a national champion of punching and kicking."

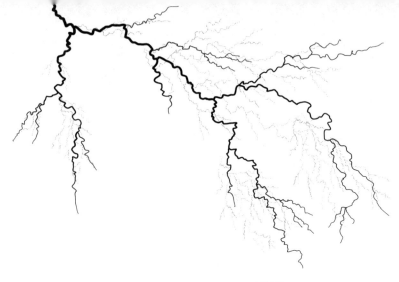

CHAPTER ELEVEN

The most beautiful things are often the most deadly. Never assume anything about anyone by looking.
—Solange Aidair Delaney

The palace was perched on top of an enormous mountain. There were actual clouds floating just below it, so if you looked at it the right way, it appeared to be resting on top of them.

A long, winding, red-dirt footpath snaked its way through the vibrant blue-greens of the lawn and nudged explosions of purple and blue flowers as it crawled all the way to the top. It was the steepest climb I had ever seen.

There were no discernable steps cut into the path.

Al was waiting for us, leaning against one of the two Grecian style pillars—that of course had attractive morning glory-esque vines wrapped around them—flanking the head of the trail, the sun gilding his blond hair. "What do you think, Im? Beautiful, right?"

I was staring up at the palace, slack-jawed, watching what I was pretty sure was an eagle soaring several feet below it.

"I have a recurring nightmare where I am stuck to the side of a breathtakingly beautiful mountain and if I move one muscle I'm going to fall to my death." My gaze volleyed between Al and Wells. "Please don't tell me we have to climb that today."

Al grinned at me. Wells gazed up at the palace as if he were having his own telepathic conversation with it. I hoped he was summoning some kind of ride, but I doubted it.

"*Please* tell me there's a floating gondola . . . a horse with wings . . . a goddamn *dragon*. I am not climbing that today."

"Oh, c'mon, Im, it'll be fine. You like hiking," Al said, still grinning wickedly.

"I am not dressed for hiking a damp garden path, much less *that*," I snapped. These stupid clothes were his fault.

"It's easier than you'd think." Al smirked. "We'll take breaks if you need to."

"Leave her alone." Captain Marc had come up behind us.

"Oh, good," Al said. "None of us have to climb." He looked at me. "Right now, I'm not allowed to wink up, neither is Wells. Captain Marc will have to take us or we'll just get bounced right back out here."

"You two will certainly be climbing." The captain's eyes glittered. "Your father set the wards for a reason, after all. I'll be winking up with Imogen and Imogen alone. We'll see you when you arrive."

They both looked so scandalized I would have laughed if I wasn't dreading being inside the palace at all. Captain Marc offered his arm to me. I hesitated for a fraction of a second—it felt wrong to leave my Wells-shaped security blanket—then released Wells's arm and walked over to take the captain's.

"I suppose I shouldn't be surprised," Wells said, hands in his pockets, a new tension lining his frame. "Even though *I* haven't broken massive amounts of protocol."

"The king thinks it would be nice for the two of you to have a little time together to chat," Captain Marc said, dark eyes landing on Al, sparkling like he was having a difficult time reigning in his glee. "You haven't had that opportunity since Imogen arrived. We've all been *terribly* busy." He grinned widely. "And exercise is so stimulating. See you in a bit."

I lifted a hand to wave goodbye to Wells—I did feel a little bad for him, being punished by proximity—but before I could so much as waggle my fingers, we were engulfed in the same black, windy void that I'd experienced when Al and I were pulled onto the ship. Only this void lasted for about the space of two blinks.

Then we were inside the enormous palace entryway. My hand still floated limply in the air, my jaw had once again dropped unattractively away from the rest of my face, and a tiny squeak bounced from my throat.

Everything was gleaming ivory and gold. Before us were several evenly spaced pillars that ringed the largest decorative indoor space I'd ever seen. The ceilings vaulted impossibly high. Like a Catholic church on steroids. High, curving skylights let in bright shafts of sunlight that played with the flecks of glittering mica sprinkled within the tile and mortar. *Is it mica? I'm calling it mica.*

I tried to get my brain to restart. This was the *entryway*.

I dropped my hand and closed my mouth. The quiet pressed in on me. I could hear the distant, echoing footfalls of an unseen person on some errand or other.

"Obnoxious, isn't it?" sighed Captain Marc, his melodious voice bouncing around the pillars near us before being swallowed by the cavernous space beyond them. "Who needs ceilings that high? I'd hate to be the one assigned to cleaning the skylights." He began strolling around the outside edge of the pillars, gently pulling me along in his wake. "By the time we arrive, King Allestair will be ready to see you. We'll walk slowly to give Aloysius and Llewellyn a chance to catch up."

His irreverence relaxed me. Still, I fought the urge to whisper when I asked, "Did Al and Wells grow up here?"

"They did. In fact Aloysius still lives here, as he's the king's son and in line for the throne." He glanced down and must have seen my face doing subtle acrobatics. "Questions, Imogen?"

"I'm not sure how to ask politely," I admitted.

He threw back his head and laughed, the sound ricocheting off the pillars and the wall next to us, which was lined with windows that must have stretched two stories high. "Please don't stand on ceremony, Imogen. I'll let you know if you've inadvertently given offense so that you can correct yourself going forward."

"Okay, thanks," I said, still trying to figure out how to word these questions and wondering if they were really any of my business anyway. But the diversion was nice. "So, if Al is the king's son and lives here and he and Wells are only half brothers—"

"They are both sons of the queen. Only Aloysuis is the result of a union between both royals."

"And that's not a ... problem?"

He chuckled. "Not in the least. The current king and queen have reigned a long, long time. Children are considered a blessing and a triumph, so after a lengthy dry spell, it's common for monarchy to attempt progeny outside of their partnership if they're not mated. I'm sure you've learned by now that reproduction is a bit more of a challenge for our species than it is for your former affiliation." I thought that was an interesting way to say that I had switched species. He continued, "Anyone joining with the royals does so with the understanding that any resulting children will be forever tied to the royal house and raised there."

I tried to peek out one of the windows as we passed. From where we were I could only see endless pale, purply-blue sky and fluffy white clouds. Earthlike enough to be calming. "Does that mean Wells doesn't know who his father is?"

"Oh, there are always rumors. And he may have some guesses. But not definitively. And none of the king's outside partnerships have resulted in any offspring. The queen is very proud of herself and for once, can enjoy the spotlight." He smiled down at me. "Something Aloysius also delights in."

"So does that mean Wells is a... prince too?" I was drifting over toward the windows when he answered.

"No, it's Aloysius's line that is the ruling one. Llewellyn is a valuable asset to the royal house, but he isn't considered royalty."

"Hm." That felt kind of like a raw deal, but I held those words back. Maybe there were perks I didn't know about. Noticing my preoccupation with the windows, the captain walked us over to one and gestured for me to look out.

The bottom of the golden window frame was level with my chin. I placed my fingertips upon it, stood on my tiptoes, and peered out. At first, all I saw were cotton candy clouds, but they blew by quickly, as if the winds were strong. All at once they parted and I got a glimpse of the city sprawled out below. It reminded me of flying into London or Paris with curving streets rather than the straight lines of a grid city like Chicago. Farther out, houses and farms tumbled along the rolling hills all the way to the blanket of shimmering azure sea. I wondered how many miles I could see. My eyesight had sharpened considerably. I saw little breaks in the waves and wondered if there were sand bars. Maybe even a barrier island to explore. Colored sails dotted the water. Red, yellow, green... I liked that they weren't all white. More clouds rolled in, obscuring my view just as I heard Captain Marc chuckling.

I stepped back from the window and glanced over to see him leaning against the wall watching me, a faraway fondness in his eyes. "You look just like my mate did the first time she stood by these windows." He offered his arm again.

I took it and we continued our stroll up the hallway that was wider than any house I'd ever lived in. "You have a mate?"

"Indeed, a former Earthling." His aura glowed with red-gold pride.

I sighed in relief to find that particular skill returning to me. "Oh, from which part?"

"Mesopotamia."

"Mesopo—whoa..."

He laughed again, his aura splashed with yellows and pinks of amusement and satisfaction. I'd given him the reaction he'd hoped for. He had to be thousands of years old. At least two thousand. I couldn't stop staring at him. He had a few laugh lines, but that was it. *He is as old as civilized society...*

"Does she ever go back to visit?" I asked.

"No." We turned a corner, leaving the windows behind. "Her civilization was collapsing when she left. She knows it's changed and wants to remember it the way it was."

"Do you have children?" I thought I could hear voices ahead and my stomach clenched. During our nice stroll I'd almost forgotten what I was here for.

"Seven!" he said, grinning. "We're very lucky." His smile faded. "We're nearly there, I believe I hear the dulcet tones of the king greeting his son now. They must have sprinted the entire way. Are you ready?"

I swallowed and nodded. "How bad can it be, right?"

Captain Marc sobered. "Be prepared, Imogen. I know you never wanted children, but you might be beginning to grasp why that's difficult for most of our people to understand. And another reason Aloysius shouldn't have taken you. You're going to be asked about it. Especially with your... unique genetics and the talents you've already displayed."

I sighed. I'd thought I was done fielding the "when are you gonna have kids" questions after I turned forty. "Does the king know I don't want children?"

"Oh yes, I required both Aloysius and Llewellyn to provide me with as many details about you as possible. Their reports and my own have all been sent to Allestair." He squeezed my arm, his aura swirling with pale blue sympathy. "No one is going to force you to do anything, Imogen, but the hope will be that you'll be woo'd by Aloysius and eventually change your mind. I thought you should be aware."

I nodded while internally screaming, *Fat chance, suckers.*

The raised voice spiked louder and clearer. We halted before two three-story-high doors, with ridiculously normal sized door handles sticking out of their swirling, ornate fronts. Captain Marc placed his hand on one. "Any last questions before we go in?"

"Do people *have* to call you Captain Marc? Does anyone ever just call you Marc?"

His lips split into a wide grin, revealing gleaming teeth. "Protocol doesn't dictate they use my title unless they're a subordinate and we're on active duty." He turned the handle. "However, I do tend to encourage it. Mainly because I enjoy the sound of it." He pushed the door wide.

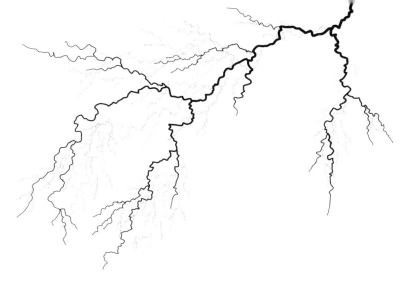

CHAPTER TWELVE

Justice isn't swift or merciful. She takes her goddamn time, she's fickle, and she's inconsistent. Don't rely on that bitch for anything.
—Solange Aidair Delaney

All conversation ceased when Captain Marc led me into another gigantic room. This one boasted several groupings of fancy, padded, gold and ivory chairs set around matching low tables. Thick rugs were tossed attractively on the floors. No one was using the chairs. Al and Wells were slightly rumpled and glisteny and panting a bit, like they'd been running. They were facing a sidhe who had to be Al's father; they looked almost exactly alike. Except the king's eyes were ice blue, he had a thin scar cutting through his left eyebrow, and his intimidating bearing held none of Aloysius's casual swagger. His clothes were obviously well made and tailored to fit him, but he had no crown, wore no . . . kingly cloak or any of the things I had been picturing in my head. Their auras all shifted when we entered. Wells's face relaxed and some of the blue-black concern receded from the dancing colors around him. Al's expression hardly changed. He'd looked irritated when we came in and he looked irritated when he saw us, his aura only swirled faster for a moment and one ribbon of pink flipped through when he first laid eyes on me. The king's darkly furious expression completely melted as his jaw dropped and his eyes widened. His aura was doing a dance I hadn't seen before.

Captain Marc was unfazed, hinging forward into a short bow—pulling me with him—then taking my hand from his arm, keeping my fingers in his lifted palm and leading me forward. "Your majesty, may I present Imogen Delaney. Lately of Earth." He released my hand.

I didn't know what to do with my limbs. It had seemed like eons since I'd been allowed to just . . . stand on my own without being attached to someone. I started to fold my arms, realized that sent the wrong body language signal, then clasped my hands behind my back. They were still staring. I dropped my arms by my sides. "Hi."

"What took you two so long?" Al barked, scanning me from head to toe, as if Captain Marc might have damaged me somehow in the interim. He took one step toward me and I backed up two. His expression darkened, but he stopped moving forward.

"We went the long way," Captain Marc said breezily as he stepped to my side. He flicked an invisible speck of dust off of a sleeve. "I thought Imogen might enjoy taking in the eastern view. Turns out she did. She's never been here before, you know."

I liked Captain Marc more and more.

"By my life, she looks just like her." The king was still gaping at me, his aura swirling with colors too quickly for me to interpret.

Exhaustion dragged at me again. I loved my grandmother, but I was very tired of the constant comparison. The staring was getting old too. "Well, my eyes used to be brown, but Al decided to change those without asking permission."

Everyone's attention snapped back to Al. He didn't look the least bit contrite. I didn't feel a twinge of remorse for throwing him under the bus.

"Right." Allestair's gaze sharpened. "To the task at hand." He waved a hand and a sheaf of papers appeared before him; he caught them in mid-air and leafed through them ostentatiously. "I am to understand that the entire ship is aware of my son's," his lip curled as his icy eyes flicked up to Al before falling back to the papers, "inability to follow certain protocol?"

"Okay, we've been over this," Al said. "I broke some rules, but not only do I think Imogen is going to be happy here, I know she's going to prove a valuable asset to Molnair."

"Marcellus, I assume the documentation held undeniable proof that Aloysius—?"

"In addition to testimony from the prince and Imogen herself," Captain Marc confirmed. "He did not make contact with her within the allowed timeframe and gave her no indication of his plans."

The king's blue eyes lasered through me. A chill swept down my spine. For one wild moment, I wondered if he would destroy me on the spot for throwing a wrench in things, unwilling participant or no. Then he fixed his glare on Wells.

"And you did absolutely nothing to prevent this?" His voice could have frozen hot tea.

Wells's expression didn't change, he didn't so much as tense a muscle, but I saw his aura gutter. "I offered to search alongside Aloysius, your majesty, but he preferred to be on his own. So I was unaware—"

"You should have *insisted!*" the king exploded, inches from Wells's face. *How fucking unfair*, I thought, splinters of anger pricking my skin on Wells's behalf. The king wheeled on Al.

"Aloysius, you claim that she is powerful, you claim—"

"She *is* powerful, father, probably more powerful than—"

"Do not interrupt me." King Allestair's voice was frost. "If you were so sure of her bloodline, why didn't you take the time to explain and convince her to come?"

"Imogen claims she was happy where she was," Captain Marc broke in smoothly. "In such cases, Aloysius was to follow protocol, glamour her memories so that he faded out of them and move on. By his own admission, he did not."

Al wasn't backing down. His feet were firmly planted, chest out, eyes up. "Imogen was only happy because she was making the best of it. Because she knew nothing about who she was and what she could become. She has too much potential."

His father glared at him from beneath his eyebrows, hands frozen mid-page-flip. He glanced back down at the words in front of him. "You knew she didn't want children, Aloysius, the primary purpose of this entire mission. Marcellus, was this aspect discussed during your meeting?"

"I don't believe that particular detail came up," Captain Marc said.

"She only had a short time to live before. Of course she didn't want them, she wanted to live her own life. She'll change her mind once she understands how much time she has now," Al said, as if this was an obvious outcome. I gaped at his presumption. Behind him, Wells sank his face slowly into his palm.

"Gods' bones..." Captain Marc muttered. "It's like he skipped half the training."

"After she stays here for a while, she'll get used to it. And I know you've heard how fast she's learning." He aimed his luminous amber eyes at me. Dread pooled in my stomach. They weren't going to keep me in this palace, were they?

"I've received urgent messages from every head of state that was on that mission and several that weren't," Allestair bit out. "All of them are demanding to know what's to become of Imogen and how you're going to be disciplined. *Everyone* on that mission knows you turned her without her consent. Rumors are probably flying around the entire country by now."

"That's not my fault, father," Al said, his tunic stretched tight across his shoulders as he folded his arms. He had the audacity to toss Captain Marc a glare. "I thought the meeting was going to be private."

"Impossible," Captain Marc said coolly. "Your majesty, word was already getting around the ship. To ban heads of state or their representatives from the meeting would have aroused even more suspicion. The prince's presence on this expedition was under scrutiny from the beginning. As we discussed."

The king locked eyes with Captain Marc for a long beat and I had a feeling many previous conversations hung in the tension strung between them. I was super pleased to have Captain Marc on my team.

The king let the two halves of his report fall together with a snap as he spun on Al once more. "In light of how public this is doubtless going to become, do you honestly believe you can get away with trapping her in the palace? It would cause a national scandal." His gaze shifted to me, addressing me for the only time during a meeting about me. "Do you want to stay in the palace with Aloysius, Imogen?"

"No, thank you," I said quickly. "I'd rather not be trapped anywhere."

Al's aura drenched dark blue. "You wouldn't be trapped, Im, and you'd love it, I know—"

"Stop talking like you know how I feel!" My voice bounced off the walls and ceiling, but I didn't care. "You've never asked how I feel. You just compelled me and drugged me when I didn't do what you wanted." I felt like electricity was crackling through my veins. I wanted to get out of here. Why had we even come? Wells's eyes bounced between me and Al as if he'd like to put himself between us, but wasn't sure he was allowed.

I realized he'd been standing so still and quiet that I had nearly forgotten he was there. I wondered if he was intentionally fading into the background. I didn't blame him if he were trying to keep from getting his head bitten off again.

"What was the final arrangement you arrived at during your . . . meeting, Marcellus?" the king asked tersely, ignoring the fact that I had just hollered at Al in a very echoey room.

The captain stepped forward. "As Llewellyn also used his kroma to help turn Imogen, he volunteered to be an alternative option for the lady. She chose to go with him."

"Llewellyn?" Allestair's voice cracked through the air like a whip. Wells didn't flinch, but he stood at absolute perfect attention, somehow even more formal than he'd been on the ship. The king stared at Wells for an uncomfortable beat. Even Al was still.

Allestair's aura crackled, shifting rapidly between a pulsing bronze and billowy crimson. He nodded his head, eyes never leaving Wells. "That will do. I trust you will train any significant powers she may possess very discreetly. At least until this mess is beyond us?"

"I will, sire."

Allestair dug into a pocket, his eyes blazing.

He tugged a small pouch free and tossed it to Wells, folding up the papers he'd been reading and sliding them into his pocket. "For her initial expenses, as the prince is responsible for her . . . unprepared arrival." His cold eyes never wavered from Wells's face. "I suppose you should take some additional time off to acclimate her, same as the other pairs. Adgemon has been doing well in your absence, I recommend him for promotion based on his performance."

"Thank you, sire." Wells pocketed the pouch, still the picture of propriety, but somehow without any of the graceful ease I'd seen on the ship. "I'm not surprised regarding Adgemon, but he'll be pleased that he has your endorsement."

The king yanked another sheaf of papers from thin air and passed them to Wells. "In the absence of an official partner, you're to publicly register yourself as Imogen's—"

"No!" Al barked.

"—for the time being. *I've already asked you once not to interrupt me, Aloysius, you are on very thin ice.*" Allestair's aura exploded into red and gold flames, shot with glittering black fractures. I repressed the urge to flinch away. Although his aura only calmed slightly, his face dropped from fury to neutrality with frightening ease. "You are to stay away from Imogen for one lunar cycle." When Al looked like he might protest, the aural flames grew hotter. "Of *both* moons." Al shut his mouth. Meanwhile, I raised my eyebrows because one month seemed like not enough time away from Al. Even if the months were longer here. And there were apparently more moons.

The king continued, "Imogen needs time to adjust. The entire populace needs to know that you've . . . had your wrist slapped. And I want this incident played down as much as possible. Even if I have to personally speak to each head who attended that meeting."

He pinned the captain and Wells with a glare while my blood boiled in outrage. No one said a word.

The king turned his laser eyes on Al, his voice deadly calm. "Llewellyn is now responsible for her and this fact will be made public. You will return to him anything of hers that you may have kept and you will absent yourself from them for one dual cycle. You and I will have a private conversation about this later." He looked at Captain Marc. "Marcellus, if you would remain to discuss this latest Sephryan attack and this rumor circulating around the failure of the shields upon reentry . . ."

So he's going to cover up my help with the shields too? I wondered.

Allestair's head snapped in my direction, as if he had heard my thoughts. He fixed his ice cubes on me and I sucked in an involuntary breath. I really hoped mind-reading wasn't a kroma. I felt like I'd just been spotted by a hungry jaguar. Without breaking eye contact with me, he gestured to Wells. "If you have no questions, take her. I'll likely want to speak with you later. You can wink out."

Wells nodded, hinged into the same half bow that Captain Marc had performed, then strode toward me.

"Wait!" Al said, his aura swirling faster. "Let me just talk to her for a second. Im, just for a second, please?"

Although tension radiated from every perfectly proper line of his frame, Wells didn't look back at Al when he reached me. "It's up to you if you want to talk to him or not."

My gaze flicked to Al, his aura spinning orange with distress, those pink ribbons occasionally winging through. "I'm not going anywhere alone with you."

"That's fine." Al's shoulders dropped, the orange receding. "We can talk right over there, by the windows. Just a minute, that's all."

I hesitated, then decided there was less danger with three other people in the room. Maybe Al needed to hear from me, in no uncertain terms, that I was not going to be with him. I dipped my chin once. Al crossed the room with long strides, reaching to take my hand. I jerked it out of his trajectory and shrank back a few steps. "No touching. That's a non-negotiable condition."

His smile faded a bit, but he stuffed his hands into his pockets and nodded.

I walked with him—keeping three feet between us—over to a collection of fancy, velvet cushioned, gold and ivory chairs arranged by one of the enormous windows lining the sides of the room. They were similar to the windows in the hallway and I guessed that they must be on the same outer wall. Neither of us took a seat. Al leaned a shoulder against the wall beneath the window and I stood with my arms crossed.

Al's aura still spun faster than normal. "So . . . how are you?"

"Ha. Better late than never, I guess." My entire experience was being downplayed to save his reputation. I was not in a charitable mood.

"I haven't been allowed to see you to ask—"

"You also mostly kept me knocked out and compelled when I was with you. I don't remember you ever asking me how I was coping then either."

Al exhaled raggedly and looked down at his shoes. "You have no idea how special you are. No one does." Thick eyelashes swept up, eyes simmering with frustration. "I knew they would take you from me if they found out. I can answer all of your questions, Im. I won't compel you and I won't give you any sleeping potion. I promise. Now that we're here, it'll be different."

"Did you ever learn the phrase 'too little, too late' when you were on Earth?"

"Im . . . can't you just try it out here? If you don't like it, I promise you can go to Wells's—"

"No."

"Just eight days—"

"Wow, you *really* don't know what the word 'no' means, do you?"

Off to the side I heard the king mutter, "It's obvious she's not going to be convinced. Now I have to keep this entire thing from becoming a scandal when she's paired with his brother."

Al heard it too. His face hardened. He chewed his lower lip and stared past me for a few seconds. I turned to gaze out the window. I was about to ask him if we were done when he spoke up again from where he'd moved right next to me.

"Nice view, isn't it?"

I flinched and backed up but my leg hit a chair so I straightened and stood my ground. He hadn't tried to paw at me yet. "Yes, it's nice. Glad I got to see it once."

He deflated, started to reach for my arm and stopped himself, letting his hand drop back down to his side. "I want to touch you so bad it hurts."

"You can't always get what you want," I said, although I knew the Rolling Stones reference was lost on him.

"Imogen, I know you were drawn to me just as much as I was drawn to you. I could feel it. I know I wasn't imagining it—"

"You kind of killed any flirtatious attraction I may have once had with the whole holding me against me will and—"

"Okay, Im, how about a compromise?" He straightened, slid his hands back into his pockets. "You go with Wells, he can . . ." He huffed through his nose once. "He can teach you, look after you, whatever. As long as you want. But I get to spend time with you every day."

"No!"

"C'mon, Imogen, give me something here. I love you—"

"You loved my grandmother."

"I did," he said, and his aura slowed, more deep purples and blues spreading through it. Still occasionally punctuated with those ribbons of pink. "Im, I promise, everything I've done has been because I care about you. At first I just wanted to see you. But . . . you're like everything Solange was . . . and more. And you weren't happy with Keane. Not as happy as you could be."

I kept my mouth clamped shut. Glaring at him. I wasn't going to give him permission to see me. I didn't owe him anything.

"Imogen." He reached for me again. Caught himself again. "Some of the happiest moments of my life were when I first found you. When you said you'd go with me. And when you first opened your eyes after you'd been turned."

I swallowed, then said softly, "You've just described some of the worst moments of my life."

Direct hit. His aura shrank completely down inside of him for a beat before creeping back out a little at a time. He shook his head and blew out a breath. "You're angry and you're trying to hurt me. It won't work, Im. You know we'd work well together. And I know you were attracted to me before, I could smell it—"

"Being attracted to someone does not necessarily mean you're going to break off your engagement and move in with them!" I unfolded my arms. He had incensed me enough that I *had* to gesticulate. "It certainly doesn't give anyone a carte blanche to kidnap and drug them."

"You said you wanted to go, it wasn't kidnap—"

"Yes, of course, I was to assume we'd be taking a stroll into another galaxy, never to return, when you asked me to come with you to learn about my grandma," I spat. I was no longer capable of reading his aura, all I saw was red.

"Imogen . . ." Al deliberately shoved his hands in his pockets and stepped closer until he was inches from me and I was forced to look up at him. His amber eyes smoldered as he whispered, "I know you were running away from that engagement. And I *know* you wanted me."

"We're done here." I stalked back to Wells as fast as my legs would carry me. I heard nothing over the roaring in my ears. My face was on fire. My entire body vibrated with rage, shame, and grief. Wells had barely lifted his arm when I latched onto it, praying we didn't need a long goodbye.

We didn't.

CHAPTER THIRTEEN

*Two things we don't appreciate enough:
the quiet times in the company of those we love and the absence of pain.*
—Henry Delaney

The windy, black void was one blink longer this time and then I was standing with Wells on a sunny sidewalk. The breeze brushed my hair back. I felt as if I could take a full breath for the first time since arriving, although my heart still galloped behind my ribs.

"I thought you could use some fresh air and sun before we hide ourselves inside," he said. I wondered if it was just me or if he was slightly paler than normal. "Do you want to walk or sit?"

"Sit." I was still shaking and that feeling of exhaustion was dragging at me again.

Wells glanced around, then pulled me into a large park. The trees were like Bob Ross doing Van Gogh. The colors startlingly vibrant, like no trees on Earth, but the landscape was serene. Calming. I felt my soul exhale. *I like it here.* Wells guided me to a bench facing away from the sidewalk, obscured by two bright blue bushes. I couldn't resist reaching out and touching the leaves as we passed. I was almost surprised when the color didn't stick to my fingers.

Once we were seated, I released Wells's arm, kicked off the dumb slippers, and crossed my too-long legs on the bench, making sure to tuck the skirt of my dress around them modestly. It did feel good to have the sun on my shoulders. I scanned our surroundings and realized we were completely concealed from passers-by. "You hiding me?"

He blew out a breath as he leaned against the backrest. "Did you *want* to take the risk of random strangers coming up to us and bombarding you with questions?"

I shook my head, staring out at the colored trees and shrubs. I thought I even caught the glint of water from a stream or river between tree trunks. "So all of this is just going to be swept under the rug? Al just has to stay away from me for a month and . . . that's fucking it? Free to stalk me to his heart's content after that?"

"I know it's not fair, Imogen—"

I choked on a laugh. "Not *fair*? He destroyed my fucking life, Wells! He destroyed my father's life, he—" My jaw snapped shut, then opened, then shut. My fingers curled into fists, I slammed my eyes closed, my clenched jaw ached as I forced back the scream of rage trying to claw its way out of my throat.

Warm fingers slid around my fist, cupping it gently. One thumb traced a gentle circle over the inside of my wrist. "I'm sorry, Imogen. It's not right. And I have no capacity for the nuances of grief and anger that you're feeling right now, but I do empathize with how unjust this is."

My fingers uncurled first as his thumb continued to trace soft circles on my skin. My lashes swept up to find his russet eyes fixed on my face, more expressive in that moment than they'd been the entire time we were in the palace. "Al is not being punished for what he's done to you. And he never will be. And I'm sorry for that." He took a breath. His eyes dropped to his hands cupping my loose fist. "But I'm not entirely sure it's a bad idea for Allestair to downplay what happened on the ship."

I felt my eyebrows snap down.

Wells caught my other hand and clasped them both. "Not about what Al has done, but about your powers."

My brows lifted.

"You remember what I said on the ship, Imogen?" He scooted closer and lowered his voice. Okay, so he was definitely hiding us. I nodded numbly. "I'll find out later how much Marc tells the king about the shield, but . . . right now knowledge of what you've done is confined to those who were on the bridge. Depending on what Marc or Allestair has ordered, some of the narrative can be controlled. And you will be safer if that's the case."

"What do you mean what they've ordered? Like, they can order people to not talk?"

"Most of those on the bridge were military or heads of state, so yes, some can be ordered and some can be strongly advised to keep quiet."

I realized I was chewing my lower lip and released it with a pop. "This is a lot."

Wells nodded, squeezed my hand, then set it in my lap and dropped an arm on the backrest behind me. "We'll take it one day at a time, but for now, let's give your mind a break. Would you like to get your bearings a bit? This is the area you'll be living in."

My spine straightened. A strange fizzing burst through my chest. I ignored it. "Sure."

"I'll just point a few things out to you, then. If you forget, I can point them out again later." Wells gestured toward the trees. "If you look straight ahead and a little to the left, you can see the palace where we just were."

I tracked the direction he indicated and spotted it just above the tree line. The mountain with its robe of clouds and palace crown. "If you look just there," he indicated a break in the trees to my right, "you can see a trail. A lot of people run on it. I thought you'd like to know where it is because I'm given to understand that running's something you enjoy."

A corner of my mouth twitched up. I could tell he wasn't a runner by the slightly perplexed way he finished the statement. I did see a red dirt path, however, and that strange tightness in my chest eased knowing I'd have access to my preferred mental escape and physical release.

He continued, gesturing to the sidewalk behind us and to the left. "If you walk down the hill, you'll end up in town. We'll head there when you're feeling up to it and you can get some clothes you actually like. My house—where you'll be staying for the foreseeable future, so your house too—is at the top of the hill." He pointed to the sidewalk uphill to the right, where we had been standing. "We can wink up the hill the first time if you're still feeling averse to climbing."

"I'm not adverse to walking up a *hill*," I clarified. "I was averse to hiking up a mountain in these stupid shoes right after that excruciating parade."

He squeezed my shoulder. "If you're up for it, I suggest we take a quick trip into town now, get you some clothes you actually like, and anything else you might need. In the event that rumors of your powers do leak, I'd rather we not be besieged by people. At least until I know what Captain Marc and the king have decided is the official truth."

I snorted at the idea of an "official truth" but pushed past it. Politics evidently existed everywhere. "Yeah, we can go. I think I'm up for some commerce," I said, then paused. "Can I see what the money looks like?"

"Sorry?"

"The . . . currency. Whatever you exchange for goods and services. I wanted to see what it looks like here." I'd always thought the United States had the most boring looking money.

"Oh, sure." He reached into his pocket for the pouch the king had given him. He tugged it open and poured something that made delicate chinking sounds into the bowl of his palm. He closed his fist and held it out to me. I cupped my hands beneath his and he dropped several small, clinking objects into them.

"It's so pretty." I pushed the colored disks around the flat of my hand. They looked like etched glass, but they couldn't be, they were so thin. I held a blue one up to the light. A crest and a motto seemed to be inscribed on one side, but it was worn, although the material was still crystal clear and unmarred other than the faded imprint. There were pink, blue, green, and clear disks. "I love them, I don't want to spend them, I want to make jewelry out of them."

That earned a half smile from Wells. "They're made of crycelite, which you don't have on Earth, but is obviously valuable here. Each color has a different value, and the larger disks are double in value to the smaller ones."

"So these things themselves actually have value?" I asked, sliding a pink one on top of a blue one to make lavender. "They don't like . . . correspond to something else in some vault somewhere? I like it. I'm here for it. Which ones are worth what?"

He spent a few seconds explaining the values of the disks to me and once I thought I had it, I handed them back. "Keep some of them," he said. "They're basically for you."

"Then let's get me something with pockets," I replied, a little smile pushing its way out.

We got something to eat first. Wells insisted, saying I was starting to look a little peaked. I refrained from saying the same could be said about him. Perhaps the drama at the palace had exhausted him as much as it had me. Regardless, I did feel better afterward.

I was thrilled that the shop we went into had short chopsticks, but thought it so weird that they were used only to pick up very tiny savory pastries. Apparently chopsticks were pretty common, but usually only for appetizers when you didn't want to get your fingers dirty.

We went through several shops to get things for me to wear. Wells didn't rush me, but I could tell that he was hoping to get us in and out quickly. Once or twice, people did come up to him, and each time he told me to go on and shop and led them away. My social battery was at about a zero, so

I didn't particularly mind, but there was now an itch in the back of my mind wondering how much of a target I'd really put on myself.

Thankfully I found clothing with pockets galore. Almost every pair of casual pants had thigh pockets in addition to the usual hip pockets. Even in skirts and dresses. Some of the pockets were even permanently sewn shut and Wells explained that they were to 'port coins into so that they wouldn't accidentally fall out.

There were some t-shirts and snaps, but tunic style tops seemed to be more the thing, which I didn't mind. Even the athletic clothes had long tails. Shorts were available, but not nearly as plentiful as pants and even athletic skirts. I had to dig for them. They also loved elastic and if they could avoid fasteners all together, they would do it. I kind of loved that all the pants were stretchy pocket pants. My butt looked great and I had storage.

We were headed back up the hill when I passed the window of a jeweler and paused.

"See something you like?" Wells stopped to see what had caught my attention.

"I forgot to ask Al for my ring back," I said, my voice sharper than intended as I turned away from the window.

Wells sighed and offered his arm again. "I can ask next time I hear from him. He'll use it as a loophole to try to see you, you know."

I grunted as I curved my fingers around his forearm and mulled that over. I still wanted my ring back.

"To be honest, he's probably going to make an attempt anyway, so may as well ask for something you want in return."

"Was he like this with my grandma?" Honestly, no wonder she'd found my gentle grandfather so refreshing.

Wells was quiet for a moment, his eyes scanning the ground just ahead of us as if it held the answers.

"The main difference in this situation is that Solange actually did like Al. She just didn't want him to be the *only* one she was allowed to like. So, he would get like this occasionally, yes, and she'd carry on with him for a bit.

Usually after letting him chase after her for a few weeks. It was part of the game the two of them played."

His ribs expanded against my arm. Blowing out a long exhale, he raised his gaze to the top of the hill as the ground tilted upward more sharply. "I can see why he's doing it; in his mind it always worked before. But I'm not defending the way Al is treating you. As much as you may look like, and occasionally act like her, you are obviously not Solange. And you've been very clear with Al." He flushed. "And he still hasn't apologized for what he's done to you."

Wells's house was at the very crest of the hill. A tall, elegant rectangle in dark browns and navy blues. It reminded me of a New Orleans townhouse, the way the upper story balconies wrapped from the front around to the side. There were even a few window boxes with bright, Perimovian blooms hanging down. A pang pierced my heart. I hadn't been able to live there long at all.

There were no mailboxes. No powerlines or telephone poles marred the skies. My youngest nephew would have been appalled. He loved powerlines. Personally, I just enjoyed electricity, but we'd had light on the ship, so I hoped there was some kind of temperature control and artificial illumination.

All of the houses were fairly close together and none of the yards were enormous, but everyone had a little patch of blue-green lawn surrounded by a fence. Wells's fence even looked like wrought iron, matching his balconies. Compared to the palace, it was humble, but it was twice the size of any house I'd ever lived in on Earth.

When I inquired about the lack of light switches and deadbolts, Wells just chuckled and said it was all kroma-based and I'd get used to it.

He gave me a brief tour. Sure enough, a soft illumination at the crown of each wall brightened as we entered each room. There were also some fixtures reminiscent of lanterns that seemed to contain the same kind of light.

Wells told me I was free to look around anywhere I wanted, but the essentials were the kitchen and main room on the first floor, training room in the basement, bed and bathrooms (yay, plumbing!) on the third floor. The second floor we bypassed as it held only the office, library, and dining room. Apparently a dining room on the second floor and kitchen on the first floor were totally normal on Perimov.

We reached the third floor and walked toward the eastern end. Wells pointed out a hall bathroom. "But the two bedrooms at the end have bathrooms attached. One is mine." He indicated a doorway on the right side of the hall. "I thought you'd like the other." He opened the door directly across from it.

My shopping was already on the bed. Wells had 'ported it there each time we paid so we wouldn't have to carry it. Apparently, telepaths had especially proficient telekinetic talents. There was a large sliding glass door on the eastern wall of the room which opened out onto a balcony facing the sea.

"Due to my position, the wards on this house are some of the strongest available," Wells said from the doorway. "You'll be safe when you're home, Imogen."

Home. I swallowed down a golf ball of feelings and stared out the window, yanking myself under control. "Not safe when I go out?"

He folded his arms and leaned against the frame. "We'll keep the outings judicious for a bit. We can change anything in the room you'd like."

A non-answer and a subject change. I didn't have the energy to press and stepped closer to the balcony. "I'll get the sunrise," I said, striving to sound appreciative and not as if I was trying to hold a flood of emotion at bay.

"Yes, unless you close the curtains..."

"I like the sun waking me up." I turned to take in the rest. The bathroom was across the room and there was a small desk in one corner, a nightstand by the bed, and a dresser.

"Why don't you take some time to yourself? Unpack. Rest. Take all the baths you want."

I looked up to find Wells half-smiling, although blue-black concern edged his aura. I pushed a small smile back. "What a time to be alive."

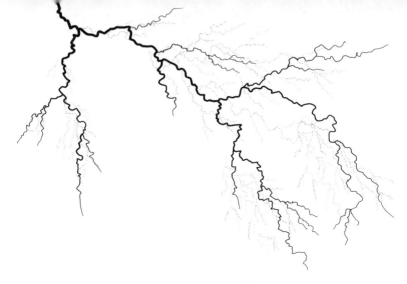

CHAPTER FOURTEEN

If you don't know what to be, be resilient.
Everything else will fall into place.
—Solange Aidair Delaney

The next day the sun did wake me, violet and chocolate tones caressing the clouds around it.

And I didn't know where I was.

When I remembered, a weight settled onto my chest, crushing my heart. I lay frozen in bed, gazing out my balcony windows, watching the dark red sun slowly climb over the horizon, pulling itself from the sea on a ladder of thin, violet clouds. *You could be waking up in that museum of a palace*, I told myself. *Things could be worse.*

I knew there would be times when I would cry again. Maybe even days where I couldn't get out of bed. But I decided that today didn't have to be one of them. Once the sun was up, I got up. I could not figure out the lamps or room lights, so I made the bed and got dressed by the light from the balcony. Had I been at home, I would have gone running, but I wasn't sure if Wells would panic if he woke up and found me gone. He hadn't exactly said that I *wasn't* safe but then again, the last time I went on a dawn run, I'd been kidnapped by Al. And I wouldn't put it past him to try it again, since the rules apparently didn't apply to him. I also didn't know how these security wards or whatever worked. Was I magically locked in the house until Wells... turned them off or something? I'd have to figure this out. I needed my morning runs.

When Wells knocked softly at the door several minutes later, he found me pushing myself up from the floor where I'd been sitting in front of the full-length mirror in the corner.

The space between his brows creased. "What are you doing?"

I shrugged. "Playing 'spot the differences.'" I had decided to try coming to terms with what I looked like now by forcing myself to take it in.

"Are there a lot of them?" He raised an eyebrow.

"Some. There are a lot of scars I used to have that I don't have anymore. That's weird. I never thought I'd *miss* scars." I examined my forearm where I'd been stabbed with a pencil in second grade. A gray dot had always remained like a tiny tattoo. The skin was smooth and perfect now. Like my entire past was erased.

I lifted my chin and made myself meet his gaze. "Good morning, by the way."

"Good morning." He scanned my face. It was an effort not to drop my eyes to the floor again. "You know, you're still you, Imogen."

I lowered my eyes. "Yeah, I know," I said to the ground. *Am I?*

Wells apparently decided to let it go. Maybe he'd already picked up on my aversion to crying in front of people. "Hungry?"

"Perpetually."

"Do you want breakfast out or in?"

"Is it okay for us to go out?"

He nodded. "I had a message from Captain Marc last night. He's downplayed your role in landing the ship by telling Allestair that although you did stumble onto the bridge, you merely lent your power to him, rather like a battery. He's requested that those on the bridge keep the entire truth of what happened to themselves. You'll still be seen as talented, but not quite the mind-blowing rarity that stands before me."

My lips twitched in spite of myself. "And what about Al?"

"He's not happy about it, since his entire defense rests on how exceptional you are and how you're certain to benefit Molnair, but Marc has convinced him that your safety is more important." Wells crossed his arms and his tone went bone-dry. "Al is also certain that your powers will out themselves and you'll rise to your inevitable position as Chosen One eventually."

I rolled my eyes. "While that's all . . . information. That I now have. I meant is Al going to be held accountable for kidnapping me and destroying my life?"

Wells's long, dark eyelashes swept down to fan his cheekbones. Any humor dropped from his expression. My stomach twisted. I already had my answer.

"The public narrative is now that Al and I both found you on Earth, that you made friends with both of us, and that you wanted to come learn about your grandmother's people." He exhaled roughly. "They're leaving your partnership status intentionally ambiguous."

Fury tore through me like a tsunami. My chest tightened as my ever-quickening breaths went nowhere. My rage ebbed as grief crowded it out. So my life meant nothing? The prince's reputation was more important than my entire life? My fingernails bit into my palms. I had nowhere to go . . .

Wells reached out a hand. "To say it isn't fair doesn't begin to cover it, Imogen. I'm so incredibly sorry."

I uncurled my fist and placed my hand in his. Long fingers wrapped around mine and squeezed. Our gazes collided, empathy shining from his warm russet eyes.

An unspoken understanding passed between us as I stepped into his embrace. He wrapped his arms around me and I shut my eyes and tried to breathe.

"For what it's worth," he said softly, his voice rumbling against my cheek, "as head of the Earth expeditions, Captain Marc insisted on the official records being accurate. If anyone does take a look at them, they'll have questions." I felt his chest expand. "But for that reason, I'm sure their inclusion in the public record hall will be delayed."

We stood together until my heart rate had dropped to a normal cadence.

"Do you still want to go out for breakfast?" Wells asked without breaking the hug.

I nodded against his tunic. "I have it on good authority that some kind of caffeinated beverage exists here?"

We went out for jatki. Which could be prepared in at least as many ways as espresso. I even got a muffin-like pastry called a pouffe which was flavored with some kind of spice I'd never heard of. As a bonus, I got to watch kromatic baking from the small table we'd picked beside the outer window of the shop. There were no knobs or buttons on any of the stoves or wood burning ovens. Nothing electronic at all, people just waved their hands at things. All sugars, spices, honey, et cetera, were in glass dispensers. Like a sugar soda fountain. I kind of liked it. There also were fewer Molnairians out this early, which was nice. Wells was more relaxed.

"What would you like to do today?" he asked, finished with his own oatmeal-esque breakfast. "You can take the day to rest if you like, no one would blame you, or—"

"I want to learn more about kroma," I said. Jesus, heaven forbid I give myself any chance to really ruminate on my situation. "Honestly, I can do *magic* now, that's all I want to do."

He stared right back at me, russet eyes gleaming, one corner of his mouth turned up. "All right, Imogen, we'll . . . do magic, as you say. But it's not all going to be impressive, power-draining military kroma like you did the other day. And you'll have to learn some control."

"I agree to all those conditions. I didn't know we were doing Military Kroma." I sipped my jatki. It wasn't the same as Starbucks, but it was good.

Kind of cinnamony. I flicked my eyes over to the window, where a baker barely glanced over his shoulder as a tray of pastries slid from the oven behind him and floated over to his workspace. "I'm excited to learn that there are different flavors of magic. What kind will we be doing?" I waited to see if he would get pedantic on me.

"Let's start with basic household magic." His eyes twinkled as he sipped his own jatki. He drank his black. In spite of having a *literal sugar packet collection.*

"Basic Household Magic," I repeated. "That sounds like the title of a book for '50s housewives. But it probably is a good idea for me to learn how to turn on lights. And then if I'm really awesome at it, maybe I can get a tour of Sachets Through the Ages?"

His cheeks reddened, but he merely finished his jatki and didn't answer me.

Before I was allowed to so much as kromatically light a candle, Wells had me sit in the middle of the main room, on the floor, cross-legged, as if we were about to meditate. He sat facing me.

"You need to come closer," he said. I scooted forward a few inches. He cocked his head, pinning me with his beautiful eyes. "I'm not Al, come all the way over here, please."

"I know you're not," I muttered, scuttling across the floor like a weird crab and settling directly in front of him.

He shifted forward himself until our knees touched, then placed one of my hands, palm up, on his knee, and the other, palm down on my own. He set one of his hands on his knee, one on mine, palm up, palm down, so that our palms connected. The pads of his fingers rested lightly against my wrists. Even my newly lengthened hands looked small next to his.

The quiet tension in the room made me jittery. *We're basically just sitting on the floor holding hands,* I thought. My cheeks warmed before I punched that notion aside. *He's trying to help you, be an adult.* A flutter of nerves brushed against my chest like the wings of a passing hummingbird.

"This does require some concentration," Wells said. "It's not combative kroma, which you seem to have a talent for, but it is essential in order to be truly effective in any kromatic conflict. As well as daily life."

My skin tingled as if little electric spiders skittered over its surface. "I feel like we're about to do some joint meditation thing. We should have chanting monks and gongs," I said, then died a little inside at how lame I was. This kind of nervous joking was usually reserved for first dates and job interviews. I wondered if they even had gongs here. Or monks.

Wells mercifully continued as if I hadn't spoken. "I mentioned before that it's possible to pull kroma from another person. It can be given as well. For instance, if you and I were in a situation where I burned myself out, but we needed some kind of kroma that you weren't adept at performing, you could pass me some of your energy."

"Like the 'official truth' of what I did on the ship?" I asked.

Wells cleared his throat. "Precisely. What I'm going to do now is gently pull energy from you, then give it back and add some of my own. For right now, just focus on what it feels like and don't try to affect anything."

I nodded.

For a moment, our auras spun normally, mine slightly faster than Wells's. Then they slowed almost to stillness. The light around our connected palms brightened and I watched as waves of light flowed down my arms and up his, stopping at the elbow.

I felt my energy leave, as if I had just sat down after a long day and didn't want to get up again immediately. After a moment, the swirling colors flowed back down then up my arms. I felt rejuvenated. Like I'd just had a good nap. The sleeves of color retreated back to our palms and our auras flowed normally again.

"Feel that?" Wells asked.

I nodded again, my mouth twisting up into a giddy grin. It was cool. I wanted to try it.

"Most people eventually learn to do it from a distance, although this is far easier. You can also block someone from taking energy from you. If you're in any kind of hostile situation, you'll want to be blocking at all times. That's one of the reasons it was so dangerous to have you on the bridge during the battle. If any of the Sephryans had realized you were vulnerable, they could have sucked your energy dry and used your power themselves."

My face dropped back into serious lines. Probably the only reason I hadn't been attacked was the presumption that only experienced fighters would be defending the ship.

"In most situations," Wells continued quietly, "the sidhe half of the pair explains all of this to their human partner well before they've even been pulled onto the ship. Had you and Al been a normal pairing, you would have known why it was dangerous for you to leave the room that day." He swallowed. "Aloysius truly told you absolutely nothing. And endangered not only you, but everyone else."

"Now you try."

What looked so simple took me over an hour to execute. Once I had shown a respectable ability to block Wells from taking my energy, we moved from sitting to standing and eventually practiced from opposite sides of the room. Sweat beaded my hairline and I was thinking I'd have to ask for a break before we'd even gotten to Basic Household Magic when a there was a knock at the door.

Wells's brow furrowed. "Wait here."

Grateful for the reprieve, I collapsed into the nearest chair and watched Wells until he disappeared around the corner to the foyer.

I heard the door open and let my eyes drop shut. Then I heard a strange voice speak my name. Magically my energy returned and I padded toward the door. The main room and foyer were separated by a wall with an open archway. I peeked around the archway to see Wells standing in front of the partially open door, his hand gripping the inside knob, his spine ramrod straight. He glanced over his shoulder and caught me, then stepped outside and shut the door behind him before I could hear anything interesting.

Frowning, I stepped fully into the foyer and leaned against the wall, folding my arms. Moments later Wells returned, his face unreadable.

"So, on Earth, when someone says, 'wait here,' what do they usually mean?"

"I heard my name," I said.

His mouth tightened. "Well, I did tell you people would be interested in you. Let's head to the kitchen. I think you have enough control to work on some basics."

Deciding I would let it go for the time being, I followed him. No sooner had I gotten the most tenuous grasp on kromatically lighting the stove than there was another knock.

"Keep practicing," Wells said, his words clipped.

This time I obeyed since I literally had fire in my hands and wood all around me. Wells was back in even less time. Once again, his face told me nothing, but his aura pulsed with irritation. Before I could even open my mouth he said, "Good. Let's move on."

I'd learned how to turn on and off lights and clean things, but was struggling with how to lock and unlock doors. Although these were apparently simple tasks that all sidhe learned as children, it took me several false starts and incredible amount of energy. Wells patiently assured me that this was normal, and like strengthening any muscle, I'd get better with practice. Then the third knock came.

I was starting to recognize Wells's blank political persona when it slid into place like a mask. If I hadn't been able to see his aura—blue-black concern now ringed the autumnal colors—that blank face would have been his only tell. "Keep working, you're almost there." He gave me a stiff smile before spinning on his heel and heading to the door.

Unease slithered through my veins like oil. *He's been gone for eight months*, I told myself, refocusing on the small box I was trying to unlock. *Maybe he just has a lot of friends who want to see him.* But why would his friends cause irritation and worry? *Maybe he has bad friends. I mean, his brother does kind of suck.*

Wells returned at the exact moment I squealed, having finally unlocked the box. To my surprise he merely nodded at it and said, "Come with me."

I followed him back to the front door, my shoulders tense. His aura was pulsing with bronze and crimson. I cleared my throat. "Are the people—the visitors—are they friends of yours?"

He laughed humorlessly as he yanked open the front door and led me through. "My friends have the courtesy to message me first. And give me privacy when I ask for it. These people are busybodies. Acquaintances who feel they have an in and want to pry, and at least one was trying to trick me into saying something he could print."

I stumbled as I followed him down the steps. "So there's like a newspaper here?"

"There are a few," he said. "But you can be sure Allestair will have people leaning on them regarding you. This one was asking about your powers. Heard a rumor."

My mouth dried out as I joined him near his gate.

He looked down at me, a slightly rakish upward tilt to his lips. "Let's teach you some light warding. We'll start by making our yard off limits to anyone not invited or on a very short list."

Wells took on the complicated bits of the warding, but I did feel like I was getting the hang of it by the time we were done. I made a mental note to ward something more manageable, like a drawer in my room or bathroom, just to try it out.

We were back inside, and I was chugging a well-deserved glass of fruit juice, when a slip of paper fluttered in front of Wells's face, appearing out of nowhere. "What *now*," he snapped plucking it from the air and running an eye over it.

His eyes dropped shut briefly as he sighed.

"Al's on his way." He glanced at me from beneath lowered brows. "Ostensibly to drop your things off as ordered. If you don't want to see him, I'd suggest running up to your room and pretending to be asleep."

I didn't wait for any additional details before I turned tail and sprinted up three stories, taking the steps two at a time. I ripped back the covers and dove underneath them, even going so far as to close my eyes. I didn't think that Wells would actually let Al come up, but he might not be able to stop him. I tried to slow my breathing to a convincing hush and may have fallen into a doze.

The next thing I knew, Wells had thrown a bundle onto the bed. "You didn't have to go that far," he said. "I wouldn't have actually let him bust in on you, I just needed the location of your scent to be convincing. These are yours, apparently."

I sat up and clambered over to the sack he had tossed on the bed. I upended it. The clothes I had been wearing when Al took me. Including my running shoes. The pouch. Nothing else. I unzipped the pouch; my phone and earbuds fell out. I dug around inside of it. Nothing. Pawed through the clothes. Even checked the tiny pocket on my running shorts.

"What is it?" Wells asked. He was leaning against the dresser watching me.

"My ring isn't here."

He sighed and massaged his forehead. "I'll ask him about it."

I picked up my phone, surprised when the screen responded. I swiped it open. 1% battery. Without thinking about what I was doing, I opened the messaging app, scrolled to the last conversation I'd had with Keane, and typed, "Hey. I miss you. I'm okay." And hit send.

Message Send Failure. Insufficient Signal.

The phone died.

Why did you do that? I asked myself as a tear landed on the smooth, black surface of the screen. *Why did you waste your last battery life on that? You knew it wouldn't send. You could have gone to look at a photo. Read the messages one last time . . .*

"Are you all right?" Wells asked. I couldn't look at him.

"I think I need a minute," I whispered.

"I'll be downstairs," he said, and left, quietly closing the door behind him.

CHAPTER FIFTEEN

Nothing will bring back the place you grew up. Even if you went back to that exact spot with those exact people. It's gone. That's what they mean when they say you can never go home again. You can only make a new one.
—Keane Battersea

It was hours before I resurfaced. I put the clothes and shoes away with everything else. I hadn't been able to bring myself to throw away my useless phone and earbuds, so I tucked them back inside the running pouch and slid them into a drawer in the nightstand. It had a keyhole, but no key; still, I warded and locked it. Not that I figured anyone would have any reason to break into the general's house and steal a useless relic from Earth.

Wells asked if I was okay when I joined him in the kitchen. After my subdued nod, he let it go and ran through a few of the basics to make sure I could at least heat up food and turn on lights.

I went through the exercises mechanically, sadness still weighing me down, but at least I was starting to get things. Wells even complimented my 'porting. "Everyone learns to 'port eventually, but it doesn't always come so quickly." He smiled at me and I could tell he was trying to be upbeat, but my chest felt cold and hollow. "Once you have a bit more instinctive ability to control your power flow"—sometimes I 'ported things much too fast and hit myself with them, not embarrassing at all—"we'll go to the park and try some more advanced kroma."

Cool. Big Kroma. Whatever that was. I merely nodded, then floated the last delicate wine glass into its slot above the sink without so much as tapping the one next to it.

"Well done, Imogen." He placed a warm palm between my shoulder blades and patted. "You should be pleased with yourself." I nodded, searching for a "pleased" feeling. Wells's hand stilled on my shoulder, his eyes searching my face. "In fact, I think you've earned a tour of the most extensive tea sachet and sugar packet collection in this galaxy."

My shoulders straightened out of a slump I didn't even realize I'd adopted. Wells's face was the color of a sunburn, but one side of his mouth was lifted in a half smile.

The hollow feeling eased. "I get to see Sachets Through the Ages?"

"You're sworn to secrecy and may not touch unless invited to do so." He held out a hand.

A genuine smile curled my lips upward as I took it.

Wells's bedroom was neat—of course—and opposite in layout to mine. Although his balcony wrapped around to the front of the house, effectively giving him two. In between the two balcony exits sat a round table that currently held a wooden box and a mess of colored packets.

We spent the next hour organizing the sugar and tea he'd obtained on this trip and rearranging the wooden box, *which he had built himself* so that the slotting was more accurate. Apparently, after his search for a partner was nullified, he traveled to Jerusalem and Germany to purchase tea and sugar packets respectively from collectors there so that he could fill out his assortment with items he'd missed in the intervening one hundred years. He had at least one tea sachet from every decade. With the sugar packets, he seemed to be going more for global variety.

"My cousins and I used to play with sugar packets in restaurants," I told him as I sorted a few into piles by shape. Different countries sometimes had different shapes. It was actually kind of cool. "We'd pretend to be playing cards with them. We were really young because my mom was still alive, so we must have made up our own rules. We called them patience."

Wells's skin tone had nearly returned to normal. Only the tips of his ears were pink. "You called the packets patience?"

I nodded, smiling at the memory. "Yeah, we would divide them up so one person had each color—I was always blue—and it was rough if you had less patience than the next person. Probably our parents told us to have patience when we were hungry and wanting our food or something and we took it literally." I gave him a sideways glance. "Anyway, now I know how you're able to put up with Al. You have an entire box of patience."

He laughed, a full belly laugh that warmed me from the inside out. I couldn't help comparing this expressive face to the stiff mask I'd seen earlier in the day. My entire being softened. "Thank you for showing me this."

His eyelashes lowered and his cheekbones flushed lightly. "You're welcome." He picked up one of my piles and slid it into the appropriate slot, eyes twinkling. "Everyone scoffs initially, but in the end one can never deny the joy these sachets bring."

I snort-laughed, scattering one of my piles.

Although Wells was obviously leery about letting me out on my own, he eventually agreed that running in the park at daybreak wasn't inherently dangerous, although he made me promise not to get within arm's length of anyone if they tried to engage me, and to come straight home afterward. He also had me leave through the side door.

Those early morning runs kept me sane in the weeks that followed. Very few people were out as early as I was and I eventually recognized most of the regulars. Only once did someone try to flag me down. I didn't know them and I sprinted home with my heart in my throat. Wells started working my shielding that same day. Since I'd shown obvious interest and aptitude in the combative arts, and conveniently they were highly related to Wells's job, he saw no issue in honing those skills.

Wells continually scanned the papers for any hint that my abilities had been leaked. The paper in Molnair all had a purply tinge to it, and their newspapers all came as a scroll rather than on big sheets like on Earth. I'd looked through one the first time Wells brought it home, but couldn't stomach the bullshit story about me befriending Al and Wells and longing to come to my grandmother's homeland. I'd involuntarily crumpled the stiff edges of the paper, making it more difficult to roll back up, before I'd tossed it away. I let Wells scan the papers from then on.

Days later, he tried to keep me home while he went to the market after several requests for invites fluttered into existence while we were making a grocery list. But I'd been looking forward to getting out.

"How are people going to know how bad-ass I am just by looking at me?" I threw up my hands and stood up from the kitchen table. "I get that it's annoying, but it seems like this is how life is, so shouldn't I be able to at least go to the grocery store?"

"No one can tell just by looking at you, but there are certain individuals with the ability to tell by touching you." He remained seated, his fingers spread over the papers that had interrupted our morning, frustration clear in every line of his face. "It's easier to get an excuse to brush up against you in a place like the market. There's also the possibility of you accidentally letting something slip. You never know when you're going to discover some new kroma. And I'm not convinced someone isn't watching the house. I can't seem to catch them but..."

Afraid of opening an additional can of worms, but unwilling to concede, I said, "If someone were watching the house, why wouldn't they pounce on me when I go running?"

Wells exhaled and pushed himself back from the table, his mouth tightening as he looked up at me.

"What?"

He ran a hand through his hair. "One, I don't think they like getting up that early, and two . . ." He grimaced. "I've a couple of friends keeping an eye on you."

"*What!* Which ones?" I knew instantly who they were when he described them. "And you didn't think to maybe just introduce us? This is so *weird.*" I plopped down in the chair next to him, shoving the papers away.

Wells covered my hand with his, looking down at the table when he spoke. "I wanted you to feel like you had some measure of independence and I didn't want you to drop your guard in case one or both of them couldn't make it one morning." He glanced up at me through the tops of his eyes. "And I hate running."

My lips twisted to the side. "Take me to the market and I'll forgive you."

He eventually agreed as long as we left the house under a cloaking shield and returned the same way.

"This will all die down eventually, Imogen," he said as we stood still in front of his gate, waiting for a person with a large dog (yay! Dogs!) to pass. The cloaking shield hid us, sight, scent, and sound, but a gate opening and closing on its own would announce our presence, and Wells wasn't going to take a chance in case his phantom person was watching the house. "I'm sure they're bothering the other twelve also, but as you're attached to two rather public figures, of course there's more interest. We just have to be patient until you've got enough control of your powers to . . ."

"Act normal?" I finished.

Wells dropped the shield once we were far enough from the house, and winked us—jarringly and without warning—to another area of the market when a "busybody" he recognized spotted us.

"Maybe I should just talk to one of them and get it—"

"Nope." We were trudging back up the hill under the cloak. Cloaking shields apparently took a lot of energy, but Wells still insisted he'd be fine to spar after a snack. "You're a terrible liar and have no control of your face."

My mouth dropped open, an indignant squawk escaping.

"Exactly." He glanced furtively over his shoulder at the empty sidewalk and winked us straight into the house, not even bothering with the gate or door. Only someone who lived in the house could wink in or out. "Training room in twenty minutes."

We trained daily, sometimes twice a day. Almost like Wells was trying to tire me out so I wouldn't insist on leaving the house. I didn't really mind. Although I was instinctively talented, Wells was far more technically proficient at a number of things that he insisted I work on. I found it all fun and interesting and Wells was a good teacher.

Constantly learning also helped push thoughts of Earth out of my head. "Do you want some water?"

We'd been engaged in some very acrobatic sparring for almost an hour. I had done things that I wouldn't have even attempted with the aid of wires when I was a human. I was dripping with sweat. "Yes, please." I plopped down on the edge of the ring, unwrapping my hands.

Wells took a seat next to me with a bit more grace, although he was just as damp. "All right, see if you can get it."

"Ha." I repressed a groan and dredged up the required energy. "Okay." I 'ported two glasses and a carafe to the floor in front of us. They only skidded a little bit, both glasses toppling over, but the carafe was still full, only a little slopping out over the side. I wasn't confident enough to fill the glasses. I tended to spill things when 'porting.

"Better! You're learning so quickly." Wells poured water for both of us before removing his hand wraps. "It's a blessing Al didn't end up with you. He would have found this far too fun and probably one of you would have ended up hurt."

I considered that information as I gulped my water. I didn't want to think about what might have happened if I'd ended up in Al's "care."

"I'd almost forgotten about Al," I grumbled.

"He hasn't forgotten about you," Wells said, dumping his wraps in a pile on top of mine and 'porting them all into the laundry before grabbing his glass. "I get at least one message a day from him asking for a blow by blow of your activities. If I thought it would do any good, I would tell his father."

"It's like he's Pepe Le Pew and I'm that black and white cat," I said, refilling my water. A spritz of static jumped from the pewter carafe to my hand, shocking me. This had been happening a lot lately. I was apparently very staticky now.

Wells blinked at me. "I wish I got your jokes. You look so happy when you make them." He took the carafe when I handed it over, refilling his own glass.

My entire being deflated. "I do too," I sniffed. "Being funny was one of my best defense mechanisms. I feel like I'm down a shield."

He snorted.

Ha! Still got it, I thought. "I should make up a little Earth-to-Perimov translation manual."

"I told you that we all lived on Earth at one point," he said, setting the nearly empty carafe back down in front of me.

I nodded. I remembered this. "And then y'all got really good at space travel super-fast and just left because . . . ?"

"Well, thousands of years ago, humans and sidhe coexisted mostly peacefully." He took a long drink. Then showed off by just 'porting more water from the carafe into his glass. "But at some point, the sidhe felt that the humans were taking advantage of them. Always pleading for kromatic assistance. Always blaming them for things that went wrong. And yes, our kroma advanced us far beyond what humans were capable of. We hid our technology from them, because they were getting too reliant—to the point of entitlement—on kromatic solutions to every challenge. Some sidhe even retaliated. Playing nasty tricks on humans who couldn't defend themselves. It only added to their narrative. So we separated ourselves further. Hid away.

"Once we were able to leave the planet, half our race went exploring off world. The other half remained on Earth, doing their best to stay away from humans. But there was still occasional contact. Still occasional romantic relationships.

"Some of the explorers returned, decades later. They had found a new planet perfect for us. We could take our powers and leave Earth to the humans. Let them learn and grow on their own, without being plagued by their demands and their accusations. Without the least scrupulous among us toying with them. Only those who possessed kroma could go. Everyone else was to be left behind.

"One sidhe didn't want to leave her human love. She and her sister found a way to use their kroma to turn him. And he became the first person turned."

"Is that why you had to help Al? Is it always a sibling thing when you turn someone?" I asked, fully engaged in the story. I'd killed the rest of the carafe.

"Any pair can do it, although out of tradition, it is usually a family member or close friend that helps in the turning," he said. "That first turning was controversial. Some believed it unnatural and even cruel. As you know, it's far from painless. And not everyone survives. However, centuries later, the sidhe of Perimov were having more and more difficulty having children. Starting a family can easily take a pair decades, but some lines weren't reproducing at all. And some only sporadically. Some terrifying years passed where no children were born. Sidhe were panicking. After extensive research, it was discovered that the only line that was consistently still fertile descended from that sidhe and her human mate, for he did become her mate once he was turned. Which they felt was proof that the act of turning wasn't cruel or harmful as kroma had blessed them with the bond. The sporadic lines were the ones who had stayed on Earth the longest and continued to intermingle. It was then that we realized we couldn't truly separate ourselves from humanity.

"As you know, not everyone took similar views. The first expedition back was primitive. They didn't know how long they'd have to stay or when they'd be able to come back pending the movements of the celestial bodies en route. They stayed on Earth for decades. Some of them brought back turned sidhe, some of them refused and brought back humans.

"You know the rest. Molnair and Sephrya split. Molnair has continued to advance, leaving Sephrya behind. And—until you—we have only turned those willing to come with us."

I stared at him. "So there used to be magical mischief makers on Earth for real. I wonder if that's why we have fairy tales."

He narrowed his eyes. "What sorts of things do your tales say about fairies?"

"Like . . . you're never supposed to dance with fairies because if you do you won't be able to stop and you'll dance until you die and then your bones will just keep dancing forever—"

"Disgusting!" The horror on his face only encouraged me.

"I know. And there was something about never eating any food a fairy gives you. But I can't remember what horrible thing it was supposed to do to you. Also, fairies take healthy babies and put their own dead ones in place instead."

He stared at me for several beats, dark red eyebrows pulling closer and closer together. "And people believe this horseshit?"

"No, Wells," I said, smiling. "No one believes it because *magic isn't real.*"

He blinked at me.

"Go take a shower," he said, tossing back the rest of his water and tugging at the edge of my tank top, which was plastered to my stomach. For a moment, I thought he *might* be checking me out. I felt the very early flutters of butterfly wings in my stomach, then he let go. "You're a bit ripe."

The wings vanished and I told myself I was absolutely not disappointed. I poked his side; his shirt was just as damp as mine. And no, I was *not* checking out his lats, they were just there. So obvious it was impossible not to see them.

"Have you ever heard the expression about the pot calling the kettle black?" I asked. Wells 'ported the glasses and carafe away and stood, offering me a hand up. I accepted and let him haul me to my feet.

He tilted his head to the side, long, dark lashes clinging together. "Do your kitchen implements usually talk to each other on Earth?"

I squinted at him. "I can't tell if you're being hilarious in a dry, British kind of way, or if you're seriously . . . I want to see Cilla."

He blinked, then gestured me toward the stairs. "Who?"

I jogged up the first few steps before my legs reminded me that we were exhausted. "Cilla. I met her at the meeting on the ship. She said we could hang out and she *specifically* promised to laugh at my jokes." I panted slightly as we climbed past the first landing.

"Oh, right, and you're both from the same country." He trailed off, frowning, and although I was too tired to read his aura clearly, I knew exactly what he was thinking.

"Look, they were both already on the ship. They were at the meeting. They know everything already. We won't even have to lie to them and won't that be nice?"

I watched his face. I'd become so attuned to Wells's subtle expressions that—unless he pulled that blank cypher on—I could read them almost as easily as his aura. And even his political mask was a tell in and of itself.

"Wouldn't it be nice to hang out with some different people?" I nudged his arm with my shoulder.

To my surprise, his eyes dimmed with disappointment and . . . my stomach dropped. Oh, no, had I hurt his feelings?

"I should have realized you'd be lonely—" he started.

Without thinking I reached out and curled my fingers around his wrist. "I like hanging out with you. A lot. I like you, I really do." Why was my face suddenly on fire? "I just . . . I thought it might be fun . . ."

He smiled softly, his cheekbones just barely tinged pink, but the disappointment had lifted. "I understand, Imogen. And you're right. I can get in touch with Zoe . . ." He edged ahead of me slightly thanks to his longer legs.

"Yay. See if we can see them tomorrow." I followed him, realized I was staring at his butt and jerked my eyes higher.

"Tomorrow?"

"Well, I thought today might be too soon," I said sweetly.

"I was going to suggest we go to the park tomorrow . . ." He let that sentence dangle tantalizingly.

I knew what he was doing. I could see the mischievous golds and greens dancing through his aura, but even as my heart leapt at the bribe of doing Bigger Kroma, and in public no less, the prospect of any kind of balm to soothe the persistent ache of homesickness won out.

"So ask them to meet us at the park. Cilla wants to do magic too," I said.

"How do you know what Cilla wants? A little presumptuous don't you—"

"Cilla is probably, what, twenty?"

"She's twenty-three, I believe."

"Okay, exactly, so she was raised on Harry Potter. And no matter how much Rowling may have destroyed her relationship with the LGBTQ community, Cilla is *still* going to feel like she got her letter from Hogwarts and just got off the goddamn train. She will want to do magic," I concluded as we reached the third-floor landing.

"I have no idea what—"

"Cilla would have understood *everything* I just said." We continued down the hallway to our bedrooms. "Just . . . get in touch with Zoe and see if you two can arrange a playdate in the park with your pet Earthlings."

He paused with one hand on his bedroom doorknob, gaze unfocused, as if he were thinking through every potentially tragic scenario.

"If Murphy's Law was a religion, you would be head priest, I swear. We'll be careful like all the times we're out, but hey, what *if*, what if . . . we don't overthink it and we meet Zoe and Cilla and have a picnic in the park and do a little magic and everything is fine?"

He sighed.

"It's a real possibility!"

He almost smiled. But opened his bedroom door and stepped through before I could really catch it. "I'll see what I can do," he tossed over his shoulder.

CHAPTER SIXTEEN

You'll find your place, Imogen. It's always the last spot you look.
—Henry Delaney

Freshly showered with a few minutes to myself, I kromatically unlocked the nightstand drawer and pulled out my phone. I'd done this on occasion. Not really knowing what I was expecting. An outlet with a charge cord to magic itself into the wall? A cell tower to spring up where no cell tower had ever existed before? A satellite to appear and bounce my signal all the way to Earth?

It had been more than a communication device though. It held my favorite music; most of it was downloaded so I could listen to it even on trail runs with poor signal. It held years of photos. Videos. Hell, it was my calculator.

I peered into the little port where a charging cord would never again make a home. *There's got to be a way to get electricity into this little guy . . .* I mused as I brushed my finger over the opening. A static shock bounced off my finger at the contact. Then a flash skittered over my entire hand.

I dropped the phone.

I stared at my hands. *I mean, there is a certain amount of electricity* in *me.* I thought again about generating electricity and brought my fingertips together. Sparks. This time I didn't jump or pull away and the charges expanded until my hands were wreathed in lightning. "Holy shit," I whispered and pulled my hands slowly apart. The lightning stretched between them like strings of gooey cheese. I shook my hands and it dispersed.

Keane was an electrical engineer. He loved trivia and had told me that the human body at rest produced enough electricity to power a 100-watt light bulb, but some people could produce 2000 watts depending on what they were doing. I was no longer human, so who knew how many watts I produced. Probably more. It took less than six watts to charge a phone. *I wonder...*

Heart pounding, I picked up my phone again and peered into the port. But it also charged on a charging pad. That seemed easier. I carefully popped the phone out of its case. Wells had been relentlessly drilling control. I'd just start with the smallest amount of electricity and see what happened. Worst case: I'd fry it. And it was currently as good as gone anyway.

I laid the phone across my flat palm, my skin tingling with excitement. *Manage your expectations. This has every chance of not working.* My eyes flicked up to the doorway. I considered waiting for Wells to help ... decided against it. He might not be into me reactivating something that most Earthlings had to leave behind.

I took a breath, steadied myself, and concentrated on my energy. I focused on the electricity, just lightly. White-blue flashes danced through my aura. Slowly, as if I were about to send a tiny bit of energy to Wells the way we had practiced, I moved the flashes up my left arm toward the hand cradling my phone. For a moment, nothing happened.

Then the screen lit up.

I yanked my hand away and the phone dropped to the bed.

It was still alight.

I was almost scared to touch it.

I took a breath and soothed my aura back down to chill, swirling blues and greens. Barely breathing. Barely daring to hope. I picked up the phone. Lifted it to my face. Swiped up. It opened. 100% battery.

An involuntary shriek exploded from my throat as I half rose from my seat on the bed.

Balancing on my knees, my finger hovered indecisively over the screen from photos to messages to ... I jabbed the voice mail app. Tapped at random as soon as it opened.

Wells burst through the door. His long hair was still wet from his own shower, darkened to a ruddy bronze and dampening the shoulders of the shirt he had thrown on. His aura was spinning with shock, concern, confusion ...

"*Haaaaaappy biiiiirthdaaaaay tooooo youuuuu ...*"

Tears ringed my eyes even as my lips curved upward. I didn't glance up from my phone as Wells slowly walked over. The sounds of my father and my uncles' voices, singing the worst rendition of "Happy Birthday" ever, filled the room.

"*Haaaappyyyy biiiiiiirthdaaaaay deeeeeeeaaaarr Im oh giiiiiiiiiiiiiiiiin ...*"

"What is that?" Wells asked softly, staring at my phone.

"My dad," I said. "And my uncles. Victor and Glenn. They were on a vacation together that happened to be during my birthday. Don't worry, they're very drunk, they don't normally sound that bad." I giggled as they finished the song, each adding an extra joke verse over the other one and then slurring out individual birthday wishes. "This is from twelve years ago or something. I saved it because it's awesome."

I sat back down on the bed, still smiling at the voices. Wells took a seat on the edge next to me.

"When is your birthday?" he asked.

"I don't know when it would be here ... I don't understand your calendar yet."

"What time of year was it?"

"It usually fell on the Spring Equinox."

"We do have a Spring Equinox here."

"And one of my great worries has been laid to rest." I flicked my eyes to his and smiled to take the sting out of my involuntary snark. My father's voice mail ended and I scrolled through the others.

"How many children did Solange have?"

"Three boys, two girls," I answered, searching for a particular voice mail. "And eleven grandchildren and . . . fourteen great-grandchildren." I found it. "Here's one I think you'll like." I tapped the voice mail and then set the phone on the bed between us, watching Wells's face.

Solange's dramatic exhale cut the silence. Wells's cheeks lifted.

"*Imogen.*" Another exhale. "*Darling, your father would have told me to leave it alone, but I can't. You know me, I can't leave it alone.*"

"Oh, gods she sounds the same," Wells whispered.

"*Honey, this boy you're dating. Man. Whatever. He's not the right one. I know, I know, but I couldn't just not say anything. Have your fun if you like, bop around with him for a while, but don't let him pin you down . . . there's more out there for you. And I know you don't believe me when I say it, but you are special, honey. You think you haven't found your place because you haven't. You haven't seen everything yet, you haven't* done *everything yet. Don't let yourself get caught up in these arbitrary milestones that everyone else your age is obsessed with. You're different. In a good way. And I don't say that to all the kids, you can ask your cousins. Go ahead, ask 'em! I don't care!*"

Wells chuckled. Solange exhaled.

"*Anyway, your father told me the kid was thinking of proposing, so I had to say something. Couldn't let it go. Don't settle, honey. There's more in store for you. Don't let him wear you down. Not on this. Love ya. . . . Call me back if you get this in an hour or so, after that you probably won't be able to reach me.*" She sighed again. "*There might be other worlds to see . . .*" She cleared her throat. "*Love you.*"

"Did you call her back?"

Wells's eyes were still sparkling. I wondered what it was like to hear a voice you'd never expected to hear again after a hundred years.

"I did," I said, swiping the app closed. "I was too late. She left this the day before she . . . disappeared. I've been moving it from phone to phone for sixteen years."

"Was she right?" he asked. "About the . . . person you were dating?"

I snorted. "She was. And she was right about me being different and she was right about me never finding my place." My heart squeezed. "And now I know what she meant about other worlds."

"There's still time to find your place," he said softly.

I didn't look up. I pulled the phone toward me. "I know I'm not supposed to have this." My stomach dipped down to my toes as I said it.

"I won't tell anyone if you won't . . ."

I lifted my eyes to his. He was giving me his half smile, aura swirling calmly. I thought I saw a ribbon of pink flip through, but I couldn't be sure.

I smiled back.

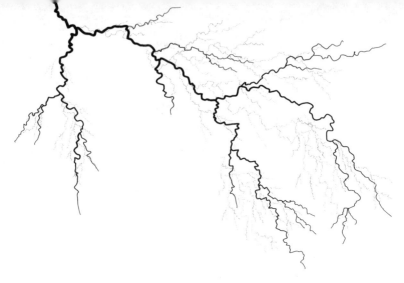

CHAPTER SEVENTEEN

Of course friends are difficult! They're worth it, too. It's a relationship just as strong as any romantic one you might have. Stronger sometimes.
—Solange Aidar Delaney

Zoe and Cilla were meeting us in the park for a picnic and practice. Neither Cilla nor I had done any work with our powers outside the house, or in front of anyone aside from our "partners" yet, so this was a step up for both of us.

Apparently Cilla's kroma was emerging at the normal rate for a recently turned person; that in addition to his constant worry about someone sniffing out my badassedness meant that Wells reminded me continuously not to "show off" when we met them.

"Everyone's levels are different," he said, shutting the front door behind us. "Things that come easily to one person may take someone else decades of practice. Kromatic talents that develop naturally in one person may never emerge in another."

"So it's like everything else in life," I snarked as we stepped onto the sidewalk leading downhill.

"Are you always so surly when you're looking forward to something?" he asked. "Remind me to stop planning outings for you."

I smashed my lips together to hold back another sarcastic retort and glared at the walkway in front of us. "Sorry, I'm a little nervous," I muttered finally.

"Why are you nervous? Yesterday you were dancing around saying everything was going to be fine."

I sighed, stuffed my hands in my pockets, and mumbled an answer.

He tugged at my sleeve. "I didn't hear you, Imogen."

My cheeks heated, but I made myself look at him. "First of all, I was not dancing. Second of all . . ." I lowered my voice. "What if she doesn't like me and doesn't think I'm funny."

Wells laughed, the sound bouncing off the houses on either side of us.

"Making friends this way is hard!" I said. I usually integrated myself in a group or activity where I could blend in until I found out if I clicked. There was no blending in here. And no activity that I was familiar with. I could feel my shoulders curving inward. "I'm kind of an acquired taste."

Wells threw an arm across my shoulders and gave me a squeeze. "You're very likable, Imogen. Try not to set anything on fire and I'm sure it will go just fine."

I had accidentally set the dining room curtains on fire the evening before with an exuberant attempt at lighting all the candles on the table at once. Perhaps Wells's constant reminders to avoid showing off were well placed.

He gave my shoulders one last hug before releasing me. "Look," he said, pointing to the park bench we were nearing.

Zoe and Cilla were already there. Cilla shot to her feet and waved at me like I was a long-lost friend. My face split into a grin.

After initial greetings and introductions—Cilla gave me an unrestrained bear hug—Wells and Zoe sat on the park bench while Wells filled her in on the current standing of our situation with Al after she'd asked about my registration status and the writeups she'd seen. None of which aligned with what she knew to be the truth.

"It honestly makes me wonder what else the prince has done that the palace is covering up," she said heatedly.

Cilla and I sprawled on a blanket they had spread on the grass nearby while she told me how a consensual turning went down.

She and Zoe met on a yoga retreat. Zoe, glamoured to look human, caught Cilla's eye right away and they started dating as soon as they returned to LA, where Zoe told Cilla she had just moved. Giving Cilla what was apparently the agreed upon line—she'd grown up in a strict household with no television and little access to pop culture—Zoe happily allowed Cilla to introduce her to all of her favorites and within months they were basically living with each other. Five months in, Zoe started to drop hints about having to "move back home" to some small island off the coast of Portugal that she had invented. An island that had no internet and very poor cell service.

"It was breaking my heart," Cilla told me, belly down on the blanket, chin propped on her hands, her bare legs lazily kicking in the air behind her. She wore a yellow sundress that complimented her tan skin, her honey blond hair cascading down around her shoulders. "I finally asked her if I could just come with her. That's when we had the big discussion and she told me what she was."

"Did you freak out?" I asked. I was lying on my side, head pillowed on my bicep, completely engrossed in her story.

Cilla shook her head. "No, she did it really well. She said if I wanted to come, she would be the happiest she'd ever been, but that if I decided it was too much, she'd understand. Then she took the glamour off and told me I could ask as many questions as I wanted and we could stay up all night talking about it if I needed to."

She dropped her arms down to the blanket and rested her cheek on top of them. "I mean, she was still the same person I had fallen in love with. She just looked a bit different is all."

"How did you tell your family?" I asked.

"Oh, they didn't agree with my 'lifestyle choice,'" she threw up some finger quotes as she rolled onto her back, "when I came out to them a couple of years ago. I didn't bother saying anything to them. They stopped speaking to me when their intervention didn't have the desired effect." The hurt was evident in the hardness of her voice. "I told my friends I was moving overseas with Zoe and spent a couple of weeks getting rid of my stuff, saying goodbye, and getting tons of pictures printed out."

"You were able to take stuff with you?" I asked, propping my head up on a fist.

"Oh yeah." She twirled a blade of grass between her fingers. "Lots of photo albums, some books, all my clothes, a quilt my friend Joanna made for me, jewelry . . ." She trailed off and glanced over at me. "You didn't get to bring anything, did you?"

I shook my head, swallowing down the tightness in my throat as I pulled a loose thread out of the blanket. "Just what I was wearing at the time. Didn't get to say goodbye to anyone either."

"That really sucks," she whispered. "I'm sorry."

I nodded. "Thanks." I decided to change the subject. "Did you get to bring any music with you or anything?"

She sighed, letting her arms flop down to the blanket beside her. "No. No electronic stuff at all. I can't believe this society is so advanced that two ladies can have a baby and they can travel through multiple galaxies in a matter of days, but they don't even have like . . . the equivalent of a record player."

"Well, from what I've gathered, reproduction has been their hot button issue for . . . I guess all of time." My fully charged phone rested in my back pocket like a ten-pound weight. I wanted to share it with Cilla so badly, but I hadn't even let Wells see that I'd taken it out of the house. He'd told me not to show it around or I'd risk getting it confiscated and destroyed.

I made a decision. I rolled onto my stomach, facing away from the park bench, sliding the phone from my pocket and cradling it against my chest. I purposefully switched to English when I whispered, "C'mere. I have a secret."

Cilla didn't ask questions, she just rolled over and scooted her shoulders next to mine. I opened the music app, turned the volume down on the phone, and pressed play, placing it on the blanket between us. Cilla gasped and clutched my arm.

"Ohmigodohmigod!" she whisper-screamed. "Do you have any Prince?"

"I think at least one song..."

Our heads were so close they were touching. We held completely still as our eyes followed my finger scrolling carefully through the list of downloaded songs. A shadow fell across the phone.

Wells sighed. "Imogen, you're not supposed to—"

Cilla threw her arms around me and the phone, collapsing us both down on top of it. She glared ferociously at Wells. "You can't take it from her! She doesn't have anything else!"

Wells knelt down in front of us, giving Zoe an amused look over our heads. "I'm not going to take it from her, Cilla. But she needs to put it away so that no one else is tempted to either. Imogen, hand me your... phone and I'll 'port it back into your room. Then we can practice before we eat."

Zoe wanted to warm Cilla up a bit with some basic summoning, so Wells decided to hone my shield skills.

He tossed his indigo projectiles at me, instructing me to shrink or expand my shield based on the power or size of the blast I was being hit with. If I was being hit with something small, it was a waste of energy to throw up an enormous shield.

After the first few attempts, I was in the zone, even deflecting Wells's blasts back at him occasionally, forcing him to throw up his own shield. In spite of Wells's instructions not to show off, I couldn't deny the giddy pride inflating my chest when we got a decent volley going. However, Wells called a stop to it a few moments after Cilla and Zoe stopped their own practice to watch. His eyes scanning the park.

"That's so awesome!" Cilla said.

"Do you wanna try?" I asked. It felt rude not to involve them.

"Oh, I can't really do any . . . I'm a lover not a fighter type of person." She blushed. "It's fun to watch though. And I'm okay with like, spells out of books and stuff."

"I keep telling you, not everyone needs to be a fighter," Zoe said, smoothing a lock of Cilla's hair behind her ear. "Your own kromas will serve you fine."

"What kind of stuff does your kroma do?" I was curious to see something new and also wondering if Wells had spell books in our library. I had not been told about spell books.

Cilla looked at the ground, her shimmering aura dimming a bit, and muttered something about "total Hufflepuff BS."

"Why is everyone down on Hufflepuffs? Hufflepuffs probably make the best friends because they don't have so much drama. I would very much like to see your Hufflepuff Kroma," I said, ignoring Wells's perplexed stare.

"Cilla showed this to me on Earth," Zoe explained to him patiently. "It's from a story about a magical human boy named Harry Potter."

"Oh!" Wells said. "Imogen was going on about that yesterday. Sometimes I have no idea what she's saying."

I rolled my eyes and turned back to Cilla, rotating my wrist in a "go on" gesture.

"Okay," she said, kneeling in the grass. "This is the only kind of neat thing . . ." She pushed her hands through the blades, spreading her fingers wide . . . and all the grass around her began to grow and bloom before our eyes. In a matter of seconds, she was surrounded by a small wildflower thicket.

"That is so. COOL," I said. "Do you have to be touching it with your hands or does it work if you have bare feet on it? Can you only make things that are already there bigger or can you grow whatever you want wherever you want it? Have you tried to like . . . grow a beanstalk or anything?"

Cilla grinned, basking in the glow of my enthusiasm. Her aura was back to its usual robust gleam. She stood up and kicked off her sandals. "I haven't tried doing it with my shoes off, that's a good idea." She wiggled her toes, burrowing them within the surrounding blades. She took a deep breath and the thicket she had just created receded. She lifted a hand in front of her, focused on her upturned palm . . . and grew a lavender wildflower.

She tucked it behind my ear, smiling. "It matches your eyes."

Ignoring the twist in my stomach, I pulled the flower out of my hair and studied it. "Oh, my God," I said, then grinned at her. "You are GROOT!"

She gasped. "I am totally Groot. That makes it so much cooler." She shot a flower at me. I caught it, smiling. It was the most I'd smiled in weeks.

"This is from a movie about some guardians of a galaxy," Zoe said to Wells. "I found it very strange."

"How many of their movies did you actually sit through? That was a bizarre experience," Wells said.

We ignored them. "What other kind of stuff can you do?" Cilla asked.

"Well, I did this new thing yesterday—"

"What new thing?" Wells snapped to attention.

"It's nothing big, I don't think," I assured him. "It's how I figured out how to charge my phone." I touched my fingertips together and focused on the electricity. Gooseflesh flashed out across my skin. I sucked in a breath. Outside among the trees and grass, with the open sky above, this felt different. The charge zipped up my spine, shot down my nerves, and my hands were wreathed in lightning instantly with no effort on my part.

"Whoa," Cilla breathed. "Can you like . . ." She punched a fist into the air. "Thor, god of thunder?"

I grinned. "I don't know, I've never tried." Before Zoe or Wells could ask what "Thor, god of thunder" was, I imitated Cilla and punched my fist skyward. The air around us crackled. The wind picked up. The current I'd felt zipping up my spine enlarged and engulfed my entire core. Clouds converged overhead and a bolt of lightning split the sky, pulsing back and forth from my body directly into the clouds. I felt heady with excess power thrumming through me. Somewhere behind the roaring of electricity in my ears I heard Wells yelling my name. With effort, I bent my elbow and pulled my fist from the current I'd created. As soon as the line was broken, the energy dissipated so suddenly I felt like I'd been dropped. I stumbled. Cilla grabbed my elbow to steady me, then Wells was there, gripping my upper arm and pushing me to sit on the blanket. Zoe followed, herding Cilla. Wells 'ported our lunch over still maintaining his hold on my arm.

"Did anyone see that those clouds came from us? Is anyone coming over?" Wells snapped.

Zoe was already glancing around the park. "There's only a handful of people in the area. And I don't think anyone knew it came from us. Maybe just thought it was a random lightning strike," she said. The storm clouds I'd gathered were already separating back into their pleasant, non-threatening, fluffy poufs.

"Sorry," I said breathlessly. I still felt like I'd been supercharged. "I didn't know that would happen."

Wells's grip on my arm tightened. His fingers curled around my chin, lifting it until I met his gaze. His eyes were blazing, more red now than brown, but concern pulsed through his aura. "How do you feel?" His words were clipped. "Dizzy? Faint? Nauseated?" He scanned my face as if checking for injuries.

I tried to shake my head, but he didn't let go. "No, I feel great actually. And no one saw..."

His aura flashed. The concern drained away replaced by red shoots of anger. I braced myself for a scolding but rallied for a fight. I hadn't shown off intentionally. "Anyone could have been hurt, Imogen. *You* could have been—"

Zoe touched his knee. "Have you set ground rules?" she asked gently.

It was as if she'd let the air out of him. His fingers slackened on my arm and he released my chin. He dropped his gaze, blew out a breath, and shook his head. Zoe patted his leg. "You need to set ground rules or she won't know..."

"I'm such an idiot," he whispered, staring at the blanket between us. My righteous indignation ebbed away. His previously spicy aura was now dulled with the ocher shades of guilt and thrumming with blue-black concern. Not just concern that we'd be spotted, but concern for me. I'd scared him.

"No, this isn't your fault," Zoe said. "Neither of you had any orientation together. The expedition heads never planned for this situation. They didn't know what to do with the three of you. And Imogen is obviously... special. There is no way she could know what she's capable of. We don't even know. Her heritage is unique. With sidhe pairings, powers and level of power are usually obvious to some degree based on genetics. Watching a turned human develop is always unique in terms of where their talents may lie, but power level is usually predictable after the first week. But turning a talented sidhe into a human and then turning one of her descendants sidhe..." She shrugged.

Wells rubbed my arm where he'd been hauling me around. "I'm sorry Imogen. I'm doing my best." He finally looked up at me. "And I know you are too."

"Set ground rules that both of you understand. Make sure she knows *why* it's a rule." Zoe ticked points off on her fingers. "Make a repetitive pattern for your days at first to avoid unnecessary stress. And be sure one of you is taking a tonic. No attempts at pregnancy for the first several weeks until her powers are more settled."

Both of us blushed.

"That's not a... we're not... partners," Wells stammered.

"Oh, right, of course," Zoe said smoothly, but I caught the sly glance she shared with Cilla, brief as it was.

Some of the lightness returned to the conversation as we ate, but I could tell that Cilla and Zoe were being intentionally upbeat for our benefit. There was a shadow clinging to Wells and me. It was still an enjoyable meal, and when we finally parted ways, Zoe and Wells agreed to add our park meetings into a routine at least until the two of them had to return to work. When Cilla and I hugged goodbye, she whispered that she thought my lightning was incredibly cool. Zoe winked the two of them out and Wells offered me his arm. I took it. We walked in silence until we reached the sidewalk and left the park behind. I searched for some way to shift the heaviness that had settled around us.

"I'm sorry, I didn't know it was gonna be so . . . big."

Wells placed a hand over mine and squeezed. "I apologize for reacting the way I did." He met my eyes and forced a smile. "Once again, you blew past me unexpectedly and it was rather terrifying."

I chewed my lower lip, unsure what to say.

"I know you didn't do it intentionally. And thank heavens no one saw, but more than that, there's a cost when using kroma, Imogen. I'm sure you've noticed that you're perhaps tired, or even hungry after practicing for a while? And you were exhausted after holding that shield on the ship, which should have been beyond you."

I nodded. "But I felt . . . like I had even *more* energy after my Thor moment."

"Regardless, whatever you did was incredibly powerful. That kind of kroma doesn't come without a cost. Whether it comes immediately or with time." His hand remained on mine as we neared the house. "It could be as simple as you burning out and being unable to wield any kroma for a few days, or it could be worse. We'd have to find someone with lightning kroma to have a better understanding."

I let that settle. Every action has an equal and opposite reaction. Made sense.

"Do you want to suggest any ground rules in particular, Imogen?" he asked me quietly.

I shrugged. "I'm not sure I would even know what kind to make."

We were at the front door before he spoke again. "I'll make the first one then, shall I?" He opened the door and we stepped inside. "Feel free to add on later if anything comes to you." He shut the door behind us.

"Okay," I agreed.

Wells took my hand from his arm, held it in both of his and turned to face me. "Ground rule number one. If you exhibit *any* kind of new power, no matter how trivial you think it is, please tell me immediately."

"What if you're sleeping?"

"Wake me up."

"What if you're in the shower?"

He opened his mouth to respond, then snapped it shut. His cheeks pinked and he narrowed his eyes at me. I really did enjoy making him blush.

I lost control of my face and my mouth twisted into a smirk, even as warmth crept across my own skin. "What if *I'm* in the shower?"

"If either of us are in the shower, you will wait until we are both decent and then inform me as soon as possible," he said evenly.

"What if it's water kroma and it only works when I'm soaking wet." I barely got the last two words out before they were swallowed by my giggle.

He flung my hand away and stalked into the kitchen. "Go upstairs and play with your phone you . . . utter child." He didn't quite turn around fast enough to hide his half smile.

That night I had another Earth nightmare.

My own memorial service. They had put up a headstone and I was stuck to the ground in front of it. My friends and family were gathered around, weeping. My father was sobbing uncontrollably, my two uncles holding him up. My heart shattered, tears streamed down my face. I tried to touch him, but couldn't reach. My legs wouldn't move.

"I'm okay, Dad, I'm here, I'm okay!" He couldn't hear me. None of them could see or hear me. I tried again, tried to shout, but my words got stuck leaving my throat.

Then my uncles patted Dad on the back and pulled him away. I struggled harder, choking on my tears, but I couldn't move. One by one, they all turned away and left.

I couldn't wrench my legs free. Sobs racked my body as each one of them turned from me. My heart cracking open. My lungs filling with my own tears. My inhales going nowhere. Keane was the last to leave, his face haggard with grief. He dropped a rose at my feet. "Goodbye, Imogen."

They were leaving me behind.

I screamed but it didn't go anywhere. Only a rasping cry scraped out. My own sobs were strangling me. I couldn't breathe. I woke in the throes of another laryngospasm, my face wet. Moonlight from both full double moons spilled in through the windows. I thrashed to get free of the sweat-soaked sheets I had tangled myself in. Wheezing loudly. Unable to pull in a breath. My door burst open and Wells came barreling in, half-dressed, still tying his pants, his aura spinning with alarm. I was reaching for him even before he latched onto my arms.

"Imogen, TAKE A BREATH."

My vocal cords relaxed. My lungs obeyed. But I hadn't stopped crying. He compelled four more breaths before he realized I was no longer choking, but sobbing. He pushed my tangled hair back from my face.

"Oh, Imogen." He folded me into his arms and let me cry. "I'm so, so sorry."

When my weeping subsided, Wells made to tuck me back into bed. Panic punched me in the chest and I hung on to him. "Don't leave! Don't leave! They were all leaving me..."

"Okay, okay, not leaving. Just...repositioning." He managed to get me under the covers, then lay beside me on top of them, leaving one arm flung across my torso for me to cling to.

My heart still beat wildly. My breath hitching. But the panic slowly drained away. "S-sorry," I whispered, embarrassed but unwilling to let him go.

He gave me a squeeze. "You have nothing to be sorry for, Imogen. Try to get some rest. I'm not leaving you."

He fell asleep before I did. I listened to the slow rhythm of his breathing. And eventually drifted off.

When the sun woke me in the morning, Wells was gone. But his scent lingered. And the covers beside me were still warm. As if he'd only just slipped out.

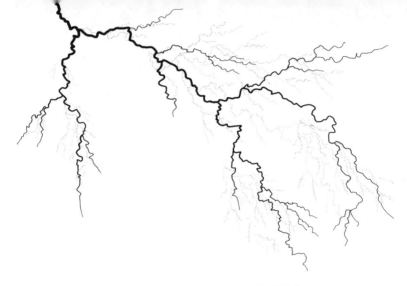

CHAPTER EIGHTEEN

Just make sure you've got each other's six. Be home by ten.
—Solange Aidair Delaney, to Imogen Delaney and friend, age fourteen,
off to roll bullies' houses.

We followed Zoe's instructions and set up a routine for our days, which included meeting Zoe and Cilla in the park every other day. The days we didn't meet with them, Wells and I trained there on our own. The attempts at ambushing us at home slacked off and with it some of Wells's tension; even so, we didn't work on lightning again. Wells didn't know anything about that particular power and until we found someone else who did, he didn't want to risk injury to me or anyone else around. I was so freaked out by his reaction the first time I was happy to comply.

Eventually the lunar cycle—for both moons—came and went and Zoe and Wells had to return to work. Zoe, it turned out, worked in the research branch of the army's compound, so she and Wells were on the same campus.

To Cilla's and my utter delight, they decided the two of us could practice in the park together in the morning. One of them would meet us for lunch and make sure we both got to our respective homes before returning to work.

"No new skills. Only the kromas you both know well," Wells said as he and Zoe dropped us at the park bench that had become our meeting place. "Everyone knows who you two are, so you might get a few people gawking, but try not to draw undue attention to yourselves." He directed that last at me. I pasted a look of bland innocence on my face. "And don't wave your dagger around, Imogen. I'm glad you like it, but keep it in your boot, please."

Wells had given me a fantastic dagger as a present to celebrate the survival of my first lunar cycle in Molnair. He said it was inspired by the one I had thrown on the ship, but this one was much prettier. The blade itself was honed from some kind of dark alloy, making it a shimmering storm gray rather than the usual silver. The hilt was inlaid with a deep blue. It fit perfectly inside a sheath nestled along my calf in my tall boots. I immediately toted it around with me everywhere. Although Wells wouldn't let me throw it at anything, which I considered a bit of a bait and switch.

"I wouldn't 'wave it around' like a prat anyway," I huffed. Cilla giggled. Wells gave me a pointed look.

"I promise we won't talk to strangers and we'll hold hands when crossing the street."

He folded his arms. "You should have no reason to cross the street, you've promised to stay in the park."

Cilla buried her snort into Zoe's shoulder as she hugged her goodbye.

I successfully choked back a laugh. "It's a joke that didn't translate. Don't be nervous, we'll be fine, and we'll stay in the park and I won't do anything crazy." I reached up and tugged him into a hug, holding for an extra beat before switching with Cilla. Wells's aura was spikey with stress.

"Have fun," Zoe said, giving me a squeeze. "It'll probably be me coming to collect you today."

"Have fun at work," I said as I pulled away.

Zoe gave Wells a pat on the arm and an understanding smile before they both winked out.

Cilla and I marched toward the tree line, our auras sparking at the prospect of several unsupervised hours stretching ahead of us. Still, by unspoken agreement, we headed for a clearing several feet back from any marked trails.

Neither of us really thought we were going to be bothered, but if someone came up to me and asked about my powers or, heaven forbid, the circumstances surrounding my turning, I didn't know if I'd be able to dissemble. And how would either of us be able to tell if they were just a curious sidhe or some evil sidhe with nefarious intentions?

"Do you have your phone?" Cilla whispered in English, although no one was nearby. We knew everyone could understand us if they tried, but it was fun to speak English together occasionally.

"No," I grumbled. "It's one of the new ground rules. I'm not allowed to take it out of the house without specifically asking if it's okay. I'll save you the suspense; it's never okay."

We found a spot among the trees and started playing with Cilla's plant kroma. She was now able to shoot blades of grass and flowers from her hands if she wished, but she wanted something more substantial and "Grootlike."

"Like vines," she said, shaking another bouquet of wildflowers from her fingers. "Vines would be cool."

"Maybe you should try touching something more . . . viney. Like . . . go stick your leg on that tree," I said.

"My leg?"

"Leg, foot, boob, whatever, I'm sure the tree doesn't care."

She chuckled and dutifully walked over to a tree. She carefully set her foot atop the hump of an exposed root. "I don't wanna like . . . step too hard."

"Cilla, the tree is huge, and much stronger than you. Your little foot isn't going to hurt it." I demonstrated by hauling myself up to sit astride the low hanging branch of the tree across from her.

It was the only one in our clearing that had bright blue leaves. It was my favorite.

"Yeah, you're probably right." She settled her left foot firmly on the root and found another foothold for her right. "Okay." She took a deep breath. "Here goes."

I held still as she shut her eyes and gathered her focus. Her aura shifted, waving around her like leaves on the wind. Her feet appeared to meld with the tree, the skin darkening. Her normal aura of sparkling blues and pinks shifted as her kroma sang to the earth. A purpley-brown glow at the intersection of skin and bark flowed up her legs, crawled across her torso, then down her arms. Eyes still closed, she lifted her hands, took a breath, and opened her fists on the exhale. Vines shot out of them both. One wrapping around the tree branch I had perched on, one shooting off harmlessly in another direction.

"Cilla!" I gasped. "Look what you did!"

"*I'm so cool.*" She stared at her hands, wide-eyed, then grinned up at me. "It wasn't that hard!"

I tugged on the vine. It was firmly attached. I waved the end back and forth. It was flexible. "Hey, make us rope swings."

Minutes later we were soaring on our own homemade vine-rope swings. Cilla had even decorated them with morning glories. I loved it when Cilla created familiar Earth flowers. With her floaty summer dress—green today—and long blond hair, adorned with a crown of daisies, she truly looked as though she belonged in this beautiful place. As opposed to me, with my dark blue tank top and sturdy gray pants stuffed into knee high boots. Although my messy dark bob had been decorated with a chain of little purple flowers courtesy of my friend.

"Are you sure it wasn't *your* grandmother who was sidhe?" I called out to her as we swung past each other. "You look like you were born here."

"I'm positive," she said. Then she let go of her swing at the apex of its upward sweep, floating gracefully to the ground. I imitated her, but tucked into a shoulder roll for my landing, springing to my feet just in front of her.

Cilla dusted off my back. "My grandmother told me I was going to hell and even described which circle I would be in. She had pictures of renaissance paintings as visual aids."

"What? Seriously?"

"I know, right?" She tossed her hair over a shoulder and bent to pick up her sandals. "It would have been funny if I hadn't been crying my eyes out already."

"That sucks, Cilla, I'm sorry that happened." I steadied her with a hand on her arm as she stood on one leg to slide her shoes on. Her aura was crimped in painful browns and dark blues.

"Yeah, thanks. But I'm way happier now and much better off. Do you wanna go see the river?" She turned to walk deeper into the forest. I saw the normal sparkling sky blues and pinks trying to force the browns and navies away.

"Sure," I said, accepting her change of subject. "I've actually never seen it."

"Really? Oh, Zoe took me one of the first times we came here. It's a bit farther from . . . you know, people."

"Did y'all go to the river to make out?" I raised my eyebrows at her, grinning.

She laughed. Cilla was the only person I'd ever met whose laugh sounded glittery. "We *totally* did," she said with a lazy smile.

It didn't take us too terribly long to reach the river, the background noise of the city faded away. The sound of running water ahead grew louder, mingling with the chirping of birds and breeze playing in the leaves. I could understand why Zoe had brought Cilla here. It was just far enough away to feel private. One of those little oases of nature in the middle of a populated metropolis.

Cilla kicked off her shoes once again and splashed right into the crystalline flowing water. "Oooo, it's a little chilly today!"

"How deep is it?" I asked from the shoreline. "It's so clear . . ."

"It's shallow until right here and then there's a big drop off. Like the edge of a cliff." The river darkened into navy past the spot she indicated.

"Scary. I'll stay here." I squatted down at the water's edge to test the temperature with a finger. "Can you drink it, do you think?"

Cilla splashed back toward me. "I don't know if you can drink it . . . I mean, it looks like you could, but we're in the middle of a city, you know?" She crouched down at the water line next to me, shoulder to shoulder, her bare toes sinking into the soft soil. "What are you looking at?"

"Look at these little stones . . ." I pointed out a purple one.

An odd wind brushed our backs. The hairs on the nape of my neck stood up. I grabbed Cilla's wrist.

"Well, hello there." A silky voice behind us.

I stood, whipping around to face two strange sidhe males strolling toward us. Both with silver hair, pale skin, and yellow eyes. Both grinning like devils. Both with swords hanging at their hips. *Okay, so I can tell when they have nefarious intentions.*

"Hello," said Cilla, frowning. I shoved her behind me. Her feet made twin splashes in the river. The two sidhe separated, one with longer hair sauntering three feet to the right. My stomach flipped. They were cutting us off.

"It's your lucky day, darlings. We thought you might like to see another country on this planet. Since you're so new," purred the shorter-haired of the two. "We could take you on a little tour." They knew who we were.

"No thank you," Cilla said. "We're fine here."

I stared them down. Watching their hands. Relaxed at their sides. Within easy reach of their swords. They didn't go for them. Not yet. Their auras were swirling just slightly too fast to be calm. Blues and greens punctuated with splashes of gold.

They were excited. They thought we'd be easy targets. And we might be. I flexed my fingers, rolling to the balls of my feet. Two of them with swords. I only had a dagger. And Cilla was defenseless. I internally cursed myself for not bringing my phone before realizing that it would do no good. Then I remembered overhearing Wells 'path to Al during the parade. How had I forgotten to ask him about that?

Wells! WellsWellsWells! I tried it desperately anyway. Throwing my focus toward that sense of him I remembered. *Zoe!* Why not try everything? *ZoeZoeZoe! Help!*

"Oh, we weren't really asking, you see," said the longer-haired one, grinning like a wolf. He took two steps toward us.

My dagger flew into my palm. "We're not going with you."

As one they reached for their swords.

Two jets of water shot out from either side of me. Straight into their faces. I saw Cilla's arms bracketing my shoulders. She'd bought us a sliver of time.

With my free hand I grabbed her wrist and sprinted away from them along the river, angling toward the trees as soon as we were clear. If Cilla could throw some vines. Even climb up and get away . . .

The short-haired one winked in front of us. Sword out. Dripping wet. No longer smiling.

Fuck. Winking. I forgot about that.

I spun around. The other was behind us. I put Cilla's hand on my shoulder and pushed out a shield with my free hand. "Stay behind me. Don't let them touch you." *Wells! WELLS! We're in trouble! By the river. They have swords! Zoe! By the river! Help! They're trying to take us!* I didn't know if it was even working. I had to let it go and concentrate on their auras.

"So cute," Long Hair purred, his eyes glinting malevolently as he shoved back a dripping strand of hair. "She's going to try to stop us and protect her little friend with that tiny knife." He lifted his sword and took a lazy stab at my face. The world slowed down and I parried easily.

I hadn't noticed the other one edging back until he thrust at Cilla. I parried, then only just managed to deflect Long Hair's slice at my shoulder.

Even with my slo-mo advantage, the fact that they had swords and I had a dagger was a challenge. The fact that there were *two* of them made it worse. The fact that Cilla was behind me made it almost impossible. I couldn't move freely. For a few minutes they toyed with us, taking turns tossing out thrusts and slices. Although I could see they were surprised at how quickly I was blocking them, they were far from concerned. They merely upped the tempo.

Their auras telegraphed their moves, but my focus was split. Cilla had slowed down with the rest of the world, her fingers digging into my shoulders as I dodged and twisted. Sweat dampened my hairline. Other than being soaking wet, they both looked fresh. If only I'd stayed closer to the river, then at least Cilla could have shot more water at them.

"Well, this really has been amusing, but I'm getting bored," moaned Short Hair. Quick as a snake he hurled a javelin of white-gold kroma at us. I spun and expanded my shield. It held, despite shuddering with the impact, but left Cilla open a second too long. She gasped as Long Hair's sword tip caressed her bare arm. I whirled and knocked it away, my eyes locking with Long Hair's as a smirk twisted his lips.

This is bullshit, I thought. "Cilla, piggyback me, now!"

She mercifully leapt right onto my back, no questions asked. Her long legs wrapped my hips and she flung her arms around my shoulders. She was a good piggybacker. She held herself up and didn't strangle me. Now I could move. They pressed harder. Both throwing orange and maroon kroma in between thrusts, trying to crack my shield. Several times they succeeded and I was forced to push more energy to reform it. But now I had complete range of motion and could go full speed. It was easier to defend the blade attacks. Which was all I could do. My mind was too occupied with reading their auras and maintaining my shield to even consider attempting offensive kroma. Our one advantage was that they didn't want us dead.

Wounding, however, didn't appear to be a concern.

My tank was soaked with sweat. My arms trembled. My only plan as I panted my way through another volley of blade attacks was get to the tree line so Cilla could get away or work some defensive kroma of her own. I caught a slice across my throat. Tilted my head in time for it to graze along the side, but it was still a hit. Healing took energy like anything else. A jab to my calf. I blocked a double blast by wrapping my shield around us, but it dropped me to my knees.

"Knock her out!" Long Hair barked, now continually hurling kroma to keep me occupied. I needed to get to my feet. I hauled one foot up. Got sliced across the knee. Short Hair pulled the hilt of his sword back. I prepared to block the blow to my head.

Twin blasts of air exploded feet from us. Wells and Zoe winked in. Armed to the teeth. Their eyes promising death.

An inarticulate cry of relief burst from Cilla. The two silver-haired assholes swiveled to see what was behind them. Barely in time to defend themselves from Wells's twin blades and Zoe's bad-ass MACE! *She has a fucking mace, that's awesome!* My inner nerd apparently still had some energy.

I staggered to my feet just as Wells yelled, "Get out of here! Back to the street!"

I didn't hesitate, launching into a full sprint with Cilla still clinging to me like a burr. I didn't dare put my dagger away. Even as part of my brain chided, *running with scissors* . . . I crashed through the woods at breakneck speed. It's a wonder I didn't trip and impale us both.

Cilla warbled in relief when the light between the trees grew brighter. We burst into the park like a two-headed bat out of hell. I didn't stop running until I reached the sidewalk. Until I was within easy sight of many, many people.

I skidded to a stop at a sidewalk-adjacent water fountain. Gasping. My legs trembling. Cilla slid off my back. I turned to face her. Dagger still out. Still scanning the area. "You . . . hurt?" I panted.

Her face was pale, her eyes were wide and bright. She shook her head. The slice on her arm was already closing. "No, but *you*!" She reached for the cut on my neck. I grabbed her hand and held it.

"Not yet," I gasped. "Stay alert . . . just in case . . . they could wink . . ."

We stood, hand in hand. Cilla petrified and windswept. Me scuffed up and breathless, gripping my dagger. We got a few startled looks from passersby but I didn't care. Let them look at us. They'd be more apt to notice if something happened.

"Do you think they're okay?" Cilla breathed.

It had only been a few minutes, but it seemed like an eternity. Her dark brown eyes were brimming with silver.

A burst of wind. I raised the dagger. But it was Zoe. As soon as she saw us, she 'ported her mace away and grabbed our wrists.

CHAPTER NINETEEN

It's always going to be hard to do some things.
To get to the end of the day sometimes.
It's the person helping to pick up your pieces that gets you through.
—Henry Delaney

We were pulled through the black void for half a blink and then we were standing in front of Wells's house.

"You'll have to let us in, Imogen, it will only open for someone who lives here," Zoe said, pushing me to the front door.

"Where's—" I staggered up the four short steps.

"He's taking them to the palace dungeons for interrogation," she answered. "In! In!"

I opened the door and she shoved us inside. "Llewellyn has stronger wards on his house than we have on ours," Zoe explained to Cilla as she herded us into the main room. Cilla tried to hug her but Zoe held her away. "Are you hurt? Let me see."

"No." Cilla showed her the half-healed cut on her arm. "I only got this little one, but Imogen..."

Zoe snapped around to me, eyes raking me up and down. "You are a bit of a mess. And you're not healing. You're drained. Sit down." She pushed me into the nearest chair and pulled off my boots. My dagger's scabbard clattered to the floor. "Good thing you had that with you after all," she said. I sucked in a sharp breath when she touched her fingers to the bleeding gouge in my calf. It slowly clotted.

"How did you know to come?" Cilla asked, settling onto an ottoman next to Zoe.

Zoe's eyes flicked up to mine. "Imogen called us. Did Wells know you were a telepath?"

"I... I didn't really know..." I flinched as she found the gash above my knee. "It just seemed like a good thing to try. I was feeling a little... out of my depth."

The corners of Zoe's mouth twitched up. "The second attempt was better. The first one I thought I was being paranoid about leaving the two of you. Making things up in my head." Finished with my knee, she pulled the dagger out of my right hand and set it on a nearby table. My hand was covered in small cuts that I hadn't registered. She gently touched each one. "You'll have little scars for a day or two. It's always like that when someone else has to help you heal. They'll go away though."

"Did you get hurt?" I asked, leaning back in the chair. My eyes kept traveling to the door. I wondered how long Wells was going to be interrogating those assholes.

Zoe snorted. "We had them down in no time. It's a shame you couldn't stay to watch, but neither of us would have been able to concentrate with you two still in the area." She shook her head. I was having trouble reading her aura. The colors had faded into transparent waves. "If one of them had been able to grab hold of you, even for a second, they would have winked you back to Sephrya and who knows how long it would have been before we'd even realized where you'd been taken."

"Why did they want to take us to Sephrya?" Cilla asked.

"That's what we need—" Zoe was interrupted by a cool breeze as Wells winked directly into the entryway.

"Imogen!" He crossed the room in three long strides.

"I'm not done healing her," Zoe said, but she moved out of the way as he hauled me out of the chair and pulled me into a hug. He didn't let go.

I hugged back, sagging against him. My head fit right under his chin. "This is nice," I said after a few seconds. "I could take a nap right here. But I'd probably bleed on you."

His hands slid to my shoulders and pushed me back. His eyes landed on my wounded neck. "Gods' bones . . ." He seized my chin and tilted my head to the side, smearing my sweat and blood-dampened hair away from the cut. I winced as he pressed his entire palm to the wound.

"I told you," Zoe said, her arms now wrapped around Cilla. "It's as if they were trying to bleed her out over a course of days. Little gashes everywhere."

"They were trying to weaken her." Wells didn't shift his gaze from me while I clung on to his arms for balance. He had my head tilted at an awkward angle. "Couldn't get through her guard as easily as expected and didn't want to kill either of them." His eyes met mine. "You surprised them." He smiled and it warmed my skin like sunshine.

My heart swelled at the fondness in his eyes. No trace of irritation or exasperation. I wished I could read his aura. It had gone transparent, like Zoe's.

He lifted his hand from my neck and ran a finger along the newly formed skin. "Good enough for now." He released my chin. "Where else?"

"I don't even feel anything," I said. The burst of adrenaline had spent itself and left me drained.

"On her arm." Cilla—still wrapped around Zoe—pointed to a wound I didn't even remember receiving. Wells clamped his hand around it. Cilla continued, "And I think the top of her head and somewhere in the middle . . . like her stomach somewhere. Because it kind of hit my legs on the way out. I'm fine, they healed."

Wells pawed through my hair. I hissed and jerked away when his fingers brushed a tender spot.

"All right, I'll go slowly, but let me find it." He stepped behind me, placing one hand at my neck to hold me in place.

Zoe gently disengaged from Cilla and gingerly lifted the hem of my shirt. "By my life, Imogen. How could you not feel this?"

"Did it tear my shirt? I like this shirt. Whoops." My knees buckled, but I caught myself. "Sorry. I'm so tired."

"All right, on the couch with you," Zoe ordered. She pushed me along and Wells after me. "You can do her head, I'll do her stomach. And I'd like to hear what happened at the palace."

I was in enthusiastic support of anything that let me lie down. Wells propped my head up with his thigh while he carefully pushed through my sweat-soaked hair. Zoe knelt down beside my stomach, already going to work. Cilla settled herself by my feet and pulled off my socks.

"Cilla, no, my feet are almost certainly gross right now," I mumbled. My eyes were drooping. Wells rubbing my head felt nice. Even Zoe demanding to know who was interrogating the Sephryans wasn't grabbing my attention hard enough.

"There are energy channels here," Cilla explained, squeezing my feet and smiling at me. "Reflexology for healing. I'm helping."

"'Kay, fine. Thank you." I sighed. "Oh, shit, your sandals—"

"I'll get them back," she said. "Just chill."

I didn't want to open my eyes. I was warm and comfortable and everything smelled good. My return to consciousness was slow, like floating up to the surface of a warm pool. I was still on the couch, but a blanket had been thrown over me. I didn't hear Zoe or Cilla. My head was pillowed on Wells's thigh. I heard the rustle of paper, as if he were paging through documents. One hand gently stroked my hair. Almost absently.

And the pet Earthling metaphor has circled around to literal truth, I thought. I took a deep breath, stretched, rolled to my side and tried to push up.

"Ow... ow..." I collapsed back down, my head smacking into Wells's leg. "Sorry. Everything hurts."

"You'll feel better after you've eaten," he said, setting the pages he'd been looking at on the table in front of him. "Food is on the way. Zoe ordered it for us before she took Cilla home. Cilla was adamant that you not be disturbed until you woke up on your own."

"I'm sorry I trapped you on the couch," I said, feeling more and more like a cat that had fallen asleep on her owner's lap. And yet, I left my head where it was. I really was exhausted.

"It's all right, I've been able to get some work done." He indicated the pile in front of him. "Eat this. It should boost you enough to clean up before the food gets here." He handed me a block.

"How did I ever exist without these things?" I shoved it into my mouth.

Wells chuckled. "I doubt you were even capable of expending the amount of physical and psychic energy in your previous life that you've been producing lately."

I swallowed the block and decided it was fine to stay where I was until it kicked in. Wells didn't seem to mind. "I thought I was getting better at controlling my energy flow," I grumbled. We'd only been working on it every damn day.

"You are." He gave my shoulder a squeeze. "You wouldn't have lasted as long as you did otherwise. Your shield control is excellent. But you've never attempted any kind of telepathic communication before. Let alone at a distance and to a location you'd never been to. You threw your focus blindly toward Zoe and myself—hitting a few other nearby people, I might add—and expended a lot of excess energy in doing so. You probably weren't even aware of it."

"Oh... sorry my cry for help... hit other people." The block was starting to do its work. I straightened into a sitting position.

"It was actually rather helpful in lending some legitimacy to Zoe and me when we grabbed weapons and fled work an hour into our first day back," he said, just as two pieces of paper materialized in front of him. He plucked them from the air, gave them a glance, and set them atop one of his piles. "Obviously both of us are doing what we can from home for the rest of the day."

"Were you and Zoe near each other when you heard me?"

He laughed. "No, we met in the armory. I 'pathed her to meet me there after your second attempt. I didn't know if your message had reached both of us." Warm russet eyes scanned my face. "Feeling better?"

"Yeah, I still can't read your aura though."

"That will probably come back after you eat." His gaze flicked to the clock. "You may want to go upstairs and clean up. I should warn you . . ." He sighed.

"What? Warn me of what?" *Could the rest of the day not just be easy?*

"Al will be here in a bit—"

"Whyyyyyyyyyyyyyyyyyyyyyyyyyyyyyyyyuh." I flopped back to horizontal on the couch. In the opposite direction out of consideration for Wells's leg. It didn't seem fair to subject me to Al after the morning I had survived.

"Reason one, as misguided as he may be, he does care about you, and it was all I could do to prevent him from winking over here immediately to see with his own eyes that you were in one piece." His brows dropped. "Which was made even more difficult as *I* hadn't seen you yet. Although, Zoe let me know you were both safe. Reason two, he was in charge of interrogation and he'll be coming over in an official capacity to let us know what they've learned and what the next steps may be." Tension lined his jaw as he took a breath. "And as he reminded me, his lunar cycle away from you is up as of today. He wants to see you."

I sat back up. "I don't want him to touch me."

"I will be sure to let him know," Wells said mildly, receiving another memo out of thin air.

I pulled my knees up in front of me and wrapped my arms around my shins. My clothes were absolutely filthy. A shower was a fantastic idea. Still I didn't move. I sat staring at my toes.

"Anything else?" Wells asked.

"I don't want him talking about . . ." I chewed on my lower lip. Swallowed against the tightening in my throat. "Talking about *being* with me," I finished. I could feel Wells watching me, but I continued to focus on my toes. My face grew warm.

"I'll tell him in no uncertain terms," he said quietly. "Do you want help getting upstairs? I can wink you if you want."

"No thanks, I'll be fine." I unfolded myself and headed for a shower, spotting my dagger as I passed the table Zoe had set it down on. Someone had cleaned and sheathed it. I took it with me.

Al had arrived by the time I'd cleaned up.

Their voices drifted up the landing as soon as I stepped into the hall from my room. They were in the dining room. My chest caved. I had been hoping to get some food in me first. I got as far as the stairwell and stopped. *I need a minute.* I leaned against the wall opposite the staircase and let myself slide to the ground. *Just a minute to gather myself,* I thought. Although there was a small part of me hoping that if I sat long enough, maybe Al would leave.

". . . don't see how this changes anything. She's still registered to me." Leashed irritation strained Wells's voice.

"We're merely offering an option. Father admits that she'd be safer—" Al. My stomach twisted with dread.

"I don't necessarily agree with that. We've been incredibly cautious. But regardless, it should be Imogen's choice." Wells. *Please don't let him take me. Please don't let him take me.* I'd run away. I'd go to Cilla and Zoe. I bet they'd let me stay until I was on my feet.

"I'm sure you did your best, but she was attacked today," Al continued. I wanted to punch him. This wasn't Wells's fault. "Anyway, I need to at least be able to see her. Otherwise, how is she going to make a decision?"

"If she wants to see you, she can see you. I'm not stopping her." Wells's words were clipped, but even. "She's also asked for her ring back. I don't suppose you've brought that with you?"

Silence for several moments. The scent of the food wafted up the stairwell and my salivary glands went wild. *I should go down. Get it over with. It's not going to get better...*

As if he'd heard my thoughts, Al asked, "Where is she anyway? She is coming, right?"

"She's cleaning up. She was a mess and she's exhausted. I had to give her a block just to get her off the couch," Wells said, his tone now ringing with concern. "Please don't push her, Al. Let her eat first before you scare her out of the room."

Al laughed. "I'm not going to scare—"

"Do not try to touch her," Wells interrupted firmly. "Do not talk about a relationship under any circumstances—"

"You've said this already." Al sighed.

"I'm adding on," Wells bit out. "You will not discuss taking her with you immediately. You won't even offer the *option* until she's eaten. All right?"

Al mumbled something about knowing how to take care of me.

"You're not responsible for her!" Wells was finally fed up. "I *am*. And until that changes, you will follow *my* rules when it comes to Imogen or you will get out."

I'd heard enough. Wells had my back. And I was going to start gnawing on the banister if I forced myself to wait much longer. I clomped down the stairs. I had intentionally dressed in my least feminine pair of pants and a soft, loose V-neck t-shirt, with my hair only towel-dried.

I swung into the room and announced myself. "Hi, I heard shouting. I guess that means Al's here." Containers were spread out on the long, polished, wooden table. Al lounged in one of the center chairs, closest to the door, directly across from the food. Wells stood on the other side, looking like he was trying to wrangle his expression down from "pissed as hell."

I gave Al a wide berth and circled to the opposite side of the room to sit near Wells. I couldn't tell if he had claimed a seat, but I intentionally did not take the one directly across from Al. It appeared as though they had been waiting for me to eat.

"How are you, Im?" Al said, leaning forward. "I was worried about you today. You okay? I feel like I haven't seen you in ages."

I felt his eyes on me, but I didn't look up, glancing down the table at the food. "I'm hungry."

Wells sat down beside me, across from Al, and slid a few containers and a plate my way. "None of these have meat," he said. "Take as much as you want."

I dove in, famished, spooning fat, curly, spring-green noodles onto my plate before reaching for the next container. Soft, poofy, bite-sized bread rolls that appeared to have different savory vegetables cooked inside. I tipped half a dozen onto my plate then poured out a measure of purply sauce I recognized. It had kind of a spicy marinara flavor and I hadn't found anything I didn't enjoy dipping into it. My plate full, I passed the containers back down, and began shoveling food in like it was my job.

"Imogen, it's not going anywhere. Slow down," Wells said, serving himself. Al was picking at a piece of bread, eyes glittering.

"You're not the boss of me." I didn't check my speed. I wanted to eat quickly and leave.

"For all intents and purposes, I am," he said mildly, placing the containers he had finished with in the center of the table. "If you start choking, I'm going to be the one to have to deal with it."

I paused, realized that was basically true, and growled. But I had already burnt my tongue, so I did slow down.

Al laughed, amber eyes dancing. "Doesn't have to be that way, Im."

Wells cut him a glare. "Aloysius, why don't you go ahead and tell us what you learned during your interrogation of Imogen's attackers?"

Al paused, his gaze bouncing from me to Wells. I wished I could read his aura. Finally, he tossed his bread to the table and clasped his hands behind his head, tilting his chair back on two legs. "Well, all right." The corners of his mouth lifted in a grim smile. "To start with, Sephrya's humans are dying."

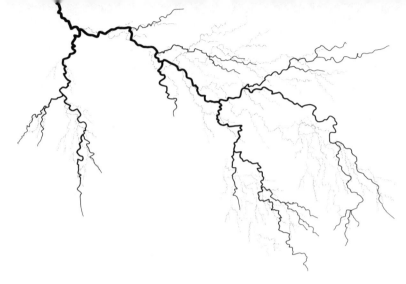

CHAPTER TWENTY

Unfortunately there will always be assholes.
Cut off the head of one and two sprout up in its place.
—Solange Aidair Delaney

"What, all of them?" Wells asked, his fork paused halfway to his mouth.

"Most of them," Al confirmed. "The ones left are either too old to have children or sterile from whatever is killing them." He dropped his chair back down to four legs. "They're probably going to put them down."

"They're just going to kill them because they can't make babies anymore?" I slammed my fork down.

"If they can't figure out how to cure them . . . yeah," Al said, frowning. "We're not talking about the greatest group of people, Im."

"How many humans are left?" Wells asked, his voice strained.

"The two you brought in—Staf and Vel, they're called—didn't know exact numbers. They guessed somewhere in the hundreds."

Wells whistled. "There were thousands last I heard . . ." He cut a glance at me.

"Yeah, well." Al picked up his bread again and tore off a piece. "Not anymore. Anyway, that's why they hit us so hard during re-entry. They were hoping to knock us off course and force us to land in Sephrya. The dual purpose of that being that they'd have our ship, they'd have us to torture into telling them how to get it to Earth and back," he looked at me, "and they'd have our newly turned sidhe to partner with in the meantime. Hypocrites."

"That's more than two purposes. That's three purposes," I deadpanned.

"What's that, Im?" Al smiled.

"You said dual purpose. That implies two purposes. Then you listed three—"

"She's being pedantic." Wells tossed me a look.

I shrugged and tucked back into my meal. "So they were trying to kidnap me and Cilla to turn us into their little fuck bunnies?"

"It would appear so," Al said, even as Wells shook his head at my coarseness. Al continued, "What's more, they're well informed. Seems like they've been watching us—"

"I knew it," Wells said darkly, giving me an "I told you so" glance.

Al continued, "Not that we've tried to keep any of this information hidden—why would we need to—but they knew that most of the partners of our Earthlings would be returning to their various jobs today. There were three more kidnapping attempts this morning—"

"Who?" Wells asked.

"Are they okay?" I said simultaneously.

"Misha, Helga, and Oriia," Al said. "And yes, they all got away, although so did their attackers. Misha was alone on the farm while Lydiata winked some deliveries out, but their dogs protected him. Helga was followed on her way into town but she managed to evade them until several people within a mile radius heard her screaming and winked in to investigate. And Oriia was supposed to be alone, but Simeon couldn't bring himself to leave her and begged a few more days off. She was in the yard when one of them approached her. Simeon winked over and whoever it was realized their mistake and winked out right away."

"So they weren't supposed to get caught," Wells mused.

"Absolutely not." Al flashed his teeth. "By the time you'd snagged Staf and Vel, word was getting around. The other seven either went with their partners to work or hadn't yet left their homes. They were trying to get them early in the day, so there would be more time before they were missed. And as they'd all been instructed to set a pattern to their days, it wasn't difficult to figure out where they might be."

"Has Allestair declared war?" Wells asked, setting his fork down and leaning back.

"You'd be the first to know, brother," Al said. "But no. No matter what I throw at these guys—and we've hurt them—they won't admit to being ordered to kidnap anyone by King Demian. They claim to have been working alone, aiming to build families of their own."

"Bullshit," Wells hissed, eyes flashing.

"Oh, total, total bullshit," Al agreed. "But as usual Sephrya walks the line to keep us from being able to officially claim an act of war. Demian probably forbade them from implicating him. We could take a chance that the other nations *wouldn't* get pissed at us for breaking the treaty and side with Sephrya, but . . ." Al shrugged.

"Allestair won't risk that," Wells finished. "We'd need proof of an actual government sanctioned offense."

"What if one of us actually *got* kidnapped?" I mused, having cleared my plate. Energy was creeping back into my body. "Like going undercover. I mean, surely they'd take us somewhere . . . I dunno, government property or something. Like, we could be a decoy—"

"NO!" they both shouted at me.

"Imogen, getting you back would be nearly impossible," Wells said. Both of them had gone a bit pale. "They'd certainly take you somewhere warded against winking out, even if you had the skill—"

"Okay, okay." I held my palms up. "I was just throwing out a hypothetical. So what happens now? Can I carry the big swords when I go out?"

"Oh, no." Al smirked, resting his forearms on the table. "You're officially on house arrest, baby."

"Do not. Call me baby." I swung around to Wells. "He's lying, right?"

Wells massaged his forehead, glanced at me, then looked back at Al. "Is that the official word?"

"Memos are winging their way to the thirteen now," Al said. "They're even warning the ones from the last mission, just in case. Who knows how desperate Sephrya is?" He turned his gaze toward me. "Are you done eating, Im?"

My stomach dropped. "Never. I am never done eating." I cast around for anything to stuff in my face.

"You look done to me," Al said, then propped his feet up on the table. "You're not going to be able to run by yourself in the mornings anymore, Im. Not until this is all sorted out and that could take months. Years even."

I froze. *I will go insane. He knows I'll go insane. Empty threat.* My gaze flew to Wells, positive he could see the panic shining out of my every pore. "That's not true, right?"

"Oh, right." Al reached into his jacket pocket. "I said the official memos were on their way and forgot to give you yours." He handed a folded, sealed sheet of paper to Wells, who broke the golden wax and read silently.

I scooted my chair loudly across the floor until I was close enough to read over his shoulder. A lot of it was jargon that I was too impatient to wade through. I started skimming.

"You know, Im, if you came to the palace there are lots of safe places for you to run. You wouldn't even have to leave the grounds." Al rocked on the back legs of his chair, boots still resting on the edge of the table. "You'd have a lot more space. A lot more to do. Cilla could even come stay with you whenever you want. Zoe too."

I opened my mouth to tell him I never wanted to set foot in the palace again.

Al's eyes locked on mine. "It's not really fair to Wells, you know."

I snapped my jaw shut, my lungs tightening.

"This whole situation was just kind of... dumped on him and now he's having to rearrange his life. Not to mention how much it costs. And how's he supposed to find anyone of his own to be with when he's taking care of you all the time?"

Barely breathing, I peeked at Wells. He'd gone utterly still. His face was set and he was staring at Al. Still holding the memo in frozen hands. As much as I tried, I still couldn't read his aura. Only colorless swirls surrounded him

Al's eyes never left mine. "Wells could come visit whenever he wants, too. You'd get to see all of your friends, whenever you want, and it would be a lot easier on everyone. You could even have your own rooms. If you don't want to share with me right away."

He might have guilted me into it, if he hadn't thrown that last bit in.

"If Wells gets tired of me," I said quietly. My chest was still tight, but my voice was steady. "Then I'll go stay with Zoe and Cilla for a while until I can find my own place. Figure out what kind of work I can do. I'm not going with you."

For a moment, Al just stared at me, his expression unchanged. Then he dropped his feet to the floor, popped his chair upright, and stood. "I think you're being ridiculous and maybe a little selfish, but fine. It's your choice. When you change your mind, the offer still stands." He ambled to the door with his hands in his pockets, then turned. "I'll be seeing you soon for another visit, Im. Maybe you'll be in a better mood when you're less tired. Bye, Wells." He walked out the door, tossing over his shoulder, "Let me know if you need any help."

We sat perfectly still, staring at the place where Al had just been.

We listened to him walk down the stairs, open the front door, and close it behind him.

Wells swiveled to face me. "Imogen—"

"Do you want me to go?" I chipped at my fingernails, felt my shoulders curving in and forced them back straight. Put my hands in my lap. Stared at the table.

"Imogen, look at—"

"I know I'm kind of a pain in the ass."

"Imogen, look at me, please."

Cheeks burning, I forced myself to meet his eyes. His aura was still transparent, unreadable swirls. His eyes were at least more on the warm brown side than red, so he wasn't pissed. I bit my bottom lip, started to chew, then made myself stop.

"From your . . . declaration that you would never be done eating, I'm guessing that you overheard a few things before you came downstairs?" he asked, eyebrows lifting slightly.

I dropped my gaze back to my lap. "I didn't mean to, I just wasn't ready to come down."

He took one of my wrists in his hand and squeezed lightly. Pleasant tingles cascaded up my arm. "Can you look at me, please?"

I did.

"I just need to know how much you overheard, so I know how much I need to fill you in." He gave my wrist a slight shake. "I'm not upset with you and I don't want you to go anywhere."

My stomach unclenched slightly. "I didn't hear much, just you giving him . . . behavioral guidelines and him saying he hadn't seen me enough."

"Then you didn't hear him make me promise not to interrupt him when he tried to convince you to come stay with him for a while?" When I shook my head, he sighed. "I thought that might have been the case. I had no idea he was going to use me to guilt trip you, Imogen. Al doesn't speak for me."

The tightness in my chest eased.

"Furthermore, everyone who comes from Earth is expected to spend at least a year adjusting. Some of them take longer finding out where they fit in. Some find a calling right away. But a year is about average."

He dropped his eyes to the wrist he was still lightly clasping, turned my palm face up and placed his other hand on top of it. My fingers curled around his. "Everyone who even applies to the Earth expedition to seek a partner is required to provide evidence of sufficient support for that partner to live comfortably with them for a reasonable amount of time without additional income. You know I went with the intention of finding someone. And yes, when it didn't happen after the first few months, I was expected to give up the idea, and I did. Resulting in my lack of preparedness when it comes to you. My point is that although you personally were unexpected, you're not causing a financial hardship."

What about that thing about you finding someone else? I thought. I didn't have the courage to ask. It was probably bordering on none of my business.

"Now, if you ever *want* to go somewhere else . . . If you don't like it here or you decide my company is—"

"I like your company and I like it here," I said. "I don't want to go anywhere else right now."

He smiled. "Good." He released my hand, stood up, and busied himself packing up the leftovers and 'porting them away. "And for the record, you are a pain in the ass, but you make things fun. How are you feeling?"

"Better," I said, taking my first full breath since Al arrived. "But I still can't see auras."

He nodded, sweeping up the crumbs from Al's bread and incinerating them in a flash. "We'll work on your 'pathing a bit tomorrow. You should take it easy for the rest of the day."

"There's another thing I wanna work on too . . ." I said, grabbing an errant crumb and incinerating it like I'd seen Wells do. It made the tiniest spark.

"Oh, really, what's that?"

My face warmed. "I want to learn how to throw off a compulsion." I pretended to hunt for more crumbs. I wasn't sure why it embarrassed me, but I couldn't look at him.

"We can do that," he said. "It's not easy, though, I'll warn you."

"Could we like, brew an antidote to sleeping potions too? Cilla does spells and potions..."

Wells made a face. "Potions are tricky, Imogen and I'm not the best at them." The table was clear, save for the memo still lying face up, partially open along its creases, like a trap. Wells sat back down next to me. "If you weren't so... atypically talented I wouldn't even agree to try the compulsion so soon. One thing at a time, okay?"

I nodded, my eyes wandering to the stiff paper. "So, what happens now? Do I really have to stay inside all the time? I don't, right?"

He took a breath and slid the paper between us. "I'll have to read this more carefully to make sure I understand all the nuances—and probably speak to the king myself due to my position—but you don't have to stay inside—"

"Yaaay!"

"—as long as you're supervised when you go out."

"Booooo."

"I know it's tedious, Imogen, but surely you understand the reasoning." His eyes skimmed the cramped writing.

"So what am I supposed to do when you're at work?" I popped out of my chair to perch on the dining room table facing him.

"We'll figure something out." He ran a hand through his hair. "I'll... work from here when I can. Perhaps Zoe and I can swap and you and Cilla can stay with each other occasionally."

"Ugh. It's like we're toddlers. I've been an adult for a *really* long time, I'm used to being able to go wherever the hell I want."

He snorted.

I narrowed my eyes and nudged his leg with my toe. "What exactly was funny?"

He leaned back in his chair. "Everyone knows humans mature quickly due to their shorter lifespan, so you are treated as adults . . ." One corner of his mouth slowly inched up in a half smile. "But if you'd been born here, you'd be the equivalent of a teenager right now."

"Well. I. Wasn't." I snatched the memo off the table and scanned it. "I thought this was all supposed to ease up. What about running in the morning?"

"You can't go out alone for a while, Imogen, I'm sorry. And having people peripherally keeping an eye out isn't enough."

I peeked at him over the top of the paper. Raised my eyebrows.

"I don't run," he said.

I kept eye contact.

"What if I wake up early and spar with you instead? Sparring is cardio."

I put the memo down. "If I don't run, I will go insane."

"All right." He crossed his arms. "How about a compromise?"

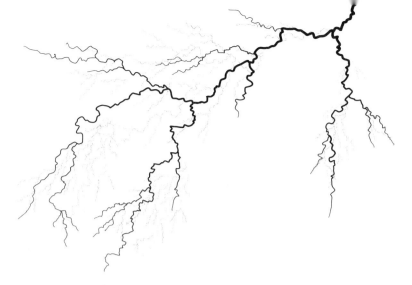

CHAPTER TWENTY-ONE

*At every given time, at every given moment,
everyone has something they need or want. Never forget that.*
—Solange Aidair Delaney

I couldn't sleep. Spending some time in the training room was an innocent enough way to burn off excess energy. I was working a kicking drill on the bag when Wells came yawning down the stairs, tying the drawstring on his loose pants.

"Imogen, do you know what time it is?" He approached as I stopped kicking and grabbed the bag to cease its swinging.

"Not really, I couldn't sleep so . . ."

He sighed and circled his hands around my bare arms, rubbing up and down. "It's very late. Or very early . . ."

I felt myself leaning toward him. "Sorry if I woke you up." My eyes traveled up to his, straying to his lips en route. A deep breath pulled in his scent. How did he smell so good when he'd just rolled out of bed?

"It's not a problem." He pushed a strand of hair out of my face, his fingers lingering on my cheek. Our gazes locked and something changed. I was suddenly too close to him and not close enough. Tension coiled low in my belly. My heartbeat somehow became more urgent.

In one fluid movement, his hand dropped to my waist and tugged me closer while my arms slid up to wind around his neck and shoulders. His other hand threaded through my hair and our lips met.

I couldn't get close enough; the heat inside me expanded fast and hard. I pressed deeper into the kiss but still needed more. I hauled myself closer, wrapping my legs around his hips. He slid one hand down to cup my rear, then pushed me against the wall . . .

I woke up—alone—mid climax.

I clamped a hand between my legs, rolling to my side and gasping until the roiling pressure subsided. *Shit. That hasn't happened in a while.* I lay still for a beat, until guilt and embarrassment slithered around in my stomach like twin snakes. I swung out of bed, walked over to the glass doors leading out to the balcony, and stared at the sky, just beginning to lighten near the horizon.

It doesn't mean anything, I told myself. *You haven't had sex in a while, you see him every day, your body was just . . . doing what it needed to do.* Another, annoying voice in the depths of my mind countered, *It hasn't been that long.*

You know what though? It's a new body. You don't know how it works. The main thing is that it was just a dream. It doesn't mean anything. You'll probably have a sex dream about Cilla next time. Let's just be thankful it wasn't about Al and . . . move on.

I pressed my forehead against the cool glass of the window. Then Wells knocked and entered.

"Imogen, if you want . . . oh good, you're up. Did you still . . . what's that sm—?"

He froze as realization struck. My cheeks flamed. I should have opened the window.

"You know what? This is *my room*." I stormed over—positive that embarrassment was wafting off me in visible waves—and shoved him out. "And when you come into my room without permission, you might smell some things." I slammed the door on him before he burst into laughter. I leaned against the wall and slid down to the floor burying my face in my hands.

"Does this mean you don't want to run?" Laughter still tickled his words.

"I will be *out* in a *minute*," I said, pushing calm into my voice. *God, just kill me.*

"It's nothing to be ashamed of, Imogen, everyone does it, it's perfectly natu—"

"Oh my God, go *away*." I was going to melt into the floor.

"I'll see you downstairs." He left, chortling.

I descended the staircase with as much dignity as I could muster. Wells seemed to have decided not to tease me further and simply opened the front door for me. Once we were on the sidewalk, I ran down to the park entrance, stopped, and ran back up the hill to Wells. I walked with him the rest of the way.

This was his compromise. We'd get up extra early four days a week and he'd take a walk while I ran. I could run until I was almost out of eyesight and then I had to come back. Wells absolutely refused to run.

"Zoe and I are trying to work something out where you and Cilla can be with one or the other of us if you want to practice out here," he told me as we swung into the park. "It may be difficult to get a schedule nailed down at first as everyone was expecting to have us back. At the very least, one of us can wink one of you over to either house for a few hours."

"Cilla should come to ours first. I want to teach her to defend herself."

"I got the impression that Cilla wasn't interested in fighting," Wells said as we stepped onto the red dirt path.

"She doesn't need to *fight*, but she should know how to throw an elbow and which end of the sword to hold." I'd given this idea some thought since our attack. "I'm not trying to sign her up for the WWE."

"Don't you think she might be more comfortable learning from Zoe?"

"I mean, if she wants to, fine." I shrugged. "But when couples like that try to do fighty stuff together, they end up making out most of the time and nothing gets done."

Wells barked a laugh.

"Seriously, you should see their auras when they meet up after time apart." I could *just* see the gap in the trees where the path exited into open space. "Can I go now?"

"I'll let the two of you work that out," Wells said. "And no, Imogen, just wait until we're clear of the trees."

"It's like, right there," I protested.

Wells sighed. "You're like Al. I give you a little bit of leeway and you can't stop yourself from pushing for more."

I shut up. Initially offended. Then I realized he was right. He didn't want to get up at the crack of dawn and watch me run around like a nut. He didn't make the rules. And I *had* been nearly kidnapped yesterday from these very woods.

Before I could apologize, Wells spoke again. "I'm sorry to have compared you to Al. You're not as bad as he is."

"No, you're right." I bumped him with my shoulder. "You're doing this for me, I should be less annoying about it."

"Well, he's had a few more centuries to work on his behavior. And, as you've pointed out, you're not used to restrictions. Regardless, we're going to work on your telepathy while we're out here, so it is dual purpose."

We finally approached the edge of the tree line. Wells gently took hold of my elbow. Pleasant shivers chased across my skin. I smiled when he blushed and cleared his throat.

"I'm going to 'path to you when I want you to turn around and come back, and you're to try 'pathing back an affirmative. It's actually beneficial to do it now when there are fewer people around while you learn how to narrow your focus."

I grinned. "Sounds fun."

It was easier for me to feel where I was going wrong immediately after having received a correctly honed 'path from Wells. Even I noticed improvement after our first morning.

For the next several weeks, 'pathing was part of our dawn outings. Once I was proficient enough that I was successfully bothering Wells at work when I was bored—resulting in a whole new crop of ground rules—we worked on 'porting small objects to each other to mark my turnarounds. I practiced 'porting (non-breakable) things all around the house and 'pathing Cilla like we were teenagers on telephones in a '90s sitcom.

Cilla even consented to learn some self-defense. Once I agreed that she could teach me yoga after each session. After quickly learning that she was very uncomfortable practicing on me, I taught her strikes on the bags first, which went much better. From there we graduated to throwing knives at targets, then eventually to disarming.

Since potions weren't Wells's forte and Cilla had a knack for them, we even experimented with some simple recipes and incantations together. After one minor explosion, which mercifully happened at Cilla and Zoe's house—Zoe was just chiller than Wells when my powers slipped—I was more cautious and respectful when mixing potions. And under Cilla's instruction, even managed to brew an antidote to sleeping potion. If you could stay awake long enough to drink it.

Yoga afterward was good too. Cilla somehow manufactured a lavender scent out of thin air during savasana. My nightmares about Earth grew further apart and lessened in severity when I started telling Cilla about them. On the now rare occasion that I did have a laryngospasm, Wells always woke up to help me breathe again.

And usually stayed with me until I fell asleep. Sometimes I could tell him about the nightmares, sometimes I couldn't, but I could always tell Cilla. Then the palace threw us a curve ball.

"I don't see why I have to freaking *perform*. Just because he's curious."

"He's the king, Imogen. Generally everyone does what he says." Wells passed me some large, flat blue-green leaves. "Here, vent your frustration on these."

We were standing in the kitchen making a big salad for dinner. I gritted my teeth as I ripped the leaves apart. It *was* satisfying. "Why does he have to evaluate me himself? You evaluate my fighting on a daily basis. And you're Lead Fighter Person of the country. Aren't you a good enough—"

"Lead Fighter Person." One corner of his mouth tipped up, but his eyes remained on the tubers he was chopping. "I'll have to get that embroidered on a tapestry or something. And I've told him we've been training regularly and let him know that you had training on Earth, but he wants an unbiased assessment. The fact that you managed to hold off both Sephryans and defend yourself and Cilla caught his interest."

I caught the thread of tension in Wells's voice but said nothing, continuing to shred greens and chuck their pieces into a bowl while he chopped a bright red fruit into long strips.

"You do have one other option if you don't want to go to the palace," he said finally, then grimaced. "You're not going to like it."

Wells dropped me off at the park. With two swords and my dagger. Al arrived minutes afterward, similarly equipped, his blond hair pulled back.

"Hey, Im." He grinned, winked. "Never knew you were so violent."

Wells took me by the shoulders, looking into my eyes. "I'm a 'path away." He glanced at Al, then back at me. "Just . . . don't kill him. It would make things very complicated."

Al rolled his eyes. "I don't know what exactly you think I'm going to do that's going to make her want to kill me, Wells."

"Maybe . . . one or two of the things you've done before?" Wells's mouth tightened, then he gave my shoulders a final squeeze and dropped his hands. "You'll walk her straight home afterward?" When Al nodded, Wells gave me one final tense smile and winked out.

And then it was just us. For the first time since...

I turned to face Al, consciously trying to relax my jaw. "Okay, how long is this going to take? What exactly do you need to see?"

"As long as it takes." He grinned. "I'll tell you when I've seen enough."

I released a slow exhale through my nose as I slid one sword from its scabbard. Slowly. "Then let's get it over with. Normal rules or...?"

Al shook his head, grinning, and yanked one of his own swords free, flinging it skyward and catching it by the hilt. "This is a whole new side of you. Didn't realize you were the combative type." He carved a few flourishes into the air.

"Like we've established," I skinned the other sword, perhaps intentionally scraping it along its sheath, "you don't know me very well."

"I understand you better than you think." He gave me the traditional Molnairian salute: swords crossed over chest, slight incline of the head, then slashing down and outward.

"And I think it's really arrogant for you to think you understand enough to rip me from my entire life after three months." I returned his salute, swords singing as I whipped them through the air.

Openings exchanged, we settled into a relaxed fighting stance. Eyes on the midline, balance shifted to the balls of our feet. The world stayed at a normal speed. Al made no move to attack and neither did I. If he wanted to test me, he could start the fireworks. When Al started to circle slowly, I followed, keeping my lead foot forward.

"You wanted to do everything. Everything you could possibly cram into your lifespan," he said. "You wanted to feel everything, see everything. You didn't want to regret anything you *didn't* do."

Al and I were sitting on a wooden fence watching the soccer games ahead of us finish up before it was our turn on the pitch.

"So, what do you think is the one thing you want to accomplish before you die?" Al asked.

"I don't have one thing," I said immediately. "I'm going to do as many things as I can. And I don't want to pressure myself with a list, so I just... pick the thing that I want most at the time and go for it, then I decide what's next."

"Wow," he chuckled, "that was a really fast answer!"

"Keane says I talk about death a lot," I said, swinging my legs beneath the fence rail. "I just think I have a healthy appreciation for how short life is. My grandma used to tell me to live my life so that I didn't regret not *having done something.*" I grinned at him. "She said not to worry too much about the things that I did *do.*"

"Your grandma sounds awesome," he said.

"That little insight doesn't mean you know me," I snapped, still circling.

"Solange said it her whole life," he countered. His aura shifted and the corners of my mouth twitched. *Here we go.* His circling slowed almost imperceptibly. "That was her whole thing, no regrets, try everything; her whole mentality was built around it. And so is yours." He struck, sword arching toward the crown of my head. The world slowed, but I went with a simple block. Shielding with one weapon and using the other to wipe his sword along the blade, away from its target.

"Just because we have the same motto or whatever, doesn't mean we're the same person." I stepped back into an easy stance. *C'mon, test me.*

"You're not the same person." He attacked again. Time shifted with his first movement. A beautiful spinning strike sailed toward my neck. Al expected me to defend and then engage. I took one step back. Avoided one blade. Angled my head to the side. Dodged the other. *Gonna hafta push harder than that, asshole.*

"I know I'm not." I was tired of playing around. I wanted this done. "I don't know if *you* know that."

I tossed one blade up. Struck the pommel. It launched straight at him, like a javelin. As I anticipated, he parried it to the side with his dominant hand.

I caught it. Stepped off to the same side and kicked his legs out from underneath him.

Normal speed resumed once he hit the ground. I kept circling until I was behind him, forcing him to get to his feet and change his angle to face me. "Can we get on with it?"

Al acted as if I hadn't spoken. "Solange was carefree." He summoned the sword he had dropped, glittering eyes on me. "She was reckless." He sprang to his feet. "She wouldn't be tied down." He turned to face me. "And she lived for the moment, almost exclusively." We circled again. "I can count on one hand the times that she chose the future over the now. And you are her exact opposite." He struck, eyes blazing. Slashing at my right shoulder.

Time slowed. I blocked on instinct. My right sword scraped down his blade to the hilt. I blocked a strike from the left. Aimed a front kick to his nose. Connected with a thunk, then spun out of range before he could counter.

"What happened to me being just like her?" I asked.

"You're just like her in some ways." He sniffed. Shook off my kick, scraped one blade along the other, circling me again. "The way you move, your temper, some of your mannerisms. But you think of everything differently. Every experience is precious to you because you've always thought of them as limited. She always thought of them as infinite. She was always bored trying not to be bored. You're always fascinated trying to take everything in. You're like her mirror, Imogen."

I blinked. Not prepared for Al to be insightful. "I'm seriously done with all this chatting." I snapped, blood heating.

I attacked. Feinted with my left sword. Slashed with my right. Al barely parried, but managed to deflect me. I launched a flurry of single sword attacks, guiding his lead hand over to one side. Then lunged with my right blade. Got inside his guard. Kicking range. I clenched my teeth. I wanted to kick him. I wanted to be up close and personal.

I got one solid snap kick to his chin, then focused on disarming his lead sword. Once he'd been rocked, it wasn't difficult. His next strike was sloppy. I blocked it at the hilt. Ran my other blade to the tip on the outside. Stepped back and shoved, using the fulcrum to twist the sword out of his grasp. The weapon flew from his fingers. Spun directly at him.

He dodged but kept his other blade up. He shook his head, smiling. Not his normal cocky, Aloysius smile. There was something raw there. He switched his remaining sword to his lead hand. Still en garde. We circled.

"Seen enough yet?" I nearly growled.

"Is it so painful to just spend a little time with me?"

My grip tightened, knuckles whitening around the hilts. "Did you orchestrate this entire thing just to get one-on-one time? Did Allestair even—"

"I told him you were special is all," Al said, his voice hard. "That combined with Wells's report of your encounter, of course he wants to evaluate you. I'm not going to stop talking about you, Imogen, I may be the only one who believes in what you are right now, but once your powers start maturing you won't be able to hide it."

"I had a good life. You took it from me," I snarled, my breath coming quicker.

"You weren't even living up to one tenth of your potential. Torn between trying to find a place to fit in and trying to do what you wanted. And your fiancé was trying to slow you down." His voice was hard. Amber eyes glinting.

"That's utter horseshit," I spat. "Keane was always up for whatever."

"Look at me, Imogen." He spread his arms wide, almost daring me to strike. "You can read my aura, right? Am I lying?"

He wasn't. I hadn't seen one black spike. I pressed my lips together.

"Keane told me he was done moving. He wanted to get married and settle down. He was hoping once you hit menopause you would chill out because he was ready to stay in one place for the rest of his life and he was hoping New Orleans would be it."

"Well, maybe I would have chilled out." My tone was defensive, even to my own ears. "Keane's known me for years. We talked about everything. We were committed. He was ready to deal with me when I was old and falling apart—"

"You mean he was ready for you to be old and falling apart," Al bit out.

Something unspooled in my chest and I launched myself at him, twin blades glinting in the sun. "You... don't... know that!"

"I do!" He defended fiercely, but to my fury, didn't fight back. "He wanted vacations and retirement, you were still hungry..."

"There's no way you can *know that!*" I threw a vicious spinning slash with no technique, no thought, only emotion behind it. Al stopped it. Knocked the blade free.

We were now evenly matched. Both breathing harder. We circled again.

"I talked to him, Imogen, I spent time with both of you. I know it wasn't the months we were supposed to get, but I didn't have that luxury. I needed to make fast decisions."

"You made the *decision* to get yourself a new Solange."

"You're so different from Solange." His face broke and my heart stopped hating him for a beat. It was swift and it was fleeting, but I marked it. "But she's in there. I can see it. And, Imogen, I know you don't believe me, but... I love how different you are."

Anger burned through my chest. I launched myself at him again with my single sword. I was better when I was being attacked and could see what was coming at me. Although the world still spun down, Al wasn't fighting back. It dulled everything. My super speed, my aural predictions, neither of them were as effective when my opponent wasn't a threat.

I finally backed off. Frustration rippling beneath my skin. "What the hell do you want from me?"

His eyes widened. He shook his head and laughed. "I want to be with you, Imogen." His face contorted with emotion. He wrestled it under control. "And I know it's not going to happen any time soon and that's okay."

"Why do you think anything is ever going to change between us after what you've done?" I summoned my other sword. Al immediately summoned his as well.

"Because you may be pissed at me now, but in one hundred years when you realize that you would be dead if it weren't for me, you might feel differently."

"I will still remember that you did all of this shit to me without my permission or consent," I snarled, twirling one blade through the air with a flick of my wrist. I needed him to attack. I wanted a physical fight.

"And you'll thank me for that."

Everything stopped. I blinked. "I'm going to *thank you?*"

Al stepped closer, I brought my blades up. He laughed humorlessly and stepped back.

"Imogen, if I had asked you if you wanted a chance to live longer, see another world, learn to do things you never thought possible . . . you would have wanted it badly. If you're honest with yourself, you'll know that's true. You would have been on board. But you wouldn't have come. Because of Keane. Because of your father, your family. Because of everyone you would be leaving behind. You would have wanted to come and you wouldn't have left. And you would have regretted it for the rest of your life, which would have been short. So I just saved you the trouble."

"Fuck you," I rasped. "You took everything I loved. Everything I had *built* . . ."

"And you will thank me in one hundred years," he snapped, then he lunged. Both blades flying toward me. He wasn't going to kill, but he was definitely aiming for pain.

Good.

I blocked every strike. In my element now. I parried. Countered easily. Remembering Wells's plea to avoid killing him. A poorly blocked stab earned him a slash to one leg. A short parry and I struck his shoulder.

"You wanted time!" he bit out, backing off. "I asked you what you wanted. You asked for time. I gave it to you."

Sitting around a fire pit. Looking out over the lake. It was the first time that Al had hung out with just Keane and I. Keane had gone inside to refill his drink. Al and I were staring at the stars.

"If you could make one wish come true, what would it be?" he asked.

"That I'd have time to do all the things I want to do. Time to find out where I fit," I said.

"That wasn't your responsibility, Al." My voice broke. "And it wasn't an invitation to—"

"Have you ever considered that *this* is where you belong? *This* is where you fit in? You're not going to die in fifty years, Imogen," Al said, his voice diamond hard. "You would never have picked that for yourself. And you know what? I don't care if you hate me." He dropped his guard, his face open, eyes bright. "I don't care how angry you are. Because in a hundred years, you might feel differently. And even if you don't, I'm not going to regret having you in this world." He sheathed his sword. "I'm done fighting with you." His aura swirled with distress.

I stared at him, my stomach coated in ice. My swords dragged at my sides.

"I love you, Imogen." Al's aura tossed with indigo and blue-black, ribbons of pink frequently flipping through. "And I don't care if you think I haven't had enough time to know you, or if you think I'm projecting. I don't need your permission to love you."

I remained frozen. I didn't know what to say.

"I've seen enough to satisfy Father. Test complete. I'm taking you back to Wells's," he said. And when he reached for my arm, I didn't back away.

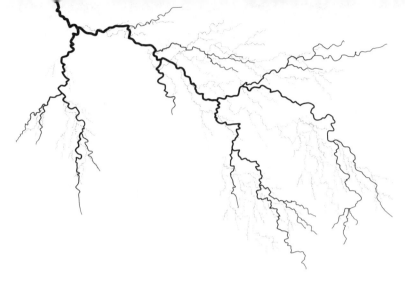

CHAPTER TWENTY-TWO

*You think love is gentle and easy? Ha! Love will smack you
upside the head when you least expect it. That's what the bastard lives for.*
—Solange Aidair Delaney

When spring crossed firmly into summer with no new kidnapping attempts, former Earthlings and their partners were chafing at the restrictions. Wells learned from Al—who did stop by the military campus to see him although he was studiously avoiding me—that the two Sephryans had yielded no additional information and were simply rotting away in the dungeons. Sephrya's monarch had denied responsibility and claimed no interest in their welfare.

Most felt that Sephrya was simply trying to lure us into a false sense of security, but there were many who wondered how long they were going to have to live their lives concerned that they might be kidnapped at every turn. Half the Molnairian citizenry bridled at how our monarchy had been "turning the other cheek," restricting our own when we had done nothing to deserve it, and felt that we should take this fight straight to Sephrya. The other half didn't want to rock the boat with the surrounding countries or have their own country at war.

True to his word, Wells did try to teach me to throw off a compulsion. It was something I worked on only with him. Never in the park and never in front of Cilla or Zoe.

And he was right, it was difficult. He never compelled me to do anything terrible or embarrassing—usually it was a simple action, like standing or walking—but after a few unsuccessful attempts at throwing it off, my emotions grew turbulent and I couldn't hide them. He only ever did these lessons when I pestered him. And after the first few breakdowns, he even tried to dissuade me. It was the only skill thus far that I hadn't been able to grasp.

We were attempting it again in the few minutes we had free before going to meet Cilla and Zoe for "normal fun" in the park. Both Zoe and Wells thought it might be nice to just enjoy each other's company without working for a change. Which made it easier for me to goad Wells into some compulsion practice before we left.

"*Come sit here,*" Wells said.

I was across the room, where he'd compelled me to walk during my last unsuccessful attempt to break free. I dug my feet in. Tried to find that switch inside my body to turn off its mindless need to obey.

My psyche thrashed around frantically as my legs took one calm, measured step after another toward the chair across from Wells. I fisted my hands at my sides, but had no control over my lower body. Anxiety spiked hot. My heart thundered in my chest as I ran mental fingers blindly over the walls in my mind, desperate for that switch . . .

"Stop stop stop . . ." I whispered to myself, but my feet kept moving until I was standing in front of the chair. I tried to lock my knees. To prevent my hips from hinging. The muscles flexed as I ordered them to, but relaxed almost immediately. I sat down.

And cried.

"Imogen..." Wells reached across to hug me, but I wouldn't move my hands from over my face, trying to stifle my hitching breath, and just collapsed against him. He pulled me into his lap, his face tight, aura blue black with concern. "I'm not doing this anymore. It makes you feel terrible and it makes me feel worse."

I want to be able to do it, I 'pathed. Not trusting my voice. I swiped hot tears from my cheeks.

"It's very advanced kroma, Imogen. We can try again after you've learned how to wink, but this is enough. It's just self-flagellation at this point. Your shields are perfect, you can deflect it if you see it coming." He tucked my head under his chin. "And I can't stand making you cry like this."

You should feel honored to have breached the inner sanctum, I tried to joke. Wells was officially the only person on the planet I was comfortable crying in front of. *I have some kind of mental block around this that I want to get through.*

"I don't think this is the way," he said, giving me a squeeze. "We've tried it over and over and it's just making you more upset each time. We're giving it a good long break. End of discussion."

I closed my eyes and deepened my breaths, leaning in to the thud of Wells's heart against my cheek. Letting the fingers he pushed through my hair calm me. In spite of my breakdown, I felt safe. Relaxed. Like I could share anything with him and be okay. *Maybe even my heart.* The thought whispered through my mind.

I shushed it. Wells had taken on enough in saving me from Al. I didn't need to complicate things with a crush.

We sat for a few minutes until I had calmed down. By then it was time to meet Cilla and Zoe.

I stood up and wiped my face on the hem of my tunic. "Is my hair okay?" I asked.

When he didn't answer, I turned around to find him still seated, his aura spinning with alarm, his eyes wide. "What's the matter?" I asked. Then

I saw it. Something was different about his aura. There was something . . . static. Shining.

Wells shook his head and stood up, his movements stiff. "Nothing. I'm sure I just imagined . . . let's go, we'll be late." He strode from the room, back rigid. My stomach dropped.

The static white light was connecting his aura to mine. It stretched thinner as he walked away until I got an uncomfortable sensation in the pit of my stomach. Like something was missing. Something important. I rushed after him.

When I caught up, the hollow, aching feeling disappeared.

What the fresh hell is this?

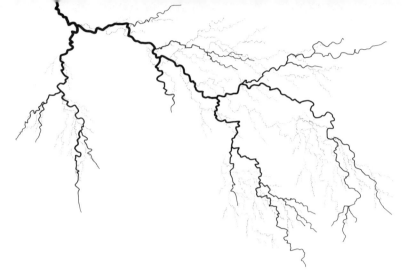

CHAPTER TWENTY-THREE

Everyone wants or needs something.
And sometimes it's the opposite of what you think you want or need.
The hard times are when you wish it weren't.
—Solange Aidair Delaney

We marched briskly to the park. Wells didn't offer his arm or touch me at all but kept his hands shoved in his pockets. His face was tight and pale, at odds with the small talk comments and stiff smiles he forced out at regular intervals.

I couldn't tear my eyes from the bridge of light between us, but when I tried to ask about it, the words caught in my throat. By the time we turned into the park, my stomach was in knots.

Zoe and Cilla were in a different spot this time. They had claimed a picnic bench underneath a bright pink tree out in the open. It was a warm, summer day and a vendor nearby was selling cream clouds, which Cilla and I had been delighted to learn were similar to ice cream, only lighter somehow and they didn't melt as quickly.

A Dagger of Lightning

Cilla jumped up to hug me right away. I closed my eyes and squeezed her back, letting the exuberance of her embrace melt some of the tension from my shoulders. When we broke, I stared at her. I felt my brows contracting. "You smell different," I said. Then sputtered, "I mean, not bad different. You don't stink or anything, it's just—"

"Zoe, Immy noticed too!" Cilla gasped, her grip on my arms tightening, her aura luminous with delight. She had started calling me "Immy." And for some reason, when it came from Cilla, I didn't mind. I would have beheaded anyone else.

Wells glanced from Cilla to Zoe, a genuine smile growing fast. "Well, that was quick. You must be the first from this group. Congratulations, both of you!"

Zoe beamed at Cilla, her aura glowing with pride even as she said, "Let's not announce it everywhere just yet. Another cycle or two."

"Oh my God, are you *pregnant*? Cilla!" I hugged her under the arms, lifting her off her feet, and spinning her around while her alto chuckle tickled my ear. "You're going to have the most charming, most beautiful baby *ever*!" I released her to embrace Zoe after Wells was done. He gave Cilla a squeeze and offered to get everyone cream clouds to celebrate. With a double scoop for Cilla.

When Wells left for the cream clouds, the three of us moved back toward the picnic bench. As we separated, Zoe shot a measured look between Wells and me. "I think congratulations are in order for you two, also, yes?" she asked me, smiling. "Have you decided when you're going to accept it?"

My face went slack and my body boneless even as Cilla slammed into me with another hug. "A mating bond! Oh, my God, Immy, when were you going to tell me?"

I just stared at Zoe, whose smile faded. "He hasn't told you?"

My eyes found Wells, standing several feet away, and the thin, glowing thread running between our auras. "I think it just happened," I answered hoarsely.

Cilla was squeezing my hand, chattering away about how rare and special it was and how happy she was for us. I could barely hear her over the pounding in my ears. Zoe shushed her. "Cilla, quiet. Think of how complicated this will be once the prince finds out."

Oh, fuck. Al. Another dramatic situation. I went numb. Staring into the middle distance.

"I'll go help Llewellyn with the cream clouds," Zoe said, pushing us onto the benches on either side of the table. "Stay right here."

Cilla touched my arm. "Immy, are you okay?"

I forced my gaze to hers, opened and closed my mouth a few times, but nothing came out. She came around the table to sit on my side, draped an arm around my waist, and dropped her head to my shoulder. "It'll all work out."

I tried again to say something. Managed a hoarse squeak.

Cilla lifted her head, brown eyes locking on mine. "Zoe and I thought you two would get together eventually, Immy. I know you were engaged on Earth and it sucks . . . how it happened but . . . you and Wells fit together."

She glanced over at Wells, now standing off to the side of the cream cloud vendor, letting other people pass him in line. His head was bowed, the sun catching on the crimson curtain of his hair. Zoe had a hand on his arm, her face calm and serious. We were too far away to hear what she was saying.

My eyes kept getting snagged on that glowing thread. I was sure it was connected to the nerves rolling around in the pit of my stomach like a marble. I suspected the marble would quiet down when Wells was near me again. *Is it going to feel like this for the rest of my life when he stands more than five feet away? Does he feel this?*

"I'm sorry, but you guys are so hot together." Cilla sighed. "With your dark, messy hair and those Liz Taylor eyes next to his long, silky, red hair and . . . what color would you say his eyes are? They almost match his hair, but not quite. I wouldn't call them brown either. It's like he's a fox or something, have you ever seen the color of a red fox's eyes? And you're both so fit." Her eyes glazed over a bit. "Ugh! I wish they had video cameras here, you could totally make a movie of your mating bond acceptance. Oh! You could do it on your phone—"

"Jesus, Cilla, are you sure you're not bi?" I asked, momentarily yanked from numbness.

"Oh, I'm *pan*, baby." She grinned. "I never told you that? I appreciate all flavors of hotness. And you two? Are hot."

My face flushed. "But we don't . . . Wells doesn't like me like that."

Cilla looked at me like I had just told her there were only thirteen states in the Union. "Yes, he does."

"No, he doesn't, Cilla." My throat tightened. Wells was really stuck with me now. This thing was permanent. And what did this mean for returning to Earth eventually? Humans didn't have mating bonds.

Cilla pressed her coral lips together and narrowed her eyes. "Zoe told me not to speak out of turn when it came to this, so I'm going to wait until you two can have your own conversation, because she's usually right. But. Yes. He does."

The marble skating around in my stomach slowed. Wells and Zoe were returning with cream clouds. *I need to be happy for Cilla and Zoe right now*, I told myself. *Deal with this later. Them having a baby is a huge thing.*

But having a mating bond was a huge thing, too. We weren't even partners. And Aloysius was going to freak the fuck out. It was a lot to put a pin in.

Zoe and Wells passed around the cream clouds and sat down across from us. Wells's cheeks almost matched his hair. His eyes met mine for half a second, then we both looked away. I studied my cream cloud. He'd gotten the kind with nut butter chunks that I liked.

"You two are going to talk about this later," Zoe said to me, saving us all the trouble of addressing the elephant in the room. "In private. And if you need someone else to talk to afterward . . . you know how to find us." Then she looked at Wells. "You could also speak to Captain Marc. He's mated. And he's very old."

Wells nodded, eyes on his cream cloud. "Thank you, Zoe," he said softly. She patted his shoulder.

"And his mate is from freakin' Mesopotamia," I was unable to resist blurting to Cilla, whose jaw dropped. "So he's at least two thousand years old."

"Older than that," Zoe said. "Because he had a partner before Allatu for decades. She died in the Wind War."

"Wait..." I raised my eyebrows. "How old are *you*?"

She just grinned hugely, showing all of her star-bright teeth.

"So..." Wells's eyes found Cilla over his chocolate cream cloud. "Any names picked out?"

We spent the next hour celebrating Zoe and Cilla. Cilla told me all about how two females made a baby together. Which apparently involved a lot of complex kromatics and nothing sexy. "We made up for that part later. After each session," she assured me with a sly smile.

They had floated a few names around, but Zoe didn't want anyone to get their hopes up this early and Cilla didn't believe in labeling someone before they'd taken a breath. Being with them, however, was a balm. Watching how Zoe admired Cilla when she commanded the conversation with her effervescent energy and open smile, seeing Cilla get lost in tracing the lines on Zoe's palm as if she had never seen anything more beautiful. They gravitated toward each other. Their auras often swirled in tandem, the colors perfectly complimenting each other.

Why haven't they mated? I wondered. *Why us? They seem so perfectly suited...*

Eventually, Cilla finished her double scoop of berry cream cloud and it was time to go.

I almost begged them to come home with us. To stay the night. To stay the weekend—always three days in Molnair—but even as I thought it, I knew it was ridiculous. We had to discuss this. Putting it off would only make it worse.

They gave us long hugs goodbye and Cilla whispered in my ear that I needed to 'path her to let her know how things went, or 'port her a note if she was asleep. She wasn't adept at 'porting them back my way, but I could usually pull them back myself if I gave her enough time to write on them.

Wells offered me his arm and I took it. My entire being exhaled in relief as soon as we touched. "Do you feel that?" I asked, quietly enough that he could pretend not to hear it if he wanted.

"I feel it, Imogen." He sighed and I sighed with him. My heart stumbled. Would we be breathing together now too? He glanced sideways at me as we turned out of the park. "Did you know? Could you feel it? Or did Zoe tell you?"

"I . . . I can see it, Wells," I breathed, my eyes caught on the bond shimmering around us. "It's visible to me like the auras. But I didn't know what it was. I just knew you started acting weird right when it showed up." I swallowed. "And my stomach feels weird and achy when you get too far away." My eyes flicked up to his. "Does yours do that?"

"It's physically painful for me to be apart from you, Imogen. I felt it as soon as you stood up earlier." He cleared his throat. "The bond must have solidified after compulsion practice. I'm sorry I didn't bring it up right away I just . . . I never expected this to happen. I'm sure I was in denial until Zoe told me she could sense it. I'm so sorry, Imogen."

My stomach dropped. *Had I caused the bond to form with my crushy feelings?*

Wells went rigid and halted. I followed the line of his gaze to the top of the hill and my breath caught. "Oh, fuck, just wink us out, we can't do this right now, we haven't even talked—"

"Hey, Im. Hey, Wells." Al was leaning against the wrought iron fence surrounding Wells's front yard.

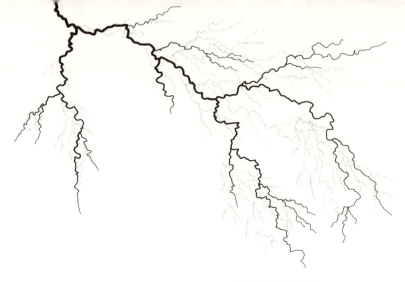

CHAPTER TWENTY-FOUR

At the end of the day, all you can do is all you can fucking do.
—Solange Aidair Delaney

"I saw you in the park with Cilla and Zoe and didn't want to interrupt so I figured I'd wait here." Al straightened away from the gate. "Since Im's all full of cream cloud sugar I thought she might be feeling less violent." He smiled.

We can't leave now he's seen us, Wells 'pathed. *He's fairly oblivious when things don't involve him directly, it could be that he won't notice. We can pretend you have a stomach ache or something and get rid of him.*

He's not that oblivious when it comes to me, I countered. *Maybe one of us can leave and the other can stay?* The marble in my stomach went wild at the mere thought.

Al was already striding down to meet us, his tawny brows coming together to crease his forehead. "Something's different . . ."

We froze. Both of us. I felt Wells tighten his hold on my arm even as I gripped him harder. *Bambi in headlights.* The thought flashed unhelpfully across my brain.

Aloysius stopped one foot from us. His eyes widened. His pupils darted back and forth between the two of us. "What did you do?"

"We haven't done anything," I said, my voice coming out in a shaking whisper.

"Al—" Wells started.

"Don't," Al spat, staring at the two of us. His gaze stripped us bare. Without conscious thought, my body leaned into Wells for comfort. I knew Wells would have stayed still if he could, but he wrapped his arm around me, hugging me to his side. I couldn't help but breathe in the scent of him.

Al's face broke.

"Al," Wells rasped, his face twisting with empathy. "This *just* happened. We haven't even processed it. Imogen didn't even know what was going on until Zoe told her."

Al's aura fractured. The normal cool sea colors turned stormy. As if the tropical beach were experiencing a rare hurricane. The pink ribbons winging through shredded as they flew. Breaking into sharp-edged confetti. Dark blue and plum-colored cracks flickered through it all like a dark lightning. He pinned me with his gaze.

I stared back. I had promised him nothing. He had taken everything. And yet.

I watched the realization move behind his amber eyes. No matter how long he waited, I would never be his. I would never love him. No matter how much he gave me. No matter how much time and space and money he let me have. I would never turn to him for affection or support.

I would always turn to his half-brother.

Despite all he had done, my heart hurt for him.

"I can't believe this." His voice cracked. One tear dove down his cheek. "I can't fucking believe this." His eyes locked on mine, agony etched in every line of his face. "I thought you needed space. I thought if I gave you some time . . ." He dashed the tear away and took a breath. His face hardened into something brutal. His glare landed on Wells. "Have you accepted yet?"

I felt Wells bristle. "I said it's only just happened."

Al's eyes flicked to me and then away, as if he couldn't stand to look right at me. "Well maybe you won't then," he said, a growl under his voice.

"Al." All empathy melted away as Wells's expression went stricken. "Al, it physically hurts to be ten feet from her . . ."

Aloysius shook his head violently, backed away.

"I've never felt anything like this, Al. We need time—"

"NO!" Al roared, then winked out.

CHAPTER TWENTY-FIVE

You're my best friend. What I want is for you to be happy.
—Keane Battersea

Wells told me that he 'pathed their mother at the palace to let her know what had happened. He was worried about Al. He'd gone so far down a spiral when Solange hadn't returned. He didn't say it, but I knew he harbored guilt for his part in turning her, even if I hadn't seen the shoots of ochre cutting through his aura.

"I'm sorry," I said as soon as we were inside.

"Imogen, this is so far from being your fault," Wells said. We were still arm in arm. We stayed that way as we walked up three flights of stairs. "Al has done this to himself in so many ways . . . and yet, I keep trying to . . ." He shook his head.

We reached our hallway. Stood between our separate doorways. Wells dropped my arm but kept my hands in his. I clung to his fingers like a lifeline.

"Is it always going to feel so weird when we separate?" I whispered, angling my body to face him.

He squeezed my fingers and dropped his forehead against mine. "I've been told the bond changes after it's been accepted. The tethers become less physically uncomfortable and more emotionally intuitive." He took both my hands in one of his and smoothed my hair down the back of my head with the other as he sighed. "It's one thing to be told all of this in a lecture, it's... quite another thing to be experiencing it."

"So what do we do now?" I asked. I knew we should probably take space to decompress. Come down from the emotional hurricane we'd left on the sidewalk. But I couldn't suggest it. Not only was my stomach revolting at the very thought of separating, but Wells had been my safe space since I'd been yanked from Earth.

Tiny charges zinged across my skin where his fingertips brushed bare flesh with no hair or cloth in between. Even his forehead touching mine had me longing to tilt my lips up to his. His scent had always been pleasant to me. Like my favorite aromatherapy fragrance. Now it was intoxicating. I wanted to drink him in. *He doesn't feel that way about you,* I told myself, keeping a firm leash on those desires.

I had never experienced feelings this strong. And that splinter of guilt still lodged in my core at the thought that I might have triggered this. I reined myself in. It was torture.

"What do you want to do, Imogen?" he asked, one hand still stroking the back of my head. "Where do you feel most comfortable? Do you want... space? I can—"

"No," I blurted. I pulled away so I could look him in the eye. We were both breathing deeply. As if we were on top of a mountain, struggling to get enough of the thin air into our lungs. "I don't know what the right thing to do is, but I hate being away from you right now." I felt my lower lids filling and blinked hard. "I need to understand what's happening."

"Okay, okay." He brought his hands up to cradle my face. "It's a lot. I've been told about it since I was a child and it's a lot for me. So... okay." He brushed my hair behind my ears. "Let's pick a place to sit and talk. It can be one of our rooms, it can be the main room, it can be the kitchen—"

"My room," I said. It was the place I had felt most comfortable since I left Earth. The place I'd felt was mine. The place I'd always been able to set my own rules. Wells always knocked—and since that one time, waited for my invitation before entering. It was my area. I felt safe there.

"Are you sure?" he asked.

"I'm sure." I spun and pulled him across my threshold.

And straight out onto the balcony. I wanted to sit in the sun and I wanted to avoid the bed.

For a minute we just sat at the little bistro table, staring at nothing.

I blew out a breath and set my clasped hands on the mosaic tabletop between us. He curved his fingers around them. We both sighed in relief. I swallowed, my mouth incredibly dry. "Why can't I stand not to be touching you?"

Wells blushed. I was starting to wonder if both of us would have permanently pink-stained cheeks after today. "It's the body's way of . . . urging the acceptance of the bond."

"Has anyone ever not accepted it?" The now familiar heat rushed to my face. I couldn't look at him when I asked, "Should we just . . . get it over with?"

"No." He shook his head. "This isn't something we're going to rush through. With both of us feeling awkward as hell. And if you *do* accept . . ." He tugged on my hands and sighed as he asked, "Imogen, I'm sorry, would you mind coming over here?"

I rose without hesitation, closed the distance between us, and settled on his lap. He wrapped his arms around my waist and I threw mine around his shoulders. A wave of calm washed over me.

"To answer your other question," he said, resting his head against mine. "I'm not sure if a bond has ever gone unaccepted or what happens if that's the case. There's always an emotional connection when a bond is formed so the pair is generally . . . happy about it. From what I understand."

My stomach twisted, the guilt sliding through. "I'm sorry you're stuck with me," I whispered. He'd only been trying to help me out of a bad situation.

"Imogen." Wells pushed me back until he could see my face. His aura had been tumbling with so many colors since we'd left the park I'd given up trying to read them. "Even with all of the familial complications this will undoubtedly cause, and the delicate feelings you and I are going to have to navigate, I don't regret that it's you." He swallowed. "Do you?"

The guilt evaporated, something bright bursting in my chest. *Maybe it wasn't just me?* I shook my head. "You're pretty much my favorite person on the planet," I said. I had never felt this connection with anyone. I had never felt at home the way I already did in the short time I'd lived in this house.

The left side of his mouth lifted in a half smile. "And here I thought Cilla claimed that title."

"Well, she's taken," I said, my chest filled with butterflies. "And I'm tragically heterosexual." Our faces were inches apart. His hands tightened on my waist. My eyes were locked on his and I couldn't tear them away. I didn't know what I wanted, even though my body was sending *very* clear signals. Everything was happening so fast.

"Imogen," he said, his throat bobbing. "I want to kiss you so badly right now . . . but I'm afraid if I do, one thing will lead to another, and I don't know if you're ready."

"I don't know either . . ." I breathed. My core heated. My entire body was so warm. He squeezed my waist again and one thumb slipped under the hem of my shirt, brushing bare skin. I sucked in a breath. His hand stilled. I felt our combined senses narrow to that one point of contact. He moved his thumb across the few inches of skin above my waistband. Flames licked up from the base of my spine to fan out across my torso. I caught the shift in our pheromones the moment we both became aroused.

I leaned forward first, my eyelids fluttering closed as he tilted his head toward mine. One hand still gripped my waist, the other circled around my back, pressing me closer. The moment our lips met, I was lost.

It was like I had been deprived of air my entire life and was only now taking in my first breaths. Electricity rolled through me, shattering me and holding me together simultaneously. His hand swept under my shirt. Anywhere he touched my bare skin was hyper-sensitive. I wanted more. The taste of him was intoxicating. I couldn't get enough. I was going to combust if we didn't get closer . . .

The doorbell clanged through the house. The sound jarred us into awareness of the world outside of our two bodies. We broke the kiss, but didn't move, staring at each other, breathless.

"Someone's here . . ." he said. The longing in his eyes as he pulled his hand from under my shirt and smoothed it back down almost undid me.

The doorbell sounded again and we stood. Wells pulled me into a hug before we left the balcony. I closed my eyes, leaned against him, and listened to his heart thundering in his chest.

"Probably for the best," he sighed. "I don't want to rush this."

He took my hand in his, interlaced his fingers with mine, and pulled me inside. We went to see who was so insistently ringing the bell.

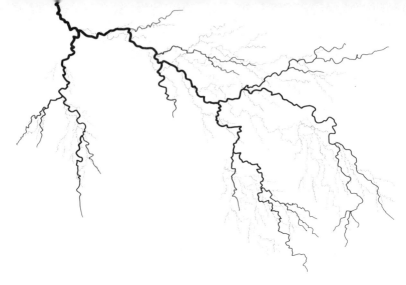

CHAPTER TWENTY-SIX

Oh, honey, sometimes words don't do the trick.
Every now and then you gotta hit it with a hammer.
—Solange Aidair Delaney

We trotted down the stairs as quickly as we could go, hand in hand.

"Do you think it's Al?" I asked. I couldn't think of who else would be so stubbornly hammering away at the doorbell.

"If it is, we'll deal with it," Wells said, eyes on the door. "We'll have to deal with him sooner or later." He didn't release my hand as he grabbed the knob and pulled it open.

Captain Marc was leaning against the frame. A bottle of sparkling wine in his hands. He raised an eyebrow. "I understand congratulations are in order?"

Moments later we were in the sitting room, each with a glass of wine in front of us, the rest of the bottle chilling in a bucket off to the side. Wells and I sat shoulder to shoulder, knee to knee in the middle of the couch across from Captain Marc.

"You haven't accepted yet, I see," the captain said, a smile dancing on his lips. "I hope I didn't interrupt the process." He took a sip of wine.

We're going to start breaking blood vessels in our cheeks, I thought as both of us reddened for the umpteenth time.

Wells shook his head. "It just happened. I want to make sure . . ." His eyes flicked to me then back to Marc. "I want to make sure it's what Imogen wants."

"I mean, is there even another option?" I asked. "Not that I don't . . . I mean . . ." I squeezed my eyes shut and blew out a breath. "This is all just really unexpected."

"I thought you might have questions, both of you," Captain Marc said, twirling the stem of his glass. "That's why I came over once I heard."

"How *did* you hear, come to think of it?" Wells asked.

"Oh, I was at the palace when Aloysius came tearing through in a tempest of emotion." He rolled his eyes, then settled them on Wells. "Your mother got your 'path, by the way. She's with him now."

"How is he?" Wells asked, his eyes cast down.

"Oh, it's not a pretty sight," the captain said. "But I'm not here to talk about Aloysius. I'm here for the two of you." He set his glass down and looked at me. "To answer your question, yes, there is a choice, although it's not a great one." He interlaced his fingers across his stomach and leaned back in his chair. "I knew a couple who didn't accept the bond."

Wells raised his gaze to Marc.

"Well before you were even thought of," Marc continued. "Her name was Elena and her partner, Joustin, was a spy during the Wind War. Before he left, he asked his best friend, an artist named Pouleau, to watch out for her. The two became close as Elena was constantly fretting about her love. Pouleau was there when she got the news that Joustin had been made. Captured spies don't live long. The bond materialized while Pouleau was comforting a grieving Elena."

"Her partner wasn't dead," I said.

Captain Marc smiled sadly. "He wasn't. He came home weeks later to his partner and his best friend, who had not accepted the bond in order to give themselves time to grieve."

"How did they live with that?" Wells asked. "I can't be in a separate room from Imogen without feeling like my stomach is being cut out with a dull sword."

"They all cohabitated at first. After a century, it got easier. Pouleau was even able to take other partners eventually, but the bond was always there. It faded, but it never dissolved. Neither of them ever felt truly whole." Marc picked up his glass again. "Once mated, the idea of being with anyone else becomes distasteful. Even for a previously polyamorous person. Theirs was an extreme circumstance. This is not. Take the time you need, ask all the questions you like, but there's no reason not to accept eventually."

"What about Al?" Wells asked.

"What about him?" Marc snapped. "I've watched you put Aloysius's happiness and well-being ahead of your own for your entire life, Llewellyn. Over half the time it was never deserved nor appreciated."

Wells squeezed my hand. His gaze cut toward me for an instant but he didn't meet my eyes. "Imogen hasn't decided if she'll remain sidhe. If she chooses to become human what—"

"If she decides to turn back before accepting, the bond will dissolve. Bonds only form between pairs of similar levels of kromatic ability and as a human, Imogen would have none," Marc said quietly. "After acceptance, there is no going back. Your souls will be intertwined and as humans don't form mating bonds ... it's never been done before and I personally wouldn't risk it. It's not difficult to imagine a multitude of ways it might wreck the both of you. For instance, if one mate dies, the other is left a shell of their former self, holding the shredded halves of two souls. I'd imagine the feeling would be similar, only you'd both be alive to endure it"

Wells nodded, his face composed, although his aura split and fractured. "Imogen doesn't love me." He swallowed, as if forcing the words out was difficult. "She should get to choose her partner."

"And what about you? How do you feel?" Marc set his drink down, his eyes boring into Wells. Even as I was thinking, *I don't . . . not love you . . .*

For a few long seconds, Wells was quiet. Then he took my hand in both of his and gazed at me so earnestly I held my breath. "I've been falling in love with you for months, Imogen," he said. My heart flipped into my throat. He continued, "And I know you're not over losing Keane, I wouldn't expect you to be. I didn't want to tell you because I don't want to put any pressure on you, one way or the other. I don't want you to feel forced into anything you're not ready for, or make you feel like you can't return to humanity if you choose. I never intended to . . . entrap you or . . ."

"I never thought that," I said, squeezing his hands, my breath coming back, quick and shallow. I'd never thought he felt anything for me above a developing friendship and a sense of obligation. "I never felt like you were trying to push me into anything."

"There." Captain Marc retrieved his glass. "Give Imogen whatever time she needs—hell, some couples like to drag acceptance out for months to enjoy the intensity—but forget about Aloysius. This isn't about him. It's time he learned he's not always the most important person in the room anyway. Being mated is rare and fantastic. You both deserve it." He lifted his glass. "My sincere congratulations."

We raised our glasses and murmured our thanks. Both blushing furiously, of course.

"Does it . . . feel different after it's accepted?" I asked. I couldn't fathom living life attached at the hip, and yet right now, I couldn't fathom being farther away from Wells than the edge of the couch.

The captain chuckled. "Yes, you'll be able to leave each other in another room without feeling physically ill. And the physical urgency in general will abate after a few weeks. Emotionally and intuitively, however, you'll be perfectly in tune with each other after accepting." He sipped. "If your mate is in distress, you'll feel it. Even if you're on the other side of the world. And the two of you being telepaths will probably make the connection even deeper."

Captain Marc finished his glass, set it down, and removed the bottle from its nest of ice to refill, indicating that we should accept top-ups as well. "I should warn you, however," he said as he poured. "You'll have to bring Imogen to work until you accept. Or Imogen becomes human again and the bond dissolves. You won't be able to tolerate leaving her behind. Get ready to field questions about when you'll be having your acceptance party."

Wells groaned and fell against the backrest.

"Thousands of people are going to want to attend, Llewellyn. And several are probably going to give you acceptance advice, whether they've mated themselves or not."

Wells took a deep pull from his glass.

"Cilla already wants us to make an acceptance video with my phone," I said, taking a sip of my own. Wells choked.

Captain Marc roared with laughter. "That's right," he said between guffaws. "I heard you were harboring a bit of contraband." He winked at me.

"We are *not* making a video, Imogen," Wells gasped, trying to dislodge sparkling wine from his windpipe. The captain wiped away a tear of mirth, still cackling.

"I didn't say *I* wanted to make a video, I said Cilla wanted us to make one." I took another sip of bubbles, perversely enjoying Wells's squirming. "She thinks we're hot together."

Suddenly an envelope burst into being before my eyes and dropped to the table in front of me. "Imogen" was written on the front and nothing else.

"That's Al's writing," Wells said. The atmosphere shifted.

I snatched it off the table, setting my glass down, and tearing open the flap. "I'll just get it over with." Inside was a card with the word "congratulations" scribbled across it, but what caught my eye was the familiar ring that tumbled out.

My lungs turned to concrete. I reached a trembling hand toward the shining circle and dragged it to the edge of the table. My heart pounded louder and louder until the sound filled my ears. I lifted my hand and stared. My engagement ring sat on the polished wood, vibrating slightly from my touch, winking up at me.

"Imogen." Wells rubbed long, soothing strokes along my spine. "You're shaking."

My heart slowly splintered. The sharp edges of the fractures cutting and slicing me. Tearing me apart from the inside. I was going to break down. I was going to collapse right here, turn into a puddle. How could I . . .

NO.

I pressed my palms to the table on either side of the ring and the note and took a deep breath.

He sent this to hurt me. I will not fall apart.

I stood up. "I want to see him. Now." My voice was granite.

"Imogen." Wells stood with me, a hand on my low back. His face was so pale.

"Now."

And bless his soul, Captain Marc didn't ask any questions. He grabbed our hands and winked us straight into the palace.

Al was pacing in front of a gracefully seated sidhe who had to be the queen. Her golden hair was a few shades darker than Al's, but her amber eyes were twins to his. She blinked once when we appeared, but otherwise showed no signs of alarm or surprise.

When I locked eyes with Al, all I saw was red.

"Your majesty," I said to the queen as I strode across the floor, my footsteps echoing loudly. "Nice to meet you."

"Aloysius," I snarled. "Got your note."

I punched him in the face.

CHAPTER TWENTY-SEVEN

Sleeping with someone is one thing. But lying with someone, trusting them enough to get complete rest in their company, that's magical.
—Henry Delaney

My aim was dead on. I heard his septum crack.

Wells leapt forward and snaked an arm around my waist, pulling me away before I could follow up.

"I knew you were self-absorbed, oblivious, and arrogant," I snapped, trying to shove Wells off. "But I never would have called you cruel until today."

Al let out a roar as he wrenched his nose back into place, the snap reverberating across the room like a shot. He wiped the blood from his upper lip with the back of his hand, glaring at me. "You've been asking for your damn ring back," he snarled. "So, I sent it to you."

"I've been asking for it for *months*!" I yelled, almost breaking free of Wells. "You only returned it to me when you could weaponize it. When you could use it to *hurt me*, you insufferable bastard!"

"*You* hurt *me!*" he shouted, his glare now including Wells. "Both of you!"

"Everything that you are going through right now is your own damn fault!" My arms were now pinned to my sides, Wells bear-hugging me from behind. "Maybe you should try taking ownership of some of the goddamn pain in your life instead of trying to push it off as someone else's problem. Take a look at what *you've done* to get to this spot." My voice started to break. Hot, angry tears burned behind my eyes.

"I didn't search through every damn human in your family, find you, turn you... bring you here... give you this life so you could be my *brother's* mate!" Al's face reddened. He opened his mouth to continue but I cut him off.

"For the last *fucking* time, I never asked you to bring me here! I never asked you for any of this! I was fine where I was and you acted with no thought for anyone's feelings but your own!" My breath started to hitch with unshed tears. I stopped fighting Wells and sagged against him. "I'm sorry you lost someone important to you. But when you really love someone, all you want is for them to be happy. And she was. Solange was happy on Earth. Maybe you should try making yourself happy instead of putting that onus onto someone else."

"We're going," Wells said, backing away with me. I was barely holding tears at bay. Wells loosened his hold enough that I was able to turn around and wrap my arms around him.

"Sorry to disrupt your evening, mother," he said.

"Not at all," she replied. "Do come back and visit when things are less... volatile."

Captain Marc winked us back home, saw us inside, and then took his leave, telling us to get in touch anytime we had any questions or needed to talk.

For a few minutes we stood in the entryway, arms wrapped around each other. Wells rubbed my back until I had stopped shaking. "I'm sorry I had to hold you back," he told me. "But my mother is unaccountably fond of both of us and I didn't want her first introduction to you to involve you murdering Al."

"I wouldn't have killed him," I sniffed. "If I'd killed him, how would he learn?"

Wells snorted. We released each other, but didn't go far. I looked back at the table where my ring still sat, glinting in the evening sunlight filtering through the curtains. My heart hung behind my ribs like a lead balloon.

"I'm sorry," he said. "I'm sorry it hurts."

I walked to the table, leaned over, slid the ring onto my palm, and straightened. I traced its bright edges with a fingertip. Images of Keane's proposal and our engagement party flashed across my mind's eye. Faces of friends and family I would never see again.

A wave of guilt pulsed through me. Just as Al knew it would. He did, actually, know certain parts of me well. This time I didn't push it down. I let myself feel it, squeezing my eyes shut for a few breaths as it rolled around me. I swallowed against the burning in my throat until it had ripped through me and subsided.

My eyes were clear when I folded my fingers over the ring and tucked it into my pocket. I picked up the note and the envelope, focused my energy, and set them on fire, banishing the ash as it formed, until nothing was left.

We tried to sleep in our own rooms that night.

I lay awake after an hour of tossing fitfully. The urge to get up and go to him like a physical hook dragging at my core. My stomach churned so intensely that I was on the verge of 'pathing Wells when he knocked on my door. "Come in!" I called out. *Thank Christ.*

He opened the door and stood in the doorway, in a t-shirt and loose pants. I knew from laryngospasm experience that he didn't normally wear that much clothing to bed. "Imogen, I'm sorry, I just—"

"It's fine," I said, my muscles already relaxing as he stepped across the threshold. "I don't think I would be able to sleep like this either."

"I can throw a blanket on the floor," he said and grabbed a pillow from the other side of the bed.

"Don't be ridiculous." I sighed and tossed the covers back. "C'mon in. The water's fine."

He hesitated half a second before sliding between the sheets as if he were indeed inching into a cold pool. Once we were both settled, I reached out and took his hand. I knew I wasn't the only one to experience a wash of relief.

"Goodnight," I said, feeling sleepier already.

"Goodnight," he replied, squeezing my hand. We fell asleep side by side.

We woke up completely entangled.

I was sprawled across Wells, my cheek pillowed on his chest, both of my legs wrapped around one of his. He had one arm flung over my back, hugging me to him, his other hand was tangled in my hair, cupping the back of my head. I didn't want to move. He'd always smelled so good and I was warm, relaxed, and comfortable.

Yes, I was conflicted. I'd made a promise to Keane. He'd been a friend to me for most of my adult life before we'd started dating. My intention had been to stay with him forever. The fact that I hadn't purposefully left him, that I hadn't flung myself at Wells indiscriminately, alleviated the guilt, but didn't erase the loss.

The ring lay in the locked nightstand drawer with my phone, earbuds, and running pouch. My most precious things. I'd put it on when I'd first come into my room alone. Even though I'd only been without it for a few months, it already felt strange. I'd pulled it off and studied it. Remembered how happy I'd been to receive it. Mentally reliving Keane's proposal, every moment of our engagement party, and several memories of our friendship together. "I hope you can heal," I'd whispered to the ring. To Keane. "And I hope you find someone new to love." Then I'd tucked it away.

I'd 'ported Cilla a note, telling her that we'd seen Captain Marc, we hadn't accepted yet, that Al had sent my ring back, that I'd met the queen, and broken Al's nose. And that I was fine. And to name the baby after me. Then I'd drawn a smiley face.

Wells stirred beneath me. I allowed myself to stay heavy, sleepy, and limp, curious about his reaction. I felt him stiffen, then slowly relax. He dipped his nose toward the crown of my head and inhaled. Then dropped the softest of kisses on my hair. His chest expanded in a sigh and he gently rubbed my back.

"Imogen," he said softly, "time to wake up now."

I inhaled deeply. *God, how does he smell so good?* Then mumbled, "Five more minutes."

His chest dropped as he huffed a laugh. "Okay, five more minutes."

We ended up dozing together for another hour.

Going to work with Wells was interesting on a number of levels. Not the least of which was that I got to see him in full uniform for the first time.

And it was hot.

"You have actual *armor* as part of your uniform?" I said, touching a finger to the rigid plates over his shoulders. "They don't have that on Earth. Not the... everyday uniforms anyway."

"Which is surprising to me considering there are so many guns on Earth," he said. "Our entire planet has banned them. We do enough damage with swords and kroma."

I'd surreptitiously taken a few pictures of him on my phone to show Cilla later. I used my phone to record her during our self-defense practice—she did better when she could see where she was going wrong—and I'd taken some pictures since living in Molnair, but I'd shown no one my pictures from Earth. I'd only scrolled through them a few times myself. I didn't get very far before my heart was wrapped in grief. I hoped that someday I'd be able to look at them and remember good times.

Then there was enduring the reactions of everyone that Wells worked with once they noticed the mating bond. Which was almost immediately. Everyone was genuinely happy for him—I read each of their auras—and curious about me. Although the palace had effectively installed their version of events as the truth, people were undeniably interested in me and my involvement with Al and Wells and, of course, just being one of the thirteen meant I was known.

Some people liked to tell me my history, which was new. And odd. They'd say I was from New Orleans in the United States and originally spoke English, as if these were things I didn't know. I did my best, smiled, and told them they were correct, which seemed to make them happy. It didn't seem worth the effort to point out that I'd only just moved to New Orleans, was born in Nashville, Tennessee, and had lived all over the place.

Captain Marc was right: everyone wanted to know when we were accepting, if there was a party planned, where it would be, etc. Wells deflected gracefully by saying we were going to enjoy this part for a while and that when we had scheduled something, he'd let everyone know.

The most interesting was when we observed some of the training. Regiments doing coordinated combat kromatics together was fascinating. Some would fling out glittering shields—all visible to me due to my aural sight, but I learned that not all shields were visible to everyone—while others tossed out attacks from behind their safety. The individual colors of their kroma streaked across the training field in different shapes, depending on what offensive blast was being used. Beautiful and deadly.

"Maybe I should join the army," I said to Wells one night over dinner. He had taken me out to a place in the city. It had an outdoor patio in the back that faced the river. Less people to walk by and stare. I had a feeling that he was trying to take me on "dates" to ease me into the mating bond, although he hadn't explicitly said so. I liked it, so I didn't try to make him label it for me. "I'm good at fighting."

"Gods' bones, Imogen... I don't know." He swirled the amber liquid in his glass before taking a large gulp.

"Why?" I narrowed my eyes and popped a piece of cephlaang into my mouth.

"You're... yes, you can fight, but I don't know that you have the temperament to be a ground level soldier. You'd have to blindly follow instructions, without question, which you *never* do." He examined his drink as he spoke. "You do have a talent for one-on-one combat, you're intelligent, admit when you're wrong, and self-correct. You might make a good officer, but in order to jump the ranks into officer, you'd have to have shown some remarkable, live-battle combat skill or have been educated specifically for the role in a university."

I frowned at my glass of wine. Everything he'd said about me was accurate.

He reached over and took my hand. As usual, we both sighed at the contact. "If you decide that's something you'd like to try, we'll get you enrolled, but please remember that you have centuries rather than decades to work with now. *If* you decide not to return to Earth. You're under no pressure to find a calling right away, Imogen. I know you're used to trying to get as much done as possible because time was short, but allow yourself to explore a bit before trying to cram into any particular box. You never know what skills you might find in the coming months. Give yourself some breathing room. You can try as many things as you like."

Something bright burst inside me. *You can try as many things as you like.* "But eventually I'll have to settle on a career or something, won't I? I mean, how long have you—"

Wells shook his head, a half-smile inching up the left side of his face. "My situation is different. Many people explore different careers throughout their lives. When you find something that inspires you, try it out."

My answering smile could have cracked my face in two. I really did fit here.

The following days were some of our best as Wells and I slowly eased in to our new relationship. His affection and steady support lifted me and I began to see glimmers of a happy life in my future as we relaxed further into our routine.

I should have known better.

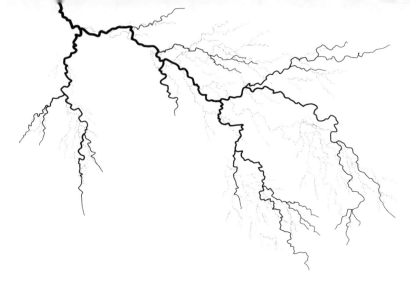

CHAPTER TWENTY-EIGHT

Have each other's six. That's what you do for your friends.
—Solange Aidair Delaney

Wells watched me strap my modified running pouch under my armpits and across my chest. "I don't understand why this is necessary." He crossed his arms.

"Cilla is a visual learner. She was raised on a steady diet of Snapchats and TikToks." I had cut a small window in the pouch for my phone's camera and stitched up the sides to keep it in place. Thus modified, I could wear it at chest level when we sparred and Cilla could see when she was leaving herself open.

Cilla and Zoe had decided to publicly announce their pregnancy in one week, becoming the first parents of the thirteen. In the meantime, Cilla had blossomed as a swordswoman. As long as we kept everything technical and never more than scratched each other, she had fun and enjoyed the exercise.

Zoe encouraged it, as movement and blood flow was good for the baby. And of course, they trusted me never to thrust at Cilla's center, no matter how lightly we sparred.

"Is it worth the risk of someone seeing it, though?" Wells asked.

"I'm wearing a black tank top and pants, the pouch is black, the phone is black. Someone would have to be searching for it to even see anything odd. They're more likely to be checking out how hot Cilla is with a sword than examining my activewear." He was still frowning. I stepped nearer and lightly circled his waist with my arms. "If anyone starts looking too closely, I'll 'port it back," I promised.

"All right, fine." He relented, uncrossing his arms and wrapping them around me. I'd recently discovered he had a much more difficult time arguing with me when I was touching him. Devious? Yes. But we were already running late and Zoe had to go into work today.

Although we knew many of the thirteen were easing up on the restrictions, Wells stuck to the official guidelines, insisting something was off. That we hadn't had so much as a peep from Sephrya worried him. He did occasionally let me start running before the tree line but that was as far as his rule bending went.

The bond still made it uncomfortable for us if I went too far anyway. At least we could shower now without the other one sitting in the bathroom, facing away from the shower curtain, pretending hard not to be trying to catch a glimpse.

I strapped my sword at my hip and I threw another across my back for Cilla. My dagger was already at home in my boot. "We're late," I said. "We should get going, we don't want to hold up Zoe."

"Right, I'm ready." Wells opened the door.

Al was seated on the steps.

"Oh, great, you're armed." He hopped to the ground and raised his hands. "Don't hit me."

I rolled my eyes and tried to walk past him. "We don't have time for this."

"Imogen, please." Al moved in front of me. I jerked to a halt, feeling the warmth against my back when Wells stepped behind me. I would have shoved Aloysius out of the way if the heartbroken expression on his face hadn't stopped me.

"Look, I've been thinking about everything you said after you . . . well, you broke my nose. You were there, you know what you did." He ran his thumb and forefinger down the sides of his now perfectly straight nose. "And you're right, Im, I do want you to be happy. And I'm glad to know that Solange was happy and I think I'd like to hear more about that sometime. But isn't there a way that all of us can be happy?"

"I . . . I dunno." I glanced at Wells for help. We were late.

"Al," he said patiently. "I do think we all need to talk about this, but now is not the best time. Maybe we can arrange a dinner or—"

"I can't sleep," Al said, his face drawn. "I can barely eat. I need to figure this out. I need to find a way for Imogen to be in my life and be happy—"

"Oh, my God, you're so *mind-blowingly* entitled," I snapped. Zoe was going to be late to work because of this bullshit. "You let people know when you want to have discussions like this. You send a note or something. You don't just show up at people's houses and ambush them—" I tried again to go around him.

Al grabbed my arm, holding hard. Alarm flashed across my nerves and I froze, sucking in a sharp breath. "Imogen, I am in agony here—"

"I told you if you touched her we would have it out."

Wells's voice sliced through the air like a dagger of ice. Al released my arm as if burned. Backed up a step.

Wells took my hand. His face was set, eyes flashing. I'd never seen him look so dangerous. "We'll talk soon." He winked us to the park.

"Are you all right?" Wells squeezed my hand as soon as the sun hit our skin, back to the Wells I knew. "Your face when he grabbed you . . ."

"I'm fine, I was just—I'm fine." I pushed a smile up at him and tugged him toward our meeting place. My heart was still pounding hard. Wells could probably tell, but he let it go.

A Dagger of Lightning

No one was at our usual bench by the blue shrubs.

"Do you think they left when we weren't here on time?" My heart sank. I was really looking forward to filming Cilla in the park with a sword.

"No, there's Zoe right there," Wells said, waving toward the lithe, ebony figure striding toward us. He stepped out to meet her.

I followed, my heart inflating with relief. But where was Cilla?

"Sorry we're late," Wells said, taking the sack a smiling Zoe handed him. "We got ambushed by Al. Where's Cilla?"

The smile dropped from Zoe's face so quickly I felt like my guts had been plunged into ice water.

"I left her right here," she said, her eyes darting around in panic. "She was talking to some friends. I went to get snacks for you all at the harvest shop." She indicated the bag Wells now held. "There are so many people around, and I figured you'd be here any second..."

"Why would she—" I spun around. Cilla wouldn't wander off. I twisted to Wells. He was already scenting the air. Shaking his head.

"No one came up to her here," he said.

My head whipped to the forest.

"If they sent a púka to lure her..." Zoe's voice barely had breath behind it.

"*CILLA!*" I sprinted toward the tree line, following Cilla's lavender verbena scent. Adrenaline flooded my senses. Making me reckless. I caught glimpses of Zoe and Wells as they winked through the forest calling for Cilla. Then others. Wells had called in Al. I saw Captain Marc. A few lieutenants I recognized from the military campus. I kept running. My mental awareness sweeping the area for any hint of Cilla.

I stumbled over a tangle of vines when I reached our favorite clearing. "Here!" I yelled, my insides coursing with electricity, pinging Wells telepathically as well. They winked in around me, one by one.

Cilla had put up a fight.

Vines were everywhere. Wrapped around trunks and branches. Sliced in half. Splintered and confettied. She hadn't gone easily.

I stalked around the area. Following Cilla's scent. Something in me hardened. Emotions retreated behind gunwales. Hatches battened. Senses heightened. My being now focused on one thing. Find Cilla.

I found a bloodstain on the trunk of a tree. Eye level. Cilla was one inch taller than me. "Here." My throat tightened as I pulled two long blond hairs from a splinter in the wood.

Wells appeared beside me. "It's Sephrya," he said. "Sire, I can smell them."

I took in those around me for the first time. The king had joined us. He was in worn leather pants, good boots, and a sturdy, if ornate, tunic. His face was grave.

"Four of them," I said, panting slightly, my skin alight with adrenaline. "There were four of them. Three male, one female." My insides burned and hardened simultaneously. *I will destroy them.* My gentle Cilla. How dare they?

My gaze fell on Zoe. Silent tears coated her stricken face. Her aura fractured and reformed endlessly. The colors darkening, cracking painfully. Wells crossed to her, pulling her into his arms. She clung to him, sobbing openly. She was tall enough that she was able to wrap her arms around his neck and cry into his shoulder.

"It's all right," Wells said, rubbing long strokes up and down Zoe's back. "I can try to get a 'path on her and pinpoint a location to wink—"

"You will do no such thing, Llewellyn," Allestair said. "*I forbid it.*"

Both Zoe and Wells went rigid. My jaw dropped as the electric fizz of Allestair's kroma swept through the clearing. Sidhe were physically incapable of performing any act their king had forbidden. The injunctive pierced their psyche deeper than a compulsion. But why forbid Wells from finding Cilla?

"We need to get her back. Now." Anxiety pitched my voice louder as my eyes darted around the clearing, searching for any nods of agreement, a sympathetic face . . . no one met my gaze. Why was the king being an asshole?

"Im." Al. Eyes bright. Looking for once like he was empathizing with someone aside from himself. "We don't even know where they've taken her. What their plan is."

My entire body went numb, then cold, then hot in half a second. "We can't wait though. What if they hurt her? What about the baby?" I rasped.

Everyone looked at me then. Even Allestair's politically correct tragic mask dialed up to something genuine. Anger spiked hot as he strode to Zoe, who was still clinging to Wells, weeping. Now *Cilla's important?* I clamped my mouth shut, clinging to my temper by my fingernails. *Whatever, if it'll get everyone's asses in gear...*

"She was with child?" Allestair asked. Zoe nodded, unable to speak. "How long?"

"They were going to announce next week," Wells said, giving her a squeeze.

Everyone deflated. I spun in a circle, taking them all in, my eyes wide. Disbelief punched me in the chest when I realized they *still* weren't going after her. They were just more upset now that they'd lost a precious kid.

What the fuck?

"So let's go, let's get her back," I nearly shouted. I was *not* going to accept this.

"Imogen." Allestair's icy stare fell on me for the first time. His words cut the air like flint. "I understand that Cilla was a good friend," the use of the past tense lit a fire in my belly, "but we don't know where she's been taken. We don't know what Sephrya wants with her. We don't even know for certain it was them that took her."

"Yes we do, Wells just said he could smell it was them!" I snapped. Several people cringed on my behalf. I knew I had addressed the monarch rudely, but I didn't give two shits.

Piercing ice blue eyes stared me down, his lips thinned in a grim smile. "We need to find out what they want. We need indisputable proof, before committing any aggressive act. We cannot upset our neutrality with the surrounding nations without a verified offense." He turned his back on me.

"Llewellyn, go handle your mate. She's obviously upset. Zoe . . ." I ground my teeth, staring in disbelief as he extracted Zoe from Wells's arms, took her hands in his, and told her that we might not be able to get Cilla back.

An electric charge shot through me. This was not done. I wouldn't accept it. I didn't need to listen to them. I ignored Wells's subdued walk toward me and turned to Cilla's favorite tree. I placed my hands on the bark as I'd seen her do countless times. I let the scent of Cilla's blood combine with the earthy smell of the trees she loved. I'd find out where she was my damn self. If she was in Sephrya, maybe Wells could send a unit; surely they wouldn't just let them keep her.

Where are you? Where are you? I stretched myself toward a faint sense of her . . . far away . . . A glimmer of something.

Cilla. Just out of reach.

I closed my eyes. Shut out the clearing and everyone in it. Pulled all my energy toward touching that hint of my friend. Diving after that little spark. There. Just there . . .

Gotcha! My eyes flew open as I latched on to her essence.

My gaze collided with Wells. "I feel her," I said, then let my energy rip toward hers without thinking.

A lightness swept through my veins. My very ether went diaphanous as the world around me dissolved. I heard Wells screaming my name.

But I'd already winked.

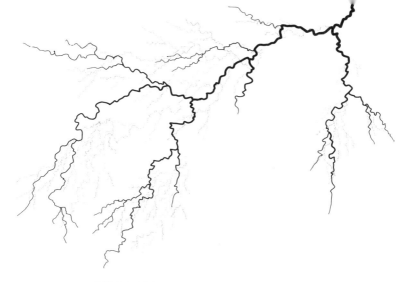

CHAPTER TWENTY-NINE

Sometimes you have to wade through shit. That's life.
—Solange Aidair Delaney

I clung to that sense of Cilla as the black void tore at me. The farther I was wrenched from Wells, the more my insides felt like they were being scraped out by dull spoons. But I hung on.

I knew that there was a possibility of getting lost in the nether or getting spit out somewhere random if I let my focus waver. Wells and I hadn't worked on winking. We'd only discussed theory. I understood enough of it to know that if I didn't make it to Cilla, there were a host of horrible possibilities I could be tossed into. I could land in the middle of the ocean. Ten feet underground.

I had nearly reached her, my energy barreling toward hers, when I flattened against a firm but flexible barrier. My essence made one last flail toward hers before it was flung forcibly back. I was bounced away from Cilla, my body solidifying as I flew. My very corporeal bones smacking against the earth as I landed sprawling in a straw-covered, muddy courtyard. Breathless, I yanked a cloaking shield up, scrambled to my feet, and searched for a place to hide and get my bearings. Wherever Cilla was, it was warded against winking.

If I had to compare the palace in Molnair to something on Earth, I would have said it was a combination of Versailles and the Sistine Chapel. The place I had landed in Sephrya was giving Tower of London vibes.

But back in the day when it was fully operational. Lots of heavy stone and thick walls. Weathered towers stretching toward a hot, pale lavender sky. Walls of stone surrounded the courtyard. A chill swept down my spine in spite of the humid day.

The Tower of London was easy to get into, but incredibly difficult to get out of again.

When cloaked, I was completely hidden from physical and kromatic senses. Which included telepathic communication. According to Wells, all my defensive shields were exceptional. Still, my nerves crackled in the midst of so many enemies.

The courtyard was alive with silver, gold, and bronze-haired assholes, armed to the teeth. I must be on a military campus. Or their palace was just more obviously guarded than the one in Molnair. I spotted a stack of hay and a cluster of wooden barrels near a break in the wall.

I darted for it, rubbed up against the hay to disguise my scent, and tucked myself into the break, making sure that I was completely hidden from sight. Then I dismissed the cloaking.

Wells? My mental voice stretched, like it was spanning an ocean. I struggled to focus my 'path on Wells's essence. That same life force that had become an addictive draw for my physical self. My belly, my spine, my entire torso ached terribly with so much distance between us. Seconds passed before I felt my 'path make contact.

Imogen! Where are you? Come back now! Please! Pain coated his 'path and my heart contracted. My insides cramped as if they were tied into a million knots, and I knew his pain was sharper. Whenever we'd described the sensation to each other, my pain was a dull ache, his was a knife in the gut.

I'll try. I squeezed my eyes shut and focused my entire being on Wells. On the sense of him that I was now so attuned to. Like reaching out my hands in the dark. My mind stretched and mental fingertips brushed his. I leapt forward...

And hit a wall. My eyes flew open as I slammed back into my body. It was as if I had been trying to cross from one room to another and run into thick curtains with no break between them.

I don't think I can wink out here. I gave myself a shake. *Cilla's here somewhere, but I can't wink to her, I was bounced away. I'm so sorry, I didn't know what I was doing.*

It's okay, Imogen, it's okay. I could feel his panic beneath the soothing mental caress he pushed my way. *We'll find a way to get to Cilla once you've returned. The king has forbidden Zoe and I from going after you.* I winced at the anguish twisting through his 'path. *You need to find your own way back. Imogen, I know you can. Please.* My heart ached.

I will. I promise. How do I know when I'm beyond the no-winking wards? I forced my breathing to slow.

You'll see shimmering. There was a longer pause. *Zoe says it's like a desert mirage. Does that make sense to you?*

Yes, it does. I peered out from behind the barrels and scanned the area. Beyond the large, arched, stone entrance, I saw a slight haze floating over the horizon. Waves in the air, like the promise of a puddle that would never exist. *I think I see it, Wells, I need to cloak.*

I sent a mental hug toward Wells and broke contact.

Then, chest tight, I turned away from the mirage and toward the terrifying castle. I felt as though I were being eviscerated but I pushed through. I had to try.

I couldn't leave without Cilla.

CHAPTER THIRTY

*If we didn't have absolutely horrible days,
we wouldn't fully appreciate the fantastic ones.*
—Henry Delaney

I kept a white-knuckled mental grip on that sense of Cilla I'd locked onto in the forest. She was somewhere inside the awful Poor Man's Tower of London. I pulled my phone out of the pouch, activated the camera, made sure it was recording, then tucked it back in. Maybe I'd be able to catch something useful. Or at least they might learn how we died if our bodies were returned. I pushed that thought away.

I summoned my cloaking shield, testing its edges to make sure I was completely covered. I flexed my kromatic muscle, relieved to find it thrumming with strength, and followed the thread of awareness tugging me toward Cilla.

There were lots of entrances. One main one. With a large, arched opening spanning the whole of the enormous wall, lazily watched by guards on either side and marching along the top. Most people filed in and out of this opening. I took two steps toward it before my senses pulled me in another direction.

One guard stood a few feet in front of a small side door. I skirted wide and eased up behind him, stepping carefully as I edged around the building. He was too close. I wouldn't get to the door without brushing him.

I blew out a slow breath and waited. This was the way, I knew it. I stared at the door, willing it to open, willing someone to come out and move this guy aside so I could slip in. A bead of sweat slid down my spine as minutes ticked by like hours. I was losing energy standing here cloaked. Nerves wrapped around my aching belly.

Just when I was about to shift position to give my muscles some relief, another guard stepped up to talk to the one in my way. He took two steps forward to meet his companion and I wasted no time in slipping behind him, pressing my back into the heavy wooden door and easing it open. Their eyes never left each other as I slid sideways through the narrow opening, then toed the door back toward the frame.

The breath I'd been holding fled in a long exhale. I gave my eyes one moment to adjust, then tore down the long, dim corridor toward Cilla.

This is like Prince Humperdinck's castle in The Princess Bride, I thought as I passed drafty corridor after drafty corridor. Everything in depressing gray stone. Even the most cheerful of realtors would only be able to point out that the corridors were wide and the tuckpointing well done. There were no other redeeming qualities.

Someone should throw up a decorative tapestry or two, I thought, trying to distract myself from the insanity of what I was attempting. *Even a suit of armor in a corner or a nice potted plant would be an improvement.* I vibrated with nerves. I had no idea where I was. No idea where Cilla was beyond a vague sense that I was heading in the right direction. No clue how much energy I was going to need to maintain the cloaking shield, rescue Cilla from wherever she was being held, get us both beyond the wards, and then somehow wink us home after having only winked myself once. Accidentally.

The deeper I went into the keep, the more my anxiety spiked. I knew it wasn't all due to being separated from Wells. Cloaking my entire self took a lot of energy. It wasn't something I could maintain for long stretches. I began dropping the cloak when I was in passageways alone. Picking it back up when I sensed someone approaching.

That beacon of essence clarified, pulsed stronger, and I knew I was close. Although even stretching my senses to reach for it was taking a toll. I was spreading myself thin. And my entire abdomen cramped like it was being scraped clean. I could only imagine how Wells felt. I drew both swords, tucked myself into an alcove, and removed the cloak.

Hi. I'm sorry.

Imogen, his mind latched onto mine with a desperate intensity. *Where are you? I thought you'd seen a spot to wink out?*

I did. I know where it is. I let my thoughts curl around the sense of him like an embrace. *I'm going after Cilla. I can't leave her in this pit. I have to try.*

Imogen. The agony drenching his mental voice scraped against my own raw nerves like nails down a chalkboard. *I need you to get back. You have to make it out. If I could come to you, I would. Please come back to me.*

I will, I will. Oh shit. Hush. I pushed his mind away roughly, fighting back a sob at the painful loss of contact, then yanked my cloak up just as two Sephryan soldiers marched up the corridor I was facing.

"All I know is he wants to see her. Not our place to ask questions, is it?" the bronze-haired one was saying. Were they talking about Cilla? My blood heated.

"It just seems like we should get some recognition, doesn't it?" said his silver-headed companion. "No one else has brought one in."

I detached myself from the wall and followed them. Keeping my cloak in place while angry and moving burned more energy, but I didn't have the space for that concern. By the way they were talking, I didn't think they had discovered Cilla's pregnancy yet.

"Don't ask for a reward for doing what the king asks," Bronze replied with a put-upon sigh. "We still have to hope she cooperates."

My jaw clenched and I had to work to pay attention to where we were going. Rage made the constant clawing at my torso easier to ignore, but left me more likely to slip up. *Remember, you have to get both of you out of here,* I reminded myself.

Then I smelled it. Her lavender verbena. Shimmering beneath a thick coat of terror. I forced myself to stay behind the idiot guards, sucking in deep breaths when they catcalled Cilla through the barred window of her cell door. Careful that the door didn't lock behind us, I followed them over the threshold.

Then I saw her.

She was still in what she considered workout gear. A fitted shift dress with a built-in bra and leggings. Perfect for fencing outside in the summer heat. Freezing if you were locked inside the basement of a stone castle. *With a metal chain around your neck.* My fury roared like a lion caged behind my ribs.

Cilla was seated on a rough pallet, the mattress stuffed with straw. It was the only place she could go in the room due to the length of her chain. They started crooning to her.

My nails bit into the hilts of my swords.

She backed away on her hands and knees. Scooting herself into the corner. Tears in her eyes. Her aura tumbling with saffron waves of fear. One hand pressed against her belly.

"The king wants you," Silver purred. "Are you going to behave or do we make you?"

"Don't touch me," Cilla spat. I could see her trembling from feet away.

My arms shook with barely contained wrath. *Unlock her chain. Just unlock the damn chain.*

Bronze grabbed her by the hair and yanked her to the chain's limit. She yelped as the metal collar bit into her neck. Thrashed against him. Clawing his hand with her nails. Pulling at his fingers.

Silver kicked her in the ribs. Twice.

A red haze descended. I stripped off my cloak.

"Hey," I said. Their heads jerked toward me.

They dropped Cilla and moved to grab their own swords but the world had already slowed. I sliced through Bronze's neck first, then spun back around to completely behead Silver. They collapsed. Blades still sheathed.

"Immy!" Cilla cried.

I vomited by the edge of her straw mattress.

"Immy, are you okay?" She tried to reach me, but her chain wasn't long enough.

"I'm fine," I said, coughing. "I just killed my first people ever and it's nauseating." I wiped my mouth on my shirt and dropped to my knees beside her, reaching for the chain on her neck, fumbling to focus. It wouldn't unlock for me. "Shit." I turned back to the bodies. Pools of blood spread steadily around them.

Gagging, I went through their clothes and found the keys on Bronze. I unlocked the chain as quickly as I could with shaking hands and flung it off her. My stomach roiled with nausea coupled with the unbearable ache of being so far from my mate. "Are you okay? Baby okay?"

Cilla nodded. "I'm just a little sore. Where's Wells?" she asked, as if she sensed my pain.

"I accidentally winked to you on my own." I pulled her to her feet and handed over the second sword. She took it without question and strapped it on. "The king forbid Zoe and Wells from coming after us."

My throat closed up. Longing for Wells crashed into me like waves. The bitter, metallic smell of blood coated my tongue. I squeezed my eyes shut and doubled over, fighting the urge to retch.

Cilla's delicate fingers wrapped my shoulders. She shoved me upright and flung her arms around me. "We'll get back to them, Immy." She squeezed hard, then pushed me away, wide brown eyes locking on mine. "Let's go."

I nodded, gripping her arms. I took a deep breath, then coughed, choking on the smell of blood. "I need to get out of this room," I said. "I can't believe I killed two people."

"They would have killed you or locked you up like me," Cilla said, a hard set to her jaw. "I don't think life would have been pleasant for either of us if that had happened."

I knew she was right. I turned to the two guards, locked my emotions away, and bent to strip their bodies of weapons, coughing against the bile trying to crawl up my throat. Cilla and I ended up with two swords each. Our own familiar weapon and one shorter, wider, and strange. I found three daggers total and gave two to Cilla since I already had my own.

I risked contacting Wells once more, knowing I had limited power.

Still alive. I've got Cilla. Getting out now. Energy is low.

Will you be able to wink?

I guess we'll see. Gotta go. I cut off contact. A little moan pushed up from my throat.

Cilla rubbed my shoulder. "We're going back, we're going back to them now."

I nodded and crept to the door, listening through the barred window and summoning my cloaking shield. It was more difficult to drag over myself now and even harder to position around Cilla. I'd used up a lot of energy. "I'm going to keep us both cloaked as long as I can," I said, linking arms with her. "Once we get beyond the courtyard there's a place where I think winking is possible. I don't know if I'll be able to do it, but maybe I can pull energy from you or they can send someone."

Part of me hoped that Al would be beyond the king's injunctive and I could call on him to pull us out. It was a long shot, but I was willing to grasp at any chance. Worst case maybe we could hide somewhere in the countryside until my energy came back.

The journey back through the dreary corridors was arduous and seemed to take twice as long. Cilla told me that she'd seen her childhood dog at the edge of the woods.

She had been Cilla's only companion through adolescence and the one being she was devastated to leave when she was kicked out of her family's home.

A púka. Shape-shifter. Native to Sephrya. It appeared as soon as her friends had taken their leave. She'd run toward it without thinking and was deep in the woods by the time her mind caught up with her emotions. Once she'd realized she'd been lured away, it was too late. They really should put this kind of thing in the *So You Used to Be Mortal* handbooks.

I couldn't move as swiftly when I was cloaking both of us and I didn't dare pull the cloak off. It took too much effort to pull it back on. Instead, I made Cilla stop occasionally. We pressed ourselves into corners several times so that I could regroup. Not only was cloaking us enervating, the clawing pull inside of me was wearing as well.

I nearly wept with relief when we finally made it out to the courtyard. It was an effort not to sprint to the stone archway and the shimmering mirage waving tantalizingly beyond it. We wove our way through people and goods. Careful not to knock into anything or anyone.

We were halfway across the courtyard when my cloak utterly failed.

CHAPTER THIRTY-ONE

*Imogen has continually surprised me throughout her life.
And most of the time the surprises were good.*
—Chester Delaney

There was no blending in. Nothing nearby to dive behind and hide. Heads snapped toward us as soon as our scents were exposed. The scraping of multiple swords yanked from scabbards filled the air.

"Run." I pulled my own swords as we sprinted toward the archway. *Maybe we can fight our way through...*

We were surrounded within an instant.

I felt it when Wells locked on to me telepathically. A part of me thought I should push him out to avoid the distraction, but I couldn't bear to break contact again.

I couldn't risk speaking to him. I felt him thrashing against the compulsion to stay where he was. Straining to come to me, forbidden or not. If I could get us beyond the gates...

The world slowed down for me, but not, of course, for Cilla. There was no water here, nothing green or growing for her to pull from with her own kroma. She did her best, and my blades flew like a tempest, but they managed to separate us.

I fought like a demon.

I clocked their auras. Moved ten times as fast. My skill with weapons had been honed to a deadly edge. I blocked nearly every thrust. Each time I struck, I hit. I lost count of how many I took down.

It didn't matter.

There were too many of them.

I lost the short sword to an especially skilled assailant, earning a slash across the cheekbone as I replaced it with a dagger. The dagger spent even less time in my hand. I shoved it into the heart of a sidhe who had run his sword into my right bicep. They both fell away from me. I shifted my sword to my left hand, all my energy focused on defense.

Cilla screamed my name. Four soldiers had backed her against a wall. Most of them were focused on subduing me. She defended amazingly, but there was nothing I could do for her and no way for her to get to me. I pulled my own dagger from my boot and redoubled my efforts. My right arm trembled with the strain of wielding even the dagger's light weight. They were herding me toward Cilla. I didn't try to resist. I didn't have the energy to spare and I wasn't leaving without her anyway.

I grunted as a blade pierced my right side just as I dislodged a knife from my left shoulder. I started to wonder if I would be leaving at all. The world remained in slow motion, but I was exhausted and ridiculously outnumbered. It was torture to watch the strikes I was unable to block arcing gradually toward their marks. Like a long, protracted march to death.

A sharp strike to my crown brought me to my knees. I finally 'pathed Wells. *Wells, I'm sorry. There's too many . . .* My mental voice was strained. I only reached him because his mind clung to mine.

Don't you dare stop fighting! Get back here, Imogen, please! My heart squeezed at the desperation, the pain I felt from him.

I'm sorry. My sword was knocked from my hand. I now had only my dagger to defend with.

Imogen! Do not quit!

Do not...

quit.

Something stirred. Like a pilot light in my subconscious.

Something from Earth.

Delaneys do not quit.

I was eight.

My grandparents argued in the waiting room of the ER. There'd been an accident.

My father was in critical condition. My mother was already gone.

"He can't survive, Henry, I saw him! No human could survive those wounds. He's gone! We've lost him!" My grandmother was hysterical, hands tangled in my grandpa's worn flannel shirt. I'd never seen her like this. I sat on a bench nearby. Watching. Numb. Twisting a comic book into a tight roll. I'd lost interest in reading it long ago.

Grandpa pulled her fingers from his shirt. Held them in his hands. Looked her in the eye. "He's a Delaney. And Delaneys don't quit," he said. "You don't know what's happening in there, Solange. But our boy is fighting for his life. He's not going to leave us. He's not going to leave Imogen unless he has to. And we're gonna fight with him. We do not give up until he's taken his last breath. As long as he's fighting, we're fighting too. Got it? Delaneys. Don't. Quit."

She took a few shuddering breaths, shining green eyes locked on his face. Then straightened. Nodded. Wiped her cheeks. Stepped away to speak to my aunts and uncles who were just arriving.

Grandpa crooked a finger at me. I scooted off the bench and stumbled over. He kneeled down and covered my thin shoulder with his warm hand.

"You remember this too, Imogen. No one in this family is going to give up on you. So never give up on yourself. Delaneys don't quit. Got it?"

"Delaneys don't quit," I repeated.

My father had survived that night. I had needed him. Cilla needed me.

I tossed my dagger out like a boomerang, slinging it so that it caught at least three throats. Then it was gone.

I'd bought myself two seconds. I pushed to my feet. I needed to get Cilla and her baby out. I took a risk.

And thought of the lightning.

Instantly, I felt its pull at my core. My blood heated.

I punched my fist skyward.

Heavy clouds gathered in thunderous tumbles. A bright gash of electric current split the darkened sky with a crack. Pulsing from clouds to fist. I gasped as my energetic tank filled to bursting. My power surged. Wounds knit together.

Someone slashed at me. I dodged, knocking the blade to the side with the back of my wrist. Lightning shot up the sword. Engulfed the sidhe holding it. He dropped like a stone.

Interesting.

I made wild guesses.

I pulled the current from my center, focused on my hand, then flung it outward as if I were tossing birdseed. Electricity scattered through the crowd. Some screamed and writhed, some dropped instantly. A stack of hay caught fire. I continued to fling lightning with my free hand, the other still extended heavenward, pulling energy from the skies. Buildings sparked and burned. People scattered. I tossed lightning again.

And again.

And again.

I backed toward Cilla. She'd lost her weapons and was huddled in the mud by the wall. "Cilla, get up," I said. "You are fighting for two. Get up." I tugged my arm from the sky, thrust both hands outward, and *pushed*. The courtyard was netted in white-blue electricity.

She struggled to her feet, her eyes wide. "I'm up." She collected her blade. "Immy. You're glowing. Your eyes are glowing and everything."

I tossed out another arc of lightning. The clouds still rolled above us. Ready, should I need more. Electricity circled my arms like living bracelets. I vibrated with power.

I summoned my dagger. Summoned my sword. They flew into my hands, my skin glowing with hot, white light.

The Sephryans were regrouping. A mass of people gathered. I saw arrows with flaming tips fitted to bows. They were no longer interested in simply capturing me. They wanted me dead.

I sheathed my sword, pulled the energy back from my hand, and grabbed Cilla's arm. I focused on Wells, the now-distant pull in my core showing me the way. I felt those wards between us. Blocking our way out. Preventing me from winking. I pulled the remainder of the lightning's power to my center.

And ripped them down.

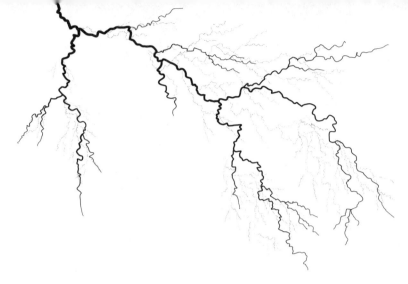

CHAPTER THIRTY-TWO

You have a place, Imogen. And when you find it, you'll know.
—Solange Aidair Delaney

We crashed to the floor in the entryway of Wells's house, the ferocity of my amateur wink sending us sprawling, a filthy, blood-coated tangle of limbs and blades. Somehow we avoided stabbing each other. A large clay vase I had bumped into wobbled . . . wobbled . . . then fell to its side with a hollow thunk.

Cilla and I locked eyes, both panting slightly. Smashing the wards and winking us home had taken all of my lightning energy. I released her wrist, leaving behind a smear of blood, and pressed myself upright with trembling arms before staggering to my feet alongside Cilla.

Movement and voices coming from the second floor indicated that the delegation from the woods had relocated. The agonizing twisting in my stomach finally relaxed. He was here.

Cilla was coated in mud from the waist down. Her long blond hair was a tangle of damp knots. Her sword hung limply from one mud-gloved hand.

"Immy you are *covered* in blood." She sheathed her sword, unbuckled the belt, and leaned it against the wall. "Your face, your hair . . . there is no spot on you that isn't red."

"Is it hot?" I croaked, my voice as tired as the rest of me.

The bridge of her nose crinkled; she rolled her eyes and shook her head, grinning. Then Zoe called her name. Feet thundered on the landing above us as Cilla sprinted for the stairs.

"I just saved your life, that's not sexy?" I quipped, smiling in spite of my exhaustion. We were safe. My eyes followed Cilla who streaked around a tall figure on the landing. Wells, his aura spinning quickly. My smile faded away as we locked eyes. Cilla continued to the next floor and out of sight. I heard Zoe sobbing, repeating Cilla's name over and over.

Wells clattered down the stairs and I crossed the entryway in three strides. We smashed into each other. A sound bubbled up from my throat as he squeezed the breath from me in a bone-crushing hug. My recently stabbed shoulder protested when I tried to hug back just as hard.

"Imogen . . . gods . . ." He pulled back, his eyes raking every inch of me. Blood now stained the front of his blue-green tunic. He ran a thumb over the half-healed cut on my cheekbone. "You look like . . ." He pulled the dagger from my hand, 'porting it away. "You look like a demon escaped from hell."

I tilted my head back. My eyes found his and I leaned into him, tears burning the back of my throat. "Would you like a hell demon of your very own?"

His face split into a wide smile. He pulled me back into his arms, tucking my head under his chin. "I would love a hell demon of my very own."

I shut my eyes and melted into him. I could have stood like that for hours. Breathing him in. Basking in the physical relief of being near him again. And the mental and emotional relief of having survived. But the king's voice floated down the stairs.

"Llewellyn, if you wouldn't mind bringing your mate, we can continue our discussion," he called blandly, as if he were asking if Wells would bring some tea. "Perhaps with her input."

Wells sighed but didn't release me. I didn't move to pull away.

"His bedside manner needs work," I said. Wells's chuckle rumbled against my ear just before he winked us upstairs.

The large oval table in Wells's office was surrounded. In addition to the king, Zoe, and Cilla, Captain Marc, Aloysius, a slight, but intense-looking sidhe I recognized as Admiral Kavlo—who I'd met briefly once—and two of Wells's higher ranking lieutenants—one I recognized as the delicate strawberry blonde who had given Wells one of her blocks after the space battle—were all crammed into the space.

"Gods' bones, Im," Al said, taking in my macabre appearance. "Please tell me that's not all yours."

"Most of it isn't."

I removed my sword and set it to the side before melting into the chair Wells pulled out for me. We were going to have a lot of weapon cleaning to do later.

"What a fitting partner for a general," the king said, gaze scraping me from head to toe. "You see, Llewellyn, you needn't have worried. She managed to save herself after all."

Wells's jaw tightened, but he said nothing. Al glowered in his father's direction.

"Your majesty," said Kavlo. His uplifted, almond-shaped eyes were grave. "I assume we will now declare war? Cilla has specifically stated that Imogen saved her just before she was to be dragged to Sephrya's king. It's obvious that Demian has sanctioned these kidnappings."

"It's not enough proof, Admiral," the king answered. Protests erupted all at once.

"... can't just let them walk all over us..."

"This is an insult of the highest degree!"

"... may as well just hand a few of our Earthlings over to them..."

"*Enough!*" the king roared, cutting through the din. "I will not risk our stability with the surrounding nations based only on the words of two, recently turned, traumatized young females."

Cilla's jaw dropped and Zoe's face turned to stone. Wells's hand tightened on my shoulder. Even Al's expression darkened. I merely pulled my phone out of its modified pouch, stopped the recording, and checked the battery. Full. Probably due to my dance with the lightning.

"You don't need to take our word. I have video of the entire thing." I selected the most recent recording and handed the phone to Wells. "Wells knows how to work it. You can fast forward through some of the parts where we're escaping the depressing castle."

"Imogen . . ." Wells took the phone from me but didn't move from my side.

"It's okay," I told him, although my stomach dipped. "Once you get what you need . . . just let me look at the pictures one more time before you destroy it." I unclipped the running pouch and let it drop to the floor with a wet smack. A few drops of blood sprayed out to adorn the floorboards around it. *Oh, that was rude. I'll clean it up later.*

Wells ran a hand down the back of my blood-soaked head and carried the phone over to Allestair. The admiral, Zoe, Captain Marc, Al, and the two lieutenants jostled for position around them as Wells set the phone on the table and pressed play.

Cilla crossed to me. Gaze trained on the ground, almost shy.

"So how does it feel?" she asked. Brown eyes flicked up to mine.

"How does what feel?" I twirled my chair around to face her. In the background my own voice on the video cursed. "*Fuck fuck fuck, what are you going to do now, Imogen?*" I cringed. I hadn't realized I'd talked to myself out loud. I'd had many variations of those thoughts several times during my journey through the castle to find Cilla.

"How does it feel to be the *real* Inigo Montoya?" she asked, eyes twinkling, her mouth sliding up to one side. She traced a finger along her cheekbone.

I clapped a hand to my face. "Oh, shit, Cilla. I *am* Inigo Montoya. Look!" I pointed out my shoulder, arm, and torso wounds. In nearly the same places that my hero had received his in the movie. "If only someone had cut my other cheek."

Cilla grinned, stepped forward gingerly, and plopped her muddy butt right in my lap.

"Ow. Cilla. Inigo is very sore." I hooked an arm around her waist.

"You're even cooler than Inigo," she said, circling her arms loosely around my shoulders and gazing down. "You're also Westley. You saved the princess. Twice."

I scanned her face. Her dark brown eyes were shadowed. I wished I could read her aura. "Cilla..."

"You've saved me twice." A tear cut a track through the grime on her face, her alto voice slipped up an octave. "I don't know how I'll ever be able to repay you."

"Cilla." I wrapped both arms around her still slim waist, well aware of the life growing inside. "You offered me a friend when you first saw me. I was alone, I was scared, and everything sucked. You came up to me and gave me your friendship and a piece of home. With no agenda. You didn't even know what kind of person I was."

A second tear cleared a path on her opposite cheek. In the background, I heard the two guards on the video abusing Cilla, my *Hey,* and the sounds of metal slicing flesh.

"I knew what kind of person you were," she whispered.

I pressed my lips together to keep them from trembling. Squeezed her again.

"I would have been so lost here without you, Cilla. Without your big, generous heart and your ability to laugh at my bullshit." I swallowed. The sounds of my vomiting and Cilla telling me we were getting out of there as an underscore. "You saved me first. And many, many times. I—very literally and truly—do not know what kind of hot mess I would be today if you hadn't found me after that meeting and offered to be my friend."

A loud sniff to our left distracted us.

Zoe and the strawberry blonde lieutenant were dabbing their eyes on handkerchiefs—yes, actual handkerchiefs—as they eavesdropped on Cilla and me.

My name is Inigo Montoya . . . you killed my father . . . prepare to die . . . floated up from the phone in my voice. Several eyes swiveled in my direction. Wells had obviously fast forwarded to the battle in the courtyard.

"I . . . did not know I was speaking aloud . . ." I said, as my entire body flushed.

Cilla chuckled as she hugged my neck, earning new bloodstains on her dress. "You said so many things out loud. You're a total nerd and I'm here for it. Never stop."

"As you wish," I said, hugging her back and hiding my burning face against her shoulder.

"There's so many of them . . ." The admiral's eyes were glued to the tiny screen. "How did you ever manage to survive?"

"She did 'Thor, god of thunder,'" Cilla said, lifting her chin. My chest swelled a little, at the pride gilding her words. "It was absolutely sick."

Wells and Zoe exchanged the briefest of glances, their faces tight, before training their eyes back on the video. A shimmer of unease glazed my stomach like tar. My lightning definitely wasn't secret anymore. I didn't have the energy to hang on to that worry, however. I didn't regret getting us out of there. It was strange, hearing myself almost give up. I hadn't realized I had been apologizing to Wells aloud either. I hadn't realized I had said *Delaneys don't quit.* And I now knew how lightning sounded when summoned and subsequently thrown.

Immy you are covered *in blood. Your face, your hair . . . there is no spot on you that isn't red.*

Is it hot?

"Okay, that's the end, that's . . . that should really be enough." I felt Cilla shaking with suppressed laughter.

I just saved your life, that's not sexy?

"Okay! Please stop the video," I implored Wells. "God, I sound like fucking Han Solo." I raised an eyebrow at Cilla and dropped into a Harrison Ford impression, "You like me because I'm a scoundrel. There aren't enough scoundrels in your life."

"I appreciate you so much." She chuckled.

The corners of my mouth quirked up. "You're my favorite."

"This is a very convincing . . . item," the king said, weighing the phone in his palm. My attention swiveled to him, heart in my throat, watching him toss and catch it. "Could do without all of the running about in the corridors but . . ."

"I can edit it down to the important bits if that's helpful," I offered.

His ice blue eyes stabbed into me as he nodded slowly. A chill rippled down my spine. He passed my phone to Wells without breaking eye contact with me. "Draw up the declaration. Admiral, General, Captain . . . we're going to war." Still, he stared through me. I was reminded of a time I'd stared down a tiger in the zoo. The same icy feeling coated my insides even though I knew I should be perfectly safe.

"Llewellyn." The king gestured between the two of us. "Get this accepted. Make it official. Before the fighting starts. You've waited long enough. We'll have the celebration at the palace. Your mother will be thrilled."

Al blanched, throat working. His fingers curled slowly into fists at his sides. But he stared down at the table and said nothing.

I reflexively gripped Cilla harder. Bristling at the king's dismissive tone.

Cilla leaned into me, whispering into my ear. "You and Wells are good together. He loves you so much. And you like him too. He's a good partner to you. You would have chosen this for yourself eventually. Let the king think he's got control. It's fine. Now nothing Al says will matter."

She had a point. The king, Al's father, had just sanctioned my partnership with Wells. There was nothing Al could do to possess me now. It had even been implied that the acceptance celebration would take place at the palace. Very public. It made me wonder what advantage the king saw in my bonding with Wells.

I remembered Captain Marc telling me that Wells was not considered royalty, just a "valuable asset" to the monarchy. I supposed that as his mate I'd be considered an asset as well.

It also meant that this was my permanent life. No going back to humanity if I accepted. *But what would be left for you in one hundred years anyway?* I hugged Cilla tighter, my heart hammering.

Papers were drawn up. Demands and negotiations would come first. In order to pacify the surrounding nations, a verifiable offence must be documented, followed by attempts to reconcile via good faith negotiations. Notes ported in and out. Documents flew around the room. All but forgotten, Cilla and I fell into a doze against each other.

"Sire." Captain Marc eventually spoke up. "If we're done with Imogen and Cilla, I'd imagine they both might like to get cleaned up. Maybe take a rest after their ordeal."

"Of course." The king glanced up from a memo he had been reading, remembering that we were still in the room. Covered in mud and blood. "Llewellyn, take a few minutes to settle your mate. Zoe, you and Cilla can go home. We'll speak soon."

Once out of the office, Wells turned to Zoe. "I have plenty of room here if you're tired," he said. "You're both more than welcome to stay." I understood the additional offer beneath his invitation. He'd tell Zoe everything that was decided in the meeting as soon as it was over if she wanted.

"Thank you, very much appreciated." Zoe smiled. "But I want to get Cilla home and have a medic check her out. Just to make sure..."

Wells nodded. "I understand. Let us know, please."

"Of course." She wrapped him in a hug, her eyes bright. "Thank you for being there while she was... while they were..."

Wells squeezed her back. "You helped me, too."

They released each other and Wells gave Cilla a hug goodbye. Zoe flicked a tear from her cheek and turned to me. "Oh, Imogen. Thank you for my partner. Thank you for being so brave and selfless." She pulled me into a tight embrace. "I'm so glad Cilla chose you as her friend."

"That makes two of us," I said, hugging her back. "You know, you could always name the baby after me . . ."

She laughed and let me go. I winced as I saw rust-colored stains on her white shirt. I was ruining everyone's clothes today.

After they winked out, Wells walked me down the hall to my room, his fingers twined with mine. "I'll be okay cleaning myself up," I said. "If you need to get back."

"Allestair told me to take a few minutes and I'm taking them." He smiled and squeezed my hand. His voice softened. "We can talk about all of this later, by ourselves. But we don't have to rush things between us. No matter what he says. You can take your time."

In the bathroom I finally caught a glimpse of myself in a mirror.

"Holy bloody massacre, Batman!" I said. "I literally look like I've bathed in the blood of a thousand virgins."

Wells started the water. He'd learned to ignore any of my pop culture references he didn't understand unless he was ready for a dissertation-esque monologue. He turned back to me and tilted my chin up. "Rinse off," he murmured. "I'm going to change my shirt and I'll be back." His lips brushed mine in the softest of kisses, sending shockwaves through me. It was an effort not to grab onto him and dive in deeper. From the sound he made when he shoved from the room—some combination of moan and sigh—I could tell he felt something similar.

Showering off was heaven. The water ran red for minutes and my soapy lather foamed a bright pink. Eventually, I was clean again. I had half-closed wounds on my side, shoulder, and face, as well as several smaller scars all over my limbs. But they would heal.

And I survived.

Wells was sitting on the edge of the bed when I emerged. I'd changed straight into a nightshift.

"You smell one thousand times better." He took my hand and tugged me toward him. "Do you think you'll be able to rest for a bit?"

I nodded. There wasn't a muscle in my body that didn't ache.

"I'm a 'path away if you need me. I'll come right here as soon as we're done." He pulled the covers back and settled me beneath them. "Thank you for making it back."

"Thank you for not letting me quit."

When I woke up the first time, the sun had moved. I reached out to Wells's mind and found him occupied. They must still be making war plans. I left him alone, content that he was merely a floor below.

I 'pathed Cilla instead. Asked her if she'd seen the medic. If she was okay, if the baby was okay, if she was resting. She had, they were, she was. She was not naming the baby after me.

She's a brand-new person, she needs her own special name.

Spell my name backwards.

Her glittery chuckle bounced against my mind before she changed the subject. *What are you going to do about Wells?*

Well... I never want to go through another day like today again...

Same, Immy. Big same. But what does that mean for you?

I continued to deflect. *I'm not making a video for you, if that's what you're asking.*

As disappointing as that is... does that mean you're going to accept?

I hugged my knees to my chest and stared out the window toward the sparkling sea. *I don't know. What about Keane?*

You don't need to stop loving Keane. Or anyone you've left behind. Her mental tone was gentle. *You don't even have to stop missing them. You can love Wells, too. Your heart will grow to make room.* When I didn't answer she said, *It probably already has.*

I rested my cheek on my knees, my heart swelling and cracking. *How'd you get so smart?*

Well, it certainly wasn't during my illustrious tour of the Ivy Leagues. When her family disowned her at sixteen, Cilla got her GED and went to beauty school. By the time she met Zoe, she was giving two-hundred-dollar haircuts to LA's elite. Her trade currently seemed much more practical than my Bachelor in Graphic Design. Or my second one in Electronic Media. The majority of the sidhe in Molnair left their hair long and natural, but a significant amount had *very* specific haircuts.

I'm having Zoe 'port you over some tonic. Cilla still wasn't comfortable 'porting anything containing liquid. I heard the thunk of the bottle landing on my nightstand. *I got it from the medic. Wouldn't hurt you to start taking it just in case.*

Thanks.

You're welcome. Let me know if it happens.

Can I wait until we're done?

Her mental chuckle had the corners of my mouth twitching upward.

Dork. Yes. Tell me in the morning if it happens. I'm going to eat all of the food in the house now and then go to sleep until I'm in labor. You should eat something too if you haven't.

My stomach growled as soon as I thought about food. I said goodbye to Cilla and broke contact, swinging my feet over the side of the bed. My eyes rested on the bottle of tonic. The smooth, brown glass gleamed in the fading sunlight. I left it there.

I pulled on a pair of pants in case I ran into anyone on my way to the kitchen and padded out onto the landing. Voices floated from the office as I passed the second floor. I caught something about the distance to Sephrya and wondered how many miles I had winked today. I made a note to ask Wells to see a map of *all* of the countries, not just Molnair, as I continued to the first floor.

I found some bread and soup, which was about all I had the energy to fix for myself, and dumped the soup into a pot. I waved my hand, igniting the stove, then plunked the pot down, thinking as I stirred.

Cilla was right. I didn't need to cut Keane out of my heart. How I felt about him didn't change the fact that I was never going to see him again. My breath shuddered at the thought, but it was no longer as painful as it had been months ago. My thoughts turned to Wells and I found my skin warming, my lips twitching upward. I did like him. A lot. When he had told me he had fallen in love with me, it was a surprise, but nice, like sunshine exploding through my chest. When Al said it, it inspired eyerolls and indigestion. I knew Wells better than I'd ever known Al. And I was certain he saw me as my own person, not a replacement for anyone else. *How do I feel about him being in love with me?*

"It doesn't suck," I whispered to the soup, that now familiar warmth flooding my ribcage. "Today sucked though. I never want to go through that again."

What sucked about it? I asked myself. The physical pain of the bond pulling at us had been horrible, yes. But . . . I wanted this to be a choice *I* made. Not some dumb, animalistic, physical thing. Regardless of how rare and mystical and permanent it might or might not be. My choice with Wells. Not the king's directive. Not my body's demand . . .

It sucked because I wanted to see him again. Because if I didn't make it back . . . A chill slid down my spine in spite of the heat from the stove. I didn't know what happened to an unaccepted bond if one mate died, but I couldn't imagine it would be painless. And if I was honest, Wells and I had cared for each other before the bond. My death wouldn't have been painless for him either way.

Losing him would wreck me, I realized. I swallowed down the burning in my throat and shoved those thoughts aside. We weren't going to lose each other.

I poured the soup into a bowl and brought it over to the kitchen table. I dipped bread into it and munched while I turned the situation over in my head. For the first time, I forced myself to think of what I really wanted. What *I* wanted. I let it all run through my head. How I felt living with Wells now. How I felt when we argued. How I felt when we had fun. How I felt when we did mundane things. How I felt when our situation was terrible. How I'd felt when we'd kissed . . .

Then I made myself imagine leaving Perimov and returning to Earth.

A pang of regret, sharp and unexpected, hit the base of my throat. I missed Earth, but I liked it here. I took a deep breath and pictured going back. Back where, if I were lucky, I could find some of my nieces and nephews in their old folks homes.

My throat closed as I imagined leaving Wells. Saying goodbye to him. And Cilla. The bond dissolving. My heart twisted. My vision blurred.

And what if I stay? My body relaxed. I let out a breath I hadn't realized I was holding.

I finished the soup, washed up after myself, and headed back to my room. The meeting was still going strong when I passed the second floor, but I didn't even take in a passing comment. Another thought occurred to me, blotting out everything else.

If Sephrya didn't capitulate to Allestair's demands, we'd be going to war. And Wells led Molnair's army.

He'd have to leave. And if our bond remained unaccepted, I'd either have to be right beside him the entire time or we'd both endure constant pain. My mind traveled back over the agonizing events of the morning and how draining that pain had been, and I'd only had to endure it for a few hours. And I'd still nearly been killed.

My stomach lurched and I stumbled on the stairs. I couldn't let the bond distract Wells. Not during a war.

I took a breath and marched onto the landing, lifting my chin. I would make a case for going with him regardless. I'd proven I could fight. But I knew there would be resistance to that idea. And it wasn't a solid solution either way.

The sun had set by the time I made it back upstairs. I shucked my pants off and climbed back into bed after brushing my teeth. Wells 'pathed me as I pulled the covers up.

Were you just in the stairwell?

I just went to the kitchen, I was hungry. I'm back in bed now.

Oh, shit, Imogen, I hadn't even realized the time, I would have brought you something.

I smiled. *It didn't hurt me to move around a little bit. I didn't want to interrupt all the plans for violence.*

His mental sigh brushed my bones. *I'm hoping this won't take too much longer. There will probably be more meetings tomorrow. Go to sleep. And don't worry about interrupting if you need something.*

Okay. Thanks.

I'll try not to wake you when I come in. He broke contact.

We were capable of being rooms apart now, but we'd continued sleeping next to each other every night. Sometimes in his room, sometimes in mine. Neither of us had suggested we stop.

I didn't want to suggest it. Because I didn't want it to stop.

I plucked the tonic off the nightstand and took a dose.

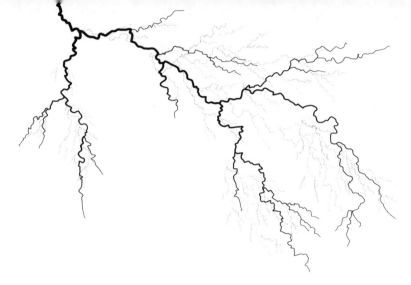

CHAPTER THIRTY-THREE

Don't settle. You want someone worth fighting for.
Someone worth losing everything else for.
—Solange Aidair Delaney

I woke up when Wells slid into bed beside me. As usual, my entire being melted in relief. I scooted over to his side and snuggled up next to him. He moved his arm out of the way and then draped it around my back once I had settled my head on his chest.

"I'm sorry I woke you." He sounded exhausted. I wondered what time it was. "I was trying to be quiet."

"You were quiet," I said. "And I don't mind." I slid an arm around his waist. "Did you eat?"

"We all ate. The office is a mess." He exhaled. "I'll take care of it tomorrow."

"Are they coming back over here?" I asked, rubbing my hand back and forth across his stomach. My insides already coiling.

"I don't know. I'm sure messages will be 'porting back and forth first thing in the morning."

I let my hand slip beneath his shirt. Both of us inhaled sharply at the skin-to-skin contact. My fingers continued to explore the defined planes of his torso. I swallowed. My heart beating faster. And dared to sweep higher...

He pressed his hand on top of mine, holding it still on his chest. "Imogen—"

"I'm done waiting if you are," I whispered, the words trembling off my tongue. "But if you're too tired—"

He rolled toward me, pulling me against him. My breath quickened as I shoved his shirt upward. He stripped it off. My own shift had ridden up to my waist. He tugged it higher. I lifted my arms. He yanked it free and tossed it against the opposite wall. I still wore my underwear and he still had on loose pants, but we were distracted by the amount of skin we'd already bared. Our hands hungry. Famished. Every cell in my body was hypersensitive. His calluses scraped against my tender skin as he explored.

His scent hit the back of my tongue and I lifted my face to his. Our lips met and the world narrowed. A sigh that was nearly a groan whispered from my throat as Wells took the kiss deeper. Bombs could have detonated around us. Earthquakes could have shaken the foundation of the city. We wouldn't have registered anything beyond the feel of skin on skin.

I was once again drunk on his scent. Our hands guided themselves, desperate but lingering. Soft caresses and firm grabs. I needed more. I needed to taste more, feel more...

He snapped his fingers and the clasp of my bra released. I shrugged out of it. Flung it away. He threaded one hand through the hair at the back of my head, holding me into his kiss. The other stroked slowly from my jaw, down my throat, across my collarbone, stopping to palm my breast, his thumb scraping across the sensitive skin of my nipple, then moving lower, across my stomach, sweeping around my waist to grip my rear... He wandered everywhere except the aching spot building between my legs.

We still had too many clothes on.

I tugged at the hem of his pants, shoving them down as far as I could before bending my knees, hooking my toes around the waistband and pushing them the rest of the way, baring his legs. He kicked them off and made sure my underwear followed.

I needed to be closer.

Our auras were mingling. Coalescing. The static, shimmering light of the mating bond pulled tighter and tighter. Wrapping around us. As if it could force us into one single body.

I pushed further into the kiss. Pressing myself against Wells until there was no space between us. I hooked a leg behind him and rocked my hips into his. Needing to relieve the intense ache at my center.

He flipped us over. He was on top of me. Pinning me. I couldn't so much as wiggle. I let out a moan of frustration. Wanting to move, appease that sweet ache. Get closer. He held me down and broke our kiss, leaving both of us gasping. "Imogen, I need to know that this is what you want."

In answer, I pulled his lips back to mine. Tried again to move against him.

He fisted his hand in my hair and pulled me back. The desire and longing on his face mirrored the unbearable, aching need I felt in every trembling cell. "Imogen, I need you to say that you want this. That you understand—"

"Yes," I said, straining against him. "Wells, I want to be your mate."

He crushed my mouth against his. Gave me space and moved his hips with mine. I dragged my hands down his back. Every place we touched was raw nerve. The urgency roiling within me bordered on desperation. He pulled away from the kiss, still grasping my hair, and dropped his cheek next to mine, his breath tickling my ear. "I love you, Imogen." Then he entered me fully in one thrust.

I gasped. Clinging to him as he held us still. Letting me adjust. Kissing and nibbling along my neck and shoulder. Then he began to move slowly. Too slowly. Almost teasingly. I wanted more. I shifted my hips, trying to urge him faster. He pressed me back into the mattress. Holding me still.

"Impatient little demon," he whispered. I growled and squirmed against him. I *needed* to move. The bond was squeezing so tightly. It wrapped us both from shoulder to hip. If we'd tried to stop now, I don't think it would have let us go.

Wells moved again. I twined my legs around his and rocked with him, heat and pressure building at my center. Both of us increasing in speed, hurtling toward the edge. Neither in control any longer. The bond pressed tighter around us, then disappeared beneath our skin as we shattered together.

Waves pulsed from my core, down my aching thighs, and up through every nerve. Pins and needles flashed across my face. White noise filled my ears. Then the bond clamped painfully onto our souls. Wrenching. We both cried out, clinging to each other, still riding the final throes of our climax while our souls were forcefully twisted around each other. Stretched. Pulled. Changed.

"Wells," I gasped. No one had mentioned this part. I was simultaneously lifted and dropped. Caressed and crushed. Held together and ripped apart. Tears streamed down my face. Breath sawed through my chest in shuddering gasps. My entire body shook. *We're going to die. No one could survive this.*

Then it stopped. Our souls snapped back into place. Different. But whole. The bond stopped squeezing and retreated. I felt it still inside me. As if it had carved out a home and curled up in it. For a moment we both remained where we had collapsed, shivering and entwined. Then Wells summoned the covers and tucked them around us, wrapping me in his arms. I held on to him. Both of us were still trembling.

"Are you okay?" He was breathing heavily. His head resting next to mine as if he were too tired to hold it up. His long hair draped across our entangled limbs.

"I think so," I breathed. "No one mentioned that . . . other part."

"No one fucking mentioned that other part to *me*!" He propped himself up on his elbows. Smoothing sweat-damp hair back from my face. "You'd think that would be a notable inclusion." He pressed a kiss to my forehead, then touched his own against it. "I thought we were going to get torn apart from the inside out."

"Me too," I said. "I would have been so mad if we died."

He chuckled, then brushed a soft kiss against my lips. It no longer made me feel like I was going to combust if I didn't devour him. It felt nice. And right. My heart expanded.

"I love you," I said.

He froze. And I *felt* the joy thrumming from him as if it were bouncing around my own chest, even before I saw the glittering gold flecks dance through his aura. "Imogen, you don't have to say that just because—"

"I *know* I don't *have* to do anything," I said, a touch sassy. "I'm definitely the bossy one in this relationship. I do what I want." Then softer, "I say what I want."

A half smile. He kissed me again. A little less gently. "I don't suppose that soul shredding experience has scared you off sex?" He murmured, moving down my neck, teeth scraping lightly against my skin.

I arched against him. "We still have time to make a video for Cilla . . ." I whispered.

"You truly are a demon from hell," he growled, his hands wandering.

"Mmmm, but I'm *your* hell demon," I said, my voice already husky.

Apparently sidhe males don't need any recovery time.

We didn't get much sleep.

The clanging of the doorbell jerked us awake after what was surely only an hour of slumber. We blinked at each other, both groggy and disheveled. The bell peeled again. Wells groaned and attempted to detangle himself from me.

I hugged tighter. "Tell them to go away," I mumbled into the pillows.

"In order to tell them to go away, I have to go downstairs," he replied, collapsing when he couldn't pry my arms from around his chest. "All right, little demon, do you want to answer the door?"

A Dagger of Lightning

"Just 'path whoever it is from here," I moaned, releasing him. "Ask them if they brought jatki. If they didn't, they need to leave."

"I'm not going to 'path a random entity at my front door." He swung out of bed, untangled his discarded pants, pulled them on, and headed for the hallway. "With any luck I'll be right back," he yawned.

I snuggled down into the comforter, dozing almost instantly. Then Captain Marc's roaring laugh rolled up the staircase. I sighed, tossed back the covers, and hunted for some underwear.

Minutes later I was stomping blearily down the stairs in Wells's discarded shirt and my pants from yesterday. *There is no way we don't reek of sex,* I thought. Then decided it served whoever was down there right for barging in at whatever ungodly hour this surely was.

I dragged myself into the kitchen to find an indecently chipper Captain Marc and Admiral Kavlo loudly congratulating a blushing, barely dressed Wells, who dropped to a seat at the table with a resigned sigh.

"Go away," I said.

"There she *is*!" A beaming Captain Marc pulled me into a hug that I submitted to limply. "Cranky from lack of sleep, I understand." He released me, dropped his hands onto my shoulders, leaned down to my eye level, and gave me a little shake. "And maybe a little sore?"

I batted his hands away as he chuckled. "I said go away!"

Admiral Kavlo smiled and brandished a thermos at me. "We knew it was a little early so we did bring jatki."

I took it from him and sank onto Wells's lap. "All right, you can stay." I didn't care who was in the room; now that my decision had been made, I was all in and ready for PDA land.

"Is that my shirt?" Wells asked, wrapping an arm around me and pulling me closer.

"What's yours is mine," I answered, taking a gulp of jatki and sighing at the warmth.

"I thought you might be nice and bring me a shirt to throw on," he said, tugging at the hem of the one I'd stolen.

I leaned against his bare chest. "No. No more shirts for you. I like you this way." I gave him a peck on his gradually reddening cheek as the other two giggled at us like high schoolers.

The doorbell chimed again followed by a pounding at the door. Admiral Kavlo went to answer it. His muted greetings drifted from the entryway, and within moments he was back with the king.

King Allestair took one look at Wells and me. His expression didn't shift. "Oh, good. So that's done. May as well start the meeting here anyway, give Llewellyn a moment to get decent clothes on. 'Path your mother, while you're at it and let her know. She can start planning. We'll get the celebration scheduled this week." He turned to Marc and Kavlo. "I've received communications from the leaders of four other countries who've already heard rumors..." He waved his hand in a "come on" gesture as he marched up the stairs to the office. Captain Marc and Admiral Kavlo fell into step behind. Kavlo threw Wells a wink over his shoulder.

"So strange," Wells murmured into my hair as he hunted for a spot to plant a kiss on my cheek. "I can *feel* how irritated you are right now."

"I don't like the way he talks about me," I said, jerking my head in the direction the king had gone. "Like I'm a cow or something."

"He has been ruling for a very long time." Wells reached around me for his own jatki. "I'd imagine centuries of moving people around like chess pieces would tend to make one a bit dispassionate." He took a sip. "He's demanding, but a good ruler, Imogen. I'm sure he doesn't mean any personal insult."

I grunted. It was much too early for me to be feeling charitable.

I felt him sigh against me. "I should probably get cleaned up." His fingers drifted to the nape of my neck, toying with my hair. "You can go back to sleep if you want."

"No, I have caffeine now," I said, taking another swig. "And I told Cilla I'd 'path her 'if it happened.'" I made air quotes with my free hand. Cilla and I had done air quotes often enough that Wells and Zoe understood them. They rarely incorporated them, however, because they were just off enough that Cilla and I couldn't help laughing at them.

"I'm sure she'll be happy for you. As long as she doesn't give you any more . . . artistic ideas." He gave me a squeeze and gently shifted me off his lap as he stood.

"She'll be saddened by your prudishness, I'm sure." I stretched and we shuffled toward the stairs.

We didn't get far before the doorbell was abused again. "I'll get it." I sighed, set my jatki on the table, and stomped over to the door muttering about our foyer becoming Grand Central Station.

Al was standing on the threshold. His aura spinning and fracturing around him. "Al . . ." I stepped back to let him in. "What's wrong?"

"Where is he?" He pushed past me but froze when he saw Wells. I closed the door behind him as his eyes jumped back and forth between the two of us. His aura degraded further. The colors exploding in bursts and shattering. "So, you've done it," he snarled at Wells, chest rising and falling rapidly. "I guess father told you to get it done, so you had to—"

"That's not why—" I stepped between them, my fingers curling into fists as I glared up at Al.

"I can't even look at *you* right now." He pivoted away from me and into the kitchen, tossing a bound document onto the table and flipping it open. Wells followed him, brushing a hand down my arm as he passed. His aura was still controlled, but spinning slightly faster than usual. I felt his concern twinging behind my own breastbone. I wondered how my anger felt inside of him.

"I've been going through some old records from the last Earth journey," Al snapped as he violently turned pages. I was surprised that none of them tore. Then I saw Wells stiffen and that twinge of concern bloomed into a wash of dread. Al continued, "You know, the ones no one would let me look at when she didn't come back?"

"You were in such a state, Al, no one wanted to upset you further . . ." Wells trailed off, his eyes fixed on the pages Al was tearing through.

"Well, I was missing her a bit yesterday." He sneered at me for an instant before dropping his gaze back to the document. "Wonder why.

Anyway, no one tried to stop me from reading these this time." He found the page he was looking for and jammed his finger into the center. "There. Right there."

Wells closed his eyes for a breath, then looked directly at Al. "It's what she wanted, Al."

"*You* turned her. *YOU*." The purple and blue-black colors of devastation flooded through Al's entire aura, leaving no space for any other hue. "And the dates. You signed an entire week before she was turned. You helped her *plan* this."

"She asked for us specifically, Al," Wells said calmly, fractures splitting his own aura. "She made the decision on her own."

"You said you'd watch out for her." Al's face broke. "You said you'd bring her back safe."

"Al . . ." Wells started. I felt my mate's heart crack and crossed to him, putting a hand on his shoulder.

It was the wrong thing to do.

Al's face hardened. His aura exploded into red-black flames. I almost flinched back.

"And now you've stolen Imogen from me, too," he growled.

I was rallying my usual comebacks to Aloysius's delusional belief that I had ever been "his" when Wells's entire being changed. The sympathy, guilt, and dread drained from his aura. I felt the cracks in his heart seal shut. He straightened.

"I'm done apologizing for my relationship with Imogen," he said, eyes flashing, voice ringing. "If anyone's stolen her from anything, it was you. And she's coped remarkably well. She's made her own choice to be with me time and time again. I've never tried to push her or coerce her in any way. If you want to dissect Solange's decision to remain on Earth for the umpteenth time, I'll indulge you, but I'm through defending this." He took my hand and I squeezed back.

"What in the name of hell is going on down here?" The king marched into the kitchen and took in the tableau: Wells and I standing, hand in hand, facing down Al, who was glaring accusingly, one finger still jammed into the open records.

"Bones of the gods, not this again." The king rolled his eyes. "Aloysius, get home. Go do something productive. Your half-brother has mated and you need to accept it. Find someone else and move on from Solange for the sake of everyone's sanity."

Al's face tightened. He slowly straightened away from the table. His aura stopped actively fracturing, but darkened. Bright pink cracks continually splitting the glittering black. He walked stiffly from the room and slammed the door as he left. My heart couldn't help a flutter of sympathy. Yes, he was basically a selfish ass, but he was obviously not handling the situation well mentally, and his father's brusque manner was painfully dismissive. I only had a moment to worry about the potential fallout, however, before Wells was being ordered to clean himself up and join the meeting and to "get his mate taken care of" as well. Like I was a horse Wells needed to feed and water. Then Allestair stormed back upstairs muttering about telling everyone how to wipe their own asses.

I ignored him. As soon as he left, I walked over to the folio that Al had left open on the table and pulled it toward me. The calligraphy was regal and official. I scanned the words and gleaned that it was a consent for transformation from sidhe to human. My eyes snagged on the looping, curling sigil that I recognized from my youth. My finger traced my grandmother's name. The indentations in the page still discernible. There was no hesitation in that signature. My eyes drifted down to two other names... Wells and Captain Marc had signed as agreeing to turn Solange human. My heart skipped when my gaze landed on Henry C. Delaney, registered as her partner. I felt the warmth from Wells's body against my back.

"Do you want to keep this for a bit to look at?" he asked, trailing his fingers down my arm. "We can return it to the Hall of Records later. Since Al's the one who took it out, I doubt we'll get in trouble for hanging on to it."

"Does everyone sign something like this?" I asked. I had never been asked to sign anything.

He wrapped his arms around me. "There is a record of you being turned," he said, answering my unspoken question. "But since you didn't actually consent, no one asked you to sign it. There's a note about what happened in that space instead. Since you appeared . . . physically distressed when Al brought you on board, turning you first and getting paperwork done later seemed appropriate. Especially as we were so short on time to leave the orbit. Delaying the paperwork for a day or two isn't unusual. Although, again, this situation may have changed that."

"Why did she stay?" I asked, touching my grandfather's neat script. So different from my grandma's flourish. "Why didn't she bring him back with her?"

"Henry wouldn't come," he said. "His father had run off shortly after the birth of his youngest sister." I remembered that Grandpa had been the eldest of five. "His mother died from the flu shortly before Solange met him. Henry promised his mother that he would keep his brothers and sisters together. He was twenty-two, but his next eldest sister was only thirteen. Henry refused to run out on them to pursue his own happiness like his father did. And we don't attempt to turn children. There was no question of bringing the whole family." He sighed. "All of this has been explained to Al countless times."

I made to close the volume. Wells stopped me and flipped back a few pages. "It's up to you, but if you do decide you want to look at it . . . we're all required to make reports once we've met someone we're considering bringing back. There are records of what Solange submitted here." He swallowed. "I don't know if Al cared to look through those pages."

I slid the record off the table, closed it, and tucked it under an arm. "Maybe I'll keep it for a bit."

Wells and I reluctantly separated. I considered going for a run, realized I probably still wasn't allowed to go on my own in spite of being a big damn hero, and also that I was incredibly sore. Both from mating-related calisthenics as well as my epic swashbuckling escape from Sephrya. I opted for a long soak in an herb-strewn bath.

Once I had submerged myself and settled in, I 'pathed Cilla.

She was ecstatic. She wanted details, which I didn't give her. She wanted to know when the celebration was; I didn't know, but told her it would probably be at the palace. This sent her into transports of delight. She had never seen the palace. Never been inside *any* palace. And dismissed me when I said it was overwrought and obnoxiously large. She and Zoe wanted to take me shopping for a dress *immediately*.

I told her I'd check in with her when I was done with my bath and risked interrupting war discussions to 'path Wells.

Do I have to wear a dress to this ... celebration being foisted upon us?

His amusement tickled the back of my mind when he answered. *If we were allowed to do it the way we want, I'd say you could wear whatever you liked, but since it's happening at the palace, you should probably wear a dress, yes.*

Cilla and Zoe want to take me shopping for one. Like now.

Excellent idea. Zoe will have been to enough of these to know what's appropriate. Have fun.

I just managed to catch the money pouch he 'ported to me before it landed in my bath water.

You almost dumped coinage all up in my aromatherapy bath.

That sounds nice ... maybe I could get away for a few minutes and join you...

I'll set up the camera.

Demon.

He cut off contact.

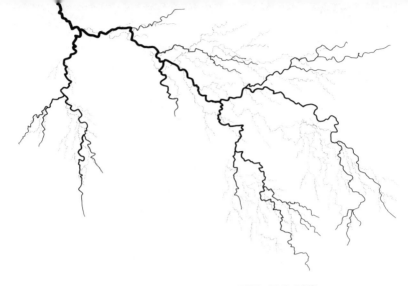

CHAPTER THIRTY-FOUR

Oh, parties can be fantastic! They can be awful too.
Depends half on your attitude and half on who else is there.
—Solange Aidair Delaney

Dress shopping was just the beginning. Between plans for the celebration—which was to be a mere two days after our acceptance—and increasingly frustrating negotiations with Sephrya, Wells and I had very little time to ourselves to enjoy our "just mated" status. I had hoped the short notice meant not many people would be able to attend, but I was mistaken. Acceptance celebrations were few and far between and very few people living could recall the last one that had been thrown at the palace. Wells was also very popular and I was a national curiosity. Everyone who received an invitation had accepted. It was going to be enormous.

The only thing that offered some relief was that Wells and I didn't actually have to *do* anything. Just show up and look pretty. Queen Iphigenia was happily taking care of all the arrangements, having only inquired what color my dress was so the decor wouldn't clash. Wells had handed over a list of people he wanted to make certain received invitations and that was it. There was to be no ceremony, we didn't have to make any speeches, we just had to accept gifts and congratulations.

I still would have preferred to skip it.

"I don't like crowds," I said to Wells before we fell asleep, the only time we had alone. We were in his bed tonight. Neither of us had possessed the mental energy to discuss moving into one room yet.

"You don't have to speak to the entire group at once," he said, lightly stroking my hair as I laid my head on his shoulder. "Just concentrate on the person right in front of you."

"Everyone's going to be looking at me." My eyes dropped shut. It always put me to sleep when he rubbed my head.

"Everyone will look at you at first, and then they'll focus on other things. You may have to endure five seconds of *everyone* looking at you right when you walk in. I think you'll be able to handle it."

"Mmmph. You'll have friends there?" I yawned. "I'd like to meet your friends."

"We'll both have friends there," he said as I drifted off. "Zoe and Cilla will be with you the entire time."

Wells and I were herded out of our own house in the afternoon, although, blessedly, we'd finally been allowed to sleep in that morning. Palace staff had arrived a few hours after lunch and ordered us to collect everything we would need for the rest of the day and the evening. My dress and bag that I'd put together were plucked from my hands and 'ported to the palace ahead of me. The staff were to stay to watch the house in our absence.

We had permission to wink directly into the palace for the day, but as soon as we were outside, I asked Wells if we could walk for a bit first.

"Doing all right?" He squeezed my hand as we cut through our park.

"I think so. That was just a little overwhelming."

"Ah, not used to being fussed over and pushed around simultaneously?"

"No. And I don't *want* to get used to it." I kicked a purple stone. "Why do they have to stay and watch the house? That's weird."

"Well, if negotiations go badly—and right now they are—we are declaring war on Sephrya. My position has been public knowledge for decades and you've recently made yourself very interesting by putting certain talents on display." He paused to open a small gate at the edge of the park for us to pass through to the main road. "If I were Sephryan, I wouldn't mind one or both of us being put out of commission."

It all made sense, and I supposed it should have scared me, but the palace looming ahead and the celebration that I was facing currently seemed much more frightening.

"What's to stop assassins from breaking into the palace tonight?" I asked as we found ourselves back on the parade route from disembarkation, once again crossing beneath the arch that led to the palace grounds. "Where I shall be much more vulnerable in a dress and heels with no weaponry on my person."

He laughed. "Not to mention inebriated."

"Most *definitely*," I agreed. "I'm going to drink anything that sparkles."

"The mountain palace is the most secure place we could be." Wells told me. "As you know, winking in or out is impossible unless you have the king's permission, which he can change with a thought. The palace itself has never been breached. Not once. The wards surrounding and protecting it are of an ancient Blood Kroma, currently keyed to King Allestair and Aloysius. I'm positive there will be more wards placed around the celebration hall for tonight. None of the invited guests would even be able to wander around if they were so inclined. The wards will keep them only to the rooms they're allowed into. It's probably the safest place on the planet."

"Fine. How long do we have to stay?" While my mind turned over the concept of *Blood Kroma*, we'd reached the pillars at the foot of the mountain, where I'd stood with Wells, Al, and Captain Marc when I first arrived from Earth. The base of the palace was completely obscured by clouds today.

"We're going to be expected to spend the night, Imogen, especially if you're planning on getting ridiculously drunk." He turned to face me and took my other hand. "As much as I would prefer to wink us straight home to our own beds, Allestair has reminded me that the palace is conferring public honor upon our union by hosting. We should do our best to be gracious." He tucked a strand of hair behind my ear. "It's one night out of centuries we'll have together. And it is supposed to be fun. Try to enjoy it?"

I sighed and wrapped my arms around him. "Okay, I'll stop being so grumpy."

"Do you mind if I wink us the rest of the way, or would you prefer to hike up the mountain?" he asked as we pulled apart, his eyes twinkling. I made a show of considering hiking until Wells threatened to make me carry him.

We winked right into the palace entryway, which had been transformed since I'd seen it last. Floral decorations adorned the pillars and corners, small tables set with candles were scattered about attractively, and musicians were setting up in one corner.

We didn't have time to see much more before two servants, evidently charged specifically to wait for our arrival, hurried us away through a labyrinth of corridors and hallways. They hustled us along so quickly that I lost my bearings immediately.

My heart rate picked up. I had no idea where we were and the people guiding us didn't care. They shoved us around like self-moving parcels. I couldn't have found my way back to the entrance if I'd tried. Wells kept hold of my hand, but I was also wrapped around his arm by the time they thrust us through the doors into a suite of rooms we were to occupy that evening.

I almost sobbed in relief when my eyes landed on Cilla and Zoe, who were already there with Captain Marc and, to my great surprise, Al. Everyone's auras were brimming with golden sparks of excitement and blue-green waves of happiness. Even Al's, although another strange crimson color pushed through his occasionally. I wasn't sure what it meant.

Cilla tried to hug me. "Immy, you can let go of Wells now, you get to hug him for the rest of your life and he's going to need his arm."

My muscles locked up. I couldn't let go. I tried to take a breath, but my chest was too tight. Everyone was staring at me now. "No, I'm overwhelmed and nervous and people keep dragging us around and I don't know where I am. I need his arm more than he does right now."

"My poor baby girl," Cilla cooed, one corner of her mouth lifting as she smoothed my hair back from my face. If she felt me trembling she didn't mention it. "No one in this crowd is going to try to attack and kill her so she doesn't know what to do. I'll get you some booze and you'll feel better. Then I get to do your hair. Which I'm very excited about. C'mon, let go. You'll be okay."

Cilla managed to unwind me from Wells long enough for everyone to hug us as separate individuals, but I smashed right up against him on a loveseat as soon as we all sat down to have drinks and snacks. There was even a separate bottle of purple-colored, sparkling liquid especially for Cilla.

Wells put an arm around me and gave me a small shake. "Don't worry, Demon, I know where we are. These used to be my rooms when I lived here." He glanced around at the silver and blue paint scheme, at odds with the abundance of gold and ivory everywhere else. "I'm actually surprised it hasn't changed much."

"You know Mother's always dying to get you back here," Al said, twirling the stem of his glass between his fingers and smiling pleasantly. "She's probably had it preserved as a shrine to the prodigal."

Wells rolled his eyes. "I moved a mile away, I'd hardly consider that going prodigal."

Al laughed. "You should have seen her getting everything ready for tonight. Gods' bones, you'd think *she* just accepted a mating bond . . ."

I 'pathed Cilla discreetly, keeping my eyes on whoever was talking. *Has Al been nice and normal this entire time?*

She blinked, then took a sip of her purple drink, keeping her focus on her glass. *We've only been waiting together for about fifteen minutes, but . . . yeah, he's actually been really chill. He showed us around a little bit. There's a garden off one of the rooms.*

Are you and Zoe staying with us tonight? I asked hopefully. That would make it feel more like a fun sleepover in a hotel rather than being obligated guests in a labyrinthine palace.

No, everyone else has to leave by midnight, I think. But, sweetie, you don't want us to stay. You'll be wanting to have sex in every room, on every surface.

I snorted and covered it by coughing.

Apparently it was tradition for family and close friends to hang out and help the newly bonded get ready for the celebration. Aloysius continued to be genial and brotherly. I watched his aura for any sign of the devastation or heartbreak I'd witnessed two days ago, but saw nothing. Not even the black spike of a lie.

That strange crimson color periodically washed through the green-blues of contentment and the golden glitters of excitement. I felt like I had seen it before, but couldn't remember when. Wells seemed to be enjoying himself, and even if Al had decided to put aside the drama just for tonight, I would consider that a gift. Still . . .

A servant popped in to replenish refreshments and to remind us of the time. Cilla and Zoe pulled me into a bedroom to get me ready. Zoe made sure to grab drinks.

"Why do we have to get ready separately?" I asked, straining to look over my shoulder to where Captain Marc and Al were steering Wells away.

"Tradition—" Zoe started.

"Oh, Immy, it's *fun*. Then you get to see each other next when you're all prettified and it'll be fucking adorable. Just let it be fun and stop stressing. Zoe, baby, give her more champagne, bubbles, whatever the booze is." Cilla smashed my cheeks between her hands and put her nose up to mine. "Now I'm going to do your hair. And it will be *fun*."

It was fun.

I pulled out my phone and let Cilla pick the music. She chatted happily to Zoe, who changed into her dress—a shimmering, gold, floor-length sheath with a long slit up one side that showed off her lithe form—while Cilla washed my hair.

She put me in front of a mirror, towel-dried my waves, and set out various scissors and clips that she had brought with her from Earth and a few that she had purchased in Molnair. "This is so great," she said, meeting my eyes in the mirror. "It's like being back in LA." She scrunched my hair and her eyes lit up. "Except now I have *magic!*"

After a brief discussion about her vision for my cut, Cilla turned me away from the mirror while she gave me a trim and styled my hair. I faced Zoe, who filled me in on a few acceptance celebrations she had been to before to dispel some of my nerves. It was not like a wedding on Earth. There was no ceremony to speak of, and although people may give gifts, it wasn't a requirement. Sometimes things like Cilla doing my hair were considered a gift. The king and queen throwing the celebration was considered their gift. People may send breakfast to the couple the next day as a gift. Some guests may wait up to a year to give the couple something they needed or treat them randomly during that time.

The king may give a public welcome at some point, but there were no traditionally required speeches. There would be dancing and people may want to dance with Wells and me, but there was no obligation around it. Food and drinks would be available but without any order to the dining, just grab-as-you-can. We'd walk in after most guests had arrived so that everyone could get a good look at us, but then it was just socializing. My shoulders relaxed a fraction.

"Be prepared for people to ask you about children," Zoe said. "Word may have gotten around that you didn't want any on Earth, but people here will not understand that. Especially given your pedigree—"

"Pedigree? What pedigree? I have a pedigree?"

"Immy, keep your face still." Cilla had finished with my hair and was now applying makeup, which she promised to keep minimal, although she insisted on emphasizing my eyes. *I know they aren't your original eyes, Immy, but they're gorgeous, they look great with your dress, and I need to pick a feature.*

"Solange was the last in a line of very powerful sidhe," Zoe told me. Cilla let me open my eyes while she applied lipstick and Zoe smiled. "I knew your grandmother," she told me. "She was very unique, very charismatic, and a great kromatic talent. This is one reason Aloysius's parents tolerated his preoccupation with her until she left. She would have been an excellent match. She had no children before she went to Earth. It was thought that her line was extinguished. But now here you are."

Cilla had finished with my makeup, cleared up her tools, and stepped into the adjoining bedroom to change into her own dress.

"I didn't realize you knew her," I said, my throat tight. That would have been nice to know.

"I spoke to Wells about it some time ago," Zoe said. "He wanted you to come into yourself without being constantly compared to Solange or being harassed about offspring. Many families were obliterated completely during the Wind War. The majority consider it a duty to one's ancestors to continue the line if you are the last. Regardless of your preference." Her eyes darkened. "Even gender preference wasn't considered centuries ago until kromatic advances were made. It's one reason Wells has kept you from meeting more people. And he asked me to respect that." Her mouth tightened. "But you're going to be thrown into many conversations tonight and you're already nervous. Wells may be able to stay with you, but it's very likely that you'll get separated at some point during the evening. I didn't want you to be completely unprepared if this happens."

"Thank you," I said.

She smiled, some of the tension dropping from her face. "Now that you are mated to Llewellyn, rumors of your lack of attachment and knowledge of your unusual power won't matter. You'll be considered unavailable and off limits. Hopefully he'll relax and let you stretch your powers a bit. And get out more."

Cilla came slinking back in the room. Her shimmering turquoise dress was similar in cut to Zoe's, but short. It perfectly complimented her coloring, clinging to her form attractively, revealing the smallest hint of a bump. And she and Zoe looked fantastic together.

"You guys look amazing! You're like the sun and the sky!" I said. Zoe laughed and Cilla twirled, the short skirt of her dress fanning out around her thighs.

"Okay, now you get to see what I've done and then we'll get you into your dress." Cilla spun my chair around.

"Cilla," I breathed, staring at the person in the mirror. "You *are* magic."

My dark hair, which I'd always wished would just pick a shade, brown or black, reflected the light softly. She'd trimmed it back to a shattered, chin-framing bob like I'd had before I left Earth. The waves weren't perfect. They were perfect for me. Softly defined, but kicking out at the ends with a little bit of sass.

She'd somehow woven tiny wildflowers in certain spots, no doubt conjuring them as she went. The makeup was light, as promised, a deeper red than I'd expected on my lips, but I liked it. My eyes were lined and my eyelashes had been lengthened. The eyeshadow she used emphasized their deep violet.

"You're welcome." Cilla pulled me toward the bedroom. "Now stop staring at yourself, we need to get you into your dress."

My dress was a dark cobalt blue. The bodice was fitted to the waist, and the skirt flowed softly to the floor. Cilla had talked me into special underwear as spaghetti straps held up the front and the back was completely open to the waist.

"Immy, God," she said, giving me a once over to make sure everything was in place. "Your back is so cut. I want to start doing crazy workouts with you after the baby."

"I will only say it once, I promise." Zoe was smiling softly. "You look *so* much like my old friend. You're both very beautiful."

"Thanks," I said, my cheeks warm.

"Okay, you ready to go into the other room and show the guys?" Cilla strode to the door, grinning.

I shook my head and backed up a step, suddenly feeling very exposed.

"You are unbelievable." Cilla's eyebrows dropped. She put her hands on her hips. "A few minutes ago, we couldn't pry you away from him, now you don't want to go in?"

"I need more bubbles," I said, holding my cold fingers against my flaming cheeks.

She narrowed her eyes and cocked a hip. "Bubbles are for closers."

"Cilla, stop, she's shy." Zoe wrapped cool fingers around my hand and pulled me closer to the door. "We'll go in first and leave the door open for you."

Which is what they did.

I stood several feet away and listened as Al, Wells, and Captain Marc bestowed well-deserved compliments on Cilla and Zoe which they returned, as "the guys" had changed also.

"Immy. Come *on*, this is getting ridiculous," Cilla called. "If you don't get out here, I'm drinking all the bubbles without you, preggers or no."

I shuffled my feet. I knew it was silly but I couldn't make myself move forward. I looked down at my hands. *I'll tap each finger one time, and then I'll go out.* I promised myself. I was on finger number six when Wells took my hands in his.

"Hi," I said, not looking up. My cheeks continued to burn.

"Hello," he answered, kissing the top of my head. "Don't you want to see what I look like?"

I lifted my eyes slightly. "Oh, dear." The corners of my mouth twitched. "We match. One of us is going to have to change."

His jacket was the same cobalt blue as my dress, with black accents. His dark red hair was neatly pulled back. Black pants and shirt all cut to fit him perfectly.

"Well, it's not going to be you," he said, brushing a hand down my arm. "You're stunning."

I reached up to tug on his lapels. "Hm, I guess we'll just have to match." I finally raised my eyes to his. "'Cause you look pretty good too."

He slid his arms around my waist and pulled me close, his eyes still locked on mine. "Maybe we should just skip the party and stay in here..."

My insides coiled. I breathed him in.

"Llewellyn!" Cilla barked. I had never heard her use Wells's full name before. "Are you bringing her out here or is this turning into a horror movie where I send person after person into the dark room and no one ever returns?"

I giggled. Wells mouthed his name, eyebrows lifting.

"This stress is not good for the baby," Zoe added, laughter bouncing through her voice.

Wells offered me his arm. "Shall we spare Cilla any further histrionics?"

I wrapped both hands around his elbow and allowed him to escort me out.

It was the only time that night I saw Al's aura fracture.

He recovered quickly and joined Captain Marc in complimenting my appearance while Cilla handed me a glass of sparkling as a reward for "getting my ass in gear finally," then insisted on using my phone to take some pictures of all of us. Captain Marc offered one toast to me and Wells, for our continued happiness and success, and then it was time for our four companions to head out. Wells and I would take a few moments together before someone came to fetch us.

Al stopped in the doorway. "Congratulations again, Wells," he said, his hand on the doorknob. Amber eyes shifted to me. "Im, you look gorgeous. Save me a dance?" I gave a stiff nod and he ducked out, closing the door behind him.

"Look how tall you are," Wells said, pulling me into a hug and running a hand down my bare back.

"I am wearing the *highest* of heels." I circled my arms around his neck easily, still a few inches short of looking him in the eye. "So, was Al all nice and normal to you the whole time?"

"He was," Wells said, glancing around the room. "It's really strange being back here. With Al behaving . . . the way he was when I was living at the palace. It was nice, not arguing with him for a change, but . . ."

"What?" I prompted when he didn't continue.

"I don't know how to put it," he said, brow furrowing. "When we lived here together, we got along, but sometimes I felt it was because—"

He was interrupted by a knock on the door, which was immediately opened by a servant who told us it was time to go. Now. We were hustled out and I had to ask them to slow down twice to navigate my long skirts and heels. By the time we arrived at the ballroom entrance, I was once again wrapped around Wells's arm like an eel.

They stopped us just before two ornate, overly tall doors in a dimly lit hallway. The buzzing of a sizable crowd on the other side had my shoulders creeping toward my ears. Two servants fluffed and arranged my skirts as if I were nothing but a mannequin. Another one stepped in front of us, pushing my shoulders back and down, then pulling at my arms to force me to release my death grip on Wells. My spine locked up, my entire body tensed. Wells politely asked them to back off and give me a second.

Once they had, he pressed a kiss to my temple. I relaxed a fraction. "Just five seconds," he said. "Everyone will gape at how beautiful you are for five seconds, then we can go see our friends again and you can drink all the wine."

I nodded. Slowly unwound myself from him. He bent his elbow and I forced myself to politely take his arm with just one of my hands. I fisted the other in the skirts at my side. I nodded again. Five seconds. I could do it. I looked at Wells and gave him a small smile. He smiled back and nodded at the servants by the doors. They simultaneously winked to the other side and opened them wide. The crowd ceased conversation and broke into cheers and applause.

It was more than five seconds.

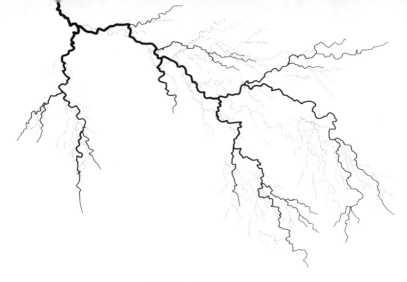

CHAPTER THIRTY-FIVE

*I know you don't like games, darling, but you should
at least learn to recognize when you've fallen into the middle of one.*
—Solange Aidair Delaney

We were situated at one end of an enormous room—at least half the length of a football field—with the king, queen, and Al seated at the other side. A wide aisle had been cleared between us and them. We had no choice but to walk all the way to their thrones. I felt like a thoroughbred being trotted out for show before a horse race. My fingers tightened on Wells's arm and I scanned the crowd for signs of Zoe, Cilla, Captain Marc, even Admiral Kavlo. Any familiar face to ground me.

Just one foot in front of the other, Demon, you're doing fine. Wells smiled at someone he knew in the throng. *I should have let you hide some kind of weapon in that dress, just to make you feel better.*

How do you think I'm holding it together right now?

You didn't.

I have a small knife in my bra and the dagger you gave me strapped to my leg.

Oh, Imogen.

What? You just said it was a good idea! And you didn't even notice, so.

The reminder of my friendly weapons did calm me down. By the time we reached the dais where the royals perched—each crowned this evening and looking regally resplendent—I was even able to smile a bit. As soon as we stopped, two servants handed each of us a glass of sparkling. The king, queen, and Al all stood and raised their glasses as Allestair thanked those assembled for coming.

He'll give us a toast, most likely wishing us well, we'll reply "thank you, majesty" the five of us will drink, you curtsy when I bow. Then he should let us go.

I was told there were no ceremonies.

Hush. Pay attention.

"Llewellyn, Imogen." The king lifted his glass to each of us. "Well matched. I rejoice in your presence here in the palace. We look forward to seeing what this new pair can accomplish in service to Molnair. May your mating be blessed with many talented children."

I managed to rasp out, "Thank you, majesty," in time with Wells, even as my stomach slipped at his blessing. My gulp of wine may have been slightly larger than politeness dictated. I managed to keep my feet under me during my curtsy. Then we were released.

I wanted nothing more than to find my friends and some food, but we were instantly surrounded. Other nobles were positioned closest to the royal family's dais. There was no way of politely excusing ourselves until they were done with us. Zoe had been right to warn me. Several of them asked if we had already started trying, all of them wished us luck with our familial efforts, and a few even went in for deep speculation on my strong sidhe bloodline coupled with my recent turning and how that might enhance my ability to bear children and how many.

By the time we had extricated ourselves from the scrum, I was near fainting with hunger and emotionally exhausted by having my hypothetical pregnancy stats discussed so cavalierly. Wells pulled me over to a bistro table and beckoned to a servant to get us some food just before we were besieged by more well-wishers. Some of these seemed to be, if not personal friends of Wells, then at least genial acquaintances, and were less intrusive in their conversation. The servant did bring over healthy servings and Wells assured me that it was not impolite for us to eat while a never-ending stream of people came to greet us.

After an hour, it slacked off enough for us to try to locate Cilla and Zoe. Wells snagged some drinks off a passing tray and handed one to me. I finally had a chance to take in our surroundings. The tall bistro tables scattered around the perimeters of the room were draped in flowing fabrics of silver and blue. Perfect for guests to set a plate or a glass on while they took a break from dancing to converse. The floral arrangements were boughs of indigo, cobalt, and violet, tied with silver ribbons. Candles of all four colors adorned the tables, sat in fat clumps on pedestals, and hung from chandeliers. Musicians played in one corner and the center of the hall was alive with people dancing. I noticed there was no place to sit if you didn't have your own throne.

Cilla and Zoe were out on the dance floor. We finished our drinks and joined them. For about an hour, we actually had fun. We danced and drank with Cilla and Zoe. I met Captain Marc's mate and tried not to fan-girl over the fact that she was from Mesopotamia. She promised she'd have us over for dinner sometime and we could tell each other about our different Earths. Wells introduced me to a few of his friends, who ribbed him good-naturedly for being so preoccupied the past several months, and seemed genuinely pleased to meet me.

I was on the verge of asking Wells if we could find a place to sit down when Al came to claim his dance just as Queen Iphigenia asked to dance with Wells. There was no way to politely decline.

For a few moments, we danced without speaking. It was the first I'd allowed Al to touch me for any length of time. I couldn't stop my imagination from replaying that first night on the ship and had to wrench my mind back into the present and force my shoulders to relax. He kept one hand on my waist and held my hand with his other. My opposite hand rested on his arm. I took a deep breath and reminded myself that we were surrounded by people. I was safe.

The dance was simple and worked with most of the music. It could be embellished if desired, but it was possible to dance entire songs with just the basic steps. I'd already danced this way with Captain Marc, Admiral Kavlo, and Zoe, who had been the one to gleefully add the embellishments.

"Are you having fun, Im?" Al asked.

"I think so, some of it's fun," I answered honestly. "I'm getting tired though."

"You look great, I really like your dress."

"Thanks," I said, then decided to put in a polite effort. "Are you having fun?"

"Yeah, I am." He smiled, eyes sparkling. "It's probably easier for me, though, because I know most everyone here."

I nodded. That was a lot of people to know. But I guessed that Al had been alive long enough to meet thousands of people.

"I'd like us to be friends again, Im," he said. I noticed that he'd pulled me slightly closer. "Do you think you could be friends with me?"

"I think so," I said carefully. "If you think you can stop accusing Wells of stealing people from you."

His hand tightened on mine for half a second. I thought I saw his aura fleetingly flood with indigo, but I couldn't be sure. A combination of wine, fatigue, and too many auras in the room made them difficult for me to read. "You're going to need a friend," he said, ignoring my last comment. "Fighting is going to start up and eventually Wells is going to have to go lead the armies down there." Al's gaze flicked down to mine, amber eyes dark. "What are you going to do if he doesn't come back?"

My insides froze. Of course I knew Wells would lead the armies, but he was the general. Didn't he strategize from a safe hilltop somewhere? He wouldn't be on the front lines, surely. My skin prickled as my entire body went ice cold. Then flames, starting at my core and spreading, slowly melted me. A crack of lightning followed by rolling thunder sounded outside, although the sky had been crystal clear.

What's wrong?

Al just implied that you're going to DIE in this war is all.

He's being dramatic. I'm not going to die.

Because I will be going with you to prevent said death from occurring.

We'll discuss that later.

Hello? Thor, god of thunder, here. I'm going.

Later.

He broke contact.

"That's rude, Im, we're having a conversation," Al said mildly.

"Sorry, my mate checked in to see what had upset me when you implied that he was going to be *killed* in the near future during our acceptance celebration," I spat.

Al laughed lightly and pulled me in for a hug. "Sorry I upset you." He released me before I could protest the contact, but I noticed that now I was closer still. One hand was resting on my bare back. "Do you like your rooms?"

I blinked, adjusting to the topic shift. "Uh, yeah, they're fine."

He rubbed my back once. "You can make any changes to them you like."

"Why would I want to change anything, it's just for the night?" The hair on my arms rose to attention as my stomach tightened.

He shook his head, smiling slightly. My bones went brittle.

"I've been talking to my parents and we all agree it would be safer for you and Wells to stay here indefinitely. We've had servants packing up your things so you won't have to worry about it." He pulled me even closer. His hand now high on my back, near the base of my neck. "You know, no one's ever seen anything like your lightning power before. Not even my father. And now Sephrya knows about it too. They'll want to take you or kill you. Better for you to stay here."

"Wells doesn't want to live here," I said, swallowing against the dryness in my throat. "He's not royalty."

"He's not," Al agreed. "But he belongs to us." His eyes burned into mine. "And now so do you." He ran his fingertips down my spine.

I tried to pull away, but Al held me hard. I scanned the room wildly for Wells and spotted him. By the stricken expression on his face, I guessed that his mother was having a similar conversation with him.

I tried again to pull free, but Al squeezed my hand, grinding the bones against each other. "Don't make a scene," he said. "*Smile, Imogen.*"

My throat constricted as my mouth curved up in a bright smile all on its own. My lungs heaved. Tears instantly burned behind my eyes. A sob pushed its way out from behind my grinning teeth.

"Oh, all right, you can stop," Al said, rolling his eyes and holding me against him. I was shaking. "I don't know why that freaks you out so much."

What happened? What did he do?

I want out! IwantoutIwantoutIwantout!

Okay, okay, get through the song and we'll find each other. See where Cilla and Zoe are?

I scanned the room over Al's shoulder, not daring to push out of his embrace for fear of what he would do, and for fear that I would fall over. My feet automatically moved through the simple steps as Al guided us around. I spotted Cilla and Zoe by one of the bistro tables. Cilla was having one of her pregnancy-safe purple drinks.

I see them.

Head over there when the song ends.

But that's not how it happened.

CHAPTER THIRTY-SIX

You've got a good family, Imogen. Be thankful. Not everyone does.
—Henry Delaney

The song ended, Al slackened his hold and I immediately turned to go. He grabbed my arm and hauled me back. "I want another dance with you, Im. It's been too long since we've hung out."

I heard myself whimper as he pulled me back into his arms and steered me onto the dance floor.

I wondered for a moment what would happen if I stabbed him, then I saw the king talking to Wells. I'd have to stab a lot of people to survive. I'd have to fight every guard in the palace and probably every member of the military present.

And some of them might be Wells's friends.

"Why are you shaking, baby?" Al said, rubbing my back again. "We're just dancing, nothing's going to happen to you."

"Aloysius." King Allestair tapped his son on the shoulder. "Might I steal Imogen for this dance?"

Al hesitated for less than a second, then handed me over. "Of course, father. She's so stunning tonight, I'm surprised she doesn't have a line waiting."

The king took Al's place. Al ambled over to where Wells was glaring at him by Cilla and Zoe. Wells said something sharp, eyes blazing. Al smirked and grabbed a glass of wine before sauntering away. Not even a bit cowed. Wells couldn't very well fight him here after all. My stomach dropped at the realization. Then the king threw me into a spin and I was forced to pay attention to how we were moving.

"I'm glad you're so light on your feet, Imogen," Allestair said. "Everyone tends to watch when their king dances and so I'm afraid a certain amount of pageantry is necessary." He spun me again, guiding me behind his back, so that he turned also, catching my opposite hand when we were back-to-back and continuing the rotation, stopping me when we were once again facing each other.

I was never a trained dancer. Aside from a few ballet lessons as a child and being forced into a few numbers on stage, cardio kickboxing was the most dancing I'd ever done. I was always good at following someone else's lead, however. If I paid attention, I'd be fine.

"Llewellyn claims that Aloysius was intentionally upsetting you," the king said, taking a breather from flourishes. "He was about to come over himself and make a scene, but I thought it better if I stepped in." He took the basic step up to double time for a few measures and I followed.

"Thank you, sire." I fought to keep from blurting out "we're not staying here!" remembering a talk Wells and Captain Marc had with me the day after my Escape From Hell, as we started calling it. Because of the shock of Cilla being suddenly taken, I'd been excused from my rudeness in the woods. Because of my heroism and exhaustion following our escape, my lack of deference in the office had been overlooked. But I shouldn't count on getting away with cavalier language with the king a third time. Especially not in the palace. Best to say nothing and listen if I wasn't sure. Wells said I'd eventually learn to read between the lines.

However, in my dealings with arrogant assholes in positions of power on Earth, I'd discovered that pretending to be confused and asking them questions until they tripped themselves up was often an effective tactic.

"Sire, is it true that Wells and I aren't being permitted to return home? Have we done something?" I managed to get both questions out politely before he threw me into another spin.

Allestair stopped me abruptly mid-spin with a hand to my waist, lifting our clasped hands high and pulling me to him until we were nearly nose to nose, his other arm landed high on my back, the blade of his thumb against my shoulder, steering me where he wanted me to go. Caging me in. "This is your home, Imogen. You'll get used to belonging to the palace just as you got used to belonging to Llewellyn." I bristled, but kept my face smooth. He continued, "As for what you've done, I think it's patently obvious that your powers have manifested so rapidly as to be beyond your ability to control them and beyond your mate's ability to monitor."

I opened my mouth to argue, but he increased the pace again, and with my feet so close to his, I had to concentrate to avoid stepping on him or tripping.

"We're fortunate that your inadvertent winking when you were distressed over the loss of your friend didn't result in both of you being killed or taken," Allestair continued, his ice blue eyes piercing me. "Better to have you here where you have plenty of space to do what you like, but are incapable of accidentally winking anywhere you're not supposed to be."

My hand tightened on his ornate tunic and I compelled my fingers to relax. He threw me into another spin, allowed me one step, then tossed me into another, a step, a spin, a step, a spin, until he had spun me in a full circle around him. People *were* watching. A few of them applauded. My face flushed. He allowed me to drop into the basic steps for a few measures. I fought to keep my teeth from grinding. My knife and dagger burned against my skin, begging to be used.

"I'm given to understand that they do not have a monarchy in the area of Earth that you originate from, is that correct, Imogen?" he asked, once again pulling me into the cage of his arms.

"Yes, sire," I said, fighting to keep my voice even. "There aren't many places on Earth that have a monarchy anymore."

"Is that so? Hm. I'll have to refresh myself sometime. Been so long since I've looked into the place personally." He spoke as if he were thinking about perhaps taking a vacation there someday, but it had dropped off his list for whatever reason. "Be that as it may, I understand that your life was fairly unrestricted as a human. Basic rules and such to follow, but no real hierarchy. No one really knew where they stood. No formality. Is that an accurate assessment?"

"Well," I started carefully. "There were certain people who considered themselves above others, but we were working as a society to eradicate that . . . ingrained attitude."

"Interesting in theory." He increased the pace again. "And perhaps it wouldn't cause chaos among a people with no significant power. But here, Imogen, you'll find that everyone has a place. In accepting Llewellyn as your mate, you've now found yours. Aloysius has indicated that because of your background, you may need some assistance adjusting to the idea. This is really the best place for you to learn." He slowed, spun me once more, then said almost to himself, "Llewellyn lived here for over a century, he'll remember."

My blood turned to ice. What was this? Some campaign to break us down? My mouth went dry. I must have dropped my poker face because the king said, "Oh, I know you're concerned about Aloysius. Don't be. Interfering with a mated pair is criminal; I've already spoken to him and forbidden it." He rolled his eyes. "He does seem taken with your line, though. Perhaps you and Llewellyn will produce a daughter and he can have her when she comes of age."

Bile rose in my throat. I started salivating. I swallowed desperately against the nausea roiling through me.

Tell him you're sick and you need to stop.

Wells . . . Even I could hear the desperation coating my 'path.

One thing at a time. Say: "Your majesty, I apologize, I'm feeling ill, I may need to sit down."

"Your majesty," I gasped. "I'm sorry, I feel ill. I need to stop."

He paused, released my hand and gripped my chin between his thumb and forefinger, his laser blue eyes scraping across my face. "You do look rather pale. Oh, dear. You're trembling. Perhaps too much wine. Let's get you back to your mate and let him take charge of you." He hooked my hand around his arm and led me over to Wells.

It was an effort not to sprint off the dance floor and tell Wells we had to make a break for it. I had been thinking through everything I had been told about the security of this place. I knew there was no way for us to simply walk or wink out.

The king handed me over to Wells, telling him that I was ill and he should take care of it. Like I was a vehicle he had borrowed that was in need of repair.

Wells tucked me under his arm, brushed my hair back from my face, then pressed his cool fingers to my burning forehead.

"I think she just needs some water," he said. Then 'pathed to me, *Just stay quiet until we get rid of him. I've told Cilla and Zoe about this . . . situation we're in. Captain Marc was apparently informed by Al minutes after he told you.*

"Here, Immy." Cilla slid her own glass of water across the table and motioned to a passing servant for more.

I thanked her and took it, horrified to see ripples caused by my own shaking. I managed to get a few sips down, then set the glass on the table.

The king glanced around the crowd. "You know, things will be quieting down in an hour or so. Perhaps you should take her to your rooms. She's had a lot of excitement this week and probably hasn't had enough rest."

I looked at Wells. I didn't want to leave my friends.

"She hasn't eaten enough, I should—" Wells looked up as if searching for someone to bring us sustenance.

"I'll have someone bring something. Say goodbye to your friends, Imogen," Allestair said.

"But—" I started.

Wells squeezed my arm. *He's not asking. If he has to tell us again, it will get ugly.*

Zoe saved me by stepping forward and pulling me into a hug. "I should get Cilla home anyway. We'll have you over soon," she said, then released me to hug Wells. "I'll see you around the campus, I'm sure."

I breathed a little easier. Wells still had work. I still had friends. We'd find a way out. Cilla hugged me as if I were about to take a voyage on the RMS *Titanic*. She even had tears in her eyes. Zoe made some excuse to the king about Cilla being emotional at this stage of her pregnancy. Cilla didn't release me when she hugged Wells, choosing instead to squeeze us both.

"I'll have someone show you to your apartments." Allestair lifted two fingers to the side of the room and crooked them toward his palm. "It's been a while since you've had to navigate the place on your own, Llewellyn. Although I'm sure it'll come back."

It wasn't two servants who detached themselves from the wall at his signal, but two guards. My chest constricted. I glanced up at Wells. He had visibly paled, but kept his face neutral. He thanked the king for the celebration. I managed to stammer out some thanks also.

Captain Marc strode up as we were being led away, a genial smile on his face, asking a moment to say goodnight. The smile dropped as he embraced Wells and said something in his ear, then returned as he folded me into a hug, telling me he was sure we'd meet again soon. He stepped away and let the guards take us.

CHAPTER THIRTY-SEVEN

*One of these days, my girl, you're going to end up in
a situation you can't get out of by just kicking, punching, or running.*
—Henry Delaney

No one spoke as the guards led us through the maze of corridors to our rooms. As soon as the ballroom doors shut behind us, the music and noise of the crowd were silenced. My heels clicked too loudly on the floors. I wished I could ask to stop and take them off, but I didn't dare speak. Wells and I didn't even 'path. I hung on to his arm with both of my hands and he covered my fingers with his.

The guards opened our doors for us and we stepped inside. I could see at a glance that our life had been moved from Wells's house to this one. His tea and sugar box rested on a side table. They'd even unpacked.

The door shut behind us and the lock clicked. Everything constricted. My lungs refused to expand.

I couldn't breathe. Adrenaline spiked.

I tore at my dress. Desperate for air. Wells grabbed my hand and hauled me into the main bedroom. A pair of French doors burst open kromatically before we got to them. He pulled me through the doorway and on to an open terrace. I staggered toward the stone railing, then quickly stepped back when I saw the steep drop, snagging a heel in my skirt. Wells caught me and spun me toward him. "Look up at the sky, I've got you."

I forced my gaze upward. Saw stars. Unfamiliar constellations. No Big Dipper to look for. No Cassiopeia to find.

"I've got you," Wells said again. I leaned into him. Still looking at the sky, letting my head rest on his chest so I could hear his heart, beating fast but beginning to slow. I felt the breeze brush against my back. Panicking wouldn't help anything. I tried to match my breaths to his.

"Are we hanging off the mountain right now?" I asked finally.

"Are you afraid of heights?" he asked, rubbing slow circles on my back.

"I am *bothered* by edges," I clarified. "I'm okay if I'm contained in something. Like looking out a window or flying in an airplane. I just don't like naked edges off cliffs and such."

"Well, then I guess no one has to worry about you trying to escape off the terrace," he said.

"Could we?" I could get over the edge thing.

"No," he sighed. "We'd fall to our deaths before we reached the wards, which I'm sure have been altered to keep us in. But whenever I needed to *feel* like I wasn't trapped, I would come out here."

"You were trapped before?" I had always imagined Wells's relationship with the royals to be kind of congenial. And when he left to get his own place, it was like . . . he went off to college or something.

"I wasn't . . . trapped like we currently appear to be." His hand stilled on my back. "But I was on a short leash until I was allowed to leave. Occasionally I'd be restricted more than normal. It ebbed and flowed." He dropped a kiss on my temple.

"When were you allowed to leave?" I asked, pulling my gaze from the stars.

"When I was promoted to First Lieutenant and in line to become General," he said. "I'd proven myself an asset that didn't need to be constantly monitored." He smiled humorlessly down at me. "It's one of the reasons I wanted to go on the Earth expedition the first time."

"No one watching you all the time?"

"No one watching me *like that*," he said and hugged me. "I'm so sorry, Imogen, I never thought they'd do this. Al found a weakness I hadn't anticipated."

I leaned back so I could see his face. "You think this is all because of Al?"

"I think Al exploited what may have at first been a casual interest in your abilities." He stared into the blackness beyond the terrace. Then pulled me toward two lounge chairs. "I'm not sure if Allestair believes in the prophecy or not, but it's undeniable that your powers are formidable either way. I think Al is angry with us for mating, he's been angry at me since I offered you the option of staying with me, he's angry with you for deciding to stay with me, he's still not over Solange, he's not over you, he feels betrayed by me, and now he's put us in a nice little cage where he can play with us whenever he likes."

The chairs were set where they might catch the sun if it were daylight. I sat down and removed my shoes, moaning as my feet were freed. Wells hauled his chair around to face mine, pulled my feet into his lap, and pressed his thumbs into my left instep. I sighed, going boneless and letting my head fall against the backrest.

"Can I come with you to work when you go?" I asked. I did not want to be left alone here.

His fingers paused, then resumed massaging. "I've been given an unasked for two days off." He cleared his throat. "To acclimate you to the palace."

I snorted.

He moved to my right foot. "During those two days, an office is going to be set up for me here. I'm not to leave the grounds for the foreseeable future."

"That's *bullshit!*" I said, sitting up. I subsided when he made a shushing gesture. *How are you supposed to fight a war from in here?* I 'pathed.

They'll expect to hear us talking. If they didn't, there would be something off. We just don't want to give them a reason to come check on us or listen harder, so try not to shout. If we 'path everything they'll put wards up preventing us from speaking to each other that way.

There are wards against telepathy?

Have you tried to 'path Cilla since she left the palace?

My stomach turned. "No," I said. "I've been here with you having a breakdown and on the verge of an existential crisis." I focused my energy on Cilla. Ever since I'd winked to her, I'd always found her easily. A flicker of triumph had the corners of my mouth lifting as I locked onto her essence and speared my thoughts toward her. "Ouch!" I smacked my hand over my right eye where it felt like I'd been shocked. I lowered my hand and cautiously blinked. The pain wasn't subsiding.

Wells dropped my foot and came to sit on the edge of my chair. "Oh, shit. I'm sorry, Demon, I didn't know they'd have *that* one up." He massaged my temples. A headache was blooming fast. "C'mon, let's get you ready for bed before it gets worse." He pulled me to my feet.

"It's going to get worse?" I let him tug me into the bedroom when my vision stuttered.

"Depending on what they moved over from my medic supplies at the house . . . yes." He unhooked my dress, then hunted around in the dresser until he found where they'd put my sleep clothes, pulled out a nightshift, and tossed it on the bed near me.

My head was already throbbing steadily. I heard him rummaging around in the bathroom as I slipped my dress off. Wells came back in time to see me remove my knives and fling them against the pillows with a smack. They'd been useless.

"This is a different kind of fighting, Demon. We'll get our bearings. Here, take a swallow of this." He pushed an opaque glass bottle into my hand. "It's not what I was hoping for, but it will take the edge off."

I took a gulp and handed it back to him, making a face. It tasted like chewing on a juniper tree.

"Is that . . ." He stopped. "I hesitate to say anything because it looks amazing, and now is not the time, but . . . is that underwear comfortable enough to sleep in?"

I shook my head and then regretted it as the world spun and my stomach pitched. Wells had to undress and re-dress me as my condition degraded. The only thing good about it was that I didn't care where I was sleeping. Wells crawled into bed and tucked me against his chest, rubbing my head. It was like a migraine on steroids. My eyeballs felt like they might just explode. I couldn't uncurl from an upright fetal position.

"When is that stuff I drank supposed to kick in?" I mumbled. Nausea floated on the edges of my lake of pain.

"Any minute now. If I had ash root it would be better, but they don't seem to have brought any over. Either that or I was out." He brushed a light kiss to my forehead. "If I had known that ward was up, I would have warned you against trying."

"This has happened before? Don't stop rubbing."

"Yes, there was a period of time when I was about your age when 'pathing anyone outside of the palace was deemed 'rude,'" he said. "It was right about the time my powers became strong enough and I became proficient enough to 'path anyone I wanted over long distances. I hit that ward and within minutes I thought I was going to die. Al actually came looking for me because I hadn't been down for meals the entire day. He found me curled up on the floor and took care of me until I was through it."

"Wells, this is some serious abusive shit they put you through," I hissed. "Locking you in rooms? Not letting you outside? Causing you pain so bad you skipped meals and thought you were going to die? You were the human equivalent of a teenager then? CPS would have taken you away and they would have gone to prison if this was Earth. Well, some parts of Earth."

He didn't answer, continuing to rub my head. After a few minutes my muscles relaxed out of their clench. The nausea floated further away.

I uncurled slightly. "Oh, I think it's working."

"Good," he said. When I stretched out, he scooted down next to me. Our heads on the same pillow. "You'll still have a headache, but you won't feel like you want to rip your eyeballs out."

"That's amazing, thank you," I sighed. My eyes drifted closed. "Can I be the small spoon?"

"Roll over."

I did. He settled my back against his front.

"What did Captain Marc say to you?"

I felt him take a deep breath and let it out. "Life is long if you're careful, keep your wits about you, remember what's important."

I didn't have the brain space for the captain's riddle. "Any more bear traps in these woods I need to be aware of?" I muttered.

"I'll alert you to them as I remember." His exhale ruffled my hair. "I can't believe I'm back here again."

"Oh, I should tell you, the king said that if you and I were to 'produce a daughter,'" I sketched some finger quotes in the air with one hand. "We could give her to Al when she's old enough since he seems to be into—"

"WHAT?"

"Shhh, inside voice." I couldn't help myself. "Why do you think I got sick? So much to unpack there."

Wells growled and hugged me hard. I started to drift off in spite of the dull ache in my head and the strangeness of my surroundings.

"Everything I thought was bad is so much worse when I watch them doing it to you," he whispered.

I still had a headache the next day. I couldn't even see auras. Wells told me not to try 'pathing at all.

When we still hadn't emerged the morning of the second day, Al came to check on us. To his—marginal—credit, he seemed as shocked as Wells that the headache-ward had been added and brought us the medicine Wells asked for. The ash root obliterated my headache within minutes. But it didn't change the fact that all unmonitored communication to the outside had been cut off for Wells and me.

I learned that we were the only telepaths in the palace—although everyone eventually learned to 'port at least basic items, 'pathing was apparently a rare skill—which made me even angrier that they'd set that painful trap up just for us. Especially as there were several gentler prevention wards available. I tried to 'port Cilla a note and earned another headache. At least we had the ash root on hand. Wells showed me how to check for these kinds of wards without attempting a 'port or a 'path first.

"Maybe I can just tear them down like I did the ones at Sephrya," I mused.

"No, don't try. Bear trap," Wells said.

"But if I did the ones there—"

"Blood Kroma is *different*, Imogen," he explained patiently. Then he sighed, regret shadowing his eyes. "Honestly, it's so tied up with the ruling family that I was hoping you'd never have to deal with it. Most people don't." He shook himself, falling into that business-like mask I'd become even more familiar with since we'd been pulled into the palace. "It is literally linked to the royal family's blood. The king can make rules around anyone he wants to give an exception to, but no one else can. Even Al has *some* restrictions as he's not yet a monarch. But he wouldn't get damaged as badly as you for attempting some of these things. The wards you ripped down—still impressive, by the way, we've heard rumors they couldn't repair them, they had to start from scratch—those were standard wards placed around any structure with some sort of security to keep people from winking in and out. Libraries even have them."

"So you're saying there's no way around them? None at all?"

"Not for anyone without royal blood. The best we can do is ride this out."

I absolutely refused to accept that.

CHAPTER THIRTY-EIGHT

*Patience may not be your first choice,
but sometimes you have to slow down and think things through.*
—Henry Delaney

When the leaders of other countries—completely different species, I can now say that I've met a merperson—wished to discuss the inciting incident behind war negotiations with Sephrya, I was allowed in meetings. I got to bring out my phone, show them the video, and answer any questions about my Escape From Hell. Although I was starting to think I'd only moved from one level to another. Other than that, I was kept away from the military offices so I wouldn't "distract" Wells while he was at work. I had large swaths of time on my own.

And I wasn't going to sit idly by.

I cultivated an interest in the garden outside the smaller bedroom. Al found this to be charming and encouraged it. I spent long stretches of time in the library, ostensibly looking up plants and gardening techniques.

Sometimes I was. I managed to plant a few unobtrusive herbs that might be useful in potions, diverting suspicion by adding some pretty flowers and fruit plants. I used kromatic techniques I had learned from Cilla to encourage them to thrive. She would have had an established and flourishing garden in an hour, but I knew she would have applauded my efforts.

And the garden was a nice cover for my Blood Kroma research.

Winking was prohibited in the library and cloaking shields were kromatically stripped upon entry, so it was either prowl at night or do it right out in the open. When I wasn't in the garden, I was in the library, surrounded by stacks of books on herbs, flowers, and gardening. It only took a little creativity to hide the occasional text on ancient wards, spells, and potions among my piles.

My enthusiasm for gardening was probably the only thing about me that didn't get under Allestair's skin.

I'd never gotten the impression I was his favorite person. From the moment I met him, I'd felt like he was either blaming me or sizing me up. I wasn't sure what exactly he wanted from me, except perhaps to meekly obey like his queen. Or at least pretend obedience, like my mate.

"This is intolerable," I said to Wells one evening. He'd come to remind me to change for the enforced family dinner—we had to dress for dinner. Every. Single. Night—and found me in my garden ripping out weeds. I could have used kroma, but even Cilla agreed that there was something cathartic about physically tearing them from the dirt.

Wells plucked a spent bloom off a flowering moon blossom as he crouched in the dirt beside me. "We just have to be patient, Imogen. Allestair goes through cycles. Eventually the war will heat up and he'll have less energy to focus on us. Even if that's not the case, he will move on to something else after a few years. If we keep our heads down and avoid making waves, we'll find a way to earn our independence again."

My blood chilled, just as my heart broke for Wells. I glanced at him once before pushing my gaze back to the patch of weeds I was working on. How long ago had he learned to lay low and make himself small so that

Allestair would eventually forget about him? How old had he been when he developed a tolerance for existing within his step-father's oppressive parameters, biding his time for *years*?

Well, I was not going to live like that. Neither was Wells if I had anything to say about it.

As if he sensed my aversion to blind deference, Allestair tightened the leash almost immediately. It started when he discovered I didn't eat meat because I didn't want to eat any being that I wouldn't have the stomach to kill myself. Not only did this become an awful dinner conversation where he pointed out that I had killed hundreds of sidhe escaping from Sephrya and I responded that I didn't eat them afterward, but he also ordered meat served almost exclusively from that point on. Wells tried to order food in the room for me after the third day, which worked once. The next time, the servants informed him that they'd been told not to bring any additional food if I hadn't eaten what was served. What I didn't realize was—as far Allestair was concerned—this was merely a warning shot.

A week into our captivity, Wells offered me his arm after another horrible family meal. At least Iphigenia had insisted on including a large salad, as tired of the Atkins diet as the rest of us. I wrapped my hands around his elbow and we headed to the dubious sanctuary of our rooms.

I have two small yellowfruits in my left pocket and bread and cheese in my right, he 'pathed.

Have I mentioned lately how utterly sexy you are? I responded. He covered a smile by lifting my hand from his arm and kissing it.

By the way, I found something interesting in the library today. I really think—

"Llewellyn." The king approached and we both tensed. Had he scented the yellowfruit? "I wonder if I might have the pleasure of taking a short stroll with Imogen. I'll bring her to your rooms when we're done."

"Of course, sire." Wells squeezed my hand and kissed my cheek as he handed me over. *Remember to breathe. You can tell me what you've found when you get back. Think of yellowfruit sandwiches.*

"See you soon." I smiled at Wells as he left to escort the queen with Al, who frowned at his father's back. Although this was ultimately Al's doing, neither of them liked it when the king was alone with me. I composed myself by arranging the skirts of my stupid dress before taking his arm. At least the horrid things had pockets in this world.

Allestair guided me outside. The night was a little breezy, but otherwise mild for fall.

"I thought I might give you a treat," he said as we stepped out of the dining room and onto a terrace. "And show you a place you're not normally permitted." As soon as we turned, one corner of the stone railing faded away, allowing us to step out onto the thick, lavender grass.

So we were headed to a place that was warded against anyone not of royal blood for whatever reason. I was not excited. Anything he ever said was a "treat" was usually the opposite. "That sounds lovely, sire."

He led me downhill, toward a foggy ravine. As much as I wanted to glance over my shoulder and reassure myself that the castle was still within sight, I kept my eyes forward. I'd learned that much from Wells. Things were always worse if the king could pull a visible reaction.

Allestair didn't warn me, but I felt it the instant we slid through the wards. Like I had walked into a large, viscous bubble. It sucked at my skin as we passed. As if it knew I wasn't supposed to be there, but reluctantly allowed me because I was with the king.

I checked the wards surrounding me and immediately knew I was unable to 'path Wells from the inside. My heart beat faster. I concentrated on keeping myself relaxed. I wouldn't allow any fear to creep into my scent, no matter what he did.

The hill leveled out; we were now on a red clay path running parallel to the ravine. "It has come to my attention, Imogen, that you are still taking a tonic against pregnancy."

Ah, here we go. "I've never been secretive about the fact that I don't want children." *And if I did, I wouldn't bring them into this cesspit for you to get your grubby mitts on them.*

"I was hopeful that your acceptance of your mating bond meant you had changed your mind. In fact, I think the entire nation was hopeful," he said.

The path he led me down seemed to drop off the side of the mountain. My stomach hollowed out. *Who the fuck told him I don't like edges? Probably useless Aloysius . . . or maybe he's just going to push me off since I won't perform my "continuation of the Aidair line" duty.*

"Fighting in Sephrya will begin shortly," he said. I was no longer surprised by this family's abrupt subject changes. I'd come to learn it was a way of putting me off balance.

"Negotiations aren't going well?" I shifted with him. I'd been in enough meetings to have a grasp of the big picture. And Wells always told me as much as he could when we were alone.

"They sent back our ambassadors today in pieces," he replied, inspecting his nails. "I'm going to have Aloysius start on those two that we have in the dungeons tomorrow morning in a similar manner. Perhaps he'll be able to get more out of them if they see the state our ambassadors were left in while he questions them. I'll have him drag it out for a week." He straightened the lapel of his jacket, sighing. I blinked, but forced myself not to react further, even as my insufficient dinner tried to climb up my throat. I wondered if Al knew he was going to be torturing people in the morning.

My mouth dried out as Allestair led me down the narrowest walkway in the universe. It flowed off the grassy mountainside in a smooth stream of red clay, only to be suspended over the clouds as it continued with no apparent support. Its denouement was a floating gazebo. I'm sure some people would have found it beautiful. "I like to come out here to think occasionally," the king said. "I find the view stimulating."

"Mm," I managed. I willed my hand to stay relaxed on his arm. Forced my feet to keep pace with his. Tossed a thanks to the heavens that I'd worn slippers instead of heels.

"The fighting will begin with Marc and Kavlo of course..."

This I knew.

Our aerial technology was far superior to Sephrya's and the navy would be engaged in keeping them from landing on our shores. The issue was that Sephrya was six times the size of Molnair. The armies would have it the worst.

"But once Marc gets a foothold, Llewellyn will be sent in immediately." We reached the Gazebo of My Nightmares and he drew me all the way to the railing to gaze out. I kept my eyes on the horizon and forced my breathing to stay even.

I could feel Wells's worry throbbing behind my breastbone through our bond. No wards or potions could completely obliterate those senses. I'd been told the mating bond was one of the oldest forms of kroma. I knew Wells could sense my nerves. Could probably even feel me trying to control myself. I sent a pulse of affection toward my sense of him. Sometimes this worked, sometimes it didn't. We'd become so used to 'pathing each other that we hadn't had much occasion to flex this other muscle.

"I would think you'd be happy to nurture a piece of your mate, should the worst happen." The king looked sideways at me.

I fought the urge to laugh in his face. That was no reason to bring a child into this mess. "If Wells dies," I said, something in my chest beginning to harden and take root, "nothing will bring him back and nothing will bring me peace." *I will become a black pit of rage and destruction if you orchestrate his death.*

"Well, consider that it might bring him peace," he said, placing a cold hand over mine. "To know that you might have created something together. If the worst were to happen."

Fucking manipulative asshole! I managed not to yank my hand away. I kept my face blank, my breathing smooth, but something was changing inside of me.

Shifting. Awakening. Something dark.

"I'll consider it," I said finally. I had a lot of things to consider.

I kept my composure until I was inside our rooms. Once the guards had shut the doors behind me, I stormed past Wells and Al, already unzipping my dress and tugging it off my shoulders. Not giving two shits that Al was there too. "Who the fuck told him about edges?" I bit out, throwing Al a glare. "Was it *you*? I'm going to change." I slammed the bedroom door.

Their voices drifted in from the sitting room as I stepped out of my dress and slippers and into a loose shirt and sleep pants.

"Shit," Wells said. "He must have taken her to the floating gazebo. That's why I couldn't 'path her."

"I didn't tell him anything, I swear." Al. I wished I could read his aura to see if he was telling the truth.

"He takes everyone out there when he wants them to think he's going to push them off," Wells grumbled.

I spotted the yellowfruit and cheese sandwich on my nightstand and pounced on it. *I love you.* I 'pathed to Wells, my eyes on the door as if I could see him on the other side.

And I love you. Eat all of it; Al doesn't want you angry at him, so he's 'ported up some wine.

Well, too bad. I'm angry with him forever.

Wells's amusement brushed against my mind. *Should I tell him you're abstaining?*

No thank you. I bit into my sandwich as if I were tearing a chunk out of this stupid monarchy. *Be out in a bit.*

I concentrated on the luxury of my mini-meal, but couldn't help overhearing their conversation while I chewed.

"I didn't think he'd press Im so hard." I could smell the wine when Al opened it. "Solange was talented too, and he was never like this when she was over."

"Solange knew how to play the game," Wells said. I wondered if Al noticed the subtle chill in his tone. "She knew how and when to dissemble and when to fudge the truth if she needed to. Imogen doesn't like games and doesn't like dishonesty, however slight. She's also very willful, and Allestair is not accustomed to being questioned or defied by anyone he considers under him. And she's incredibly talented, so he'd like to be able to wield her."

"What's wrong with that?" Al asked. "You're Molnair's general, she's your mate." He bit off the word. "You should both be willing to use your powers for your king. Imogen was almost kidnapped, she saw what the Sephryans are capable of—why would she resist aiding her country? We're going to fight a war she basically helped start. You should talk to her before this gets worse."

I heard the splash of wine into crystal. Then, "Imogen has asked to participate. She requested a place in my—"

"That's not what I mean. Her powers are too valuable and unpredictable. She lacks training and control. Father wants to use her strategically."

There was a pause. I finished my sandwich and stood, but stopped two feet from the door when Wells spoke again.

"There are young sidhe with less training and far less power in the infantry. The issue isn't Imogen's training and you know it. She can be taught. She's exceedingly adaptable and an incredibly fast learner. But . . ." I could just picture Wells swirling his wine. "Allestair wants total, subservient obedience. I doubt Imogen has ever given that to anyone. She won't be a mindless weapon. She resents being trapped here." He cleared his throat. "And she won't change her mind about children."

Al sighed loudly. "Both of you belong here."

"I respectfully disagree."

A tense silence followed.

I pasted on a smile and went out to join them. The dark thing the king had awakened in me stretched and flexed.

Al handed me a glass of wine. "I promise I didn't tell him anything about your fear of heights." He flashed me that grin.

"*Problem* with *edges*," I corrected. I saw no black spikes in his aura. I didn't take the wine. "I didn't eat much, I probably shouldn't have any."

"I can get something," he said, setting the glass down. "I'll just wink down to the kitchens. Be right back." He winked out.

Wells crossed over and wrapped his arms around me. "Well done. You won't go hungry tonight at least."

I hugged him back, pulling him closer, breathing deeply. "I don't like that they think they can send you away without me. If I found a way to get past the wards, we could both just go early."

His chest expanded beneath my cheek, his sigh brushing my hair. "There's no way past blood wards, Imogen."

"But if I found a way, you would go, right?"

He tensed. "Imogen—"

"I found a reference to Blood Kroma spells that can be used by non-royals in the library today." I spoke rapidly, wanting to get it out before Al returned. "So they *do* exist, I just need to find the actual spells. We don't have a ton of time. I know it's happening soon."

He loosened his embrace enough to look at me. "I haven't been told anything definite. The last I heard we're still in negotiations."

"Your ambassadors were sent back in pieces today," I said, just as Al winked in with cephlaang and chopped vegetables. "Al's supposed to torture and kill Staf and Vel this week and send them back in response. And I already know Marc and Kavlo will be sent out before we even hear back." I left the rest unsaid. Wells would go as soon as there was a foothold on land. And hell if I wasn't going with him.

Al placed the food on the table then finished his almost full glass of wine in one gulp. He immediately poured another.

"I'm sorry," I said, arching a brow. "Did I spoil a surprise?"

Al pushed the fish toward me without meeting my gaze. "I'm sure he'll tell me at breakfast."

For a moment, I felt for Al. He'd been brought up to believe that every non-royal was below him. That his younger brother was basically his vassal. And yet, he'd had to endure being his own father's servant and tool. I wondered what he might have been like if he'd really been that charming, soccer-playing, happy-go-lucky guy I'd met on Earth. I wondered if he might have chosen that life for a few decades, rather than centuries of this, if he'd ever truly considered his options. I wondered if something like this had influenced my grandmother's choice.

Not my problem, growled the thing inside of me.

I applied myself to the fish.

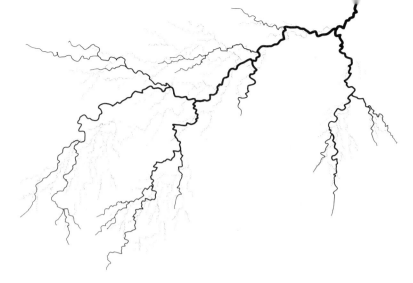

CHAPTER THIRTY-NINE

One of these days, honey, you'll learn the art of subtlety.
—Solange Aidair Delaney

The longer I lived at the palace, the more impressed I was that Wells had endured this passive-aggressive existence for a century and come out on the other side with a functional personality. I felt like the floors were paved with eggshells. Sometimes I unintentionally cracked one with a false step, and sometimes I got fed up and stomped.

I had laryngospasms more frequently. Wells was always there to help me breathe again, but it interrupted our sleep. And was obviously a symptom of something worse.

I asked permission to go see Cilla and was told it wasn't safe for me to leave the grounds. I asked if Cilla and Zoe could come see me. Yes, of course.

Once I was more "settled." Whatever the fuck that meant.

The only bits of relief were physical. I could run anywhere on the grounds I wanted, on my own, there was no shortage of outdoor paths for me to choose from, and Wells and I were allowed to train daily.

The morning after Allestair's gazebo threat, I emerged from my preferred long route through the palace forest to find Wells perched on the lip of a tiered fountain in the clearing, his long legs stretched out before him, two swords leaning against the edge.

I trotted toward him and watched a grin split his face, the tense lines dropping away when his eyes met mine. The corners of my mouth lifted. My entire being felt lighter. All the bullshit we were enduring faded into the background for a beat.

Wells stood and pulled me into his arms for a quick kiss, ignoring the sweat coating my body. "We're going to head straight to the training grounds today if that's all right with you. Al stopped by to inform me of an earlier meeting."

"Can I come?"

Wells shook his head. "Not to this one. Al also dropped off the tonic refill you asked for. He's going to meet us on the training grounds."

"That's fine." I took the sword he offered me and strapped it on. Wells had noticed that if the fighting dropped to weapons or hand to hand combat, I tended to forget I had control of any kroma other than shielding. He wanted me to get comfortable doing both. "I'm surprised I was able to guilt him into that."

"I think your jab about me being distracted and unable to focus with a pregnant mate to worry about made a mark." He started toward the training ground, a muscle flexing in his jaw.

I tucked my hand in his and squeezed, but didn't apologize. I still hadn't changed my mind about children but I was not above manipulating Al. Wells didn't like the idea of leaving me behind in the palace but he wasn't convinced I'd find a way out. Although forcibly separating a mated pair was criminal, we both knew that if I wasn't right beside Wells to publicly protest when he was ordered to Sephrya, everyone on Molnair would assume I was dutifully waiting for his return within the safety of palace walls. Which would be even more convincing if I was pregnant.

Al was already on the training grounds when we arrived, warming up with two of the guards. Al joined our sessions often. He was a decent fighter and offered good feedback, so I didn't mind. Now that he had us where he wanted us, he'd become almost an ally. Wells said they had a similar relationship when he had lived at the palace before. Which explained why Wells was continually trying to pick up Al's pieces in the outside world among normal people. But I never forgot who was ultimately responsible for making sure we were trapped here.

We'd been at it an hour when a tingle at the back of my neck alerted me to a new presence. The king had come to watch.

Wells and Al were tag-teaming me, which was how we finished lessons when Al joined. Wells felt that it was good practice for me and it would tire me out enough that I wouldn't be too bored when he left for work. At the very least, it made it easier for me to sit still in the library for hours on end.

I faked an attack at Wells. Spun and shattered Al's shield with a blast of blue-black kroma. Flipped in midair to avoid Wells's indigo counterattack. Knocking him over before I hit the ground with an immobilizing strike. I turned the same move on Al. He dodged and threw a pine-green stunning blast. My shield bloomed immediately. I deflected it back at him. Clocking him square in the chest. Knocking him on his ass. Game over.

"Reginal, Swelven," the king called over the two guards who had been watching. "Let's see what you can do against Imogen."

"Father, she's spent," Al said, brushing himself off as he stood. "We've been at it for an—"

"When I want your opinion, Aloysius, I'll ask for it." The king didn't even look at Al as he answered, his piercing eyes leveled on me. "You'll want a sword, Imogen."

When I'd disarmed and disabled Reginal and Swelven, the king called over three more guards while Al paced on the sidelines, fist clenched around his sword hilt, and Wells stood stiffly, arms crossed and jaw hard.

I panted, my arm trembling when I returned the guards' salute. Fresh and quick, two of them instantly circled around to my blind spots. I hauled up a shield at my back just in time to deflect a blast. My shield held, but I was knocked forward two steps and brought my sword up just in time to block an attack from the guard in front of me.

The other two alternated between throwing kroma at my back and sides, not even bothering with their weapons when they could drain me energetically. It didn't take long for the first one to disarm me and knock me off my feet.

All three guards instantly backed off, having won. I let my shield drop and lay there, sucking in breath, staring at the clouds and thinking I might want a nap later.

"On your feet, Imogen, that was a poor showing."

I turned my head to the side to find Allestair staring at me while the three guards tried to wipe the shock from their faces.

Wells had pulled on his neutral mask but his aura bled blue and black. "Sire—"

"On your feet." His icy stare stabbed into me, challenging, practically begging me to refuse.

I gritted my teeth and shoved the ground away from me until I was standing, covered in dirt and sweat. I summoned my sword.

Without taking his eyes from me, Allestair waved the three guards forward.

It took four more rounds.

"Get up, Imogen."

Allestair had eliminated the first blood rule. My arms bled from dozens of small cuts I hadn't been able to block. A trickle of crimson cut a path through the dust coating my skin from elbow to wrist as I shoved myself upright, but my arms buckled and my chin cracked against the packed dirt when I fell. I blinked, trying to clear the stars from my vision.

"Llewellyn." The king's voice was sharp, but I didn't miss that satisfied purr beneath it.

Before my eyes had refocused, I felt Wells's hands slide beneath my armpits and hoist me up. I swayed on my feet, my vision winking out for an instant as I clung to him.

"Drop her in your rooms to clean up." My eyes readjusted just in time to see Allestair flick a speck of dust off his sleeve and turn away. "You're due in the war room in ten minutes. Don't be late."

The king kept up his *Cool Hand Luke* treatment daily until Al and Wells started holding back during training. Even the guards seemed to be taking it easier. Since the king had eliminated first blood and a knockdown as defeat, I frequently sported wounds that were barely healed by the following day. My plummeting energy was exacerbated by the lack of food. Once Wells and I tried to skip training to give me a day to recover, but Al was sent—looking pained—to collect us. My morning runs became limping walks. I still made myself get up and go because I wouldn't have this taken away from me when Allestair had stolen almost everything else. Wells even started walking with me. It became some extra time we had alone together. And in spite of my exhaustion, I ramped up my research in the library.

I'd been there enough that no one gave me a second glance anymore. The few servants assigned to dust the shelves and keep the books organized were visibly uncomfortable with my endless questions about plants. It was clear they didn't wish to refuse to help, but Allestair must have told them to report my movements and assist as little as possible. They now kept my usual table cleaned off and ready, but otherwise avoided me.

This allowed me to make an important discovery.

A restricted section. Several stacks marked "Custodians Only" hiding behind some clever glamours.

Within, I found some *very* interesting books.

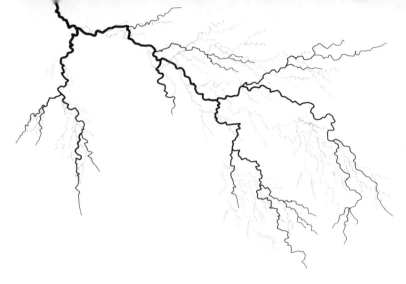

CHAPTER FORTY

*With tricky people, you've got to read between the lines.
Politicians almost never come out and say what they really mean.*
—Solange Aidair Delaney

At the end of the week, we emerged from our rooms to find Aloysius, fresh from the dungeons, dead-eyed and covered in blood. "Training is canceled today." His voice was hollow. "You're wanted in the war room, Wells." He spun on his heel and headed toward his own rooms. I followed Wells, even though I hadn't been invited.

Captain Marc spotted us in the corridor and spun toward me. "Imogen! It's been too long . . ." Before I could react, he swept me up in a hug and winked me back into our rooms. "Take this. Hide it." He handed me a canvas sack from beneath his cloak and winked back out.

I sprinted to the bathroom with it, shutting and locking the door behind me. I tore at the string around the neck of the sack until it fell open, revealing weeks' worth of nutrition blocks, carefully wrapped so that their scent would be undetectable. I almost wept at the sight of them. With them was another, smaller bag. When I opened it, several small bottles of clear liquid clinked together inside, a note stuffed between them.

> THIS IS A HEALING POTION.
> *Take it after bad training days to speed the recovery process.*
> *Keep your wits about you. Remember what's important.*

The creature inside me purred.

Negotiations were finished. The bodies of Staf and Vel were sent to Sephrya with a declaration of war. Marc and Kalvo followed immediately after the morning meeting with their forces. They would be there by evening. It wouldn't be long now.

That night Wells made love to me as if it were the last time. I made love to him as if I were swearing it wouldn't be. Afterward we lay twined together. Neither wanting to give up any time with each other, even for sleep.

"I have something for you," he said.

"Is it chocolate?" I asked. I hadn't seen chocolate in weeks.

"Less tasty, more permanent." He 'ported something into his hand, then opened his fist, dangling a sparkling silver thread in front of me. "I haven't had much opportunity to learn about your tastes in jewelry, but I thought understated might be best."

"You were correct," I said, rolling onto my back, my head pillowed on his shoulder. I took the necklace from him and examined the small, clear blue stone that glinted in the moonlight spilling in from the terrace. "It's beautiful. How did you manage to buy this?"

"I gave Marc written permission to withdraw from my accounts and had him bring the money to Zoe and Cilla. I gave them some indication of what I wanted, but they picked it out."

"Hey." I pulled the stone closer to my face; it was now a deep purple. "Did it just change color?"

"It's an augur stone. They don't exist on Earth and they're rare here. It bonds with the wearer and changes color occasionally. No one is really sure what affects the color. Mood, power..." He tugged on a strand of my hair. "Matching what you're wearing..."

I giggled. "I love it. Thank you." The stone shifted to the lightest shade of pink.

"I wanted you to have something..." He swallowed, his fingertips drifting over my cheekbone. "Like your ring from Keane."

I rolled over, half on top of him, nose to nose. "I'm not losing you like that. I refuse. I'm not doing it. They can't stop me from going with you. I've looked it up. If I don't agree to stay behind, it's forceful separation. So just stop thinking like that. I'll do whatever I have to—"

"You'll do whatever you have to in order to survive." He slipped the necklace from my fingers and fastened it around my neck. "That's what I want, Imogen. I want you to survive first. Everything else second."

I pressed my lips to his, my heartbeat already quickened with anxiety. I let myself melt against him when he deepened the kiss, his long fingers sliding into my hair. After a few beats, I slowly pulled back, leaning my cheek against his palm. My eyelids fluttered open, my gaze locking with his. "Wells. If I find a way out of the wards. Will you go?"

Our faces were still inches apart. His tiny exhale brushed my lips and my words tumbled out before he could protest. "I know you think it's impossible, but that goes against everything you've taught me about kroma. There *has* to be a counter. The people with Blood Kroma just don't want anyone to know about it. I know I'm close, Wells. I *know* I am. I've already found one potion that's... it's not perfect, it won't get us out, but it *does* pertain to circumnavigating Blood Kroma. I even have most of the ingredients in the garden. Just... will you go? If I find something, can we go?"

His eyes remained soft on mine, but he didn't speak for a long moment. One palm still cradled my head, his opposite fingers brushed non-existent strands of hair back from my jawline. His gaze dropped from mine, following the trail his fingers traced. I chewed my lower lip, willing myself to wait until he spoke.

His sunset eyes lifted. "If anyone could find a loophole, it would be you," he said at last. "Some of my units have already been sent out on Marc's airships. If you discover a way through . . . we can go direct to Sephrya. If we're with the army, he won't be able to pull us back without raising a lot of questions."

My lips curved upward. I curled around him, dropping my face to that spot just below his ear, giving it a little nip before whispering. "I'm going to kick so much ass on the battlefield."

He chuckled, his hand skating down my spine and lower. "I truly don't think either army is prepared for you."

Jackpot.

Excitement fizzed through my veins. My skin tingled, every hair lifting. A giddy smile spread across my face. I had to force myself to calm down enough to read the spell without my eyes skipping around. To make absolutely certain . . . I held my breath as I scanned the instructions one more time.

I suppressed a whoop.

This was it. This would get us through.

I tore my gaze from the pages to glance quickly around the stacks closest to me. Silent and unoccupied. I couldn't take this book out. And I unequivocally could not allow myself to be seen near this section. I had to memorize this quickly and leave. I dropped my eyes to the words.

"Im? You in here?" Al.

Fuck! Mouthing a string of curses I didn't dare utter, I slammed the text shut, shoved it back on the shelf, and scooped up the pile of innocuous herbal titles I was carrying around as a decoy. I darted into the main aisle and trotted a few steps away from the glamoured restricted area before answering. "Yeah, back here."

He popped out two stacks down and promptly sneezed. "I don't know how you can stand being around all these dusty shelves all day." He peered at the books I was carrying. "Need some help?"

"I'm okay," I said, just as he pulled two volumes out of my arms. I fought an eye roll.

"You in your normal spot?"

"Yep." I gritted my teeth. I didn't want Al here. I needed to jot down this spell and then show it to Wells as soon as he was off work. I took a breath. *Just be chill, don't give anything away.*

"Wow, Im," Al said, setting the books down at my usual table by the window. Where I had about ten other texts in piles and scattered about. "Are you planning on expanding that little garden into a farm?"

"What else am I supposed to do with my time?" I said, allowing some of my irritation to leak through as I plopped to a seat and pulled my notebook toward me. *Please just leave.*

"I think it's cute," he said, grinning as he settled into the chair across from me. "What are you learning about today?" He picked up the nearest book and riffled through the pages.

My internal scream could have shattered mountains. I forced a smile. "I'm trying to see if there are any records about cross pollinating moon fruit and yellow tarts." I shoved two volumes at him. "If you're sticking around, you can help."

As soon as Al had his nose in a book, I flipped open a random text, slid my alternate notebook out from beneath my herbal one, and scribbled down the spell I had seen. My heart beat faster as I wrote. I'd double check it later to make sure I'd read correctly, but this was it. Wells would have to agree once he saw it. He wasn't the biggest fan of potions, but desperate times. This would work. I had done it.

My pen slipped from my fingers as Wells's shock and grief slammed into me through the bond a moment before his 'path came.

Imogen, I'm sorry, I'm leaving now.

I jumped up from the table, knocking my chair to the ground. Al stood up too, eyes wide. He didn't know what was happening either.

Where are you? I'll wink—

We're already on the ship. I was told I needed to inspect the unit. My things were already on board and no other general was present. Once we lift beyond the wards, I won't be able to 'path you.

This is bullshit! I said it aloud as I 'pathed, slamming my palms into the table, my eyes burning. Al put a hand on my shoulder.

I know, Demon, I'm sorry.

My chest constricted and my heart squeezed. I couldn't tell where his sadness ended and mine began.

You stay alive. I'm going to get out so you stay alive and you wait for me, I 'pathed, snarling. My fingers curled, my nails scraping small trenches in the wood.

I love—

I felt it the moment the wards separated us. The echo of his psyche that lived in the little shelter within me, carved out by the bond, was reduced to shadow. Still there, but faint. When I stretched my senses toward him, my mental fingers brushed against that unholy wall of Blood Kroma.

"Imogen?" Al shook my shoulder gently.

"He's gone." I dashed a tear from my cheek and forbid any more from following. "I want to be alone." I grabbed my notes and stalked out of the library, leaving the gardening books where they were.

The creature inside me roared.

Time to let the demon out.

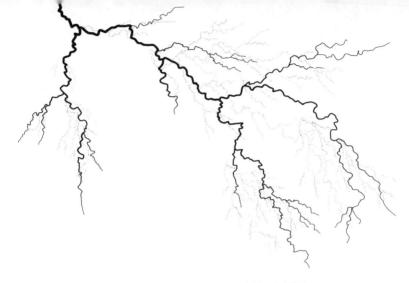

CHAPTER FORTY-ONE

Never show your cards right at the outset, honey.
Leave something to the imagination.
Always good to have a little surprise up your sleeve.
—Solange Aidair Delaney

They left me alone for the first two days. Other than Al occasionally peeking in to find me sleeping.

I slept during the day. During the night I worked.

For the first time in my life, I knew exactly what I wanted and where I wanted to be. And I wasn't going to let anyone take it from me without a fight.

I cloaked myself and moved easily around the castle by winking directly into the servants' passageways. Less chance I would accidentally bump into anyone in the dead of night, and less chance of anyone noticing anything I stole. I had two hiding spots for my contraband, both between wall studs in different spots of the bedroom.

Working my kroma became another nocturnal activity.

Wells had told me that my powers wouldn't be "settled" until I'd been sidhe for at least a year, maybe a year and a half. Until then, it was possible that more would manifest.

There was so much space in my brain now. I remembered chemistry lessons from tenth grade in their entirety. I remembered how to make a Tesla coil from a sound design class I'd taken in the late '90s. I remembered more algebraic equations than I thought I ever learned.

I honed my lightning in secret, during thunderstorms. And I got creative with things I found in strange areas deep in the castle storerooms. Weaving my kroma into my own little chemical experiments.

Completely by accident one night, I discovered I could call the wind. This became especially interesting when I was able to ride it. It was also terrifying, but I forced myself to work with it. I rode the wind farther and farther away from the terrace, in stages. Until one night I pressed right up against the wards. Like a smooth, silky fabric draped shimmeringly in front of me. The ward edge wasn't far from the terrace. Maybe twenty feet straight out. The first time I'd touched them I made the mistake of looking down, panicked, lost the wind and had to wink myself back into my room. It was so terrifying that I forced myself to go back immediately.

On the third day, Al was ordered to drag me from bed and take me to the training grounds. I was prepared for more abuse, but it never came. I now trained only with Al. The king would stop by from time to time, but never ordered the guards to jump in, and rarely stayed for long.

I was even allowed to skip the formal dinners occasionally.

If I had dinner with Al in my rooms.

I knew what they were doing, and I let them. I was no longer the directionless Imogen who could be worn down into going along, but pretending worked for my purposes. Al bribed me with pescatarian dinners and maps. I wanted detailed maps of Sephrya and Molnair and I wanted to know everything about them.

He always found a way to get me snuggled against him during this. I allowed it. He was still forbidden to interfere with me while I was mated.

He never did more than hold me and occasionally kiss my hair. I dusted off those old acting skills and turned them toward my new objective.

"What's this part here?" I pointed to a jagged area along the coast. Al had me seated beside him, his arm draped across my shoulders, as if I wouldn't notice him slowly tucking me against him. I had a large map of Sephrya spread across my bent knees. We had just finished a seafood pasta dinner.

"Those are the red cliffs," he said. "Impossible to approach from the sea along that entire coast."

"And where is Wells now?" I asked. I used his company. I needed this information. I tolerated his touch. I needed this food. And I needed the king to think I was folding. But I did not ever let Al forget that I was in love with his brother.

"Last I heard his unit was somewhere around here." He circled his finger over an area near the center of the country. No easy way back. The farther inland one went, the more distance there was to wink to safety. And entire units were impossible to wink. My mouth tightened. I blew a sharp breath through my nose. Al took the opportunity to wrap his arms around me and squeeze.

"I'm sorry you miss him," he murmured.

I bet you are. "Do you?" I twisted out of his embrace to face him. I wanted to see his aura. "Do *you* miss him?"

He gazed at me. He had to know I was reading him. "Sometimes," he said. True apparently. He swallowed. "But I like being able to spend more time with you. I like being friends again." He offered a hesitant smile.

I pushed one back. Then popped a leftover crustacean from his plate into my mouth. A subtle reminder of the price of my solitary company. I turned back to the map. "Tell me about this area. Adgemon's unit is here, correct?"

During the day, I continued to research the remaining herbs I needed and where I might be able to find them. That final spell was, indeed, able to do what I needed. It was also complicated and dangerous. However, I hadn't been able to find anything else, and I didn't want to waste time. It brewed the exact kind of temperamental potion Wells would hate, but I didn't care.

Some items had to be fresh, some could be dried. A few had to be picked during certain moon cycles.

And since there were two moons above this planet, I had to fake interest in a dinner under the stars with Al—who was thrilled—so I could grill him on the phases of these moons. All the spell books assumed the caster would be familiar with them. Waiting for those ingredients was painful, but I made use of the time.

In a few weeks I had almost everything I needed. I was getting close.

"Let's take a break from archery today," I told Al. I'd been obsessively working on shooting and throwing skills the past few days. I was now a dead shot. "We haven't done swords in a while, I don't want to forget how."

He laughed. "I don't think you could ever forget, but that sounds fun. We'll go for first blood."

Perfect.

For a few minutes I let myself warm up. Then I caught Al's aural telegraphs and worked with them for a bit. I allowed him some close shots. I let him think I was getting frustrated and made a few sloppy parries.

"Maybe you are a little rusty, Im," Al said grinning.

I made a show of gritting my teeth and narrowing my eyes as if redoubling my efforts. I let him come close once . . . twice . . . then slashed open the inside of his forearm. He dropped his blade and I dropped mine.

"Oh, shit, Al, I'm so sorry!" I ran over, yanked out the hem of my shirt, and used it to cover the wound. Blood seeped quickly into the white fabric. "I can't believe I got so sloppy. I'm really sorry, does it hurt?"

"It's okay, Im," he said, although he did look a bit pale. "It just surprised me is all. Maybe we should work blades for a few days and get you back up to speed."

"Yeah, good idea," I agreed and lifted my now blood-soaked shirt from the wound. It was already closed. I found a clean area of fabric and wiped any remaining blood off, then traced a finger over the scar. It would fade by morning. "Sorry again."

"It's okay," he said, glancing at my shirt. "You better go change before my father sees you and gets on you about deportment. I'll clean your sword."

Excellent.

"Okay, yeah, thanks." I winked out.

And straight into my rooms where I hurtled into the bathroom, tugging the shirt off as I went. I shut and locked the door behind me and then 'ported a large vial from a hiding spot. I sat on the floor and carefully summoned the blood into the vial before it could dry.

"Be enough be enough be enough be enough..." I chanted. In less than two minutes the vial was three quarters full. Enough. I started the bathwater in case someone decided to verify where I was and chucked the stained shirt into the sink. Then I 'ported in my other supplies and instructions to double check.

"Enough for one test and the big one," I breathed. I pulled out one test vial—'porting the others that I had optimistically prepared away—and my big vial. "Big one first."

I took a deep breath, willing my galloping heart to slow, and rallied my energy. Remembering my potion work with Cilla, I forced myself to slow down, be precise, and use control. I set the instructions where I could read them—the pauses and wording had to be exact—then let my kroma flow through the vessel as I repeated the incantation. My focus narrowed, letting a ribbon of my power wrap the interior as I poured most of the blood into the large vial. This spell was temperamental: too much kroma pissed it off, too little made it whiney. I kept my thread of energy steady as I chanted.

Smoke wafted from the opening. The potion morphed from a muddy green to a ruddy gold. I slowly pulled myself back once it was complete. Nothing had exploded. Cilla would be so proud of me.

It needed to sit for five-times-five hours before reaching full potency—why it couldn't just say twenty-five, I didn't know, but all sidhe spells were full of unnecessary math like that—and its hue was supposed to go more golden when it was finished. I had to keep it at room temperature, so hiding it in my wall was risky. I had poured the water out of a vase of flowers this morning and 'ported the vial into it. I poured the rest of Al's blood into the small test vial. This one only had to sit five hours. I would try it tonight.

I was so getting out of here.

CHAPTER FORTY-TWO

Sometimes you gotta be your own damn superhero.
—Imogen Delaney

After an excruciatingly fake dinner where the queen inquired about my gardening progress and I pretended interest in her suggestions of seasonal flowers to include, Al escorted me back to my rooms. As soon as the king and queen had turned off toward their own chambers, he leaned toward me. "My arm is fine now. Can barely even see the scar anymore."

I affected a relieved sag against him. "Oh, good. I'm glad. Sorry about that again." *Sorry not sorry.*

"It's fine, really. Don't worry about it anymore," he said magnanimously.

Well, then stop talking about it. I smiled up at him.

We'd reached my doors and the guards stood back slightly to let us pass.

"Do you wanna hang out for a bit?" he asked, his hand on the doorknob. "Look at maps or..."

"Not tonight," I said. His smile fell. I woke the fire in my veins, letting it creep to my face. "I'm actually feeling weirdly tired. I think I might turn in early. Maybe take the day off training tomorrow."

"You not feeling well? You do look a little flushed." Al pushed the hair back from my forehead and laid his palm across it. I leaned into his hand.

"Mmmm your cold hands feel good," I said, closing my eyes.

"You are a little warm," he said, sliding both hands to my cheeks. I pretended to enjoy it. "You have been kind of stressed lately. That might explain why you were a bit clumsy this morning. Get some rest. If I don't hear from you by lunchtime tomorrow, I'll come check on you."

"Okay, sounds good," I said. *By lunchtime tomorrow I'll be gone or dead in here.* I walked through the door he'd opened, tossing a little wave over my shoulder, and for the first time, rejoiced at the sound of the lock clicking shut.

Moments later, I was changed into comfy clothes and seated in the darkened bedroom, in front of the terrace windows, holding my test vial. Its color had changed to a deep burnished gold. I reread the spell for the umpteenth time out of nerves. I knew it backwards and forwards.

"Should be just enough to get through and stay through for fifteen minutes." I shook out my hands and rolled my shoulders. "Okay, just do it, Imogen. That's all that's left."

I slammed the liquid back. Wincing at the metallic taste. As soon as it hit my stomach my entire body went fizzy. I was reminded of that '80s sensation: Pop Rocks. The goofy candy that fizzed in your mouth. Except I felt like I had pop rocks running through my blood. *Don't be killing me, don't be killing me...*

As suddenly as it started, the fizzy feeling zipped back. First from my fingers and toes, then up my limbs, almost as if it were being called back into my stomach. It left behind a pleasant, floaty sensation. "Okay, here goes..."

I tentatively stretched my mind toward that essence of Cilla that I had so sorely missed. A burst of joy zinged up my spine when I reached the wards and speared right through them, as if tumbling past a wall of feathers.

Cilla?

Oh my God, IMMY! Relief coated her mental voice. *I've missed you so much! I've been so worried about you! We heard they sent Wells off to fight and you weren't allowed to go with him . . .*

Captain Marc and Admiral Kavlo had both petitioned for me to join their forces also. Their petitions were rejected.

. . . and you've been stuck in that stupid palace with those awful people. Please tell me they haven't been beating and starving you?

Well . . . how much lying do you want me to do here?

Immy! I could almost feel her gasp of horror. God, I had missed her.

Cill, I don't have much time. This potion is going to wear off. Tell me about the baby. Tell me about Zoe. Tell me everything.

A potion got you through? I felt her satisfied cackle. *Oh my God, you're getting so good. I'm so proud of you.*

We talked until the floaty feeling started to dissolve and I felt the claws of the wards scraping against my mind. I told Cilla I loved her and I'd find a way to check in again soon. I didn't tell her about my plan. She'd only worry. She'd learn soon enough if I failed or succeeded.

I barely slept that night. I packed up my healing potions and remaining blocks—setting one out for the morning—along with a spare set of clothes, my phone, and my ring in a compact pack that I 'ported back into one of my hiding places. I wasn't taking any chances of anything being discovered until I was about to walk out the door.

I checked the weapons I planned on taking with me, then busied myself putting little semi-permanent shields around some of my more delicate experiments, also prepped for travel. No sense in anything exploding prematurely. I didn't want to die winning a Darwin Award.

I was up with the first rays of sun. The bond pulled at me, adding to my nerves. I wondered if it could somehow sense that I was close to reuniting

A Dagger of Lightning

with my mate even shadowed by the wards. *I'm coming. Not long now.* I still had a few more hours before my potion was ostensibly ready so I forced myself to take a bath since I didn't know when I'd be getting another one. I dressed in sturdy leather pants, my best boots, a warm shirt layered over a tank top, and a short leather jacket. I secured my dagger to my hip, a few small knives in concealed areas, and then paced, chewing on a block.

I stepped out onto the terrace and tested the wind. It brushed my hair back willingly. It would come.

Leaving the terrace doors open, I went back into the room and checked the time. Less than thirty minutes left. I 'ported my pack out, then heard the click of my door being unlocked.

Fuck.

I tossed the pack onto my unmade bed and yanked the covers over it just as Al, the king, and Captain Marc opened the door to the bedroom.

"Captain Marc!" I said. "I thought you were stationed in Sephrya."

"I was called back . . ." He cleared his throat. Why did they all look so serious? Why was Marc's aura shattering with devastation? "It was thought my presence might be helpful . . ."

"Helpful with what?" I asked, dread latching onto my ribs one at a time.

Al stared at the floor. Tension in the lines of his face. His amber eyes bleak. "We think we know why you weren't feeling well last night, Im." His voice was hoarse and his aura painfully crimped and cracking.

I was totally faking. I didn't say it aloud.

Everyone's auras were spinning with various dark, distressing tones. Everyone except the king.

"It's difficult to have to bring this news to you, Imogen," Allestair said, his face a mask of false sympathy. His aura pulsed crimson with flashes of gold. "You know as well as we do that Llewellyn was a fierce fighter." My heart stuttered. "If anyone could have made it through the center of Sephrya victorious, I would have thought it would've been his unit."

Numbness blasted across my chest. Was. Past tense. No. Nonononono. I was *so close!*

My throat closed up. I sucked in a breath that went nowhere. My entire body shut down. Spots danced in front of my eyes. "No," I croaked. I couldn't pull in air. *This wasn't supposed to happen. I was getting out. I was going to him...*

"I'm so sorry, Imogen." Captain Marc's voice cracked as he stepped forward, an envelope caught between trembling fingers. My name was written across it. I recognized the writing. My heart was shredding itself to pieces inside me.

"He left this with me and asked me to give it to you if..." His words choked off, his eyes were ringed with silver. He placed a steadying hand on my shoulder as I pulled the letter from his fingertips.

My vision blurred. I blinked and twin tears slid down my cheeks. Gasping for breath, I tore open the envelope. *This cannot be happening.*

"I've spoken to Allatu," Marc continued, his voice painfully gentle. "You're welcome to stay with us for a while until—"

"That won't be necessary, Captain," the king interrupted. "Imogen has developed a close friendship with Aloysius. I'm sure he'll be able to help her through this. The best place for her is still here, among Llewellyn's family."

For an instant, my grief was pushed aside by the angry dark creature forged in this place. *He did this,* it hissed. *He's all about appearances. He moves people like game pieces. He got rid of my mate to give me to his son. In a way that will be publicly accepted. I will kill...*

My eyes dropped to the letter and grief crashed forward again, threatening to drown me.

Imogen. My heart.
I'm so sorry. I know you're strong enough to survive this...

"Do you have any idea of the pain a mate goes through when their bond is severed, sire?" Marc said harshly, his hand dropping from my shoulder as he spun to face the king. "She needs to be with someone who understands what her bond meant to her."

I stopped reading. The bond. I touched it. Still there. Still whole. Pulling at me. Faint and shadowy, but not gone. Angry flames curled up from my core to burn my grief away. I crumbled the note in my hand and tossed it to the bed. "I'm not reading this shit," I snarled. "He's not dead. I'd fucking feel it. He's still alive. The bond is still there."

I yanked my pack from under the covers and strapped it on. I couldn't wait for the potion any longer. I was just going to have to hope it was done. I threw a shield up between me and the rest of them.

"I was supposed to give that to Imogen upon Llewellyn's confirmed death *only*," Marc bit out. The king's face slowly darkened. Al's brows drew together as his gaze bounced between his father and Captain Marc.

"He'll be dead soon enough," Allestair said, his eyes like ice. "Their unit was completely surrounded and requested immediate aid."

"And why didn't we send—" Captain Marc was interrupted when I summoned my box of experiments straight through the wall. Leaving a gaping hole. I flipped it open, pulled out the little pouches, and swiftly buckled them onto my belt.

"What in nine hells is that?" the king growled.

"Contraband," I said. "Kind of like this." I held my hand out to the opposite side and my modified bow and arrows burst through another wall. I could have 'ported them to me. But I wanted to smash shit. I wanted to leave holes in these walls. "You have one chance to alter the wards and let me wink to my mate." I slung the quiver and bow crossways over my back.

The king grinned at me like a wolf. He tossed a beam of dark gray power at my shield. Testing. "You're not in a position to make demands, young lady."

"I'm not young." I stretched my hand toward the flower vase. It shattered to pieces as my potion flew to me. "And I'm definitely not a lady." I pulled out the cork, tossed it away and chugged like a college kid doing a keg stand. Then I mazel tov'd the vial, hurling it to the floor to explode at their feet, shards bouncing off my shield and scattering across the floor.

This was not a gentle fizzing sensation.

Every muscle in my body seized. My stomach clenched, yanking my spine into a curl. I doubled over and fell to the floor. My blood was on fire. Razors tumbled through my stomach, slicing up my throat. Roaring filled my ears. A cry punched from my chest, but I barely heard the sound. I could see Al lobbing pine-green shots at my shield, calling my name. I had to get off the terrace before they took my shield down. The king hurled a vicious blast of kroma. The impact buffeting me as my shield was rocked. I forced myself to crawl forward. Clawing the floor with spasming fingers. Dragging my protesting body through the plaster and shards of glass. I couldn't let them get a hold of me. I forced my gaze to my fingertips. Forced myself to put one hand over the other as I burned from the inside out. My breathing shuddered, then caught. My fingertips were glowing, as if they were in a sunbeam while the rest of me stayed in shadow. As I hauled myself painfully across the floor, the glow spread to my hands. I flexed my fingers; my hands were no longer on fire. Another blast of gray kroma and my shield cracked down the center. I had to go faster.

I called on the wind. Praying the potion would work in time. My arms and then my legs were aglow. I staggered to my feet ignoring the cutting ache in my stomach. The glow reached my hips. I sprinted for the terrace just as the king shattered my shield.

The roaring in my ears ceased and I heard Al screaming my name. Heard their footsteps just behind me.

I stomped on the railing and launched myself into the air.

My stomach dipped but the wind caught me. The pain receded. Away from my shoulders, my chest, my back. It zipped up and tugged just behind my belly button right as I passed through the wards like sliding through silk curtains. I twisted in midair to see them all standing on the terrace. I gave the king the finger.

Captain Marc, standing just behind the king and Al, tossed me a salute.

Then I winked out to Sephrya.

To the battlefield.

To save my mate.

ACKNOWLEDGMENTS

Acknowledgments are challenging because you're going to forget someone essential. No matter how much you try not to. So here I go. I apologize in advance to whoever I've missed.

I wrote the first draft of *Dagger* in twenty-eight days, which is insane. So, yes, there were several re-writes and a few beta arounds. Thank you to the Richland Park Long Form Group, especially April Bailey, Kyle Gordan, and Samanatha McEnhimer. Thank you to Justin Verstratae and Joe Ramski for reading two drafts. Thanks also to Jackie Johnson, Patti Moore, Suzan Kidman, Brooke Favillo, Rea Frey, Cheryl Rieger, Emily Whitson, Melissa Collings and Stephen Collings.

Thank you to Lauren Thoman for reading the version of *Dagger* that I pulled out to look at after a year away from it. For drinking wine with me and telling me honestly the ways in which it could grow and getting me to the version I ultimately submitted.

Thank you to Helga Schier. Even though you ultimately weren't the editor on *Dagger*, your encouragement throughout my fledgling writing career has been invaluable.

Elana Gibson! I knew you peripherally, and had been told by other CamCat authors that you were "brilliant," but my God, you floored me with your edits. You pulled me out of the forest and showed me the trees. I can't wait to send you book two.

MC Smitherman, if I could bottle your spirit and sell it to writers having downtimes I could make the writing community a better place. Thank you for getting it. Thank you for your honesty in both directions. I am so thrilled to have you on my team.

Thank you, Maryann Appel, for the gorgeous cover. We switched genres on you a couple of times. But as usual, you managed to capture our eventual vibe of "Fantasy With a Spaceship On Top" with aplomb. I am spoiled for any future cover artists.

Thank you, Bill Lehto. As the Business Director, you probably don't ever get a huge section in the acknowledgments, but you're so responsive and transparent in the best way, you absolutely deserve kudos. Whether I'm selling books at a tiny library in my parents' hometown or trying to get a preorder code for an event in New York City, you always let me know immediately what is and isn't possible and always sign off by telling me to have fun. You're the best, thank you.

Laura Wooffitt, Marketing Director extraordinaire, how do you constantly smile, look on the bright side, find the humor, and pluck up the positive in every situation? I can't even imagine you cranky. And yet you manage to give honest and straightforward marketing advice unflinchingly even when things aren't tilting in a positive direction. You're a treasure, thank you.

Abigail Miles, you are a genius. No one will convince me otherwise. You are ostensibly a marketing associate, which you excel at, but also my copyeditor. And you know the difference between lay and lie. Literally anytime someone says, "we're having Abigail do it" I stop worrying. Because you will do it better than 99% of the population, guaranteed.

Gabe Schier, I am positive that I have no idea how much work you put in behind the scenes. I know there's so much more work involved in the digital media side of CamCat than anyone sees. I loved my time on the podcast and I look forward to seeing what else you have planned.

Jessica Homami, I know that you help with the podcast and social media, and I thank you for that, but can I just say that you are the best virtual panel moderator that I've ever had the pleasure to be questioned by? Your charm and personality shines through webcam and computer screen.

Kayla Webb, I haven't had the opportunity to work one on one with you as much as I would have liked, but I have experienced your commitment to sensitivity, justice, and accountability. I thank you for it. We should all be willing to listen, and your voice has affected my writing in a positive way.

Nicole DeLise, I have met you at book events, received your ad pool notifications, and countless other small things. I'm not sure you realize how big an impact you have. I so appreciate you.

When I was young, there was a period of time where I felt that my emotional pain fueled my art. I'm happy to say I'm in a better spot now. And this is where I thank my husband, Dean. It's amazing the creative leaps your mind will take when your heart feels safe. We've had our ups and downs, but I can confidently say that you have always supported my creativity, I have always felt safe with you, and I have grown as a person in ways that wouldn't have been possible if you hadn't taken such care with my heart.

And thank you to my parents, who have supported every creative endeavor I've ever thrown myself into: enthusiastically telling people about my books, coming to my events, and letting me talk about the rollercoaster that is publishing whenever I call. For always giving me a soft place to land from the very beginning.

Although she can't see it, I have to thank Sue Arroyo once again for making it rain chances. I still can't quite believe she's gone. You created something beautiful with CamCat. I hope it lives on for a long time in your memory.

ABOUT THE AUTHOR

Meredith grew up in New Orleans, collecting two degrees from Louisiana State University before running away to Chicago to be an actor. In between plays, she got her black belt and made martial arts and yoga her full-time day job. She fought in the Chicago Golden Gloves, ran the Chicago Marathon, and competed for team USA in the Savate World Championships in Paris. In spite of doing each of these things twice, she couldn't stay warm and relocated to Nashville. She owns several swords but lives a non-violent life, saving all swashbuckling for the page. When not writing, she enjoys knitting scarves, gardening, visiting coffee shops, and cuddling with her husband and two panther-sized cats. She's a member of International Thriller Writers, Sisters in Crime and the Women's National Book Association.

Her debut novel, *Ghost Tamer*, is a 2023 Amazon Editors' Pick, a 2024 IBPA Gold Winner for Best SciFi Fantasy, and a 2024 IPPY Award Gold Winner for Best First Book. *A Dagger of Lightning* is her second novel.

If you liked
Meredith R. Lyons's *A Dagger of Lightning*,
you'll enjoy her first book,
Ghost Tamer,
a paranormal mystery.

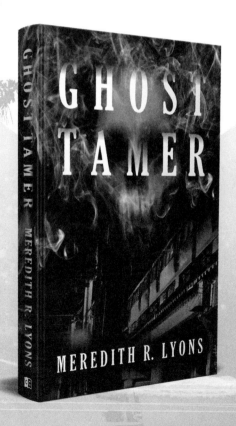

1

"IT'S COMING. LET'S RUN."

Joe and I sprinted through the thick snowflakes toward the El platform, pounding up the salt-strewn stairs two at a time. Scanned our passes lickety-split and leapt onto the very first car just as the warning bell chimed and the doors glided shut.

"Winners." Joe held his gloved hand up without turning around and I smacked my mittened palm against his for a muffled high five. He pointed to the front of the car. "Hey, Raely, your favorite seats. Must be your lucky day, girl."

"Excellent!" I clamped onto my friend's shoulder and wove after him through the passengers as the elevated train bobbed and swayed.

It was a few hours after the rush, and the train was not uncomfortably packed. Joe and I lucked into those first two seats at the front behind the driver. I loved being able to see out to the tracks in front. Made it almost like a carnival ride. As soon as I was settled in my seat, leaning back against the side window, Joe launched into an impassioned critique of my stand-up set. We were both out of breath from our sprint. Still buzzing from the adrenaline of recent stage time.

"I mean, you have to feel good about that bit with the birthday cup," he said. "That one is solid . . ." We had just finished five-minute solo sets at an early evening open mic. I liked the earlier ones, fewer people. Although Joe was trying to get me to commit to a 'real' one— 8 p.m. or later, true show time—sometime before spring.

Other passengers surrounding us in our little section of the train stood either reading or plugged into music or podcasts. Everyone created their own space. Joe's ardent critique of my set didn't register to the average commuter, although a few smiled to themselves, glancing over at him, perhaps catching some of his clever turns of phrase. Since he was in flow, he was still standing, gesticulating, while I gazed up at him. I flung my legs across the seat he had not yet taken and studied him. He was one of those guys who would always be okay. He could easily transition from his office job to any bohemian shenanigans that he may get the urge to dabble in with a simple change of clothes and an alteration of mousse pattern. His set had been perfect. He'd nailed every bit. And for some reason, he always wanted me to do just as well.

"Okay, now you do mine," he demanded, one gloved hand gripping the upright post as he swayed with the train, the fluorescent overhead lights gilding his dirty-blond hair, bleaching him into overexposure. "What did you think? Where do I need to tighten it up? I thought the part about the reunion email was a little *meh* . . ."

"Joe, none of it was '*meh*.'" I'd spent much of his set resisting the urge to tell the people next to me, *That's my best friend up there.* "I think you should just go for the whole ten minutes next time. It was spot-on. The audience was with you the entire time. I think they were disappointed when you were done, honestly."

"I still think if we got into Second City, it would take our skills to the next level." He scooted a little closer as the train made another stop, but only a few people pushed through the doors before they slid shut again. "Improv is an essential skill."

"Oh, for sure," I said. "I just don't know that I'm—"

"Stop saying you don't think you're ready, you never think you're ready for anything. You just need to *do*." He leaned toward me, grinning and pointing. The train jostled, but he swayed with it. I couldn't help but smile back. City lights flashed by in the windows behind him as we sped through the Chicago Loop, leaving the near south side. The tiny squares of high-rise windows carved bright, symmetrical specks into the dark winter sky.

It had finally stopped snowing. I peeked out the front window. The train gobbled up the line of track before us ever more quickly as it picked up speed.

"So," I nudged his leg with my boot. "We're done with our sets, no more secrets. What's the big, exciting thing you're doing this weekend that trumps game night? I was ready to clean up at Telestrations."

Joe's smile broadened. He smacked my boots, pushing them to the floor, and took the seat, leaning toward me. "I'm proposing to Mia."

I straightened away from the window. "Shut. UP!"

He grinned and grasped a finger of his glove, wiggling his hand free and reaching for an inside coat pocket. "Wanna see it?"

"Yes, I wanna see it! Oh my God! Joe!" I scooted closer, a silly grin spilling over my face, and extended my palm. I loved Mia. And I loved who Joe was *with* Mia. Joe grinned back at me and unfastened the first two buttons of his coat to access the pocket.

The full moon gilded the metal of the tracks ahead of us as the train whipped toward the river, to the turn just ahead. The hairs on the back of my neck stood up.

"Joe," I said, catching his eye. "The train is going too fast."

We turned away from each other, gazes locked on the front window. The curve was looming. Shiny, bright metal, arcing gracefully to the left. And the train wasn't slowing down. My heart expanded, uncomfortably filling my chest. Electricity shot through my limbs. Our car sped forward relentlessly.

My eyes found Joe's. The metallic taste of fear coated the back of my tongue. I meant to say that we should grab on to something, even as my body compelled both hands to grasp the railing of the seat beside me. Joe opened his mouth to say something and then . . .

There was a wrench. A screaming of metal fighting metal. The train tore off the rails. For one second, we were all suspended together. As if existing inside a gasp. Not a human sound. Conversation ceased. Silence was our collective scream.

Then chaos. Everyone yelled, cried, cursed. The lights strobed, then cut out. Every body and bag on the train hurtled toward the front of the car, tagging every metal guardrail along the way. Gravity found us again with a sickening crunch.

Pain sliced into my side, but I couldn't move. Couldn't make space. Pressure increased. I couldn't breathe. Panic clawed at my ribcage. I wanted to fight but there was nothing to defeat. No air to breathe. I couldn't move. Nowhere to go.

Blackness.

When consciousness found me again, I was disoriented.

My head hurt. My lungs heaved as if I had been underwater. I wheezed like a drowning victim. Someone pulled at me. Under my arms. Hauling. My feet were caught. Yanked free.

A yelp died escaping my throat. I struggled to open my eyes, my eyelids impossibly heavy.

"Joe?" Raspy. Rusty voice.

"I'm getting you outside. They'll find you more easily outside. You need to stay very still."

I wrenched my eyes open. I watched my legs being pulled through the shattered window of the train as if they belonged to someone else. My booted feet thudding to the ground. Dragging trenches through the fresh powder. I had never given thought to how big the trains were when I rode them every day, but now, seeing one crashed in the snow, it was like a blue whale.

"Joe . . ." I croaked.

"You need to think about surviving. You're hurt. You need to stay relaxed and then you need to do what the medical people say. Look up. Look up and stay calm."

He laid me down in the fresh snow and I looked up. I could see the moon. Full. I could even see a few stars. *Never see stars in Chicago. Not downtown.*

I heard sirens. Helicopters. Someone was in trouble. I knew I should help. But I was so tired. Lying in the snow and looking up seemed the right thing to do.

The edges of my vision blurred. Whoever had been pulling me was no longer nearby. I heard voices. Turned my head to the side. It seemed to take a long time. The world went in and out of focus. I saw people. Lights. Lots of lights, painting the glittering snow with pulses of pink. I wondered why I didn't feel cold. I didn't feel anything. A crimson semi-circle blossomed through the snow at my left side. The bloom slowly grew. It was beautiful. Red against the white.

People. Running closer. Boots spraying the fresh snow. Shouting, lights flashing, the whirring of the helicopters throbbed against my eardrums. I pulled my gaze back to the train to search for Joe. I tried to call for him, but my mouth wouldn't move.

2

DAYS IN THE HOSPITAL PASSED BY IN A BLUR. I'd had surgery and was going to have a ginormous scar on my left side, sure to be very attractive come bikini season and fun to explain the next time I managed to sustain a relationship to "that stage."

I was the only one in the first car to survive.

My mom drove up from the suburbs immediately and had the sense to contact the personal injury lawyers I used to work for part-time.

No one would tell me anything about Joe. Not that I was conscious much at first. They waited until I was "out of the woods" to break the news that he hadn't made it. Apparently, that kind of shock can affect the healing process.

Mom was neatly Tetris-ing flowers and get-well cards into a box she had coaxed from hospital staff, which had "lubricating jelly" stamped on the side. Mia had just left. Her visit had been awkward and painful with neither of us knowing how to talk to each other. Now I slumped in my wheelchair, exhausted and hollowed out from that halting attempt at conversation, cocooned in my invisible blanket of grief and pain, a stuffed Pooh Bear wedged next to me.

When Mom had placed it in my lap, I'd rolled my eyes and reminded her that I was twenty-six but tucked him under my arm when she turned her back.

Another nurse finished a chatty farewell with Mom—who, of course, had befriended the entire staff by now. She reminded me to take it easy and swept out of the room with my recently autographed discharge papers.

"Where's that tall dude with the shaggy hair? Is he coming to say goodbye, too?" I sounded crabby. But crabby was one of my more pleasant moods lately.

"Who?" Mom didn't look up from her packing.

"That guy. He came here like . . . three or four times? Usually during the night? I figured he was a night shift person. He never stayed long or did anything useful, but he sure did come by a lot. What?"

She had stopped packing and was staring at me, brow furrowed. She looked much too concerned to be merely trying to come up with someone's name.

"What?" I repeated.

"The first few nights after surgery you talked to yourself sometimes. We assumed you were . . . sleep-talking, like you used to do when you were little. You would ask about Joe or—"

"So, you never saw that guy?"

"I think you must have been imagining it. You've had a lot of morphine."

She nodded to the stack of get-well cards in her hand and resumed collecting bouquets.

Exhaustion pulled at me. The ever-present ache in my chest flared, reminding me that Joe was dead. In the end, I didn't care who had visited, and so I let it go.

THREE WEEKS LATER, I limped up the well-salted sidewalk to my lawyer's River North office, buzzed the receptionist from the street-level intercom, and announced myself. After yanking the door open, I debated taking the stairs up to the second story, decided to heed the throbbing ache in my leg, and opted for the elevator. I was on track for a full recovery, they said, but it sure was taking a hell of a long time.

Minutes later I was in the small, familiar conference room with a bottle of water in my hand and a notepad on the shiny wooden table in front of me. I'd worked part time for Dubin and Cantor for almost three years and still came in to help occasionally if they were short-handed. They'd apparently managed to grab the cases of a few more of the survivors in adjacent cars. And some of the . . . not survivors. Anyway, it was nice to have lawyers you trusted.

James Cantor, my former boss, came striding in. He was short, athletic, and energetic, with an accordion file under one arm and a coffee in hand. I managed to wrestle a weak smile from somewhere to meet his blast of energy. Normally, I blasted right along in tandem.

"Raely! You look tons better. How do you feel? You feel like crap, right? Yeah, well, just keep putting one foot in front of the other. I promise you. Night and day. You may not feel it yet, but you're healing."

"Thanks," I said, the corner of my mouth creeping up the left side of my face. I hauled my latest batch of medical records out of my messenger bag. "My ortho has started emailing me these directly, so I printed them off at the comedy club."

"Excellent!" He dived for the records. "So you don't need copies? Great. I'll have Helen enter them. Hey, you want a coffee? You look like you could use a coffee. Fake plant milk, right? Helen!"

Helen shuffled in briskly, a warm grin already in place. Her iron gray hair and sensible sweater-and-skirt ensemble contrasted with James's artfully faded jeans and black button up—rolled to the elbows, of course. He gave her my coffee order, which I knew was coming out of a Keurig, so I didn't feel too guilty about it, and passed her the records.

"Yeah, I guess the doc likes me. Is it true love? Or am I merely a fascinating case? We may never know," I said. Helen chuckled and trotted off.

James teased a folder out from the large accordion file with 'Raely Videc' printed on the side in large block letters. So strange to see one with my name on it.

"Got your police report back and even have photos of the scene."

"Really? Wow, that was fast."

"Yeah, so, we gotta work on your statement. I know you were in shock and it's completely understandable that your memory may be hazy or incomplete." He carefully spread the papers and photographs across the shiny table, placing each 8 x 10 as if it belonged in a specific spot. I accepted my coffee from Helen with a nod of thanks and scooted closer to the table.

"I don't think my memories were too hazy." I took a gulp of coffee, summoning patience. We'd had several versions of this conversation before.

"You said you were pulled from the car."

"I was pulled from the car."

"You said someone pulled you out through the window of the car and dragged you away from the rest of the train."

"Yeah. 'Cause that's what happened."

He pushed a photograph toward me. I spun it around and slid it closer. It was an aerial view of the wreck, obviously taken from a helicopter. Maybe stills from a video. I could see the smashed front car, the second car dangling, and the third car teetering. I could see myself. A lone, tiny figure, limbs splayed like a snow angel, a crimson blotch at my side. I forced my emotions into a little box. Stuffed them into my mental basement. I would deal with them later. Or never. Never was fine.

"Yes, look." I jammed my finger at the photo, pushing it to the space between us, suppressed emotion thickening my Chitown accent. "You can see drag marks from my legs. I was sitting on the opposite side of the train. How could I have been thrown from the window on *this* side? There woulda been glass all over me. I woulda hit my head or something."

"Look here." As James circled his finger over the snow surrounding my body, his accent broadened in response to mine.

I glared at the section he indicated, then clung to a polite tone with effort. "I don't see anything."

"Precisely."

What was he talking about?

"What *don't* you see?"

My brow furrowed. I looked at the photo, then shook my head.

James leaned forward, palms on the table. "Footprints."

My breath caught. I snatched the photograph off the table. Held it close to my nose and scanned. He was right. Other than the trenches my feet had dug into the powder and the craters pocked by fallen debris, the snow was perfect.

"The paramedics came immediately after this was taken. You can see them off to the side. They saw no one nearby. If someone had pulled you from the train, there would be footprints somewhere."

3

MY FIRST NIGHT SHIFT BACK AT THE CLUB WAS A TUESDAY. As soon as my physical therapist cleared me for long-term standing, I'd called up George Rosen, the owner. He put me on the floor that week. I did the weekday shifts while my leg was still sore. Less running around. Even at a comedy club, working behind the bar can get intense during breaks between sets.

On my first Friday night shift, I was working with Luck, my favorite fellow drink-slinger. He had been there a while but never gave you the impression that he was "too senior" to do side work or help a coworker in the weeds.

He was a comic himself, as were most of us in some iteration, and his set wasn't half bad. It didn't hurt that he was easy on the eyes. He had perennially bronze skin, light gray eyes, and short, dark curls. And a killer understated callback joke for every conversation that would have you chuckling when it popped into your head two days later. If

I had an option, and Luck was either on the schedule or doing a set, that's the night I'd choose. Luck was always down to hang out afterward, too. A not-so-small bonus.

During the first two hours of the shift, my heart felt lighter than it had since the accident. The easy banter with patrons and Luck—who seemed just as happy to have me back on Fridays as I was to be there—the feeling of doing something normal, and the *almost* complete absence of pain . . . it was a balm. There were even stretches of time where I didn't consciously mourn Joe.

I spotted the shaggy-haired hospital guy at the end of the bar. I gave him a small smile and a wave to let him know I'd be down there when it was his turn. His hair looked more anime than shaggy in this light. Perhaps he'd applied product for a night out.

"Hey!" I raised my voice over the din of the crowd once I'd taken care of customers ahead of him. "From the hospital, right? Nice to see you in the real world."

He stared back at me like I had grown three heads.

My professional dazzling smile dropped a watt or two. "Well, what can I get you?"

"Are you talking to me?" said the guy behind him. I started to tell him to wait his turn, but as he squished his way up to the bar, giving his order, he *walked right through* the anime-haired guy.

My blood turned to ice and a dull roaring filled my ears as Anime shook his head and backed away. Through at least one other person. It took tremendous effort to wrench my focus back to the man in front of me and ask him to repeat his order.

Maybe it was a blessing that my thirty-second chat with Anime had put me one inch away from the weeds. I was forced to concentrate on taking orders and slinging drinks until the next set started. Luck was working furiously, too. I waited until the next act was going strong—an experienced standup, thank God, because he had the crowd fully contained within seconds—and told Luck that I needed some air. I got his blessing, pulled a bottle of warm water from one of the cases in the storage closet as I passed, and pushed open the stage door to the alley, being careful to leave the worn, wooden doorstop in its jam to avoid being locked out. I plunked down on the steps with a raspy exhale, sipped my tepid water, and tried to think through what I had just seen. Some kind of PTSD effect, maybe?

I put my water bottle on the step beside me, closed my eyes and pressed the heels of my hands into them. I was wearing contacts, so I had to be careful, but sometimes I still enjoyed seeing the little stars I could create. When I lifted my face, he was there.

I closed my eyes. Assessed the position of my contact lenses and found them to be fine. I blinked several times upon reopening. He was still there. There had to be a logical explanation for this. He looked totally normal; I must have imagined him misting through people.

I stared him right in the eye, grabbed my water bottle, and took a pull. Sad that it was not whiskey. "Who are you, and what do you want?"

He glanced around, settled his gaze back on me, then took a step forward.

I dropped the bottle and jerked to a standing position. Neither of us watched it clunk down the remaining two steps, splashing its contents over the concrete, and rolling to a stop at his feet.

"You can see me?" he asked, tilting his head as if *I* were the one behaving oddly.

"No fucking shit, Sherlock, now why are you stalking me?" I edged up a step closer to the door, never taking my eyes off him.

He blinked. Stuck his hands in his pockets. It was then that I noticed he was wearing dark jeans and a light jacket in the middle of winter. No scarf. No gloves. Not even a hipster hat.

VISIT US ONLINE FOR MORE BOOKS TO LIVE IN:
CAMCATBOOKS.COM

SIGN UP FOR CAMCAT'S FICTION NEWSLETTER FOR
COVER REVEALS, EBOOK DEALS, AND MORE EXCLUSIVE CONTENT.

CamCatBooks	@CamCatBooks	@CamCat_Books	@CamCatBooks